Edmund M. Barttelot

The Life of Edmund Musgrave Barttelot

Captain and brevet-major Royal fusiliers, commander of the rear column of the

Emin Pasha relief expedition. Being an account of his services for the relief of

Kandahar, of Gordon, and of Emin, from his letters

Edmund M. Barttelot

The Life of Edmund Musgrave Barttelot
Captain and brevet-major Royal fusiliers, commander of the rear column of the Emin Pasha relief expedition. Being an account of his services for the relief of Kandahar, of Gordon, and of Emin, from his letters

ISBN/EAN: 9783337196905

Printed in Europe, USA, Canada, Australia, Japan

Cover: Foto ©Raphael Reischuk / pixelio.de

More available books at **www.hansebooks.com**

Major Barttelot's Diary on the Congo.

'HONORIS CAUSÂ.'

EDMUND M. BARTTELOT.

MAJOR, SEVENTH ROYAL FUSILIERS.

London: Richard Bentley & Son, 1890.

THE LIFE OF
EDMUND MUSGRAVE BARTTELOT

Captain and Brevet=Major Royal Fusiliers
Commander of the Rear Column of the Emin Pasha
Relief Expedition

BEING

*AN ACCOUNT OF HIS SERVICES FOR THE
RELIEF OF KANDAHAR, OF GORDON,
AND OF EMIN*

FROM HIS LETTERS AND DIARY

BY

WALTER GEORGE BARTTELOT

LONDON
RICHARD BENTLEY AND SON
Publishers in Ordinary to Her Majesty the Queen
1890

CONTENTS.

CHAPTER VIII.

CHAPTER IX.

CHAPTER X.

CHAPTER XI.

CHAPTER XII.

CHAPTER XIII.

CHAPTER XIV.

JUNE 10, 1888.

CHAPTER XV.

THE MARCH TO BANALYA.

CHAPTER XVI.

LAST DAYS.—'FAITHFUL UNTO DEATH.'

JUNE 24—JULY 5, 1888. END OF DIARY.

APPENDIX I.

LIST OF ILLUSTRATIONS.

LIST OF NAMES REQUIRING EXPLANATION.

Maniapara	- -	A head-man over some ten or twelve porters.
Manioc	- -	A root (of poisonous nature) from which sago is prepared.
Chimbeck	- -	A native hut.
'Bulla-Matari'	-	'Stone-breaker,' a name given by the natives on the Congo to Mr. Stanley.
Metako	- -	A metal wire used for money purposes.
Manyuema	- -	Natives of the region between the Congo and Lake Tanganyika (north), slaves to Tippu-Tib, and cannibals.
Melafor	- -	Palm wine.
Swahili	- -	The name of a race (a mixture of Arab and Negro blood) with a language of its own spoken by the Zanzibaris.
Washengies	-	Zanzibari term for all natives.

i

LIFE OF

EDMUND MUSGRAVE BARTTELOT.

INTRODUCTORY CHAPTER.

NOT a line of this book would ever have been written, not a word of its contents would have been published, if justice, even partially, had been done, or any kindness shown by the leader of the Expedition for the relief of Emin Pasha to the officers left at Yambuya with his impedimenta, his stores, and his sick.

The story of Major Barttelot's life represents to us a brave English officer and gentleman, who loved his profession, gloried in the work it gave him to do, and highly prized the only reward he coveted, and sometimes gained, namely, the appreciation and the thanks of those under whom he served. He is only an example of the true English nature, and there could be no need to place his actions before the public but for the manner in which his name has been treated by Mr. Stanley since his life was taken by Sanga, a Manyuema porter of Tippu-Tib's, Governor of the Falls Station.

I

When the news first came home in September, 1888, announcing the death of Major Barttelot on August 17, the shock was great; but when Mr. Stanley's letters arrived, almost devoid of even the usual expressions of regret, and hardly noticing the event at all, we were more than astonished. We hoped that one of the family might hear from Mr. Stanley; he had written to geographical societies —would not he send a line to us? No, not a word. And then came the great blow: my brother lying dead, murdered far away in the great forest of Central Africa, the bright hopes of his future career crushed out; and then the cruel tongue speaks words that wound and a pen traces sentences that, if not disproved, will blast a reputation.

Mr. Stanley writes that the rear-column was wrecked 'by the irresolution of its officers, neglect of their promises, and indifference to their written orders.'

To a soldier of the Queen and a gentleman this is a serious accusation, and should not be allowed to pass. I have already written to the papers to point out that the instructions had been carried out; but Mr. Stanley took no notice of this. If on his return to Cairo, or when he arrived in England, he had retracted in some degree what he had said, or if in his book he had been able to explain his accusations, I would gladly have held my hand, and told his officers so.

In April, 1890, Mr. Stanley, knowing possibly

through his officers, some of whom I had seen, that we considered his silence to us something more than remarkable, pens a letter to my father, in which he emphasizes his accusations in such language as to arouse our indignation, and to raise a suspicion that there must be some motive for casting blame, in a manner apparently so unnecessary, upon one who was dead, and upon his comrades of the rear-column.

I went carefully into the matter, and wrote a reply for my father to Mr. Stanley (see Appendix), going fully into all points. Mr. Stanley acknowledged this through his secretary, saying he was too much engaged to reply to so lengthy a letter.

Mr. Stanley's book, 'In Darkest Africa,' proved misleading on so many points that it became necessary to warn the public of its character, and in a letter to the press I gave instances of the 'suppressio veri' and the 'suggestio falsi' which characterize the work. These accusations still remain unanswered.

I felt it, therefore, my duty to collect and arrange the material necessary to place my brother's memory in a true light, and to lay before the public an outline of the charges made against Major Barttelot, for which, if he had lived, he would have demanded redress from the proper authorities at home as well as for the conduct of Mr. Stanley towards himself while on the expedition, and would have claimed a searching inquiry into Mr. Stanley's reasons for leaving the rear-column without proper food, deserted for fourteen months, without carriers, and in the power of Tippu-Tib.

As an example of Mr. Stanley's manner of writing, the following is almost incredible. In 'Darkest Africa,' vol. ii., p. 220, he ridicules Emin Pasha for not having explored the Albert Lake :

'There are some things I have wondered at in Emin ; he was earnest and industrious in making observations upon plants, insects, birds, manners and customs, but I was somewhat staggered when I learned that *he had not explored Lake Albert.* He possessed two steamers and two lifeboats, yet he had never visited the southern end of the lake ' (or) ' examined the affluent at the south side,' etc., etc.

There happens, however, to be a book, called ' Emin Pasha in Central Africa,' edited by Professor Schweinfurth and others, published in 1888, in which is a map showing by a red line Emin Pasha's many journeys through his large province ; this red line passes to the south end of Lake Albert, and up the affluent Mr. Stanley lays claim to have discovered, which flows from the mountains Mr. Stanley also claims to have discovered.

Emin Pasha wrote a letter to Dr. Felkin from Wadelai, October 26, 1886 (before Mr. Stanley had ever seen Lake Albert at all), p. 507, same book, as follows :

' I send you an account of a tour to the Albert Nyanza. Since I wrote it, I have made two other excursions to the lake ; the chief result of my work is

*the discovery of a new river flowing from the Usongora
Mountains.* It is of considerable size, and flows
into the lake at the south. The river is called
Kakibi by the Wasongora, and Duéru by the
Wamboga. On account of numerous cataracts it is
difficult to navigate ; it pours into the lake throughout the whole year a large volume of water.'

So Mr. Stanley's Mountains of the Moon are
Emin Pasha's already-discovered Usongora Mountains, and Mr. Stanley's Semliki River is Emin
Pasha's already-discovered Kakibi or Duéru River.
Surely Emin should not lose the credit for his dis-
coveries, as well as his province and his wealth,
as the result of the Expedition for his relief.

It will be remembered that Emin Pasha, whom
Gordon had made Governor of the equatorial province of Egypt, was in distress for want of
ammunition, and his communication with the coast
and Zanzibar had been cut off by the Kings of Uganda
and Unyoro, while the Mahdists held Khartoum and
the Nile. England was set aglow with articles
written to fan the flames of generous enthusiasm in
an effort so noble as the relief of Emin Pasha.
Money was freely subscribed ; officers, burning to
distinguish themselves in the cause of honour, volunteered their services, and the Expedition was quickly
got ready to start.

*Mr. Stanley was selected as leader by the gentle-

---

* Copies of the papers presented to Parliament on this subject
are in the Appendix.

men who had formed themselves into a committee
to manage the relief.   All England was proud of the
thought of this gallant Expedition, of the singleness
of its aim, and of the integrity and purity of motive
displayed by the committee in organizing so chivalrous
an enterprise.   Yet it was considered necessary by
the committee, and by Mr. Stanley, that all the
officers should sign an agreement to publish nothing
until six months after the official report of the leader
of the Expedition—a circumstance of a very unusual
character !

Careless of what the consequences might be, they
signed away their freedom, and placed themselves
in the hands of Mr. Stanley.

I bitterly regret the necessity, which has been
forced upon me by Mr. Stanley, to undeceive the
public, and to remove the mask which has so well
concealed the true features of the Expedition for the
relief of Emin Pasha, of which they had formed so
lofty an ideal.

In the following pages will be found clear proofs
of the many objects for which the Expedition, and
the money subscribed to it, were made use of by Mr.
Stanley, other than the actual quest or relief of Emin.

The conduct and management of the Expedition,
which was essentially military in character in every
respect, except in that of its leader, was conspicuous
for its total want of that prudent foresight which
would have contributed so greatly to the comfort
and well-being of officers and men, by a sufficient

provision of food and transport, and which would have utilized the rear column by a proper disposition of his forces.

I would particularly draw the attention of the reader to the threats of Mr. Stanley to ruin Major Barttelot's reputation, and to the arrangements and understanding existing between Mr. Stanley and Tippu-Tib ; to the leaving Major Barttelot in Tippu-Tib's power ; and to the terrible consequences —in the death of Major Barttelot and Mr. Jameson, and the increase and impetus given to the slave-trade in the regions west and north of the Falls Station.

There is one feature of the camp-life at Yambuya on which it is pleasant to dwell—I refer to the touching friendship which existed between my brother and Mr. Jameson.

Of the character of these two men, of their loyal devotion to one another and to the interests committed to their charge, of their sufferings and sacrifices, and of their splendid maintenance of the camp in peace with natives and Arabs, notwithstanding every temptation to war, ample proof is given in the following letters of Major Barttelot, and in his diary, which was so fortunately sent home by Mr. Jameson to my father from the Falls Station, in August, 1888, shortly before his own sad death.

When the box containing them was opened, we found the contents—clothes, Bible, everything—falling to a damp dust. The diary, and some letters in a writing-case, although much injured by damp, and in some places illegible, were mercifully preserved. The box seemed to have been in water for months.

It may be well that I should state that, by permission, I have read Mr. Jameson's diaries, and find they corroborate my brother's in every way, especially in reference to Mr. Stanley's conduct to his officers. It is sincerely to be hoped that they will be published, as a matter of justice to the two friends. If they had lived to come home Mr. Stanley would not have dared to write a word against them. But he knows the law cannot defend the dead, that against the dead he can make accusations and the law cannot touch him. By the law there is no libel against the dead.

References in my brother's diary to Mr. Stanley's conduct towards himself and the officers of the expedition on the journey up the Congo have also been confirmed and corroborated by the statements made to me by nearly every officer of the Expedition.

But the diaries and letters direct from the hands of the dead form evidence of supreme value. ' Litera scripta manet.' They have not been able to alter or to add a tittle to what was written at the time, and the words of these two brave men call aloud for justice.

My brother's life was short and eventful ; born in 1859, he was murdered in 1888, being twenty-nine years of age. He had served as an officer in the Royal Fusiliers in three campaigns, and his experiences, prior to the Emin Relief Expedition, are given from his diary in the first two chapters.

Before closing this introductory chapter, I would take the opportunity to add a word of very sincere thanks to the press and the public for the marked kindness and courtesy with which they have uniformly treated the name of Major Barttelot, and for the fairness shown in reserving judgment on Mr. Stanley's statements concerning him, until the gag upon the mouths of his representatives is removed by the expiration of the six months (*since reduced to four*) of silence imposed by the agreement with Mr. Stanley.

Mr. Stanley's statements concerning Major Barttelot are answered in the order of sequence of events in the narrative.

I must ask the reader kindly to remember that it is not my aim to write only what will please or interest, but to do a duty to the dead by writing what I have been able to gather of the truth. If the facts recorded in the diary are at times somewhat startling from the manner or brevity of their narration, or from their nature, it will be recollected they were not written down for publication, but for reference for personal use only, and that it was not the intention of my family to publish a word of this pathetic story.

But the painful necessity to do so is rudely thrust

upon us, and may, perhaps, be urged as an additional plea in this appeal to the English people, with whom the love of fair play forms a court of honour whose judgment is unimpeachable, and whose justice is world-famed.

Records of an Officer

of the 7th Royal Fusiliers.

CHAPTER I.

EDMUND MUSGRAVE BARTTELOT, the second son of
Sir Walter B. Barttelot, Bart., C.B., M.P., of
Stopham, Sussex, and Harriet, daughter of Sir
Christopher Musgrave, Bart., of Edenhall, Cumber-
land, was born on March 28, 1859, at Hilliers, near
Petworth, Sussex. The morning of his birth has
always remained clearly impressed on my mind from
the vivid recollection of an amusing incident, typical
of Sussex wit. We children—myself and two little
sisters—had, after breakfast, carefully locked the
door to keep out the nursery-maid who was coming
to remove the breakfast things. After vainly trying
the door, in desperation she shouted out: 'Well,
then, I won't tell you your little brother's just been
born.'

At this we chuckled tremendously, and, having got the information, let her remain outside some while longer. Our mother died in 1863, and about 1868 we all went to live at Stopham.

Edmund was educated at Mrs. Cook's, 23, Montpellier Crescent, Brighton, and then at Rugby under Jex Blake. Thence he went to Mr. Fowler's, Tunbridge Wells, and then to the Rev. G. Faithfull's, Storrington, Sussex, where he prepared for his army examination. Having gone up for the line in November, 1877, he failed to pass by twenty-two places, was admitted in March, 1878, owing to the Russian War scare, and entered Sandhurst College on May 1, General Napier being governor, and Colonel Middleton commandant. He was of a bright and cheerful disposition, full of light and life, daring, impetuous, and of extremely active habits. He never could remain at home for a day without being off some long distance. He was a keen sportsman and a warm friend, quick-tempered but forgiving ; anything mean, untruthful, unmanly, or low he despised, and was apt to show his dislikes perhaps too much. From his childhood there was a certain reserve of power about him which compelled acknowledgment, and shadowed the outlines of a true and noble character.

The summer vacation of 1878 he spent at Honnef on the Rhine, Prussia, with Frau Hauptmann Moritz, a highly-cultured friend who receives pupils to prepare for the army and other examinations. My brother was of very abstemious habits ; he never smoked, and seldom took stimulants.

He now entered his twentieth year, and on Friday, January 22, 1879, was gazetted to the 2nd Battalion 7th Royal Fusiliers, *vice* Conolly, promoted to be Captain. The battalion was in India, and on March 4 we went to Southampton to see him off on the *Poona.* For companions he had three brother cadets, Spencer 44th, Corbett (Crow) 13th, Mockler (Ferryman) 14th. On April 4, having landed at Bombay the day before, he reported himself to the adjutant, C. D. M. Gall. Tommy Marsh, who was gazetted with him, joined on April 6.

In the February following the regiment embarked for active service in Afghanistan, going by sea to Kurrachee, and then by rail to Sibi, where he had good sport, shooting and riding with Drummond Wolff, Marsh, and De Trafford. The regiment then marched to Kandahar, *via* the Bolan Pass and Quetta, and were quartered in the cantonments with the 66th.

'On July 27 the siege of Kandahar began. By evening all the stragglers had come in, poor Hector Maclean being taken prisoner. Ayoub Khan regularly invested the city, firing shell at us daily, and attacking our working parties. De Trafford was shot in the leg.

'On August 16 a sortie was made against the village of Deh Kojah, as Ayoub's regulars held this in force, and annoyed us greatly; so it was determined to drive them out. We started at 4 a.m., and it was all over by 10 a.m. We drove them out, but could not hold the village. My regiment lost 170 killed and wounded, and three officers killed, viz., Lieutenants Marsh and Wood, and Major Vandeleur, and Captain Conolly wounded.

'On September 3 Roberts arrived with the relieving force, and the battle was fought, in which the Fusiliers again took part. For this we received the Afghan medal and clasp for Kandahar. The Fusiliers then went up to Maiwand in brigade to bury the dead there, and returned after six weeks. Colonel Daubeny died of small-pox, and Major Butler now took command.'

COPY OF A LETTER FROM E. M. BARTTELOT, LIEU-TENANT ROYAL FUSILIERS, TO HIS SISTER.

'Kandahar, *May* 16, 1880.

' DEAR E.,

' I got all your letters of April 15 last Friday, 14th inst., so you see they just about take a month. There has been a good deal of excitement prevailing during the last week here. On Sunday evening last, 9th inst., four men of the transport—of whom Captain Garrett was one—were out riding, paying a visit to a native chief. As they were returning they were fired upon by seven natives, and Garrett had his arm broken just above the elbow, and one of the sirdars (they had two for an escort) was shot in the wrist. They had some difficulty in getting them back to camp; however, they are doing well now. It was at first thought that Garrett would lose his arm. They never caught the men, because I think they never took any trouble about it. They sent out a party twelve hours after it had happened, and all they did was to find out the number of men, five of whom had guns and two swords only; this information they derived from a peasant boy who saw the outrage committed.

'On Wednesday last the Wali Shere Ali was proclaimed Governor of Kandahar, and on the same day received several handsome presents from the Viceroy of India, as a token of respect from the English Government. These presents were given to him by the *political* Colonel St. John, R.E., and General Primrose, who went down to the Wali's house for that purpose. Amongst the presents were a very handsome presentation sword, a gold watch set with diamonds worth 2,000 rupees, and a silver basin. On receiving the sword he said that before God he would never draw it against the English.

'To make it a day of general rejoicing he re-mitted two taxes, one on copper and the other on silver, which had before been rather irksome to the natives. After having received all the native chiefs, muliks, sirdars, etc., he gave everyone some-thing to eat and drink, and the meeting broke up.

On the next day the Wali paid a return visit to
General Primrose and Colonel St. John at the
former's houses in the cantonments. To celebrate
this visit all the troops were turned out to line
the road from the Shikapore gate of the city, from
which he came, to the General's house, a distance
of some two miles. We paraded in tunics, white
helmets, spikes and grenades at 4.15 p.m., and
did not get back to barracks till 6.45 p.m. The
Wali rode through us, accompanied by his two sons,
his brother and his interpreter, who is a Persian.
He wore the sword and watch given to him on the
previous day. Each company presented arms to
him by turn as he came past, and the colours were
shouldered. He stopped before the colours and
saluted them most religiously. He is a very fine,
handsome-looking man.

'The fruit here now is getting rapidly ripe, and
very good it is, apricots and peaches growing like
apples do at home. I always eat them in the
morning, as they say then they do you no harm,
and they certainly are much fresher; but the chief
fruits are grapes and mulberries.

'I have been buying a lot of curious things, and
shall send them home at the earliest opportunity,
whenever that may be. They manufacture capital
knives and first-rate gunpowder here, while the
boots that come from Herat are simply splendid. All
trade between Kandahar and Herat is stopped now,
however, as the road is closed ; it is a great nuisance,

as you cannot get any horses here now, because they all come from Heratwards, as there is scarcely any breeding here at all, but nearly all crop-farming. The horses that come from Herat and Cabul are splendid animals, especially those of the Turcoman breed. We have picked out a beautiful polo-ground, a grass one; before that we played on bare ground without a vestige of grass to it, and in appearance something similar to the Aldershot parade grounds. We are all playing on transport *tats* now, and capital ponies they make. I rode through the city the other day; it is a most wonderful place: part of it is covered in and like an arcade, and there are some very pretty things displayed for sale; but I did not buy any, as I had no escort, and it is dangerous to loiter. Whenever we ride through a village we always gallop through as hard as possible, so as to make being hit harder. I forgot to tell you what our field service kit is like. It is simply our white clothing dyed brown, and covers to the helmets worn over the spike, and a puggaree. It looks rather a neat kit, I think. Last Friday we were inspected by General Primrose, who found no fault with any-thing. They are going to send some of the troops away, I believe, for the hot weather, to a place some five or six miles from here called the Argendab Valley, but only two or three companies out of each regiment, so as to make more room in barracks, and not crowd up the men so much. The flies here are a perfect pest. . . .

'The body of poor —— of our regiment has been found at last. He must have been drowned in a fit.

'Please give my love to father and everyone at home, and, with much love to yourself,

'Believe me,

'Ever your most affectionate brother,

'EDMUND M. BARTTELOT.

'Royal Fusiliers,
    'Kandahar Field Force,
        'Afghanistan.'

COPY OF A LETTER FROM E. M. BARTTELOT, ROYAL FUSILIERS, TO SIR WALTER B. BARTTELOT, BART.

'Kandahar,
    'Sunday, *September* 5, 1880.

'DEAREST FATHER,

'I am all right and well, though I have had some narrow squeaks, as we have all had.

'The siege was raised on August 30, Monday last, and we came in here on July 28, so we have had rather a long time of it. Yesterday evening we got your letters of July 5, the first news we have had from England at all since we came in here, for we were entirely isolated and cut off from all communication. A mail arrived the day after we came in here, but was taken by Ayoub Khan. We held communication with Roberts's advanced guard on the 27th and 28th ult., by heliograph. What a splendid march they made! and in the face of it were not the least fatigued or done up ; in fact, they had an engagement with the enemy the evening of the 30th, when they marched in, and fought and licked them the next day. I hope you got my few lines written on the 29th all right.

'I hear the feeling in England about Maiwand was profound ; but it is not half so bad as it was made out at home, I expect. The brigade stopped Ayoub from going to Ghuznee, and though they did not beat him, they crippled him greatly, and carried out their orders to the full. The retreat was certainly a mistake, but the panic was great, and you do not know what it is ·to see these Ghazis fight : they come on by thousands, and don't care for bullet or shell, but when one rank is mown down another takes its place.

' Besides that, they had innumerable cavalry, about 4,000, I think, ours being only about 900, if so much. There was some report about the Scinde horse refusing to charge ; but when you come to think that they were under shell-fire for four hours, and that when the order came to charge the Ghazis were among them, it isn't likely they would. The 66th behaved splendidly, so did the 1st Grenadiers R.I. The 66th lost 400 men and ten officers. Our brigade was 2,400 strong, Ayoub's 20,000. On August 26 happened that fatal affair of Deh Kojah, when we lost three officers and thirty-nine men killed besides the wounded, most of whom have died. On that day we had a force of 1.000 strong to take one

of the strongest place simaginable, hold it, and drive
the Ghazis out, who numbered, as far as can be
judged, 10,000.   Our regiment went out 300 strong,
and was the only regiment which really got into the
village and went right through it.   In fact, we held
it for about fifteen minutes, but finding we could do
no good unaided, we retreated, as we were getting
surrounded.

'Poor Major Vandeleur, who had just come out,
young Wood, and poor old Tommy Marsh, who
joined with me, and was my greatest friend in the
regiment, are all killed ; Captain Conolly and
Trafford wounded.   Trafford was not wounded at
Deh Kojah, but when out on a working party about
a week before.   We have only got ten officers for
duty now — one major, two captains, and seven
subalterns—so we have lots to do.   Our Colonel,
Daubeny, is a Brigadier-General now, vice Brook,
killed.   After Deh Kojah, nothing happened till
Roberts marched in on August 31 and fought Ayoub
on September 1, and licked him ; all which the
papers will tell you far better than I can, as they
were lookers-on, whilst we were actors.   Our
regiment was out on the 1st, and the two companies
I was with were the only part of the whole army
that was under shell-fire : we were under it about
two hours, and, as we had no shelter, it was not very
comfortable.

'I must hark back now to our life during the
siege.   We were always on guard every night,

except when orderly officer. During the day we were on working parties, outside the walls sometimes, knocking down anything that might afford cover; sometimes inside, knocking down houses and searching houses. These working parties outside were so dangerous they had to be given up, for we were always being shot at and shelled, and lost several men ; so the work done was little compared with the loss. They shelled us in the city nearly every day. One day thirty-two shells came in, but hurt no one ; in fact, only one boy and three horses were killed by their shells. The first day we came in we turned out about 10,000 Pathans, including women and children. The reason why we left cantonments so hurriedly was because the city was rising, and if they had done so, the chances are that none of us would have been seen again. In fact, as it was, if Ayoub had only known how weak we were really, he would certainly have attacked, and the chances are, if he had persisted, he would have got in. I think Deh Kojah did good, insomuch as it made them leave the village after the affair was over, and it was from them the attack would have been projected ; in fact, from so many men being found there, especially regulars, it may be presumed that they were projecting one. Do you know that we ourselves on the 16th lost more men than all Roberts's European force put together, and just the same number of officers as when he beat Ayoub on September 1 ? And the number of the enemy we killed was five times as many as they did, though we helped them on the 1st, we not losing a man. In the enemy's camp were found no end of scaling-ladders, so that an attack was projected is certain. The only thing that sullied the 1st was the sad and horrid death of poor Maclean, R.H.A. He was, you know, Ayoub's prisoner, who had treated him with the greatest kindness, and when he saw how it was going, told him to escape, and in so doing he was killed by a Ghazi, his head being nearly separated from his body, the backbone being cut clean through. Phayre was yesterday at Abdool, about twenty miles off. Yesterday some of the 15th Hussars came in, among them Pocklington, whom I dare say you know; but I believe they are going back to India, as they are not wanted now.

'Roberts is in supreme command now. Nothing is known of what is going to happen, except that Roberts's force will go down at once.

'I do not expect to leave this till the other side of Christmas, if then, for I expect fresh complications will arise, as they are always doing, and that we shall be detained. During the siege, though we were packed closely, we never had the slightest illness among the troops or followers.

'Our supplies never failed us, thanks to the able management of Colonel ——, our Commissary-General, who died last Thursday from a wound received at Deh Kojah. I hope you are all quite well. You must excuse bad writing, as I have a

bad finger. F. A. Fortescue is up here, as also
" Bumpy " Lang. Please send this letter all round.
With heaps of love,

> ' Believe me,
>> ' Ever your affectionate son,
>>> ' EDMUND M. BARTTELOT.'

COPY OF A LETTER FROM E. M. BARTTELOT,
7TH FUSILIERS, TO HIS SISTER.

> ' Kandahar,
>> ' Sunday, *October* 11, 1880.

' MY DEAR E.,

    ' I got all your letters this morning just in
time to answer them by the mail, and am much
obliged to you for them. I want to know whether
you got a letter I wrote on half a sheet of foreign
paper in pencil, addressed to father, and dated
August 2. I wrote it a few days after we came in.

    ' I heard from poor Mrs. Marsh this morning.
She says she got the letter her son wrote to her on
that date, and we both wrote together, and so I
wonder if it is lost, as I have never heard you
mention it. We are still in the same place—outside
the city, under tents—and as the wind has risen the
dust is simply awful.

    ' I am afraid our chance of going down this year
is very small, because, though our health is so bad,
yet our strength is as large, and in some cases
greater, than that of other regiments. Besides,
there is, speaking with the utmost truth, at the

present time not enough transport to convey us down, for Roberts's forces have taken it all, or nearly all, and the remainder that was available has been taken by sick convoys. . . .

'Everything is most expensive up here now except grass and oats, but all the necessaries of life are terribly dear. We are going to have a great field-day to-morrow, under Phayre—a kind of sham-fight, I believe.

'Of course you know that Generals Primrose, Burrows, and Nutthall have gone down, and Daubeny has returned to regimental duty, or, at least, will do as soon as he is fit. I am very sorry for Primrose and Burrows, for, personally, they were the kindest men I ever met, and the latter was undoubtedly most plucky, and whoever doubts it or says anything to the contrary cannot know much about him.

'Our new Major, Butler, has arrived, and an awfully jolly sort of man he seems; he came last Wednesday.

'Everyone seems to think that Roberts's victory was a most wonderful affair, and frightfully hardly contested. That it was a most brilliant victory, and following on such a march, is not to be doubted; but that it can compare in any way with the fighting at Maiwand or Deh Kojah is simply ridiculous, as the difference of the enemy's casualties on those three days will show. We never touched their regulars on the 1st, and I don't believe we killed anywhere near a thousand of them. I rode round the battle-field two days afterwards, over the actual ground we fought on, and I did not see more than sixty dead over the whole space, and none had been buried then. I do not wish to detract from the victory in any way, especially as I was there in it; but if there had been hard fighting it would not have been accomplished so quickly. We began to storm the Kotal at 8.30 a.m., and the whole thing was over by 1 p.m., and we were back in barracks by 5 p.m. . . .

' I hope we shall retain Kandahar. Not that I wish to stop here myself, but should not mind going on to Herat next spring ; in fact, hope we do.

> ' With love to all at home,

> > ' Ever your affectionate brother,

> > > ' EDMUND M. BARTTELOT.'

CHAPTER II.

'FROM October, 1880, to April, 1881, at Kandahar,'
says my brother, 'was one of the happiest times of
my life. November, December, and January I was
very ill, from exposure to damp and cold, but we
hunted, shot, raced, drilled, dined *ad lib.*, and had a
real good time.

'We then went to Madras, when Grant Duff was
made Governor, and Sir F. Roberts, V.C., Commander-in-Chief. We formed both the escorts—I
was right guide on each occasion.'

[Soon after this my brother came home on leave,

from May 17 to August 11, 1882, and while at home the bombardment of Alexandria took place. He applied to be sent out, and]

' For that purpose was attached to the 18th Royal Irish Regiment, under Colonel Gregory, whom I liked. It was at this time that I formed the acquaintance of Harry Mansel Pleydell, who from that time to his death became my dearest friend, and formed in me whatever good there is in my disposition. Harry Pleydell, Drummond Wolff, and Neddy Edwards and myself were all attached to the 18th for this expedition.

' I left home after dinner on August 9 ; Captain Gilpin was dining with us, and sang a song. On August 11 we sailed in the *City of Paris* from Portsmouth ; the boys in the *Victory* manned the masts and cheered us, while the band played " God Save the Queen," and our drums played " Brian Baroo." We disembarked at Ismailia, and bivouacked under the trees by Mons. de Lesseps' house—I slept in his veranda. We worked hard August 26 and 27, and I worked with my men, and was noticed so doing, and was offered the post of staff officer to Sir Owen Lanyon ; but I was ordered off to Nefish before I could accept it. Here I was ordered to join the Mounted Infantry, on their way to Kassassin, where I caught them up, riding a pony bare-backed for the Duke of Connaught as far as Mahouta—thirty miles—and walking the rest of the way—twenty-five miles. Harry Pleydell and

Neddy Edwards had already joined. Our going to the Mounted Infantry from the 18th caused Gregory much annoyance, as he said we were the best officers he ever had, and he could not afford to lose us. *We did work, but Fusiliers always do.*

'On joining the Mounted Infantry, then commanded by Lawrence, 5th Dragoon Guards, I became Quartermaster and Paymaster, and subsequently Adjutant. Nothing happened worthy of note till September 9, when Arabi attacked us, and we beat him off from our camp at Kassassin. We had no casualties. On the night and early morning of the 11th I and Alderson, also M.I., with seventy men, went for a reconnaissance with Sir Redvers Buller and General Wilkinson. We got within a mile of Tel-el-Kebir (the Big Hill); no notice was taken of us, and we returned to our quarters at 11 a.m. Commander Rawson, R.N., was one of the party. This reconnaissance determined the route and method of attack on September 13. The evening of the 12th, sunset, the infantry moved off for Tel-el-Kebir—we were attached to the cavalry, and did not move till 1 a.m., when we skirmished in front of the column of cavalry. We were to move without noise. There was nothing heard but the voice of Sir Baker Russell. We marched to within three miles of Tel-el-Kebir, and then halted; at dawn we moved on, and had turned the flank of the works by 7 a.m., and at 8 were on the road to Cairo, with the 13th Bengal

Lancers, Herbert Stewart, C.B., in command. If it had not been for ——, we should have caught Arabi. At 1 p.m. we fought the action of Belbeis with Arabi's guard, and it was this action enabled Arabi to make good his retreat to Cairo, which he did by train from Belbeis. We halted at Belbeis, to await the arrival of the 4th Dragoon Guards, and then marched to Abassiyeh September 14. The 13th a squadron of the 4th Dragoon Guards and ourselves went on to the citadel at 8.30 p.m., arriving there about 10 p.m., when the whole garrison of 3,000 men marched out disarmed before us. Thus Cairo was taken. I went back that night with twelve men to Abassiyeh as escort to Sir Drury Lowe. Arabi gave himself up the same night, and was made prisoner. Cradock, 5th Dragoon Guards, was in command of the guard on him.'

In October, the Mounted Infantry being disbanded, Major Barttelot came home.

'During this short campaign Harry Pleydell first contracted that illness which eventually killed him.

'From the date of my arrival home I began to hunt regularly, and stayed at Stopham all October, November, and December, staying three weeks with Harry Pleydell at Whatcombe, Blandford, Dorset.

'After Christmas I went for the first time to stay at Park Hatch, which has ever since been a second home to me, and from Mr. Godman I have received so many kindnesses.

' I stayed at home till June, hunting and shooting
the fore part of the year. In June, as I should have
been going out to India, I exchanged battalions, and
joined the 1st Battalion at Colchester. I took up
the supernumerary adjutancy of the 4th Battalion of
the Royal Sussex Regiment, under Colonel the Earl
of March, at Chichester, and was there till June 30,
when I went to Colchester.

' At this time I was completely broken, and had
a financial crisis, and had to apply to my father, who
kindly helped me, but it was horrid.'

The autumn was spent in Edinburgh at a garrison
class under Major Cochran.

' I remained there till January 7, when I came
home. I was still suffering from impecuniosity, and
was determined to leave England. About this time
the Egyptian army called for English officers.'

[My brother arranged to go out, and arrived in
Cairo in February.]

' I stayed till March 1 with Colonel and Mrs.
Maitland, R.E., when I went to live in the Blue
House, Abassiyeh, being attached to the 1st Bat-
talion Egyptian Army, under Colonel Chermside,
C.M.G., R.E. Here I stayed a month, and learnt
Arabic and Egyptian drill. I played a good bit at
polo, and enjoyed life generally.'

[In April he went to Suakim, and was employed
in building the water forts, and then as staff officer
to Chermside.]

' On May 16 I embarked on the *Loch Ard*, my-

self, servant, and two ponies. We were the only
passengers. The *Loch Ard* was the ice-ship at
Suakim. We towed two small water-boats (Greek),
intending to take them to Suez, their port ; but
experiencing rough weather, they both sunk, all
hands on board. I arrived in Cairo May 21, and
took up my old quarters at Abassiyeh. In June I
resigned, and on July 22 was appointed Acting
D.A.A.G. to the Transport (of the army of occupa-
tion), and had charge of 500 camels and 250 men at
Abassiyeh. These I looked after and worked till
August 18, when I was ordered to take 300 of the
best up the Nile, and to start the next day,
August 19, on the Expedition for the relief of
Gordon.'

August 19 he started, and, doing about twenty
miles a day, got to Assiout on the 29th, the last
town in Lower Egypt, a 'mooderyat,' and large
grain store, also the base of the expedition as
regarded river transport. To Assiout from Cairo
is 200 miles.

' I came the whole way by the railroad, which
ends here, as the Nile was rising and the fields
flooded. I stayed at Assiout three days. I received
a telegram from headquarters ordering me to send
the camels on to Kench, and to proceed by postal
boat to that station, and thence by desert to Kosseir
on the Red Sea, to land camels from Aden, and
bring them back across the desert to Kench, and
then proceed up the Nile.

3

'*September* 4.—At Keneh I find a telegram that the camels would be at Kosseir, per British India s.s. *Eldorado*, on the morning of the 6th, and I must be there then with all arrangements made for landing, and there was no pier at Kosseir!

' It was now latish, and by the time I had dined with the Mudir, and impressed on him the necessity of immediate action (for I had to traverse a desert of 150 miles without water), it was 8 p.m. We were lucky enough to find a sheik, Ali Hamded, who lived at Bir-Emba, some eight miles out of Keneh, who had trotting camels. At 10 p.m. I left Keneh with Sergeant Brown, Papodophulo, an interpreter, and a Gladstone bag on donkeys for Bir-Emba, which we reached at twelve—a collection of Arab tents and grass huts in the desert. Two hours elapsed in filling water-skins, catching and saddling camels. Our party consisted of six men and camels —myself, Brown, the interpreter, Ali Hamded, and two others. We started at 2 a.m.

' My camel, a female, was a ripper. We travelled without a halt till 2 p.m.—about five miles an hour (for twelve hours)—halted under some rocks, had luncheon, rested till 5 p.m. We had now left the plain, and got into the mountains, and the track was quite distinct. We travelled till 12 p.m., and halted for an hour, but as my camel was faster, and both Sergeant Brown and Papodophulo were beat, also their camels, I decided to leave them to rest, and to ride on by myself with Ali Hamded, for I was afraid of being late. Accordingly we started, but I soon left Ali Hamded behind, and went on by myself. At 9 a.m. I reached Kosseir' (150 miles in thirty-one hours). 'I found the steamer was not yet in. I went straight to the house of the Governor, or " Mehafiz," and put up. Directly I got off my camel she lay down where she was, and did not rise for two days. I slept from 10 a.m. to 6 p.m., when I got up and bathed in the Red Sea. My men came in at 8 p.m.

'Next day the ship had not come. I made preparations for landing. On the 12th the ship came with 250 camels and 500 men, chiefly Somalis. Captain of the ship, Jairus Withers. We accomplished the landing in eighteen hours - hard work. Withers gave me a present of two suits of clothes, shirts, socks, a box of stores, and a case of brandy. There is no well or fresh water at Kosseir nearer than twenty miles, so I was busy getting water-skins and mussocks, and filled them from the reserve water at the Government House. We arranged the loads, and told off a water-guard of Somalis.

'September 13 we started towards Kench, and arrived all safe on the 16th. September 18 I started again from Kench, reaching Kosseir on the 20th. The ship came in on the 24th—150 camels and 300 men. Unfortunately, they were nearly all Aden boys, who are the scum of the earth, and only 16 Somalis. We had our own mussocks (for water), and these I put under the charge of the Somalis and their

" Mukadum," or headman.   There was one scoundrel whom I noticed especially, who seemed to have great power over the Aden boys.   I refused to take him at first, but the police-officer who had brought them over from Aden begged me to, as he was such a bad lot.   I took him, but warned him.

' September 28 we started.   Next morning I had some words with the scoundrel, and later in the day he tried to cut a hole in one of the water mussocks. I pulled him away, when he hit me with his weighted stick.   I shot him dead.'   (Major Barttelot often told me of this adventure ; the man hit him twice, and broke the trigger-guard off his pistol and a small bone of the hand.)   ' His friends at the next halting-place said they would take my life.   I asked for a reprieve till the evening, and promptly sent on my guide to Kench, saying I would be in on Sunday ; this was Friday.   At 2 p.m. we started, and halted at 8 p.m. for three hours.   I then called for the people who wished to kill me, and said they could do so, but that I should resist, and I would like to know who was going to show them the way.   They replied, "The guide."   I said, "He is not here." When they found such was the case, they were puzzled, and at last said I had done right.

' I arrived in Kench, Sunday, 28th, and saw Lord Wolseley and Sir Redvers Buller, and I was thanked personally by Lord Wolseley for the work I had done.

' *October* 7.—Steele took all the camels up to

Assouan, my ponies and Sergeant Brown and Papodophulo. I had permission of Sir R. Buller, after
going for a third and last time to Kosseir, to go
straight by the desert route from Kosseir to
Assouan ; no Englishman, and only few natives, had
done this.

'At Kosseir the ship arrived on the 14th with
100 camels and 200 men, chiefly Somalis. I broke
one camel's leg landing him ; this was the only
casualty I had, excepting the (Aden) scoundrel.

'October 15 we started. On the 17th we
reached the first well, Er-Gheita, halted for the day,
and started next morning, the 18th, and reached the
next well, El-Ab, at 10 p.m. on the 20th. It took
me till 4 a.m. to water the camels and men. At
2 p.m. we started for Roderia (on the Nile), and
arrived that night, halted and gave the men sleep,
and reached Assouan October 23. On October 27
I was telegraphed for to Wâdy Halfa (Valley of
Grass), and arrived there November 3, and reported
myself. I saw General Buller, who told me Lord
Wolseley wished to employ me with the boats, and
I was to be under Colonel Butler at Gemai.
November 5 I arrived at Gemai, and Colonel
Butler told me off to paint and repair every boat
as it came up. I now became a staff-captain with
rank of Captain. I had a gang of 200 natives and
about 40 Canadians, and 100 soldiers as fatigue-men,
to do this work, and I did the work first of all under
Colonel Butler and afterwards under Colonel Grove,

to their entire satisfaction, till December 18, when
Colonel Grove, Harry Sclater, and self were ordered
to Ambigoll. We went by train to Mohrat Wells.
Grove and Sclater went ahead. I came on with
the baggage, and walked on foot all the way, thirty
miles. Thence to Tanjoin, and then to Dal, fifty
miles. I walked on foot. At Dal I could get no
food for our camels, so I took some of Sir Evelyn
Wood's—result, a row. As usual, I fell on my
feet. I was employed as a portage here, and was
reported to Lord Wolseley for the good hard work
I did.

· 1885. *January* 6.—We were ordered forward
right up to Corti, Grove and Harry Sclater as usual
ahead, self with the baggage. I told them I would be at
Corti first, for I then framed the intention of marching
across the desert to Corti from Abu Fatimeh. Starting on the 6th, I marched to Mograckal, then across
the Absarat desert forty miles. With me were Rolfe,
a gunner, a capital fellow ; Sclater's servant, and
Zenophon Zeno, interpreter, and thirteen camels.
January 8.—Marched to Kajbar ; here poor Eagar
is buried. January 9 to Abu Fatimeh. There took
Groves and Sclater's camels. January 10 to Argo
Island ; here I got a guide, bought corn, and filled
the mussocks with water. *January* 11.—Rolfe, self,
Zenophon and guide started across the desert; reached
the Boulatti Wells at 7 p.m. We did all the
loading and unloading ourselves (we had no men).
January 12 to Basseleni in the hills ; here our guide

deserted. We three travelled all next day in the desert alone. We reached Ayat village and water January 14. Here I saw a man eight feet high, called the Khedive's Giant.

'*January* 15.—We reached Difan on the Nile, and had a real good bathe. One of my camels, a splendid baggager, had worn a hole right through his foot, but he was very plucky and held out.

'*January* 16.—Reached Corti ; but we were on the wrong side of the river, and there were only three of us and thirteen camels, so I fired towards the camp and nearly killed Sir E. Wood's servant. They then sent over to us.

' The 17th the battle of Abu Klea was fought. I was ordered to go to Gakdul Wells by Sir R. Buller to look after the water and commissariat quarters, Mr. Hickie as my aide, and a very efficient one he was.

' On February 8 I accompanied Sir R. Buller to Abu Klea and Gubat, having charge of £2,000 and three camels. I walked the whole way on foot, had no servant, and did the loading and unloading myself.

' *February* 13.—It was decided to withdraw, the fall of Khartoum and death of Gordon being more or less verified. We reached Abu Klea 15th. Sir R. Buller put me in charge of the wells, the most arduous and disagreeable duty I had ever done. But I obtained commendation for the way I did it.

' *February* 16.—This night we were attacked ;

poor Walsh was badly hit, also Paget, 7th Hussars ; nineteen men killed and many wounded. We drove them off.' (After a week here the force retired to Gakdul.) 'I looked after the water and lived with the rifle company. During my brief sojourn here I managed to get into trouble. I and Harry Lysons went out after some Arabs who had been annoying the camp, but were not successful. I had four 35th men with me. Coming home, four gazelles got up : one broke towards the desert, the other three towards the camp. I fired at the desert one and got him not ; the four Sussex men fired at the other three gazelles, missed, and their bullets fell in camp and just missed a sentry. Sir E. Wood sent to find out about it, vowing he would try the officer by court-martial. Of course it was me, which, when he heard, he told Vandeleur to wig me, and would see me himself on the morrow. I saw him ; he called me a ——, and asked me to dinner. . I dined.'

On the return of the column down the Nile Barttelot was continually employed on the transport and portage. April 30 he writes : 'I was appointed Sheik of Hannek and Shaban Cataract, with head-quarters at Kaboddie. I personally conducted all troop convoys down, and was often wrecked, but enjoyed the time greatly. Colonel Greaves, 45th, was commandant of the station ; Lord Airlie on the Transport ; Daubeny commanding E.A. and Firman 23rd Fusiliers Transport. I did a good deal of goose-shooting with Mackeson of the 5th Dragoon Guards. I received letters of thanks from General Grenfell and Colonel Grant, R.E., district commandant, for my work at Koboddie.

'*July* 9.—Settle told me I was to go with my boat laden down the Dal Cataract, and report on its safety for convoys.

'*July* 10.—I started at 6 a.m. We went down the cataract all stark naked and prepared for any emergency ; we had two or three narrow shaves, but got down all right, and arrived at Accacia at noon.'

' I stayed the day here with Colonel Wynne, E.A., and having handed over my boat and gear, here ended actually my connection with the Nile campaign of 1884-85.'

[My brother then came home.]

' I stayed at home till the end of the year, hunting a good deal. The best run we had was, I think, the one from Goatcher's Furze, at Broadford Bridge, December 1. We killed at Ashington, after forty minutes.'

'*December* 2.—I went out looking after the polling-stations for my father's election, going as far as Midhurst to the west and to Northchapel to the north-east. Next day we went to Horsham for the declaration of the poll. Father was returned at 4.30 by a majority of 2,000.'

1886. [My brother was laid up for eight days by a kick received from a thoroughbred mare of

Mr. Walter Dawtrey's, of Petworth, that he was hunting.

On February 12 he embarked again for Egypt on the *Crocodile*.   Arrived at Suez on March 2, and on to Cairo, where he rejoined his regiment, being quartered in the citadel.   He remained at Cairo, enjoying his regimental life and the amusements there immensely, till May 17, when he went to the convalescent home at Cyprus on duty.   Reached Limasol Sunday, the 20th.   Healy of the Dorsets, with 250 men, and two officers of the Durham Light Infantry—Wilson and Jones—with him.]

'We marched to Polymechia, and dined with Colonel Hackett; then continued our march by Zigo, Parapedia, and Platross, to Troodos.

'I remained at Troodos till the end of June with the 49th (Berks), a very smart regiment, and very nice officers.'

'*July* 1.—I obtained five days' leave to travel, and went to Susu, seeing the monastery of Omados on the way.   We slept out that night; then to Klima, where the mounted police (Zaptieh) had sports, it being the Feast of Bairam.   We saw the harbour and ancient town of Pappho, where there is a temple of Venus.   Next day to Pania; then to the monastery of Kliko.   The monks fed us, and gave us wine and a room.   The smells awful, and made me quite ill.   Returned to Troodos July 6.'

'*July* 16.   Obtained another five days' leave, and went to Pania—twenty-five miles; then to Polis, on the sea-coast—twenty miles. Williamson showed me the Phœnician tombs he was excavating, and took me to Cimmi, where he has built himself a house, and where there are copper-mines. I went down an old shaft. Then to Pomo ; then to Lifka —thirty miles—and back to Troodos July 20.'

'*July* 24.—I rode to Limasol, where I stayed the next day. Assizes were going on. I visited the Aqueduct of Colossi, the Salt Lake, and the ancient monastery of Akroterion ; then back to Troodos.'

[My brother was laid up all August with fever and abscesses in the facial glands.]

' Colonel Hackett, Sir Henry Bulwer, and Colonels Armstrong and Ward all did their best for me. I found Albert Collins of F Company such a good servant, kind and attentive. On September 9 I was carried by my Fusiliers down to Sir Henry Bulwer's cottage, for he had kindly insisted I must come, as I should never get well in a tent. That day I was made a Brevet-major.'

[(Major Barttelot on being promoted to the rank of Captain was made Brevet-major as well for his services in the Egyptian campaign. He also received medals.)

The *Army and Navy Gazette*, September 22, 1888, published the following communication :

' Major Barttelot was more than an ordinary volunteer. He was essentially a man of action. As was happily remarked about him when last on active service, he contained "grit." Whilst others

swelled the multitude of "tuft-hunters" who hang
around commanding Generals, hoping that some
crumb of favour may be bestowed upon them in the
shape of a Brevet or C.B., young Barttelot contented
himself by throwing his energies into any active
sphere that opened to him.   In Afghanistan he did
good service.   Again, on the Nile his efforts were
untiring.   Upon his arrival at Cyprus in command
of convalescents of his regiment in 1886, he at
once offered his services to the senior Commissariat
officer, Lieutenant-Colonel Armstrong, at that time
taxed heavily with additional work, in the Transport Department, owing to the establishment of a
sanatorium upon Mount Troodos for invalids from
Egypt.   Finding that there was no opening for him
in this direction, he obtained leave, and visited—
on foot—the remotest parts of the island, seeing
more of its interesting localities in the short space of
a few weeks than almost any visitors since the days
of Savile and Kitchener.   He was a singularly
temperate man.   Rising at daybreak, he would
walk twenty miles, and then breakfast upon a bunch
of grapes and a glass of water.   Yet so active and
strong was he, that few could touch him as to
climbing or pace upon the mountain - side.   Like
all enthusiasts, he was regardless of comfort, and
suffered the penalty of reckless exposure in Cyprus,
a severe attack of sunstroke laying him aside there.
His elastic constitution, however, quickly enabled
him to throw off this indisposition, and very shortly

after his arrival in England, in the fall of 1886, he volunteered for service under Stanley. Had Major Barttelot lived, there is little doubt he would have made his mark upon the present generation, not only as a brave soldier, but as an intrepid and successful adventurer.'

On Wednesday, October 20, a board of officers ordered him home on sick leave. He came by Alexandria, Malta, and Gibraltar, arriving at Portsmouth on November 16.]

'On the 17th I went over to see Walter Dawtrey, at Petworth, about horses.'

[He hunted regularly now, and gives an account of each run ; for example, December 7.]

'Tuesday : to Stopham. Hunted the chestnut at Drunswick Bridge. Very cold. I rode my own horse on. Found a fox in Malham, Ashfold ; ring twice there, and then went away for Brewhurst, Whephurst, and the Ifold woods ; turned right-handed past Ifold House, across the canal by the lock ; turned left-handed past Loxwood, on the east to Sidney Wood ; turned right-handed, and we killed him in the open meadow below Alfold village ; time, sixty minutes. The chestnut carried me well, as it was fast throughout. Shepherd ' (Lord Leconfield's huntsman) ' gave me the brush.'

' *December* 24.—I went to town on account of a telegram Fitzgerald had sent me concerning the Emin Bey Expedition. I was introduced to Mr. Mackinnon at the Burlington Hotel, and then went

with Mr. Fitzgerald to 160, New Bond Street, to
see Mr. Stanley, who said he would take me if I
obtained leave, and could get any recommendation
from a person of authority. We then went to the
War Office and saw Mr. Strong, and I wrote a letter
to Sir Redvers Buller.'

'1887. *January* 6.—I saw Lord Wolseley at his
levée, and got him to transfer me back to the
1st Battalion of the Fusiliers, and wrote my application for leave to travel abroad.'

'Leave was given me for one year, without pay.'

CHAPTER III.

FROM LONDON TO BANANA POINT AND THE MOUTH
OF THE CONGO RIVER : 1887.

The Contract—The Start—Egypt—Aden—Zanzibar—Soudanese
troublesome —Territory acquired for Mackinnon—An Extraordinary Compact—On Board the *Madura*—Can get no
Information from Stanley—Simon's Bay—Banana Point.

(Copy.)

CONTRACT OF ENGAGEMENT FOR THE EMIN PASHA
RELIEF EXPEDITION.

1. I, Edmund Musgrave Barttelot, Major, 7th
R.F., agree to accompany the Emin Pasha Relief
Expedition, and to place myself under the command
of Mr. H. M. Stanley, the leader of the Expedition,
and to accept any post or position in that Expedition
to which he may appoint me.

2. I further agree to serve him loyally and
devotedly, to obey all his orders, and to follow him
by whatsoever route he may choose, and to use my
utmost endeavours to bring the Expedition to a
successful issue.

4

3. Should I leave the Expedition without his orders, I agree to forfeit all claim to pay due to me to return passage-money, and to become liable to a refund of all the moneys advanced to me for passage to Zanzibar and outfit.

4. Mr. H. M. Stanley also agrees to give £40 (forty pounds) as an allowance for outfit, and to pay my passage to Zanzibar, and my return passage to England, provided I continue during the whole period of the Expedition.

5. I undertake not to publish anything connected with the Expedition, or to send any account to the newspapers for six months after the issue of the official publication of the Expedition by the leader or his representative.

6. In addition to the outfit, Mr. Stanley · will supply the following : tent, one Winchester rifle, one revolver, ammunition for the same, canteen, a due share of European provisions taken for the party, besides such provisions as the country can supply.

EDMUND M. BARTTELOT,

Major, 7th R.F.

January 8, 1887.

[On Friday, January 14, 1887, Major Barttelot bade us good-bye, and left England to embark on his adventurous, and, as it proved, fatal journey as a member of the Expedition in relief of Emin Pasha. I accompanied him to Charing Cross Station, and

at 8 p.m. the train started. He travelled as far as
Dover with Mr. Stanley, who was going to Brussels.
Major Barttelot arrived at Brindisi on the 17th,
and embarked on the P. and O. s.s. *Mongolia.* On
the voyage he made the acquaintance of Mr. and
Mrs. Waldie Griffiths, and others, who were very
kind to him. On Thursday, the 20th, the *Mongolia,*
after a somewhat rough and uncomfortable passage,
arrived at Alexandria.]

'*January* 21.—I met Junker at Shepherd's Hotel,
and went with him to see Dr. Schweinfurth. I
had an interview with Sir Evelyn Baring, lunched
with Sir Francis Grenfell, and dined with the
Griffiths.'

[Major Barttelot remained in Cairo until the 27th,
spending most of his time in visiting his many
friends. The appointment of a medical officer to
the Expedition was still vacant, for Dr. R. Leslie,
who had been with Mr. Stanley and Sir Francis de
Winton on the Congo, was to have gone with
Stanley on the Emin Relief Expedition as medical
officer without pay. but he writes : ' I could not sign
the contract, which I thought unfair. I wished to
insert after the agreement to publish nothing until
six months after Mr. Stanley's official report was
written the words, "except in the case of my reputation being attacked." The committee would not
hear of this, but the attacks made on all the members
of the rear-guard show that the proviso was not an
unnecessary one. I also objected to pledge myself

to treat the sick according to his directions, which I thought the contract as worded implied.'

The Expedition being therefore without a medical officer, Major Barttelot, when at Alexandria, gave Dr. Parke, an old friend of his who had served with him in the Soudan campaign, a letter of introduction to Mr. Stanley, and he obtained the appointment.]

'*Cairo, Thursday, January* 27.—Left Cairo by the 11.45 for Suez. Went and said good-bye to the Griffiths; I hope I shall see them again. Edith (his sister, Mrs. Sclater) and Harry (Major Sclater) and Surtees, the Chieftain McLeod, Burton and Hickie came to see me off. I embarked on the *Verona*, and arrived at Aden on February 1, remaining there till the 12th, spending the time in writing letters home, in exploring the neighbourhood, playing polo with the officers, and looking out for and engaging the twelve Somalis who accompanied the Expedition.'

'On Friday, 11th, embarked on the British India s.s. *Oriental* with the twelve Somalis at noon. My cabin, forward saloon on the port side. Heaps of Germans on board—a German woman and her husband are deck passengers: jolly for them, with all these Somalis and Egyptian soldiers on board.'

'The next day the *Navarino*, with Stanley on board, came into port at 3.30 p.m. We transferred all the baggage and left port at 4.30 p.m. Stairs only in my cabin. We all dine at one table, viz.: Stanley, self, Jameson, Jephson, Stairs; Bonny goes second class. The *Oriental* is a small and rather dirty ship, full of red ants and huge cock-roaches, but they do not bother me.'

'Sunday the 13th, Parke vaccinated me.'

EXTRACT FROM A LETTER WRITTEN BY MAJOR BARTTELOT TO MISS ——.

'SS. *Oriental,*
February 16, 1887.

'But I must tell you about our party. Mr. Stanley improves decidedly on acquaintance, and has been amusing us with stories, chiefly about him-self; but he chaffs all of us, and keeps everyone alive. I think we shall get on all right, though he is a man who would be easily upset, and when annoyed very nasty. At present he has not said much about the Expedition, but that we go by the Congo is a settled question, and he hopes to be at Wadelai by the middle of July at the latest.

'The next is Mounteney Jephson. . . . He will, I believe, act as a sort of secretary and amanuensis to Stanley. He seems a very nice fellow. His cousin is the lady (I do not know her name) who gave £10,000 to the Gordon Home, and she it was who instigated him to come out here, and found the money (£1,300). For, except those whom Stanley chose himself, the rest have to pay to come on it.

'Jameson, who has travelled a good deal in Africa, both South and Central, and also in Borneo . . . comes as naturalist and botanist, and that stamp of thing. He is a married man, and does not look very strong, but I presume he is. Anyhow, as far as I can judge, he is very pleasant. (Mr. Jameson also found £1,300 for the Expedition.)

'Third comes Surgeon Parke, one of the Army Medical Department. I knew him up the river in '84 and '85, and met him first at Assouan in October, '84. He is strong, bright, and clever, I believe, and when I arrived at Alexandria he came and asked me to write to Stanley for him, which I did ; and he says it was on account of that he came, but I don't think so. Stanley wanted a doctor, and took him as being the most available. I am glad Parke has come, for it is always well to have someone who is not an entire stranger.

'Fourth, Stairs, of the Royal Engineers, is very clever and quick, and I should say strong. . . . He will do the surveying part of the business, and also has charge of the Maxim gun, and is assisting me with the black troops at present.

'Fifth, Nelson, who was in Methuen's Horse in '84 on the Buchuanaland Expedition, and in the Cape Mounted Rifles prior to that, and served in the Zulu War of '78, '79, and '80 with either Buller's or Baker's Horse, is, in my opinion, a most useful man. He has grand physique, and heaps of common and practical sense. He will be under me commanding the fighting force, which, as far as I know, will consist of about 700 fighting men. Stairs will also indirectly be under me.

'Sixth, Troup. I know nothing about him personally, as he is not here, but away at the Congo collecting stores, etc. His duties will be to look after and manage the commissariat department of the whole Expedition—no light business, and I am glad I have not got it, for it is an arduous and thankless task.

'Seventh, Sergeant Bonny, of the Army Hospital Corps, who purchased his discharge especially to come on this business. I have not spoken to him much, but he seems a good, useful, all-round sort of fellow. His duties, of course, will be with Parke.

'Eighth, William Hoffman, a German boy, and Stanley's servant.

'Ninth, myself. To me has been given the command of the fighting force, and also the care of the transport. I hope my health will last to enable me to go through with it.

'At present we have on board only sixty-three Soudanese soldiers, commanded by four native officers, and two interpreters. The men are recruited from what was known as the Black Battalion, from the remnant of Gordon's men who came down the Nile with us, and from the Mudir of Dongola's bashibazouks. They are at present a most lawless and undisciplined lot, but by the time we get to the Congo I hope to have them well in hand.

'On board this ship it is too crowded to do anything. The twelve Somalis whom I recruited at Aden are, I believe, thoroughly good men ; they will act as sort of gun-bearers and servants. At Zanzibar we are to get 600 Zanzibaris, who will form portion of the fighting force ; but as yet Mr. Stanley has said nothing to me about them, except that they are coming. These Soudanese are armed with Remington rifles.'

[After an uneventful passage, stopping only off Lamu and Freila, they reached Mombasa at 7.30 p.m. February 20. A very pretty place, and interesting now as the principal port of the great territory of the Imperial British East Africa Company.

The *Oriental* anchored off Pemba Island the evening of the 21st, and made Zanzibar at 11 a.m. next morning, the 22nd.]

' I took the Soudanese soldiers off at 12.30 to the British-India ss. *Madura*, also the Somalis ; got them all settled down by 2.30 p.m., and stored arms. Worked hard all the afternoon till 6 p.m.

'It is fairly hot here, and these Soudanese soldiers have been giving trouble. I think Chermside must have picked out the biggest scoundrels he could find.'

[In the very short space of time between the 22nd and the evening of the 24th, Mr. Stanley had, according to his book, made some hurried arrange- ments which eventually proved of much moment to the Expedition (' Darkest Africa,' vol. i., p. 68) : ' I

have settled several little commissions at Zanzibar
satisfactorily. One was to get the Sultan to sign
the concessions which Mackinnon tried to obtain a
long time ago.' (Sir W. Mackinnon was chairman
of the Emin Pasha Relief Committee, whose single
object was the relief of Emin Pasha.) 'This concession that we wished to obtain' (vol. i., p. 69),
'embraced a portion of the East African coast, of
which Mombasa and Melindi were the principal
towns.'

On page 52, vol. i., Mr. Stanley writes : ' It is
the relief of Emin Pasha that is the object of the
Expedition, the said relief consisting of ammunition
in sufficient quantity to enable him to withdraw
from his dangerous position in Central Africa in
safety, or to hold his own if he decides to do so for
such length of time as he may see fit.'

The first business concluded by Stanley in his
Expedition for the sole purpose of the relief of
Emin Pasha was his acquisition, for the chairman
of the Relief Committee, of a coast-line of over
400 miles. It must be remembered that the
subscribers to the funds of the Relief Committee,
and every individual who volunteered his services,
had one object alone— the relief of Emin.

When we view the first act in the busy Eastern
scene at Zanzibar, this action on the part of
Mr. Stanley, to acquire territory for Mackinnon
from a dying Sultan, seems out of place, and
hardly in accord with that British chivalry which,

it was believed, alone had called the Expedition into being— or with the notion that was prevalent that the Expedition had one single purpose only.

Mr. Stanley's second action was to settle a little commission with Tippu-Tib, whom he induced to embark before midnight of the 24th with some ninety followers on the *Madura*, and to journey with him to Stanley Falls. What inducement could have prevailed on this powerful slave-trader thus hurriedly, and without warning or preparation, to leave his affairs and his wealth at Zanzibar, and, with scarcely three days' notice, to rush off on a philanthropic enterprise with his quondam friend, Mr. Stanley?

It seems astonishing, but the agreement entered into was that Tippu-Tib should be made Governor of the Falls Station, and receive £360 a year from the King of the Belgians. All that Tippu was to do in return was (vol. i., p. 71): ' You must hoist the flag of the State. You must allow a Resident to be with you, who will write your reports to the King. You must neither trade in slaves, nor allow anybody else to trade in them below Stanley Falls, nor must there be any slave-catching, you understand. . . . But there is to be no pillaging native property of any description whatever below your station.' So that, by this very agreement, slavery, slave-catching, and pillaging native property were actually allowed—nay more, countenanced and permitted—to a salaried Governor appointed by

Mr. Stanley and the King of the Belgians over all the country above Stanley Falls, a vast distance of some hundreds of thousands of square miles, and with a large native population. Of the value of the agreement not to raid the country below the Falls we have sad experience later on.

The second agreement was (vol. i., p. 64) : 'After a good deal of bargaining, I entered into a contract with him (Tippu), by which he agreed to supply 600 carriers, at £6 per loaded head, each round trip from Stanley Falls to Lake Albert and back.'

Dr. Junker had informed Mr. Stanley that Emin possessed about seventy-five tons of ivory, of the value of £60,000. Accordingly, 'I wished to engage Tippu-Tib and his people to assist me in conveying the ammunition to Emin Pasha, and on return to carry this ivory.'

In consideration of these apparently hoped-for services, Mr. Stanley gave Tippu - Tib a free passage for himself and his ninety followers to Stanley Falls, with board included, at the expense of the Relief Expedition.

But, as we shall see, when Mr. Stanley arrived at Yambuya, close to the Falls Station, he did not expect that Tippu would provide the men ; at least, from Mr. Stanley's own account (see vol. i., p. 125). It will be remembered that Tippu-Tib had benefited by Mr. Stanley's Expedition of 1874, by following the explorer's route, and that he had in consequence obtained possession of all the country on the Congo east of the Falls Station, the King of the Belgians having benefited to a like extent on the west.

Was Mr. Stanley about to help his friends still more? By the agreement, he makes Tippu-Tib acknowledge the titular sovereignty of the King, and he makes the King acknowledge the right of the slave-trader to carry on his infamous traffic, and give him £360 per annum. The King lends Mr. Stanley one steamer on the Congo for the Expedition; Tippu-Tib, apparently, is not expected to help his friend in any way, for the carriers, if provided, are to be paid for.

Whenever an Arab comes into collision with a white man, Mr. Stanley generally thinks the white man is to blame; even Mr. Deane, defending native women from the ferocious Arabs at the Falls Station in 1886, is blamed by Mr. Stanley (vol. i., p. 65). Whatever understanding existed between Stanley and Tippu-Tib, such were the ill-advised and hurried arrangements concluded at Zanzibar, so fruitful of disaster to a part of Mr. Stanley's Expedition, and to the natives around the Falls Station, whose villages have been looted and burnt, and the inhabitants tortured, destroyed, and driven in chains to slavery by the bands of men who work for the arch-slave-trader, Tippu-Tib, Governor of Stanley Falls.

By midnight on the 24th the work of preparation was complete,* and Friday, 25th, the *Madura*

---

* This was the third time on this Expedition that Major Barttelot started with Mr. Stanley on a Friday—from Charing Cross, from Aden, and now from Zanzibar.

left port at 6.30 a.m., having on board the nine Europeans of the Expedition—Mr. Stanley, his servant Hoffman, Barttelot, Nelson, Stairs, Jameson, Jephson, Parke, and Bonny—and some 623 Zanzibaris (porters obtained at Zanzibar), 61 Soudanese soldiers, 2 Syrians (interpreters), 13 Somalis, Tippu-Tib the slave-dealer, and his 55 men and 35 women. The men were told off into companies. Major Barttelot, being the senior military officer, had command of the Soudanese, whom Mr. Stanley took with him for the special purpose ' to enable them to speak for me to the Soudanese of Equatoria. The Egyptians may affect to disbelieve firmans and the writing of Nubar, in which case these Soudanese will be pushed forward as living witnesses of my commission ' (vol. i., p. 68).]

> ' B. I. S. N. Co.'s Steamship *Madura*,
> ' Indian Ocean,
> ' *March* 2, 1887.

' MY DEAR FATHER AND MAMMA,

' I dare say you have got my last letter from Zanzibar, written Wednesday, 23rd. Early on Thursday, February 24, the Zanzibaris began coming on board by fifties. They were all on by 6 p.m., the total number being 623. Three of them were stowaways, and we did not find them till after we had left harbour. As soon as the last of them was reported on board, Mr. Mackenzie (from Mackinnon, Mackenzie, and Co.) and I mustered them, and found all present. We then weighed anchor and steamed

out four miles from the shore, served out biscuit to
them and water, and placed guards of the Sultan's
troops at the different gangways.   These troops I had
applied to General Matthews for, he being the Sultan's
Commander-in-Chief.   He was formerly a lieutenant
R.N., and is a very capable and able man ; but he is
not half well enough paid by the Sultan, considering
the work he does and the services he has performed :
800 rupees a month is, I think, his pay, and the
strength of the army is between 750 and 800 men
— nice soldier-like-looking men and well dressed.

'While we lay at Zanzibar I was unable to see
anything of the place, as my duties kept me on board,
where I had my hands full, with my troublesome
Soudanese, who, though only one - tenth of the
whole, give more trouble than all the rest ; and also
I had to make out and indent for the necessary
rations for all these men, as this had not been done.
On Wednesday evening I dined with Drummond,
Busty's brother ; he was with a man called Berkeley,
and Goodrich, formerly Vice-Consul at Nyassa.
Next night, Thursday, we all dined with Holmwood, acting Consul and Vice-Consul. The *Tur-
quoise* lent us her steam-pinnace, and we all came
back in that.

'Next morning I had a rare business issuing
rations.   We began at 5 a.m. and finished at 9 a.m. ;
but now we have got them all squared, and it is
done in half the time—rare hot work it is, too, down
in the hold.   They get good rations: rice, biscuit,

curry stuff, ghee, dhall, tea, sugar, salt, and meat
and potatoes alternate days. I manage the whole
business at present, detailing all the duties, and have
my hands full all day. We left our moorings at
6.30 a.m. on Friday, the 25th, and at 9.30 there was
a free fight between the Soudanese and the Zanzibaris; the former got a jolly good licking, which has
done them a power of good; blood flowed freely.
Stanley stopped it. I was in my bath at the time.
Of course you will have heard that the great slave-
dealer Tippu-Tib is on board with us. His country
is called Myama, on the Upper Congo, and I believe
he is coming the whole way with us to Wadelai.
He is an oldish-looking man, about 6 ft. 2 in.—a
fine, powerful, intelligent face. He is accompanied
by a brother-in-law and two male friends, making
with his followers ninety-one persons.

'Up to the present we have had splendid weather,
but yesterday morning early we got into the Mozam-
bique Channel, and there has been a heavy swell
ever since. The ship rolls terribly, and last night
we were obliged to have our ports closed. I kept my
scuttle open, though. Our numbers and nationali-
ties are as follows: Europeans, 9; Syrians, 2;
Africans, 1; Zanzibaris, 623; Soudanese, 60;
Somalis, 13; Tippoo's men, 91, making a total of
799 men, who are told off into squads or sections of
about 115 each, as follows: A Company: Myself,
60 Soudanese and 13 Somalis, 2 Syrians, 2 Zanzibaris, 1 African—a total of 79. B Company: All

Zanzibaris, Stairs.   C Company : Zanzibaris, Nelson.
D Company : Zanzibaris, Jephson.   E Company :
Zanzibaris, Jameson.   F Company, Zanzibaris, Dr.
Parke.   All the others have been made captains,
though all but Stairs are civilians.   I get up every
morning at 5 a.m., attend issue of rations, parade
the guard, and see that all fatigues are carried out.
This takes me till 8 a.m.   At 9 a.m. I see my own
company's quarters swept and cleared, and at 10.45
go round with the Captain to see the whole of the
decks are clean and cleared of men.   I write and
issue the orders, appointing orderly officers, etc.,
and all reports are made to me.   Stanley does not
do much at present, and rightly, when he has us to do
it.   All issues of blankets or any stores are made
through me, so you see I have plenty to do, and I
am, I believe, very fit and well.   We had a little
rain yesterday and the day before, but it cleared off.
I have got two Zanzibari boys told off to me, called
respectively Omalley and Solomon.   They are for
gun-bearers, and to look after my donkey and Sate,*
if I take him.   Yesterday and to-day we were all
busy packing Remington cartridges into loads
weighing 60 lb.—very hot work, but it will condition
me.   I have put on a lot of weight lately.   The
Somali boys whom I got at Aden are the best of the

---

* His dog 'Satan,' a Manchester terrier, who had been with
him in Egypt; he sent him home from Banana.   A few months
after the news of Major Barttelot's death, the dog drowned himself in the river at Stopham.

lot. Stanley is going to use them as his bodyguard, and they will be armed with Winchester repeating rifles.

'*March* 7.—We are now close to Simon's Bay, as last night we had a ripping breeze. Simon's Bay is the naval station, and is twenty-five miles from Cape Town. We shall have to take in a few stores and some ammunition. I have decided to send Sate back from the Congo. The more I see of these Zanzibaris the better I like them, they are so willing and tractable—such a contrast to my odoriferous and surly Soudanese. I see no reason why we should not be back next March ; but it all depends on the action taken by Emin Pasha. I hope I may find letters to-morrow, but I doubt. Do take care of yourself, dear father, and keep well and strong against I come home, to which happy event I expect we shall all look forward with no small anticipation after a few months of Africa. *It will take us ninety days to Stanley Falls*, which is where we leave the river, *and about thirty-five days' march from thence to Wadelai.* I see no reason why we should not all keep well and be successful. We are going half-speed now, and have taken in all sail, as we cannot get in at night.

'*March* 8.—Got into Simon's Bay at 7.30 this morning. The Admiral, Sir Hunt Grubbe, was away. There is a guardship here, the *Flora*, Captain Hand, the *Royalist*, a composite ship, and three gunboats (10-inch guns).

5

'We went on shore, and dined at the Royal Naval Club. They are building tremendous forts here. We went for a long walk this afternoon. It is a most lovely country, and if it were not for the south-east wind the place would be charming.

'We have yet to take on certain stores, and some 30,000 rounds of ammunition, and then away.'

EXTRACTS FROM A LETTER FROM MAJOR BARTTELOT
TO MISS ——.

'SS. *Madura,*
'*March* 11, 1887.

'Tippu-Tib is going to give us 600 fighting men, armed with rifles of all sorts, and they will meet us at Stanley Falls. We are to halt a month at the southern end of Albert Nyanza, whenever we get there, after leaving Boma, which is the town to which we hope to bring this steamer on the Lower Congo. Provisions and food of all sorts are very scarce, and we shall not get any quantity till we get to Stanley Pool. We have all been doing so well on board ship that a little starvation will not harm us. Our new man is a good sort. His name, I find, is Walker, and he has been on the Congo for two years. He only came home last October, and does not give a very glowing account of the Congo Free State. . . .

'I am often afraid I may fall short of the mark, for, of course, and naturally, Stanley expects us to be prodigies in the way and amount of work ; but no

man can add a cubit to his stature, nor can water
ordinarily be squeezed out of a stone. He is a funny
chap—Stanley ; sometimes I like him fairly well,
and sometimes quite the reverse. . . .

' I have had to send back heaps of those things
you saw at Stopham, for I cannot carry them, as I
should be over-weight ; as it is, I have to get Stairs
to carry ammunition for me for my rifle, and Jameson and I go shares in shot, wads, and caps. . . .
We are to be allowed one lamp and one candle
among us ten—the candle to last us three nights.'

' *March* 16.—Ingham and Walker, the civil
engineer, do not come with us beyond Stanley Falls.
I believe, in all probability, we shall steam up the
Albert Nyanza, or a portion of us will, as there are
two steamers there—the *Wadelai* and another.
Stanley asked the Church Mission at Stanley Pool,
who possess a very fine steamer called the *Peace*, to
lend her to us ; but the head of the mission wrote to
say he was very sorry he could not lend it to a man
whose life was accursed before God, and whose
every act was one of cruelty. Stanley told us about
it last night. . . . I had a long talk with Stanley
to-night ; he does not know yet quite what he is
going to do. He says he expects advices at Banana
Point, but expressed himself determined to get the
utmost out of us. I told him not to be disappointed
if we, and self in especial, did not turn out all that
he could wish. . . . He (Stanley) has got some
special job for me, but he won't tell me yet what it

is. I expect we shall all know before long more than we want. I wonder if any of us will ever want to come again. Stanley says we shall not. He receives no pay for this business, he says, and has given up £10,000 to come on it.'

EXTRACTS OF LETTER FROM MAJOR BARTTELOT
TO HIS SISTER, MRS. SCLATER.

'Atlantic Ocean, SS. *Madura*,
'*March* 14, 1887.

' MY DEAR EDITH,

' I must first wish you a very happy birthday; you have all my best and kindest wishes.

' What you said of Stanley is quite true. He is an extraordinary man, and I do not think, taking it all round, and leaving myself out of the question, that he treats the fellows quite fairly. He has told us next door to nothing about the business, and is very close about money matters. I have not collided with him yet, though I told him I thought he ought to be more explicit. We arrived at Table Bay, Cape Town, on the evening of the 9th, and went alongside the coaling wharf; next morning I and old Satan went on shore to see the place—very pretty, but uninteresting. Going round the Cape of Good Hope we caught it rather, but the shore landscape was lovely. Mr. Godman sent me a telegram, which I got at Simon's Bay; wasn't it good of him? I hoped to hear from home how father was, for the papers give a poor account of him.

'Our sea journey has been everything that we could wish, and we have only lost one Zanzibari, who died to-day. . . .

'I cannot tell you much about my companions at present; they seem a good lot. Parke, of course, I know. . . . We hope to be at Wadelai by the middle of June. What will happen then I do not know. Stanley expects serious fighting after leaving for Zanzibar.

'I am at my old game again of transport, commissariat, and general odd man, and have plenty to do, and am always glad to go to bed.'

'*March* 17.—We get to Banana Point to-morrow at 11 a.m., but we shall not disembark, I expect, for we may go up another sixty miles to Emboma; but it all depends. After we leave this ship, whether at Banana or Emboma, we have sixty days before we get to Stanley Falls, seventeen days of which we march.

'Mr. Stanley has given us each a donkey and a saddle. I shall bring my moke home if he lives, and give him to Evelyn's baby.

'Stanley expects fighting after leaving Stanley Falls. I do not think he means the whole of us to go up to Wadelai; he will leave some of us at the camp he is going to form on the Albert Nyanza. . . .

'I have had some long talks with him. He does not know when we shall be back, but he thinks at the least eighteen months. Lively, isn't it? Some of us, I expect, will hold our lives as not worth a moment's purchase, though the only disease that is bad appears to be fever, which apparently leaves no after-traces.'

LETTER FROM MAJOR BARTTELOT TO SIR WALTER BARTTELOT.

'SS. *Madura*,
'*March* 17, 1887.

' MY DEAR FATHER,

'We are just off the mouth of the Congo; we shall be there at Banana Point at about 11 a.m. to-morrow. It depends on the news there whether we shall go on in this ship to Emboma, sixty miles up, or whether we tranship at Banana Point. In either case, when we have completed our tranship-ment, and are again on the move, we shall take sixty days to reach Stanley Falls, seventeen days of which will be marching.

' Stanley intends halting at the southern end of Albert Nyanza, and forming a camp there. We go up this lake in the steamers belonging to Emin Pasha, but if he and they are not there we shall have to track it along the shores. I fancy Stanley does not intend taking the whole force there.

' It would be a grand chance of going on to Khartoum, but that will not be possible, I am afraid. I have had long talks with him about the business in hand; he has got something special for me to do, though what it is I do not know. He changes his plans daily, and, as he says himself, is not master of his own movements, as all depends on the news he gets at Banana to-morrow, and during our journey up the river. Tippu-Tib is giving us 600 armed men. They meet us at Stanley Falls. . . .

'When we shall be back I cannot say. I fancy some of us will regret the day we were born—at least, we ought to if what Stanley says be true, but I dare say it is exaggerated.

      *   *   *   *   *

'Satan' (his dog, a Manchester terrier) 'comes home in this ship. I do not want to lose him ; we have lost two men since leaving Cape Town.

'Now, dear old father and mamma, good-bye ; do take care of yourself and not overwork. You have done your share of work ; it is time for us to begin now.

'With my love to you both,

                ' Ever your affectionate son,

                        ' E. M. B.'

                        ' Banana Point,
                            ' *March* 19.

'Got here yesterday, and they are all gone up except myself and Jephson. We go to-morrow (D.V.—and the King of the Belgians).'

CHAPTER IV.

Start up the Congo—Matadi—On the March to Leopoldville—
Soudanese Mutiny — American Mission at Palabella —
Soudanese clamour for Provisions—Stanley threatens to ruin
Major Barttelot's Military Reputation—Stanley's Revenge—
Kindness of the Missionaries—Mr. Casement—Leopoldville
—Difficulty about Steamers—Stanley's Sharp Practice—On
the *Stanley*—March to Mswata—Barttelot hears of Intention
to leave him behind at Bolobo—The Holy Fathers of St.
Esprit, Kwarmouth—Bolobo.

Friday, March 18.—SS. *Madura*, Congo River,
Banana Point. Arrived here to-day ; went ashore at
noon to see the Portuguese Consul ; got a paddle-
wheel steamer from him called the *Serpa Pinto ;*
from the Dutch House one steamer, the *Keiman ;*
from the British African Congo Association, Mr.
R. M. Dennett, one steamer, the *Albuquerque.*
Mr. Dennett and Mr. Cobden Philips, of the British
African Congo Association, Mons. Fontaine and
Mr. Gray, of the Belgian Association, dined with
us. Banana is not much of a place, and is very hot.

'The *Heron* has been offered us by the Belgian Free State, and comes the day after to-morrow— rather amusing after the offers of help by the King of the Belgians. However, the cable is broken between the Cape and St. Paul de Loanda, and our arrival had not been intimated.

'*Saturday, March* 19.—At daybreak, 6 a.m., the *Albuquerque* came alongside, Captain Howe. Dr. Parke and his men and stores embarked on that ship at 7.10. The *Keiman* took Jameson and Nelson; only men and no stores. This boat left at 9.30 a.m.; the *Albuquerque* left at 10.15. At 10.30 the *Serpa Pinto* came up and took Stanley and his staff, the Somalis, also Stairs and his company, a great quantity of baggage, 20 donkeys and Bonny, 34 sheep and goats, Tippu-Tib and his party.

'Jephson and I were left. It was proposed we should go up on the *Heron* with the rest of the baggage; but we were told she was not big enough, and could only take our little baggage. Accordingly Jephson went and saw the Portuguese Consul, who kindly offered to lend us the *Kacongo*.

'*Sunday, March* 20.—The *Kacongo* came alongside at 6 a.m., but as the *Heron* came up, I embarked Jephson and his men in her with the portable boat; he left at 9.30 a.m. I went on packing with the Soudanese, and at 11.15 we embarked on the *Kacongo*.

'I went round the *Madura* with Captain Mac-

kennis, signed up, gave Mackennis my letters, sixteen in number, and wished him and his officers
good-bye with genuine regret, for they had been
most kind to us, and had always treated us with
great kindness and hospitality, and aided us in
every way.

'The commander of the gunboat *Kacongo* was
Lieutenant Nunes da Silva; with him were two
other officers and eight engineers. They treated me
right well. Nunes da Silva spoke French. We
got as far as Boma that night, sixty miles up. Here
I found the *Heron* and Jephson. I went on shore
and saw Major Parminter, chief of the Belgian Free
State. He gave me such a bad account of the pro-
babilities of obtaining food up to the Falls Station that
I wrote a letter to Mackennis, ss. *Madura*, to land
all the rice which we had left on board, and have it
laid up at the Dutch House. The country to Boma
is flat, but with distant hills.

'*March* 21. — We reached Noki, forty miles
further up, at 9 a.m., where we stopped; then on
to Matadi about 2.30. We commenced to wade at
5 p.m., and knocked off at 6 p.m., having unloaded
everything but the rice and eight casks of cooking-
pots.'

The expedition remained at Matadi until the
25th, getting into order for the march to Leopoldville.

'*Friday,* 25.— Began the march. Got to the
camp on the Mpozo River at 12.30 p.m., over some

terrible hills.   At 4.30 Stanley told me to send back
my Soudanese with Ingham to fetch twenty days' rice
apiece from Matadi, but they refused, and mutinied.
Stanley spoke to them, and they came round ; it
was, however, too late for them to go back, so next
morning, March 26, I left at 6 a.m. with forty-six of
them to bring the rations back.   We got to Matadi
at 8 a.m., fed, and started back at 9 a.m. ; got half-
way, when they fought among themselves about
the loads, so I halted, and redistributed the loads
equally.   We got to camp at 8.30 p.m.—the rest,
all but Walker (the engineer), had gone on ; but as
several Zanzibaris had gone back the day before
to fetch rice from Matadi, their loads were still at
Camp Mpozo.   Men came back to fetch them, but
too late to start.   I helped Walker unscrew his boat
—the portable boat, by which some had come to
Mpozo—and sent it and him to Palabella, our next
camp ; found they had left behind four sick men and
one dying.   I slept out in the open air that night,
but the dying man made such a noise . . . that I had
a bad time.   Next morning left Mpozo for Palabella
at 6 a.m., taking the dying man with me, but he
died on the road.   I got in at 11.30.   Ingham and
Clark, of the American Mission, gave me breakfast—
the road was downhill the whole way, wooded, and
covered with bracken.   Palabella is 1,700 feet above
the sea.   Bathed with Nelson and Jephson in the
evening, and dined at the American Mission with
Mr. Clark, Mr. and Mrs. Ingham, and two other

ladies.   Clark lent me a bed* belonging to a sick
man, so I slept soundly.

' *Monday, March* 25.—Left Palabella at 5 a.m. ; a
bad road, very much up and down hill, and greatly
fatiguing to the men.   This is my birthday ; I am
twenty-eight years old.   At 4.30 p.m. we reached
camp—about twelve miles—and I bathed with Jephson in a muddy stream.   One of my Soudanese
tried to kill a goat, but was stopped in time ; his
excuse was, the goat charged him, and was possessed
with a devil !   The next morning we left camp at
5.45, and marched to the deserted village of Congo
da Lemba, nearly the whole way uphill to the top
of a range deeply wooded—a horrible camp.   It
rained   in   the   afternoon,   but   not   much ;   and
again the Soudanese gave me trouble, knocking
flat a woman and a boy of Tippu-Tib's into the
water. . . .   I got up at 4.15 the next morning : an
awful day, heavy rain falling ; dirt worse than Wet
Wood or Botany Bay.   Nelson rear-guard.   We
got to a river called Bambesi, about thirty-five yards
wide, usually shallow, but now much swollen by last
night's and early morning's rain.   Here Stanley
decided to wait till the spate subsided somewhat, so
Nelson and I cooked some sausages and tea for
lunch.   About 2 p.m. a crossing was commenced,
and all were over by 4 p.m.   A rope was stretched

---

* Major Barttelot, in order to save the porters, had left his
camp-bed behind.   I am told it was a dangerous thing for him not
to have a bed, as the ground is so damp, and the fever prevalent
on the Congo.

across, and the men hung on to it, and passed the loads over. Of course, with my usual luck in small matters, my canvas bag got into the water, but took no harm; they are first-rate things, for they float in water, and keep the water out, if properly tied. Nelson and I swam over. We had fearful work after this; the men were quite demoralized. I left Nelson with a sick man, and went on with Jephson; it was uphill with variations. In the evening, at 6.30, and quite dark, we arrived at Baron von Rothkirch's camp in a wood; he is transporting the shaft of a steamer for the Sandford expedition. We thought this was our camp, but he told us Stanley was on about a mile, and a bad road. We got the men through his camp, but the darkness was so great, and the road so bad, the men refused to move on. However, Jephson and I crammed on through a wood, down the steepest pitch, and dark as ink, and it began to rain. At last we came across Bonny, who told me my loads and donkey were all safe on ahead, and they had my lantern. After a short distance we found Jameson's boys, who gave us some whisky and water. At length we got out of the wood, still going downhill. We then came across Salem and some women; and after we had gone about three miles we came to the camp—Mazamba Hill. All the way from the Baron's to Mazamba men were lying with their loads along the road. We got to camp at 7.30, and slept in Stanley's tent.

'I got up at 5 a.m. next morning, 31st, feeling very stiff and dirty, and told Stanley I was going back to fetch in the men. He said it was no use, and that the pot was boiling over, and he was getting tired of this sort of thing. He said he had dysentery, flung himself out of the tent, flogged Ulich, cuffed the Somalis, and made himself ill with passion. However, he started off with the men he had and my Soudanese, who were all in. I started at 7 a.m., and got a message from Stanley to send Parke on, as he was ill. He had to be carried in a hammock from the Lufu River to camp, and was in a fright about himself. We crossed the Lufu River by means of a rope and bamboo bridge ; the sheep and donkeys waded through.

'On April 1 we arrived at Banza Manteka at 2 o'clock. This is an American mission station, well situated on a high hill, with surrounding villages and crops. Mr. and Mrs. Richards and Dr. Small gave me a most excellent lunch. That evening there was every appearance of a heavy thunderstorm, so Dr. Small kindly put me up in his room, and at 8 o'clock it came down in buckets, with lightning and thunder, the wind blowing hard. The Richardses know Surrey well. . . . The next day Stanley paraded all the men. At Matadi I had taken a third boy, Mydedi, a ripper ; but on this parade Stanley asked me why I had three, and so I had to give up one, and Omalley left me. Jephson and

Walker, with forty men and the boat, went off to the Congo to sail up river. We left camp at 10, and arrived in our next camp at 3.30.

'*Sunday, April* 3.—Left camp at 6 a.m., crossed two rivers; the latter part of the march all uphill. I felt like a brute flogging the men to get them on.

'On Monday we left camp at 6.45, and crossed some rivers, at one of which my donkey gave me a lot of trouble; he is a rare stubborn brute, but strong. At one place, a gully, Parke and I and some men dragged him bodily right up a hill. We came to the Kwilu River, about 100 yards wide. There was only one dug-out canoe, holding eleven men and their loads. I had a rope, however, and we fastened that across, as prior to my arrival they had to paddle her over, doing three trips in an hour —very hard work. Now with the rope we did six trips; we worked up to 7 p.m. Next day, Tuesday, we continued the crossing; but at 11.30 it rained pitch, and was simply miserable. The river rose fast. It rained till 5 p.m., so we did not quit camp. Wednesday, April 6, at Mwembi, a head-man of Stairs' company, whilst looting a village, was shot dead—serve him right Also a man of Tippu-Tib's. Salem says he performed prodigies of valour, but he lies.

'We reached camp at 3.30, about seven miles' march. I shaved and washed for the first time for four days. Stanley issued four days' rice to the men and fifty rounds of Winchester rifle ammuni-

tion to the Europeans. My boy Sulieman is so
careless. I changed him for a new boy called Sudi,
a quaint little chap.

'*Thursday, April 7.*—Fine, but cloudy and hot.
Left Mwembi at 7 a.m. Stanley, as rear-guard, got
on A1. He flogged loafers, and they all kicked
amazingly. Got to camp at Wombo, in a wood, at
noon. The country from Matadi to Wombo has
been a succession of hills and valleys, though the
last three days have been more on the level. We
have accomplished 100 miles.

'The Zanzibaris are not such good carriers as I
was led to expect; some of them downright loafers.
We have lost forty men—dead, deserters, and sick.
The country is grass and jungle—very park-like.
The weather is fine on the whole, though often wet
and muggy. I have not experienced great sun-heat
at present. The missionary station people are most
kind and hospitable.

'*Friday, April 8.*—Left Wombo at 6.30 a.m.,
and arrived at Lukungu, a Belgian Free State
station, also an American mission, at 2.30 p.m.
The Belgians gave us an excellent dinner. After
arriving in camp, my Soudanese came and said they
had finished their rations, which had been given
them March 26, for twenty days nominally, to Port
Leopoldville. This was only the thirteenth day. I
told them they could not expect any more, but I
would ask Mr. Stanley. I asked him. He said he
would consider, and let them know his answer the

next morning. They were not satisfied with this answer, and said they wished to see him personally. So they saw him, and he told them they could not reasonably expect any more, but he would see what he could do. One man stepped forward as spokes-man, and said that unless they had rations given them they would not go a step further; that they had been brought there under false pretences, and if they had known how he would treat them they would never have come. This was interpreted by Assad Farran. Stanley replied: " Don't come a step further; go back ! But if you do, I will tell all the country round to shoot you down, and I will chase you from hill to hill with the Zanzibaris." Then turning to Assad Farran, he said, "And you will go with them ; your lot is with them," implying more or less he held him responsible. Of course Assad Farran demurred, and Stanley said, " I will drive you out with the bayonet myself." Then Assad spoke to Stanley very fairly, and said he had nothing to do with the Soudanese ; that he had come to Mr. Stanley as interpreter or servant, and as such he had been hired at Shepherd's Hotel at Cairo. But Stanley only gave him the same replies.

' Later on I told Stanley I was sorry the Soudanese had caused him so much trouble. He said he blamed me for it. I told him I was often away from them working with the rear-guard. He said : " I never asked you to go on rear-guard," and such-

6

like. He then said that my reputation would be blasted as a military officer if the Soudanese revolted, and had to be shot down. I said "As how?" He said it would be in every paper, and General Brackenbury would hear of it, and he had the ear of Wolseley. I replied: "Thank God, my reputation with Lord Wolseley does not rest with what General Brackenbury thought or said."'

Writing to Major Tottenham on this incident, Major Barttelot says: "Afterwards turning to me, Stanley said it was in his power to ruin me in the service. I said to him that that was an empty threat, for it would take a great deal more than he could say to do that. He punished me afterwards by making me march by myself to Leopoldville with seventy men, who were noted for their laziness and incapacity for carrying loads, and my Soudanese; warning me, if I lost a single load, to look out.'

'*Saturday, April* 9 (*Diary*).—After breakfast all the men assembled; all the goey-goeys, or laggers, were picked out, seventy in number. These men were then handed over to me, and I was told by Stanley to make the best of my way to Leopoldville, and to cross the Lukungu River that afternoon. Fifteen days' rations (rice only) were given to the Soudanese, and thirteen to the Zanzibaris. This was Stanley's revenge.

'My only rations were a little biscuit, sugar, tea, 46 lb. of rice, and two fresh loaves. I gave my two boys some additional rations, and slept in the open.

'*Sunday*, *April* 10.—Next morning I started at 5.30, and got into camp at Lukandu at noon. I had immense trouble, and my Soudanese at times absolutely refused to move ; but by threats, taunts, and persuasion I at last got to camp.

'*April* 11.—I started at 4.55 a.m. Immense trouble with the Soudanese ; left one man on the road. At 10 a.m. fetched the Mysoko River, a very frail natural rope and wood bridge only to cross it : got over every one by 2.30 p.m. Stanley caught me up. Parke told me that the Zanzibaris had informed Stanley that we, the Europeans, had opened the Fortnum and Mason boxes ; so Parke, in answer to Stanley, said " Yes," but the only person who had had any of the contents was himself, and that he should advise him to put a little more trust in his officers, who were, at any rate, gentlemen, and not accustomed to be accused of that sort of thing.

'Stanley told Stairs the day before that he had been told I had threatened to shoot Ukedi. Parke told me this, and we asked Stanley's servant if he had told him. He vociferously protested. I never threatened Ukedi.

'*Tuesday*, *April* 12.—The Soudanese are very sick and worn-out ; some stopped at Stanley's camp, some went on ; they were all over the country. I slept on a bed of rushes and waterproof coats. Jephson told Stanley, as they were talking together, that if he blamed me for the conduct of the Soudanese, he put the saddle on the wrong horse.

'*April* 13.—I started at 6 a.m. with my remnants, and reached Luteti at 9.30.

'*Thursday, April* 14.—I awaited the moving off of the column, and started at 7 a.m. ; had hardly gone 100 yards when I found my donkey stuck at some water, owing to the obtuseness of my boys, who tried to take him over a broken bridge, though there was a ford close by ; they had managed to put everything into the water, my bag included. This delayed me about an hour. I tramped on and caught the men up ; found a Soudanese so sick he could not walk. I walked back nearly to Luteti, but finding Mr. Comber in a village, I asked him to send for the man, telling him where he was. Before starting, I had left an Egyptian officer sick. The doctor went out to meet him, but he refused, and got up and walked into camp. So far the missionaries have been most kind to us. I caught the column up at 10.30 : found the Soudanese lying all over the country ; got them all close into camp, and then walked in, arriving at 2.30 ; had something to eat, and then went and fetched them all in. Three Zanzibaris, who went into a village, were shot by the natives.

'*Friday, April* 15.—Left camp at 5 a.m. and made a much better march ; camping at the village of Imbunbi, arriving there at 11.30 a.m. Stanley camped a mile further on. Parke very unwell.

'*Saturday, April* 16.—There was heavy rain and thunderstorm all night, so we could not leave camp till 7.45, and arrived at the Inkissi River at 8.30, crossing it in our boat at 2.30 p.m. ; and encamped on the other side, just the far side of a camp of Casement, an uncommon nice fellow belonging to the Sandford expedition.

Sunday, April 17.—Left camp at 6 a.m. I found my leading men had taken the wrong road. I sent Kane's pony on to bring them back. He brought back a few, but said the remainder had crossed a large river, and would hit off the right road by a cross track. After plunging through an awful jungle, I and a few hit off the right road, and came across Casement and had lunch with him ; also Jephson, who was bringing up the boat. I waited half an hour for the rest of the men, but no one appearing, at 1.45 p.m. I started to meet them, and came on the Zanzibaris, but no Soudanese. I asked where they were. " Miles in rear." So back I went to within two miles of the Inkissi, where I found the last man. Collected them all, thirty-five in number, the rest ahead, and left them with Assad Farran, and walked into camp ; arrived at 6.30 p.m.

' *Monday, April* 18. — Rained in the night. Started at 6.30 a.m., arriving at Kirfuna village at 10.30. Stanley and Casement came up in the afternoon and camped with me. We dined together.

' *April* 19.—Light rain at night and in the early morning. Left at 7.30, and arrived at the Luiia River at 11.30, where I found Stanley checked by the flood. I got over about 5.30 p.m. in the boat. Casement helped my Soudanese on tremendously ; he is a real good chap.

'*Wednesday, April* 20.—Left camp at 7 a.m. Tried to send my Soudanese soldiers on earlier, but Stanley stopped them—perfectly unnecessarily, only he hates them so. However, I got to camp at Makoko village at 11.35 a.m. Jephson had a slight fever here.

'The king of this village, also Makoko by name, has a wonderful beard, which he keeps plaited up in two rolls under his chin, but when let down it reaches the ground, so that he can stand on it. Casement came up late at night, and camped near me. Our sugar was finished to-day.

'*Thursday, April* 21.—Breakfasted with Casement ; left camp at 5.45 a.m. A very woody, hilly march, and very hot. Parke very seedy. We arrived at Leopoldville at 12.15 p.m., and helped to clear a camp ; secured some hippo meat for the Soudanese. We had now marched 210 miles in twenty-seven days over an awful country for marching ; no regular roads, and up and down, with heaps of rivers and small streams, which, though insignificant, yet delayed and impeded a large column like ours tremendously. A beautiful country' (in a letter he writes), 'densely wooded the whole way ; now and again open plains of high grass. The work of urging the men on was most wearying. I can compare it to nothing else but slave-driving. We met our first check here, for the steamers we expected were *non est.* There was only one ready, the state steamer, the *Stanley.* There were two others, the *Peace,* belonging to the English Mission, which was not ready, and which had been refused Stanley at home; and the *Henry Reid,* belonging to the American Mission, and which they also refused, unless it was sanctioned by the authorities at New York. The English mail had broken down; the intelligence, therefore, that the *Peace* had been refused was not known by the chief of the mission at the Pool, who agreed to loan it to the Expedition provided that no news to the contrary from home came before she started. The mail did come in before she was ready, but Stanley had, through the chief of the station, stopped the mail, and abstracted all suspicious-looking letters, to be delivered after we had started, and when the next mail came in. This was how we got the *Peace.*

'*April* 21.—Camp Leopoldville. I served two days' rice all round—the last they will have. Jameson went away to shoot hippo meat for the camp. The American Mission, Mr. Billington and Dr. Sims, refused to let us have their steamer, the *Henry Reid.*

'*April* 23.—Stanley sent for me, and told me to fall in the men we had to Jephson, who was to take possession of the steamer, and with the rest of the men go to Billington, demanding repayment of money paid. While falling in the men I per-

suaded Stanley to let me have another talk with
Billington before taking such measures. He agreed,
and I went with Jephson as a witness, but no good.
The Belgian Free State then slipped in and formally
pressed the steamer.

'*April* 24. *April* 25.—Monday, at 7.30 a.m.,
with 150 men, Parke, and our donkey, I embarked
on the *Stanley*. I issued three brass rods per man
to buy food with for two days; they had had nothing
to eat for two days. We stopped that night at Kui-
poko, Bishop Taylor's mission. The chief, Mr.
Keate, was very kind to us.

'*April* 26.—I had a slight fever; took large
doses of quinine.

'*April* 27.—Disembarked at Lisa Point in order
to march to Mswata, the *Stanley* returning for
others.'

ExTRACT FROM A LETTER TO MISS ——.

'Leopoldville, Stanley Pool.
'*April* 24, 1887.

'The very first day out, the Soudanese grumbled
because they had to carry their own kit, but when
they found they had to carry rations as well, they
refused to go on. However, Stanley talked them
over, and they carried their rations for twenty days;
but after ten days were up, they had eaten or
thrown them away. Stanley refused to give them
more; they refused to march. He threatened to
shoot them; they said, " Shoot! we can shoot too."

However, he gave in, but sent them on with seventy sick men and myself ahead. I never had such a time in my life—urging, threatening—wearing work. A man's load is 65 lb., and then he has to carry his rations for twelve or thirteen days—1 lb. of rice a day only.

'Certainly human transport presents a very sad aspect of life. The missionaries and station people have been very kind to us on the way up. I feel very well at present, but not always very bright, there are so many sad things happening all round: starvation, sickness, and lingering death, which nothing can avert.

'I have been busy getting ready for to-morrow's start to Mswata; I shall be away from the column about ten days, I think. I hope Parke won't die with me, but he is very ill, I am afraid. I like all the fellows, but Jameson and Stairs the best: they never complain, and are always ready. Our tent is a failure, and our beds are so heavy we cannot carry them: my boys make me a bed of sticks and grass, which keeps me off the ground, which is always wet.

'*Tuesday, April* 28.—We left camp at 5.30 a.m.; our road lay through a dense jungle and high grass. I fancy the reason of Stanley sending me on is that he dislikes me on account of the Soudanese, and hates them. Stanley intends leaving me in the rear, I think; at least, he told me so at Leopoldville—a bit of spite. Parke shot a partridge.

'*April* 29.—Arrived at Kiben village; here the

King refused to let our guides go any further. After an hour's palaver we got two more guides, presented the King with fifty metako, and bought food of him. All the women here smoke, and the men do their hair in chignons! They call food " chop."

'*April* 30.—Our guides gave us trouble. The natives here are rare liars.

'*May* 1.—Arrived at Mswata, where we stayed awaiting Stanley, and cutting a supply of wood for the three steamers. We bought supplies of food—native bread made from the root of the manioc.

'*May* 5.—The *Stanley* arrived with Stairs, Jephson, Jameson, and Nelson. Stairs told me that Ward was with Stanley' (Mr. Ward had been recently taken on the Expedition), 'and Troup was left behind—a great shame, as Troup had done good work, besides being the first chosen.

'A few hours later, the *Peace* with Stanley, and the *Henry Reid* with Tippu-Tib, Bonny, and Walker, arrived. I saw Stanley: he came to a chimbeck, and told me he intends leaving me behind at Bolobo, and that I was eventually to go up to the Falls with Troup and Bonny, who remain with me at Bolobo; I am to proceed to an entrenched camp, which he would already have formed, and assume command. Should I have enough porters, and can get guides and men from Tippu-Tib, I am to proceed to Wadelai. This sounds very well, but my stay at Bolobo would probably be of four months' duration;

and unless I obtain a distinct assurance of aid from
Tippu-Tib, and promise of proceeding to Wadelai, I
would go home. His object at present is personal
dislike to me and hatred of the Soudanese, and
his treatment of Troup is most unfair.' (Writing on
this subject to Major Tottenham, Major Barttelot
says : '*June* 19.—I was then to take command of
the entrenched camp, and if Tippu-Tib had got
some carriers ready, those which he promised to
have, I was to move on with all the loads and men
towards Wadelai ; but if I was unable to transport
all the loads, I was to await Stanley's return.') ' I
dined that night on the ss. *Stanley*, and got orders
to march to the Kwar River and await the return of
the *Stanley* from Bolobo. No word of thanks for
the wood we had cut or food we had obtained.

'*Friday, May* 6.—The steamers left Mswata early.
Parke and I marched at 9.30 a.m., got to King
Gondana's village at 2.30 p.m. It was dreadfully
hot marching.

' *Saturday, May* 7.—Left camp at 5.30 a.m., and
found Gondana had sent our guides away, as they
did not belong to his country. These village kings
are very arrogant and childish. I went to King
Gondana and told him, giving him a smart prod
with a stick, that unless guides were forthcoming in
five minutes the soldiers would burn his village.
The guides came in a twinkling, and we got to
Kwarmouth at 11.30 a.m. We put up at the French
mission-station of St. Paul de Kassai. There are

three priests of the Order of St. Esprit, and they treat us right well. They are poor, and give us of their best. Their life is holy and sad; one is a Belgian, the other two Alsatians, one of whom served in the French army in the Dragoons, and was through the war of '70-71. They pray a good deal, especially at 5.30 a.m. They have a chapel, but no light burning, and no congregation. They are much persecuted in a petty way by theft, etc., by a neighbouring King.

'*Sunday, May* 8. — I had a palaver with the neighbouring King, and threatened him with destruction if he persisted in his persecutions and did not desist from his bad practices. He went away terrified.

'*May* 9, 10, 11, 12.—No signs of the steamer; it will be serious soon, as I shall run out of metako (money). The Fathers are awfully kind to us, and we both devour such a lot, I feel quite ashamed. The *Stanley* appeared in the evening; she had been on a rock.

'*May* 13.—Got all on board the *Stanley;* had breakfast with the Fathers, and was really sorry to leave them, for they had been so kind to us.

'*May* 14.—Got to Bolobo at 4.30 p.m., when Stanley told me he should take me up to the Falls, and leave Ward and Bonny at Bolobo.'

CHAPTER V.

On ss. *Stanley*—Scarcity of Provisions—Disgraceful Scenes—
Equatorville—Letter from Stanley—Orders to escort Tippu-
Tib to Stanley Falls—On ss. *Henry Reid* with Tippu-Tib—
Endless Cutting of Wood — Peace Brotherhood — Fight
between Natives and Tippu-Tib's men—Estrangement with
Tippu—Blood Brotherhood Slaves—Arrival at Falls Station
—Tippu angry at Stanley's Breach of Contract.

'*May* 15 : ss. *Stanley, Bolobo.*—Stanley left in
the *Peace* at 6.30 a.m. ; the *Henry Reid* followed
with Parke and company and Tippu-Tib on board.
There was some slight difference of opinion between
Parke, the captain, and Stanley concerning Tippu-
Tib's smelling women occupying the only cabin. I
believe Stanley settled it in favour of Tippu-Tib.
He left Ward and Bonny (at Bolobo) with 125 men
and enough European provisions for about fourteen
days : it is disgraceful, I think ; we shall soon all of
us be without them ; he himself is pretty well off.
Stairs, Nelson, Jephson, Jameson, and myself are on
board the *Stanley*. Jameson is, I believe, to stay

behind with me at the Falls. We started at noon,
and stopped at 5 p.m. at a village whose inhabitants
refused to let us land. But on the appearance of the
soldiers they fled. The Zanzibaris got so excited
there was no holding them; they robbed and destroyed, and of course the Soudanese followed
suit.

'*Monday, May* 16.—Early in the morning, about
5.15 a.m., some of our fellows burnt the best chimbeck in the village down—a horrid shame! Nelson
was taken ill this day; he is far from strong. We
started at 8 a.m., and stopped at 4.30 p.m., and the
men had to camp in a swamp, and rain came on, to
add to their discomfort. We cut wood late into the
evening, but it got so dark we had to desist.

'*May* 17 : ss. *Stanley.*—Went on cutting wood,
and had got all the men on board ready to start,
when it was found that the port boiler had been
emptied, and we were near an accident; the heat of
the chimney set the roof on fire, and the furnace
pipes were all loosened. If we had started we should
all have been blown up. This must have been a
covert act of someone, as the cock of the boiler
escape pipe is so situated it would be nearly impossible to turn it by accident. Added to which, it
was turned off when the occurrence was found out,
and in its right position. We had to stop there all
day. In the morning I had my hair cut short
by Hamis Parry; I am now like a nigger. I
still shave and wear collars. On the port side

we seldom see the actual bank of the river, as it
is all islands. In the afternoon Stairs and I
wandered far into the bush, and found some excellent firewood. Heaps of hippo and —— about;
every day I see hippo close to the steamer. Nelson
no better, and Jameson ill. Jephson is bad, and
Stairs and I are well.

'*Wednesday*, *May* 18. –Got up steam. Everything had been made tight the day before. Nelson
a little better, and Jameson ill. Started at 6.50 a.m.,
and went on till 6.15 p.m. Our halting-place a
small fisherman's encampment, with a wretched
chimbeck and one small canoe. A dead tree in
the centre, which we cut down, and finished cutting
up by 1 a.m.

'*Thursday*, *May* 19.—Got the wood we had cut
the night before on board, and started at 6.30 a.m.
Had ham for breakfast. At 7.45 a.m. it blew so
hard we had to put in. Just then Stairs saw two
elephants, so he and I went after them. It was
raining hard, and terrible high grass; but we had to
go back before we got to them, as the whistle was
blown, and we started away at 9 a.m. Arrived at
Lukolala, an English mission-station, at 6 p.m.
Just before getting there Stanley sent the *Peace*
down to look for us, as he thought something
must have happened. On arrival I immediately
went and saw him, and set his fears at rest.

'*Friday*, *May* 20.—The morning of this day was
exciting to some of us—at least, for Stairs and

Jephson. It seems that early in the morning nearly all the Zanzibaris went from the *Stanley* to see Mr. Stanley, and complained that Stairs and Jephson had thrown over a day's rations, which they had bought and paid for. The real facts of the case are that at the village which they looted* they brought on to the steamer such a fearful lot that the steamer could not carry it, so it had to be thrown away—or some portion of it. The throwing away was superintended by Stairs and Jephson. The Zanzibaris also complained of Jephson's tyranny in striking them, etc. I sent Stairs over to find out about some business, and he found this concourse assembled, and Stanley mad with rage. He raged at Stairs about it, and Stairs told him the facts of the case, and the disgraceful behaviour of the Zanzibaris. Stanley, who was on his steamer, the *Peace*, Stairs being on shore, said that he (Stairs) began it all by going into the village first and commencing the row by shouting for arms, etc. So Stairs told him (Stanley) that about twenty Zanzibaris had gone in first, and had run away from the villagers. Stanley would not hear about it, and said that the Soudanese commenced the plunder (which they did not), and that Stairs was the real cause of the disturbance. Parke wrote a note to Jephson to come over, and he went. Stanley attacked Stairs and Jephson in a frantic state,

* The men often had no food of a day supplied by Mr. Stanley, so they were obliged to loot villages to get food.

stamping about the deck of the *Peace*. He called
Jephson all sorts of names.

' Then he turned round to the men, about 150,
and spoke Swahili to the effect that the men were to
obey them no more ; that if they issued any orders
to them they were to tie them to trees (referring to
Jephson and Stairs); lastly, offering to fight Jephson.
He also said to Stairs, before Jephson came up, that
a mutiny was brewing, and that if he only raised a
finger, the Zanzibaris would rush upon him and
crush him, or club him to death.

' I was astonished when Stairs and Jephson returned and told me about it, especially in Stairs'
case, for no kinder officer to the men, or more
zealous or hard-working officer, is there in the
Expedition, besides being most efficient and capable.
The missionaries, two of them, who heard the disturbance, and the captain and engineer of the *Peace*,
never heard such language, or witnessed such a disgraceful scene before. I believe this is Stanley's
method of carrying on in Central Africa, but I had
judged him pretty well before, and was not surprised
so much at his conduct. However, I gave him time
to cool down, shaving in the meanwhile, and then
went over to see him. We were lying 200 yards up
stream. On the way I met Parke, who told me that
Stanley had called him on to the *Peace*, and opined that
we were talking about him ; that it was apparent to
him that we had formed a compact against him and
were tired of the Expedition, and only made a row

to get sent back.   Parke assured him of our loyalty,
and earnest wishes to carry on the work.   I then
saw Stanley, and told him I was sorry for what had
happened, asking to know his wishes concerning
Jephson and Stairs, whether they were really dismissed or not.   He said they were.   Harped back
on his old idea of the compact.   I assured him to
the contrary.   He said he could carry on the Expedition without any of us.

'I asked him whether I was to tell Jephson and
Stairs that his decision was irrevocable.   He hesitated,
and then said, "As regards myself, it is."   By that
alone I knew he was blustering.   I went away, and
Jephson and Stairs came over, at my advice, and
saw him, and squared it.   It is a baddish look-out,
for, of course, the seeds of mutiny have been sown
against us, and may at any moment crop up.

'I and Stairs cut wood in the afternoon, going
over in the *Henry Reid* to an island.

'It is my firm belief that Stanley does not care
whether he ever gets to Wadelai or not.   What he
looks to are his explorations afterwards.   Jameson
and Nelson much better.

'Parke is having a wretched time of it on board
the *Henry Reid* with Tippu-Tib's women, and
Salim and others.   We killed our last goat to-day,
and have now to live on chickens, one each day.

'*Saturday, May* 21.—Stairs not very well.   Started
at 6.30 a.m.   It was blowing hard, and we were
running short of wood.

'*Sunday, May* 22.—Illegible.

'*Monday, May* 23.—Started at 5.30 a.m. Ahead of the *Peace* and *Henry Reid.* A lot of canoes came alongside with presents for Bulla-Matari,* but would give us nothing. This wood-cutting is wretched work, as we never seem to be able to cut enough, however hard or much we cut. Captain Shackerstroom says that "perhaps there is an hour's wood, but certainly not more." However, we always manage to steam eleven or twelve hours. There are lots of villages on the starboard side, and large ones. I find pea-nuts roasted are excellent ; our meals partake more and more of the native aspect every day now.

'Stopped at 10.30 a.m. to cut wood, and started again at 2.30 p.m. The *Peace* caught us up, Stanley, as usual, jumping, shouting, and finding fault with everybody.

'*Tuesday, May* 24.—Started at 6 a.m., and crossed the equator at 4.30 p.m. Arrived at Equatorville at 5.30 p.m. This station is half a mile north of the equator.

'*Wednesday, May* 25 : *Equatorville.*—This is a Belgian Free-State station, also an Anglo-American missionary station. I asked Stanley to give us a bottle of brandy on board the *Stanley* in case of sickness ; but he was so very disagreeable about it that I left him. I had a slight fever in the morning,

* The natives on the Congo call Stanley 'Bulla-Matari,' or stone-breaker.

but nothing to signify. I bought two assegais with beautifully-made shafts. In the evening we all dined with Van Gèle and Glave—a good dinner. Stanley behaved in his customary manner, and kept everybody waiting. Glave kindly gave me 400 percussion-caps.

'*Thursday, May* 26.—Left Equatorville at 6 a.m. Can only go half-speed, as we have to go behind the *Peace.* Heavy tornado at 6 p.m. Jephson has gone on board the *Henry Reid.* I am not overfit.

'*Friday, May* 27. — Tornado again during the early morning. Started at 5.45 a.m. Arrived at Uranga village at 10.30 a.m. Flogged a Soudanese for theft. Jameson secured a goat off a chief, which was given him as a present, and he expected one in return, which of course he did not get. He came for his goat late that night, but we froze on. One of our goats had a kid, so we have milk now.

'*Monday, May* 30: ss. *Stanley.* — Started at 5.30 a.m., and arrived at Bangala at 11.30 a m. Stanley told me I was to take forty Soudanese and go on board the *Henry Reid* to escort Tippu-Tib to the Falls, giving me a letter of instructions. I am glad to see the Falls, but the change from the *Stanley* to the *Henry Reid* is not nice; the latter a pokey little ship, crammed with Tippu-Tib's satellites and women, and only Walker to talk to. Baert, in the Belgian army, brother of Baert at Matadi, is chief of this station. There are four others; one is away with the steamer *A. T. A.* exploring. We all dined with them that night. Stanley made an . . . . . . speech. Baert is a nice fellow, and did all he could for us.

' My orders from Mr. Stanley were :

' " You will please take 40 of your fittest Soudanese, and the Somali Abdi, who understands Swahili, with rations : $\frac{3}{4}$ of a matako per day per man, or 2 matako for 3 days per man, for 18 days = 492 matako, and 90 matako for yourself, with sufficient rice, biscuits, etc., etc., to serve you ; and embark them in large boat now alongside the *Peace*. This boat you will secure to *Henry Reid* in place of the portable boat *Advance*.

' " Having secured rations for your detachment as above and for Tippu-Tib's people, 96 in number for 16 days = 1,056 matako, you will please proceed per *Henry Reid*, in tow of *En Avant*, and large boat to escort Tippu-Tib and his people to Stanley Falls, or as near there as your sense of prudence and care of life and property will permit, starting to-morrow morning as soon as you can.

' " I should advise, in order that you arrive quickly, that you should coast along south bank until near Rubunga, when you should sheer off to one of the central river-channels, to avoid the small rapids just below Rubunga. Arriving at Rubunga, 5 days from Bangala, purchase food again for 3 days, to Yalulimà, a large scattered settlement on south bank. At Yalulimà purchase food for 5 days, as far as Isangè, south bank, which is at the confluence of the

large affluent Lubirawyi and the Congo. You will
then have arrived in Tippu-Tib's territory, where
no doubt he will become responsible for obtaining
provisions.

' " You will please remember that, as you approach
Tippu-Tib's territory, you approach a country that
is at variance with the Congo State, and that the
people, being ignorant of Tippu-Tib's presence, are
liable to fire on your steamer with *rifles*. Great
caution must therefore be exercised by you that
your steamer, 2 days above the Yalulimà settlement,
may not be imperilled by an ambuscade of sharp-
shooters. I should advise that you should, while
keeping the south or left bank in view, skirt the
islands for greater safety.

' " Upon sighting the Arab camps or settlements,
you should consult with Tippu-Tib as to the best
manner of making his presence on board known
to them, after which of course there will be no
difficulty.

' " I consent, if it be possible, that you should
take Tippu-Tib to the old station landing-place
(Stanley Falls), but no further up on any consideration. You will then proceed to cut up wood, and
return along north or right bank, the next morning,
as fast as you can with your own people. Arriving
at the mouth of the Aruwimi, cast your eyes at the
highest tree nearest the point of landing dividing
the Aruwimi from the Congo for a " blaze," or the
bark of a tree taken off, which shall be a sign to

you that we have passed up the Aruwimi to the
Rapids of the Aruwimi. You will then steam up
the Aruwimi to camp, where we shall be anxiously
awaiting you. We hope to reach the Aruwimi on
the 12th, and the Rapids on the 16th early. You,
according to my calculations, will reach Stanley Falls
on the 15th, and return to the Aruwimi on the
evening of the 17th."

'I transhipped with Jephson. Abdi, the Somali,
and a good boy, died to-day.

'*Tuesday, May* 31 : ss. *Henry Reid.*—Nasty wet
morning.

'*Thursday, June* 2.—I did not get to bed till
2 o'clock this morning, as we were busy cutting
wood till then. Have got a cold in the head, and
feel altogether horrid.

'*Friday, June* 3.—Up the Congo.

'*Saturday, June* 4.—Up the Congo.

'*Sunday, June* 5.—Up the Congo. The captain
took the wrong channel; lost thereby about two
hours. On going up the right channel, we saw the
Stanley ahead of us. We passed her at 3 p.m. I
saw Jameson and Parke. They told me two of my
Soudanese were dead. We stopped at 4.15 p.m.,
and I cut wood from 5 p.m. till 3.15 a.m., when the
last piece was put on board.

'*Monday, June* 6.—Though cutting wood for such
a long time, I don't believe we have got more than
nine hours' wood. This wood is a perfect bugbear

to me. I make up for my loss of sleep in the day-time, but I do not think it rests me much. I had fever to-day. It commenced at 11 o'clock, and was all over by the evening.

'*Tuesday, June* 7.—Started 5.30 a.m. Stopped at 5 p.m., and cut wood till 11.15 p.m.

'*Wednesday, June* 8.—The *Henry Reid* started at 5.30 a.m., but we were stopped by a fog at 6.14, and put into a village to buy food, but they had next to nothing.

'*Thursday, June* 9: ss. *Henry Reid.*—I had the wood stowed this morning by 1.55, and we started at 5.30, but had to put in at 2.15, as we were short of wood—our normal state.

'*Friday, June* 10.—We started at 5.20 a.m. I only finished stowing the wood at 4.45 a.m. We arrived at the village of Mbunga at 7 a.m., and Tippu-Tib desired to put in, so we did. We made peace brothers with the chief before landing, and they agreed to sell to us. The method of making peace brotherhood is this : a chief comes up to the ship and holds out a piece of cane ; he holds one end, and one of us catches hold of the other. He then cuts it in two, and we hand him back our half. This is the sign of peace. All went well for an hour, and they were buying away. I was on shore, walking by myself, unarmed, towards the southern end of the village — I had already been to the other end — when suddenly I heard loud vociferations in front of me, and voices raised as in anger. I hurried on to see, but before I could get there about twenty of Tippu's men rushed past me, and two were wounded. I then met three of the Soudanese, who forced me to come back, which we four did at the walk. . . . (illegible). All this while the natives were passing us by dozens, all shouting and flourishing their spears and knives ; they never offered to touch me, though unarmed ; in fact, they ran into the long grass on either side of the road to avoid me. About 200 yards from the ship I found one of Tippu's men lying in the road, stabbed in the back by a spear. We carried him on board, when I found Tippu had six men and one woman wounded, and a Zanzibari of the ship's crew, Asani. I fell my men in and went to the northern end of the village to look for the natives, Tippu going to the southern, but they had all disappeared into the bush. So we burnt the southern and central part of the village.' (Here follows an account of the numerous wounds received by Tippu's people.)

'About 4 p.m. we passed another village, where they were assembling, and Tippu-Tib wished to put in, but I would not. He ordered my men to fire, but as Stanley told me on no account to have unnecessary rows with the villagers, I ordered them not to fire. This caused an estrangement between Tippu-Tib and myself, who said, as I had refused to aid him, he would do nothing more for the Expedition. I explained to him how matters were, and that we had already punished one village, that I

could not disobey Mr. Stanley's orders, and that my
men could only take orders from me. He agreed
to this, but was still angry with Stanley, and said he
should refer it to him.

 '*Saturday, June* 11 : ss. *Henry Reid.*—Wounded
are all doing well. The Zanzibaris and Tippu-Tib's
men fired off rifles at imaginary foes during the
night, and they wanted my men out, but I was not
going to be bothered. Dull, wet day.

 '*June* 12.—Walker has a bad fever. I had to
look after the engines ; the wounded doing well. I
wore my smock (an English labourer's) yesterday
for the first time. It is a great success in the wet
jungle. We stopped at 3.30 to get wood. I gave
Salem Mohammed a shirt ; he was very proud
of it.

 '*Monday, June* 13.—I gave Salem Mohammed
four tin studs for his shirt, and he presented me with
a bunch of bananas. We are now in Tippu-Tib's
country, and since the forenoon have been accompanied by a host of canoes. The natives are very
strong, of a coppery hue, and very ugly. They have
beautiful paddles ; I bought one. They told us
there was war between them and Tippu's people,
and that they were living on the river ; they thought
we were the Free State come up to avenge the
burning of Stanley Falls. Tippu had a palaver
with the chiefs, and told them he had been made
ruler by the State, and would protect them and stop
the war. Blood-brotherhood was made between

them by scratching each other's arms with my pocket lancet, and transmitting the blood to each other.

'*June* 14, *June* 15.—We arrived at the village of Ukanga. Tippu went on shore in a canoe; as there were a lot of his men there, they naturally thought we had come to avenge Deane and the Falls. They fired a volley at Tippu, but hit no one. As he did not return their fire, and the steamer stood off from the shore, they let him land, and he made all square. There are some fifty-eight Zanzibaris there; some of them are to come with us and form part of the 600 that Tippu gives Stanley.

' At 6 p.m. we reached the village of Tutombé, a very poor village; in fact, they all have been so since coming into his territory; his people have devastated them.

'*June* 16.—We make slow progress, and are already a day behind time. We reached Yarukombé at 10.30 a.m.; this is the first Arab settlement we have come to. There are some Zanzibaris here also. Continued my letters home. I saw about twenty slaves in a chain — men and women — at Yarukombé. I also saw some yesterday at Ukanga.

'*June* 17.—Friday we were met by a convoy of canoes from the Falls, and Tippu's brother, who, with other Sheiks, came on board. We reached the Falls at 10.15 a.m. It is very like a cataract on the Nile, except there is more vegetation. I had to

write a letter for Tippu to the Administrator-General
of the Congo Free State, to lay before the King [of
the Belgians], stating Tippu's strenuous efforts to
pacify the people and restore order.

' The efforts really consist in drinking coffee and
palavering. The forenoon we spent disembarking
Tippu and his people. The Old Falls station is on
an island now occupied by Raschid, one of his head
men. Tippu's brother looks very like one of those
Jew Arabs at Aden who come on board to sell
ostrich-feathers. Both the Old Falls station and
Tippu's village consist of mud houses, thatched with
dried palm and banana leaves, and are stockaded.
They have got three Krupp seven-pounders, and one
muzzle-loading seven-pounder; one of the Krupps
is in perfect repair ; the others have no wheels, and
the breach-pin of one is missing. The muzzle-loader
has no carriage. The Arabs call the place Singatini. The river is narrow here, but broadens out
towards the cataract, and the volume of water is
immense. I had a palaver with Tippu. He is
evidently a bit sore with Stanley about the men he
promised to give him, for Stanley promised he would
supply them with ammunition ; and to the best of
my belief the ammunition is left behind, to come up
the next trip. Tippu-Tib must have been told this
by Stanley, and asked to supply it, to be repaid
hereafter ; but he thinks it a breach of contract, and
also says his men have no powder. I effected a
sort of compromise by making him half promise

to supply, at any rate, 200 men with ammunition, to be repaid.   This will suit me admirably,
because then, directly Ward and Troup come up,
I can cut on, unless Stanley changes his mind
again.

CHAPTER VI.

'*Sunday, June* 19.—Left Stanley Falls (having
interchanged presents with Tippu). Dense fog,
and one of the pipes of the boiler got loose, so we
were forced to stop. Our clever captain got us on
to a sandbank later on.

'*June* 20.—Queen's Jubilee. We found a tree
at the mouth of the Aruwimi, which Stanley had
blazed and painted " 12 " on to show he had gone
up.

'*Tuesday,* 21.—We passed the *Stanley* downwards bound. Some natives shot a poisoned arrow
into the *Henry Reid.*

'*June* 22.—The *Henry Reid* started at 5.30 a.m. Had to stop at 8 to cut wood till 12.30, when a tremendous squall came on and a drenching rain ; it lasted an hour.

'We arrived at the entrenched camp at the deserted village of Yambuya at 5.45 p.m., being two days behind our time. Stanley was very anxious about us, and Stairs not very well. The fellows here have had nothing but rice, beans and manioc cakes ; there is not even a fowl to be had, and no big game to be shot ; a pleasant look-out for Jameson and me, who are to be left behind unless the natives come in ! Stanley told me that Baruti, his African boy, had deserted with his rifle and other things.'

YAMBUYA CAMP.

June 23.—[Major Barttelot writes to his father : 'Jameson and I are to be left here at present ; Stanley intends us to remain here till he comes back, which will be about November.'

He also writes to a friend, June 23 : 'Stanley intends to leave Jameson and me here ; we are to await his return, which will be about five months ; but I am going to try and persuade him otherwise.'

The above are extracts of letters written on board the *Henry Reid* before 9 a.m., Thursday, June 23, for the diary says : 'I stayed on board till 9 a.m., finishing my letters, four in number, to father, etc., and put them all in one envelope and sent them home by Captain Wheatley, of the *Peace.*'

Major Barttelot had his interview with Mr. Stanley that same afternoon and obtained permission to advance.]

' I had a long talk with Stanley in the afternoon, and he gave me permission to move on eastward directly Ward and Troup, etc., were up. In the afternoon the Soudanese put wood on the steamer. I called the roll for this purpose—twelve were absent ; late in the evening they returned, bringing one of their number in wounded. I finished putting the wood on board by 10.30 p.m. I had got my things on shore during the day, and had taken up my quarters with dear old Parke. I have not been well the last few days.

'*Friday, June* 24.—Alexander Hadad, the young interpreter, died yesterday ; he had been failing for a long time. We buried him to-day. Stanley has built us a house, and put a stockade nearly all round our intended stockaded camp. He has also put up a firing platform. There is an excellent spring of water.'

[On this day Mr. Stanley delivered a letter of instructions to Major Barttelot, and a copy of it to Mr. J. S. Jameson, his second in command. This will be found at the end of the chapter.]

'*Saturday, June* 25.—I went in to see Stanley, and had a row with him. He told me I nagged at him, and if I went on we should fight ; that I ought

never to have come on this Expedition, and that I
was either naturally cross or for a purpose, and that
if the former he should suspend me from all duty.
The cause of it was because I told him the truth,
and because Stairs had shown me a letter which
Stanley had written him concerning my non-appear-
ance.* He thought that Tippu had captured us,
or the Soudanese had mutinied. The former I
told him was absurd, and I could not understand
how he could have entertained it, especially after
what he had told me, viz., *that he would as soon trust
Tippu-Tib as a white man.* Stanley replied, " Yes ;
but I would only trust a white man to a certain
point, and no further, as my letter of instructions
showed." I said, " Yes, that is the worst of it ;
trust me all in all, or not at all." The day previous
I told him that Tippu† did not trust him, and
thought that he (Stanley) had broken faith with him
concerning the ammunition, etc., which had fetched
Stanley rather. The second proposition, as to the
Soudanese mutinying, I said was equally absurd, and
that when alone with me, and not continually sneered
at, they did well. I asked him where his camp was
going to be ; he said I ought to know. " Of course,"
I said, " I know the direction, and which shore of

---

* Major Barttelot was two days longer coming to Yambuya
from Stanley Falls than Mr. Stanley expected.

† ' When I told Stanley this, he said he did not want Tippu-
Tib's aid ; he could do very well without the men.'—Extract from
letter to Major Sclater.

Albert Nyanza." He said everybody else knew it. I replied very bitterly, " You have told them, but not me, for you never tell me anything." Then he burst out, and I left him. However, it did me good, and I took two podophyllin pills that night.'

[In vol. i., p. 117, 'Darkest Africa,' Mr. Stanley devotes nine pages to the questionable report of a conversation with Major Barttelot, supposed to have taken place on June 24, into which he, for prejudice, imports private matter concerning the opinions of general officers of the English army of Major Barttelot, making out that Major Barttelot was afraid of their opinions. The truth is, that Mr. Stanley had, on more than one occasion, threatened Major Barttelot with the name of General Bracken-bury, and had told Major Barttelot in March that General Brackenbury had recommended him not to take Major Barttelot. Whatever may be the truth as to General Brackenbury's remarks, Mr. Stanley has placed himself in this position: He told Major Barttelot in March that General Brackenbury had recommended him not to take him ; and then in this account of the conversation (Major Barttelot being dead, and presumably unable to speak) he makes him-self to say, ' I do not understand how General —— could have warned me,' etc. It is difficult to know what is true ; but one of these statements of Mr. Stanley's he must know to be misleading.

Major Barttelot writes (June 4, 1888) : 'Stanley and I were never on good terms. He could not

threaten me, and threats are his chief mode of
punishment.'

Lord Wolseley and Sir Redvers Buller had both
recommended Major Barttelot, and his honourable,
manly character was too well known to be injured
by Mr. Stanley's threats, or for Major Barttelot to
care for them. Hence Mr. Stanley's anger.

This, therefore, throws doubt on the validity of
the whole conversation as told by Mr. Stanley.
The writer of an article in *Blackwood's Magazine* for
August, 1890, on Mr. Stanley's book, says : ' No
one can read the pages in the first volume, headed
" Conversations with Major Barttelot "—in which
the Major is scarcely allowed to interject a remark
—without being conscious that Mr. Stanley is
laboriously endeavouring to cover his own error in
leaving the rear column dependent for its safety and
means of advance upon a person whom he himself,
from his previous experience of Tippu-Tib, had so
great reason to regard as utterly untrustworthy.'

In this quite impossible conversation Mr. Stanley
makes himself nobly say, ' Ever since King David,
those who remain with the stuff and those who go to
the war receive the same honours.' Barttelot and
Jameson, Troup and Ward and Bonny, remained
with the stuff, but where are the honours ?]

' *Sunday, June* 26.—Sayed Mohammed, the soldier
who was wounded, died during the night. A chief
from a village across the river made blood-brotherhood with me by our lancing each other's arms, and

covering the wounds with salt.   He licked the blood off my arm, and then I had to do the same; we then rubbed the places together; after this a chicken was killed, and the blood sprinkled on the people round.   He kept the head, and I the body, and the performance, an exceedingly nasty one, was over.

'*Monday, June* 27.—The companies were told off to-day.   Such a lot of wretched men as were left behind you never saw.   Out of 74 Zanzibaris, 36 are able to work and carry loads, the rest sick. The worst Maniapara (head-man), called Muni-chandi, is left, who has no authority with the men, and is laziness personified.

'Our share of European stores was also given out to each one for six months.   Jameson's and mine together consist of five 1-lb. tins of coffee, three 1-lb. tins of tea, two tins of salt, six tins of butter, eight tins of milk, one opening knife, one tin of sugar, six tins of jam, one tin of chocolate, three tins of cocoa and milk, three tins of sardines, three tins of sausages, four 1-lb. tins of biscuit, one tin of red herrings, two tins of flour, four pots of Liebig, one of tapioca, one tin of sago.

'*Tuesday, June* 28.—Stanley left at 8.30 a.m. with Stairs, Nelson, Jephson, and Parke.   The last I saw of Stanley was at 8.10 a.m.'   ('He said to me, "Good-bye, Major; shall find you here in October, when I return." '—Letter to Major Sclater.)

'I sent 1 officer, 1 sergeant, and 10 men with

Stanley, and I have with me here 45 Soudanese
(41 fit for duty), 1 interpreter, 4 Somalis (all more
or less sick), 76 Zanzibaris (40 sick), my 3 boys and
Jameson's 2, myself and Jameson—133 persons.'

[From this date begin the weary days of long
anxious waiting, with nothing to cheer, and everything possible to distress, the two brave fellows who
had given up their time, home, friends, and employ-
ments to go to the rescue of Emin Pasha. They
knew that, according to Stanley's calculations, the
relief would be effected by the advance before they
could move from this hateful camp. They were in
doubt as to when Ward, Troup, and Bonny would
arrive from Bolobo. They expected 600 carriers
from Tippu-Tib, but felt that probably they would
not be sent. If Stanley did not care whether they
were sent or not, and took no trouble to see that
they were provided, why should Tippu care? The
commissariat provided by Stanley was most miserable : not an atom of tinned or fresh meat—a few
carriers would have brought enough tinned meat to
last a year. The men had nothing to eat but the
poisonous manioc, and the health of both officers
and men was soon seriously affected by the deadly,
hopeless monotony of this awful forest camp.
Stanley and those with him were cheered on day by
day by the hope of what was before them and the
novelty of the scene, by the knowledge that daily
they were nearer the achievement of their object.

Meanwhile, at Yambuya, the bitterness of disappointment, betrayal, and death was gradually to consum-
mate the terrible sacrifice of the rear column.]

Letter from Major Barttelot to Major Sclater

'Camp, Yambuya Village, Aruwimi Falls,
'(Commenced) *July* 19, 1887
(Finished, *August* 13).

' My dear old Harry,

'I am writing this to you privately. Of
course you will have seen my last two letters home
and all about our journey up the river. But it is
about other things I want to speak.' (Here follows
an account of Mr. Stanley's behaviour to the
Soudanese, Mr. Stanley's threats to ruin Major
Barttelot's military reputation, and the disgraceful
scene with Jephson and Stairs, as given in the diary.)
' He (Mr. Stanley) is always suspecting us, and has
constantly called us all mutineers, and threatened to
treat us as such. He believes all the Zanzibaris
sooner than us, and they bring him no end of tales.
He speaks Swahili like a Zanzibari. It is my
belief, if he thought he could get rid of us, he would;
he sticks at nothing.

' Here we can get no meat, though Jameson and
I managed to secure two goats and ten fowls by
capturing a native woman; and that was her price.
We have ½ lb. of rice per diem and a few beans. Our
European provisions, which are to last six months,

are as follows' (same as given before in the diary).
' Beside the rice and beans, we have ¼ lb. daily of
weevilly biscuits. The Soudanese and Zanzibaris
live on manioc. I am far from well just now, and
cannot eat—consequently am weak. I have written
this to show you what Stanley is like, and how he
treats us in all ways. . . . If I had known what
he was, and how he was going to treat us, I would
never have come. Part of the agreement on which
Tippu-Tib was to let him have the men was, that
on arrival here he should supply them with caps
and powder ; these have all been left behind, and
Tippu-Tib knew it. When I was at the Falls
Tippu told me he thought Stanley had broken faith
with him, and that the men would not come till the
ammunition arrived. On arrival here I told Stanley
this, and he got into an awful rage, and said all
sorts of things, because he knew that what I said
was true. I was two days later arriving here from
the Falls than he expected. He was in such a
state about this that he was going to send off Stairs
to look for me, and you never saw such a letter of
instructions as he gave him. To this effect: that
Tippu-Tib had seized the steamer, or that the
Soudanese had mutinied and held her, or that on
my own account I had a row with the natives, and
they possessed the steamer. I was naturally angry
at this, and went and told him I had read his letter
to Stairs, and thought it absurd. In the first place,
he had allowed me a margin of two days, and I had

not exceeded it.* Secondly, as to Tippu-Tib, Stanley himself had said he would as soon trust Tippu-Tib as any white man. Concerning the Soudanese, that was equally absurd, and my making a raid was absurd, when I had plenty of food. My having seen Stairs' letter, which he knew was full of the lowest suspicion, annoyed him, and my catching him out at every point still more, and there was a row. He said to Stairs, when he gave him the letter, that if any of us got into danger through foolhardiness or want of proper caution, he would not move a hand's-breadth to help him. It shows you what a suspicious fellow he is. If Tippu-Tib does not send the men (and I don't think he will now), it will be a bad business for Stanley. . . . Out of seventy-seven Zanzibaris here now, thirty are fit for nothing, and most of them will die directly we leave camp. . . .

'This has been a doleful letter, but I write to you because I think one of the family should know how we are situated. I have never been on such a mournful, cheerless trip as this. The harder we worked, the glummer Stanley looked. After a long march, no smile from him or word of any sort, except to say "You have lost a box," or some sneer of that sort. . . .

'Jameson is such a real good chap, so bright and

* Major Barttelot started in the steamer *Henry Reid* by himself with Tippu-Tib on May 31, reached the Falls and put Tippu in possession on June 17, and reached Yambuya June 22.

cheery, and when I am well we don't have a bad time; but even now I am low, and hate my food.'

LETTER FROM MAJOR BARTTELOT TO MRS. SCLATER.

'Camp, Yambuya Village, Aruwimi Falls,
'*August* 3, 1887.

'MY DEAREST EDITH,

'I am writing you a line to tell you how we are getting on. At present Jameson and I, who are left behind, are having rather a slow time of it, as beyond cutting wood for the steamers, and making reconnaissances into the country, we have not much to do. . . . I did not hit anybody (on the march) for a long time, but I found that Stanley did right and left, and that really it was the only plan to get these Zanzibaris on. Stanley expected us to hit the men, though he always took their part when they complained. We have been nothing but slave-drivers since we started, and the trouble I have had to get the Soudanese along was something dreadful.

'I think this country, what I have seen of it, is a fraud. I dare say higher up, nearer the lakes, it is better. Here we are among the greatest savages in the world, and about the only cannibals who are left. They look with longing eyes at Jameson and me; they think that, fatted and stuffed with bananas, we should be ripping! Jameson is a rare good chap, and very cheery. . . . The natives come and sell us fish occasionally, and honey, and plantains; but the last two or three days they have not been, as they say Tippu-Tib's men are coming, and they are afraid they will kill them, as some few years back they killed a lot of Tippu-Tib's men who came down here to raid, and were encamped on this very spot where we are now, by making them drunk on melafor (palm wine), and then spearing them in the night; out of 300 about seven escaped. I hope it is true that Tippu's men are coming. . . . If these 600 men do not turn up, I am sadly afraid we shall have to stay here till Stanley returns, which would be about November. This would be terrible, for though we have a snug camp, life is so monotonous. The men, too, who are dying now pretty rapidly, will die much quicker when we have nothing for them to do. We can do nothing for them, for we have so little medicine, and in many cases none at all for their special diseases.

'I have brought the wrong sort of boots for this country, and I am afraid that even with the two pairs I have got they won't last me out, the roads are so bad and full of stumps, which tear and knock the boots about. The roads are only broad enough to admit of one person going at a time, and the foliage is so dense you have to stoop nearly the whole time; it tires one pretty much. I have been along Stanley's road some distance, and it is truly bad. Jameson and I have got a house apiece, but I live in my tent: it is drier, and I can tell you when it does rain here it comes down a regular dowser— our central road becomes a simple torrent.

'The camp slopes towards the west, and is in the form of a triangle, the base facing the east. In circumference it is 287 yards. On the eastern face it is protected by a ditch 6 feet wide and 4 feet deep, and a ramp. The northern face is protected by the river, where the bank is very steep. The western apex is protected by a ravine. The southern face is covered half-way by the ravine, and half-way by the 6-foot ditch. The whole camp is stockaded. . . . There are two doors : one on the eastern face, and one on the northern, to the river. The eastern gate is shut at night, and the drawbridge pulled up. The northern gate remains open always. There are sentries at both these gates, on the tower and at the western open. At retreat a picquet of Zanzibaris mount—ten in number.

'Our life is very simple—we rise at 5 a.m. ; get the men to work at 5.45 ; breakfast at 6 a.m. ; work till 11.30 a.m. ; luncheon ; work at 1.30 p.m. till 5.30 ; dinner at 6.30 p.m. ; talk till 9 p.m. ; go round the sentries and to bed. Alternate nights we visit the sentries four times during the night. Any man caught sleeping gets twenty-five lashes. Of course, the men think all these precautions unnecessary, but every movement of ours is as well known to the natives as to ourselves. They watch us most vigilantly, and it is my opinion, should we relax our alertness, they would try and rush us. Whenever we make a reconnaissance they know it, pass the word, and all the villages are cleared before we get there. Though savages, their method and rapidity of transmitting information is truly wonderful. They never steal from one another. Their punishment for individual theft is death, nor does one village steal from another, unless at war. Here they fight with nothing but spears and knives, and if we fire a gun at a parrot or a pigeon the villagers on the other side of the river sound the tom-tom, and jaw and chatter for hours afterwards. All the natives, commonly called Washengies, have left this bank and gone to the other side, which is nothing but a swamp. This side is high ground.'

LETTER FROM MAJOR BARTTELOT TO SIR W. AND LADY BARTTELOT.

'Camp, Yambuya Village, Aruwimi Falls,
'*July* 28, 1887.

' MY DEAR OLD FATHER AND MAMMA,

'I hope you got my last letter, written on board the *Henry Reid.* I was right glad to get off her, she was so dirty. This is not much of a place. Stanley went eastward on June 28. . . . The Zanzibaris don't know as yet how to use their arms, and we have not had time to teach them at present, as we have been strengthening our defences; and our great work now is cutting wood for the *Stanley ;* but as we have only two axes that cut at all, this is a slavish job. I hope to be out of this shortly after the steamer comes up—that is, if Tippu-Tib fulfils his contract, and sends me 600 men ; but I am doubtful,

as I told you in my last letter. He thinks Stanley
has broken faith with him concerning the ammunition, and, in my opinion, he has; and if Tippu-Tib
does not send the men, he (Stanley) will be the
laughing-stock of everybody, because he brought
Tippu-Tib round from Zanzibar with a huge following, at tremendous expense, and fed him, and he
took up room on the steamer here which would have
been more than sufficient to bring up all our men
and goods left behind, and, instead of there being a
camp here, we should all have gone on. If Tippu
does not turn up, I am very much afraid I shall
have to remain here till November, when Stanley
will return; but it will be sickening work. Jameson,
who is left with me, is a rare good fellow; he is a
married man, and has travelled tremendously.

'As I said, all the villages this side are deserted;
but the natives who formerly lived here have
established themselves on the other side, just above
us; but they have no manioc, and come to this side
for it, where there are acres of it. They have
charged us too much for their fish and other things,
so I warned them they must reduce their prices, or
I should punish them. We found out where and at
what time they landed, and lay in wait for them, and
caught two women and a baby and one boy. We
could have caught men, but did not want them, only
the women, as we knew they would pay a ransom
for them. The boy we let go, but the women
we kept until they were ransomed. One of them

escaped when she was taken down to bathe. The polite guard turned their backs on the lady performing her ablutions, and, hearing a bigger splash than usual, they turned round and found she had made a swim for it. Two men swam after her and caught her, but half a dozen canoes putting out and the natives threatening to spear them, they let her go.

'I have just suffered a tremendous misfortune : my watch stopped for no apparent reason at 9 p.m. last night, and has not gone since, though I can see nothing wrong with it. It is one of Dent's best. I shall send this letter home by Walker, the engineer of the *Stanley*, also my watch and other things. I hope Tippu will turn up, as it will expedite my return home ; and I can tell you even now I look forward to that tremendously : never have I done so so much before. I hope I shall find you all well and happy, and everything prosperous. By the way, I must wish you, my very dear old father, a very happy birthday, and many happy returns of it, and also a happy Christmas and New Year. It seems strange to be writing of these things now, but you will not get this till the end of October.'

LETTER TO HIS NEPHEW, MASTER WALTER
BARTTELOT.

'Camp, Yambuya Village, Aruwimi Falls,
'*August* 9, 1887.

' MY DEAR LITTLE BOBBIE,

'How are you and Nigel and Irene ? I am now living amongst bloodthirsty savages, who

delight in eating the flesh of the white man and
drinking his blood while yet warm. Their favourite
dish is English boy roasted whole and stuffed with
bananas. They are copper-coloured, and rejoice in
the name of Watuku. They are armed with spears,
shields, and knives, with the latter of which they
whip off your head before you can wink. They
wear but little clothing, and are of such savage
aspect that if you look long enough at them you
don't feel at all afraid. Their bravery is such that,
always on our approach, they immediately run away
with lightning speed, and go on the principle that
he that runs away lives to fight another day. We
live in a stockaded camp; my friend Mr. Jameson
in a house, and I in a tent. Mr. J.'s house is so
waterproof that there is never a shower of rain
without all our things getting wet through. I say
our things, for my tent is so large that it will not
hold all my kit. When we are inside our camp,
with the gates shut and everything made fast, we
look out over the top and scan the natives; but as
they are all across the river, some three-quarters of
a mile away, they don't much mind. Their chief
mode of getting about is by canoes, which are
hollowed out of the trunks of trees; some are large
enough to hold fifty, others only three or four.
They propel them with paddles, and go down stream
with tremendous swiftness. This is not exactly the
place one would choose to spend a happy day in,
only two white men, and our posts arrive once in a
hundred years; we are shortly expecting one now,

and a few more white men. At present I am suffering from over-eating, as we killed a goat the other day, and have been stuffing ourselves ever since; but two or three long walks in these delightful glades, where the roads are so good you cannot walk upright, and are in danger of falling down every other step you take, will soon make me right. Here the wild parrots whistle and the wood-pigeons coo, which at times we throw violently down with powder and shot, and then eat them. Now, my dearest little boy, I must wish you a very merry Christmas. I hope I may spend the next one with you, when we will have the biggest turkey, plum-pudding, and mince-pies that can be got; we will have a rare merry time. Good-bye, dear little Bobbie; grow your teeth, and don't forget your antique relative, who with many kisses and much love will always remain

'Your very affectionate uncle,

'E. M. B.'

'*Monday, July* 18.—Had a better night, and feel stronger. We pursue our usual routine. Jameson is a dear old chap; if it was not for him I don't know what I should do.

'The butterflies have come right into the house, and on to my writing things; there is a large and beautiful variety of them, also of birds. Jameson is making a collection. A beastly beetle has got at some of them, and done them damage.

' *Tuesday, July* 19.—Jameson shot a pigeon this morning—we had it for lunch ; also fried plantains. I completed a new year's almanac, which I have been at work at for the last six days, and it is a most complete one. Commenced a new collar to-day, having used two in four months.

'*Sunday, July* 24.—Went on exploring expedition : got to the place I wanted ; found it deserted.

' *July* 27.—My watch stopped suddenly at 9.5 p.m. —a great misfortune.

' *July* 28.—A man brought us a lot of honey. One of the men died to-day.

'*July* 30.—Started at 6.45 a.m. with twenty Soudanese and thirty Zanzibaris. We had not gone far before it came on a regular downpour, and rained more or less all day. We came to a huge village, but they had cleared everything out and gone across the river. Their fires were still burning, but they pass the word so quickly we never can get up to them.

' Rats in my tent have eaten a hole in one of my coats, and the buttons off one of my gaiters. The soldiers eat them when they catch them.

' *Sunday, July* 31.—Stayed in camp. Fine and very hot. Continued letters home. Paid the men.

' *Wednesday, August* 3.—In the evening Washengies came to see us to claim protection, presumably against Tippu-Tib.

' *Monday, August* 8.—Our old friend the chief

9

came in to see us; he reports that the men of
Tippu-Tib came from the north, and that they
are not far from us: when they heard we were here
they said they should not stir from where they are,
a village a day's journey hence, and they have a
stockaded camp.

EXTRACTS FROM A LETTER TO MISS ——.

'Camp, Yambuya Village, Aruwimi Falls,
'*August* 8, 1887.

'Jameson and I are left here by Stanley ; I
in command, and Jameson to help me. I could not
well be with a nicer or pleasanter fellow ; instead of
life being intolerable, he has made it bearable, and,
in a fashion, we don't have a bad time. After our
work is over, after dinner over our wine (alias tea
without sugar or milk), we talk about home ; it is, in
my idea, the pleasantest time of the day—Jameson
is such a help in every way to me, that all the
monotonous work we have had has passed away like
a dream. Stanley left here June 28, and I hope, if
T.-T. comes, and the *Stanley* arrives in time, to be
off with all loads by the 21st of this month. The
natives report T.-T. on the road, but they may
not speak the truth. I shall enjoy that march
tremendously, for I shall have three real good men
under me, viz., Jameson, Troup, and Ward. The
latter is a nephew of Ward in Piccadilly, and is a most
energetic fellow ; he has been out here a long time,
and speaks Zanzibari. Troup is a son of General

Troup, and is the man who wrote to me about tobacco when I was at Park Hatch last January. I have never seen him yet, but by all accounts he is an excellent fellow, and has also been out here before.'

'*August* 11.—Had an axe stolen. I suspect Munichandi.

'*August* 12.—A straggler from Stanley came in, who says the men are terribly emaciated for want of food; he left them a month's march from here at a river running north.

'*Sunday, August* 14. — The steamer *Stanley* arrived at 12 p.m., and Troup, Ward, and Bonny, and 125 men. Jameson and I lunched and dined on board. We had some wine.

'*Monday, August* 15. — The steamer *Stanley* discharged cargo. In the afternoon the Arabs came down to the village opposite, and fired two or three shots; the natives cleared out, and came over to this side, and in the afternoon begged we would come over and turn the Arabs out. As I wished to get word with these Arabs, and the chief and other natives said there were but five, I sent over Ward and Bonny and five Zanzibaris; but the Arabs had left. I am not much better; have got a slow fever.

'*Tuesday, August* 16. — Not much better: I cannot get my food down. I gave Walker all my letters for home, my watch and spears.'

Among the letters was the following, to Mr. W.

Mackinnon, published in the *Times*, November 28, 1887 :

'From Major Barttelot, commanding Camp, Yambuya Village, to Mr. William Mackinnon.

'Camp, Yambuya Village, Aruwimi Falls,
'*August* 15, 1887.

'Sir,

'I have the honour to inform you that Mr. H. M. Stanley went eastward from here on the 20th of June. A lagger on the march came in on August 12, and reported he had left Mr. Stanley at a river flowing north into the Aruwimi, eighteen days' march out from here. He reported all as well.

'Since Mr. Stanley's departure, Mr. Jameson and myself have been employed in fully carrying out his instructions, a copy of a letter of which is attached for your information. The trench has been dug, the platforms put up, the bank of river cleared, and the clearing to the east side kept clear.

'I have ascertained the position of all villages within a four-mile radius on the southern, eastern, and western sides.

'Our relations with the natives are most friendly. They trade with the men in a small way, and the chiefs come in constantly to see us. Lately they have come to claim our protection against some marauding Arabs, who may or may not be Tippu-Tib's people. I have tried to ascertain, but cannot obtain any information.

'The steamer *Stanley* arrived yesterday, August 14, with Messrs. Troup, Ward, and Bonny, three donkeys, and 479 loads.

'Our present strength is : Soudanese, 44; Somalis, 2 ; Zanzibaris, 200—total, 246. The sentry duty is entirely furnished by the Soudanese, the Zanzibaris only finding picquets. Up to the time of writing this, Tippu-Tib's men have not arrived, though these marauding Arabs before mentioned may be them. Should it turn out to be so, or should they eventually come, I should march at once in Mr. Stanley's track. If, however, they do not, I shall be compelled to stay here till November, when Mr. Stanley expects to return, or till such time afterwards as he may return.

'Since Mr. Stanley's departure our casualties have been : Soudanese, 1 ; Somalis, 2 ; Zanzibaris, 4—total, 7.

'Attached is a sketch of the camp by Mr. Jameson, which will show you everything for the safety of the camp as regards the fortifications.

'Attached, also, is a copy of the camp orders for your information, which will show you that all has been done to preserve discipline, alertness, and cleanliness.

'I have the honour to be, sir, your most obedient servant,

       'EDMUND M. BARTTELOT, Major,

    'Commanding camp, Yambuya Village.'

COPY OF MR. STANLEY'S LETTER OF INSTRUCTIONS.
'TO MAJOR BARTTELOT, ETC.

'Camp, Yambuya Village, Aruwimi Falls, Africa
'*June* 24, 1887.

'SIR,

'As the senior officer of those accompanying
me on the Emin Pasha Relief Expedition, *the
command* of this important post naturally devolves
on you.   It is also for the interest of this Expedition
that you accept this command, from the fact that
your Soudanese company, being only soldiers, and
more capable of garrison duty than the Zanzibaris,
will be better utilized here than on the march
(road).

'The steamer *Stanley* left Yambuya on the 22nd
of this month for Stanley Pool. If she meets with
no mischance she ought to be at Leopoldville on the
2nd of July. In two days more she will be loaded
with about 500 loads of our goods, which were left
in charge of Mr. J. R. Troup. This gentleman
will embark, and on the 4th of July I assume that
the *Stanley* will commence the ascent of the river,
and arrive at Bolobo the 9th of July. Fuel being
ready, the 125 men in charge of Messrs. Ward and
Bonny, now at Bolobo, will embark, and the steamer
will continue her journey. She will be at Baryata
19th of July, and arrive 31st of July. Of course the
lowness of the river in that month may delay her
a few days, but, having great confidence in her

captain, you may certainly expect her before the
10th of August.

'Though the camp is favourably situated and
naturally strong, a brave enemy would find it no
difficult task to capture, if the commander is lax in
discipline, vigour, or energy. Therefore I feel sure
that I have made a wise choice in selecting you to
guard our interests here during our absence.

'The interests now entrusted to you are of vital
importance to this Expedition. The men you will
eventually have under your command consist of
more than an entire third of the whole Expedition.
The goods that will be brought up are the currency
needed for transit through the regions beyond the
lakes ; there will be a vast store of ammunition and
provisions, which are of equal importance to us.
The loss of these goods and the men there would
be certain ruin to us, and the advance force would
in its turn need to solicit relief. Therefore, weighing
all these matters well, I hope you will spare no pains
to maintain order and discipline in your camp, and
make your defences complete, and keep them in
such a condition that, however brave an enemy may
be, he can make no impression on them. For this
latter purpose I would recommend you to make an
artificial ditch of six feet wide, three feet deep,
leading from the natural ditch where the spring is
round the stockade. A platform like that on the
southern side of the camp constructed near the
eastern as well as the western gate would be of

advantage to the strength of the camp. For, remember, it is not the natives alone you have to fear, or who may wish to assail you, but the Arabs and their followers may through some cause or other quarrel with you and assail your camp.

'Our course from here will be true east, or by magnetic compass east by south, as near as possible. Certain marches that we may take may not exactly lead in the direction aimed at ; nevertheless, it is the south-western corner of Lake Albert, near or at Kavalli, that is our destination. When we arrive there we will form a strong camp in the neighbourhood, launch our boat, and steer for Kibero, in Unyoro, to hear from Signor Casati (if there) of the condition of Emin Pasha. If the latter is alive and in the neighbourhood of the lake, we shall communicate with him ; and our after-conduct must be guided by what we learn of the intentions of Emin Pasha. We may assume that we shall not be longer than a fortnight with him before deciding on our return to this camp, along the same route traversed by us when going east.

'We will endeavour, by blazing trees and cutting saplings along our road, to leave sufficient traces of the route taken by us. We shall always take by preference tracks leading eastward at all crossways where paths intersect. We shall hoe up and make a hole a few inches deep across all the paths not used by us, besides blazing trees when possible. It may happen, should Tippu-Tib have sent the full

number of adults promised by him to me—viz.,
600 men able to carry loads—and the *Stanley* has
arrived in safety with the 125 men left by me at
Bolobo, that you will feel yourself sufficiently competent to march the column, with all the goods
brought by the *Stanley* and those left by me at
Yambuya. along the road pursued by me. In that
event, which would be desirable, you will follow
closely our route, and before many days we should
most assuredly meet. No doubt you would find our
bomas intact and standing, and you should endeavour
to make your marches so that you could utilize these
as you marched. Better guides than these bomas of
our route could not be made. If you do not meet
them in the course of two days' march, you may rest
assured that you are not in our route.

'It may happen also that, though Tippu-Tib has
sent some men, he has not sent enough to carry the
goods with your own force. In that case you will,
of course, use your discretion as to what goods you
can dispense with to enable you to march. For this
purpose you should study your list attentively—viz. :

'1st. Ammunition, especially fixed, is important.

'2nd. Beads, brass wire, and cowries rank next.

'3rd. Private baggage.

'4th. Powder and caps.

'5th. European provisions.

'6th. Brass rods, as used in the Congo.

'7th. Provisions (rice, beans, peas, matamas,
biscuit).

'Therefore, you must consider after those sacking tools, such as shovels (never discard an axe or a billhook), how many sacks of provisions you can distribute among your men to enable you to march, whether half the brass rods in your boxes couldn't go also, and there stop. If you still cannot march, then it would be better to make marches of six miles twice over, if you prefer marching to staying for our arrival, than throw too many things away.

'With the *Stanley's* final departure from Yambuya you should not fail to send a report to Mr. William Mackinnon, of Gray, Dawes, and Co., 13, Austin-friars, London, of what has happened at your camp in my absence, when I started away eastward, whether you have heard of or from me at all, when you do expect to hear, and what you propose doing. You should also send him a true copy of this order, that the Relief Committee may judge for themselves whether you have acted or purpose to act judiciously. Your present garrison shall consist of eighty rifles and from forty to fifty supernumeraries. The *Stanley* is to bring you within a few weeks fifty more rifles and seventy-five supernumeraries, under Messrs. Troup, Ward, and Bonny.

'I associate Mr. J. S. Jameson with you at present. Messrs. Troup, Ward, and Bonny will submit to your authority in the ordinary duties of the defence and the conduct of the camp or of the march. There is only one chief, which is yourself; but should any vital steps be proposed to be taken,

I beg of you to take the voice of Mr. Jameson; and when Messrs. Troup and Ward are here, pray admit them to your confidence, and let them speak freely their opinions.

'I think I have written very clearly upon every-thing that strikes me as necessary. Your treatment of the natives, I suggest, should depend entirely on their conduct to you. If they do not molest you, suffer them to return to the neighbouring villages in peace; and if you can in any manner, by moderation, small gifts occasionally of brass rods, etc., hasten an amicable intercourse, I should recommend your doing so. Lose no opportunity of obtaining in-formation respecting the natives, the position of the various villages in your neighbourhood, etc.

'I have the honour to be,

'Your obedient servant,

'HENRY M. STANLEY.

' P.S.—In the bottom of your ditch put splinters; keep four or five weak men doing this light job; cut fuel ten days for *Stanley*. Give one brass rod per week to each man to buy fish, etc. In five months these will amount to 2,580. Give also six cowries per man per week. In five months these will number 15,480. Let Mr. Jameson attend to the sick daily.—H. M. S.'

'I certify this is a copy of Mr. H. M. Stanley's original letter.

'EDMUND M. BARTTELOT, Major.'

'Camp, Yambuya Village, Aruwimi Falls.'

'Camp, Yambuya Village, Aruwimi Falls,
June 28, 1887.

General Orders.

' I. (*a*) Reveille will sound at 5 a.m.

'(*b*) General parade at 5.30 a.m. (examine arms,
etc.). Soudanese guard mounts (detail duties and
punishment).

'(*c*) Commence work at 6 a.m. till 11 a.m.   Fall
in again at 1 p.m. for work till 5.30 p.m.   This is
always except on Sundays, when there is no work
in the afternoon.

'(*d*) Retreat at 6 p.m.; gate shut and Zanzibar
picquet mounted.

' II. No man to leave camp without permission,
except on duty, and if with permission and by himself, not to proceed beyond the line of sentries or
out of sight of camp.   Parties proceeding out for the
purpose of gathering manioc not to be of less
strength than five, and all must be armed with rifles.
No man or party is ever on any account to leave
camp at night.

' III. In case of an attack strict silence is demanded; no rifle is to be fired until the order is
given.   The signal of the attack will be continuous
beating of the big drum, when the men will fall in
at their allotted stations under their respective com-
manders.   Indiscriminate firing will be met with

punishment, as it tends to raise false alarms, and is a waste of valuable ammunition.

'IV. All stealing from or injury of any sort to the natives will be met with severe punishment, as conciliation is the object aimed at.

'V. The latrines situated outside the northern gates are on all occasions to be used. Any man found committing a nuisance within the stockade or within a radius of 300 yards of the camp will be punished. All rubbish to be thrown into the river below the northern gate. The camp to be cleaned up every morning at 6 a.m. The commanding officer enjoins the strictest attention to cleanliness, as the good health of all depends upon it.

'VI. Obedience to these orders is demanded by the commanding officer, as order and discipline must be maintained.

'VII. The following punishments for the following offences :

' 1. When on sentry go, sleeping on his post—twenty-five lashes.

' 2. Minor offences—confined to barracks, or such punishment as the case may seem to deserve.

' By order,

'EDMUND M. BARTTELOT, Major, commanding
'stockaded camp.'

'*Special Order to the English Officers.*

' I. One officer must always be in camp (the orderly officer).

'II. An orderly officer to be detailed daily. Duties as below :

'(*a*) Mount guard and picket.

'(*b*) Visit guard and sentries twice by day and four times by night.

'(*c*) Superintend all work in camp.

'(*d*) Send in a report to the commanding officer on the expiration of his term of duty of anything of importance that may have occurred.

'III. All working parties to be commanded by an English officer.

'By order,

'EDMUND M. BARTTELOT, Major, commanding

'stockaded camp.'

[These orders of Major Barttelot require attention, as they explain the discipline he maintained from the commencement, and are referred to later on. It will also be noticed that Major Barttelot states in his letter to Mr. Mackinnon that if Tippu-Tib's men do not come, 'I shall be compelled to stay here till November, when Mr. Stanley expects to return.']

CHAPTER VII.

YAMBUYA CAMP.

MR. STANLEY'S SUGGESTION TO THE REAR COLUMN TO ADVANCE
BY MARCHES OF SIX MILES FOUR TIMES OVER, I.E., TO MAKE A
MARCH OF 4,200 MILES !!!

AUGUST 17—DECEMBER 31, 1887.

Mr. Stanley's Accusations—Impossible to move—Total Force at
Yambuya with Loads—Jameson and Ward go to the Falls—
Their Return—Reports of Men coming in—Report of
Stanley's Return—Barttelot and Troup go to the Falls—
Singatini—No Chance of getting Men—Return to Yambuya
—Much Sickness in Camp—They determine never to partake
of Stanley's Hospitality—Christmas Festivities—A Year of
Disappointment.

'*Wednesday, August* 17, 1887. The *Stanley*
left at 6 a.m.—our last connecting-link—taking with
her Jameson's boy, and one interpreter with the
natives ; also 10 lb. of powder, taken by mistake.'

[On page 7, vol. i., of 'Darkest Africa,' Mr.
Stanley writes : ' The misfortunes of the rear column
were due to the resolution of August 17 to stay and
wait for me, and to the meeting with the Arabs the

next day.'   On page 6 he writes : 'While I possess positive proofs that both the Major and Mr. Jameson were inspired by loyalty and burning with desire throughout those long months at Yambuya, I have endeavoured to ascertain why they did not proceed as instructed by letter, or why Messrs. Ward, Troup, and Bonny did not suggest that to move little by little was preferable to rotting at Yambuya, which they were clearly in danger of doing, like the 100 dead followers.   To this simple question there is no answer . . . their journals, log-books, letters, teem with proofs that every element of success was in and with them.   I cannot understand why the five officers, having means for moving, confessedly burning with the desire to move, and animated with the highest feelings, did not move on along our track as directed.'

Mr. Stanley ignores his own letter when he overlooks the obvious fact (an important one when bringing grave accusations against dead men) that his letter of instructions only provides for a move to be made under two circumstances — firstly, if Tippu-Tib should have sent the full number of adults ; secondly, if Tippu-Tib should send some men, but not all.   The case of Tippu-Tib providing no men is not alluded to, and the choice of moving or waiting Mr. Stanley's return is allowed to Major Barttelot in each of the two circumstances provided for.

Mr. Stanley, not being a military man, cannot

understand that the simple reason why the rear
column did not advance was that he had made it
utterly impossible for them to do so at this date.
Though I believe he was a war correspondent in
Abyssinia and Ashantee, yet, not being trained to
appreciate the requirements of humanity when on
the march, even in ' Darkest Africa' he willingly
fails to grasp the situation, and talks of 'the mystery
of Yambuya life' (vol. i., p. 7). The truth, as
Mr. Stanley well knows, is that he had, very shrewdly
for his own well-being, and with a masterly compre-
hension of what he was about, taken all the strong,
all the able, all the good-character men, and left the
sick, the feeble, and the incorrigible at Yambuya.
But these 380 picked men of his were not all to
carry loads ; some 250 to 300 loads only were taken,
while he left 660 loads at Yambuya, with 250 odd
people, of whom 165 only were able to carry.

Anyone who knew Major Barttelot would be
aware that he would rather be inclined to fall into
the error of attempting a task rashly than leave any
possible task unfulfilled. He was of an eager, keen
disposition, and both he and Jameson and the other
officers were bitterly disappointed at being left
behind. If they could have gone on, they would ;
no one can read his diary without feeling this to be
the case.

Mr. Stanley actually tells us that he suggested to
Major Barttelot that if the carriers of Tippu did not
turn up, the rear column should advance by making

10

marches of six miles at a time four times over
(' Darkest Africa,' vol. i., p. 518).   No one but himself would dare, I should think, to put such a suggestion on paper, for fear of the storm of derision it
would provoke.   The idea (if the subject-matter
were not so serious) is a splendid conception of the
ridiculously impossible.   Just think what this brilliant
suggestion meant.   The distance to the Albert Lake
is over 600 miles ; to go there by journeys of six
miles made four times over means to go over every
six miles three double journeys and one single
journey—that is, seven times ; so that to advance
one mile the suggestion is to travel seven ; and in
order to cover the 600 miles a march of 4,200 miles
is to be made, which, supposing they march 50 miles
a week backwards and forwards through the forest (a
great deal more than Stanley did), would take them
eighty-four weeks, or more than a year and a half,
always supposing that there are no accidents or
troubles—such as desertions, starvation, or attacks
by Arabs or natives—and fair roads.

Imagine the five officers at Yambuya with such a
proposal before them, together with instructions that
the loss of the loads would be absolute ruin to the
Expedition !

' What !' says Mr. Stanley ; ' count your hundreds
of loads !   What are they ?   The path of duty is the
way to glory.'   ' Yes, Mr. Stanley,' they might
answer ; ' but " The path of folly is the way to
shame." '   A leader who provides for a portion of

his expedition in this sort of manner deserves trial by court-martial, only this was not, unfortunately, a military expedition.

The Zanzibaris, too, poor creatures! never forgot the lessons ‘Bulla-Matari’ had taught them of insubordination and mutiny against the white officers —‘the little masters.’ The painful scene on the Congo on May 20 had left a permanent effect on officers and men. It almost seems to have been part of Mr. Stanley's method of dealing with his officers and men to create suspicion and ill-feeling between them, and so to acquire a sort of fictitious advantage and command over both by weakening the authority of the officers, and causing the men to look upon him as the only person to be regarded.

Barttelot and Jameson had been some six weeks alone when the others arrived from Bolobo, and right glad they must have been to see them. It was at once patent to all that no advance was possible without carriers, and soon some Arabs were heard of in the neighbourhood, whom they joyfully anticipated were the men expected. ‘However,’ they would say, ‘if they don't turn up, and the worst comes to the worst, the delay is not to be such a long one—Stanley returns in November, and then we shall move.’ Such were the thoughts that would be present to the minds of the five brave officers now assembled at Yambuya.

There would be present now in camp at Yambuya :

The Bolobo Contingent, consisting of		The Yambuya Contingent, consisting of
Zanzibaris . .	125	70
Boys (servants) ..	3	5
Soudanese . . .	0	44
Somalis	0	3
European officers .	3	2
	131	124

Out of these, 4 Soudanese, 30 Zanzibaris and 3 Somalis were sick, leaving a total of 165 Zanzibaris fit and able to carry loads, and 40 Soudanese* soldiers fit for duty.

The conduct of the Soudanese on the march from Matadi to Leopoldville twenty-seven days, and the difficulties experienced by Major Barttelot in getting them along, as already detailed, had shown him their worst qualities, and probably was one of the main reasons of Mr. Stanley's dislike to them, and the reason he left them at Yambuya.   Notwithstanding that, he says (vol. i., p. 67) 'my object has been' (in taking them) 'to enable them to speak for me to the Soudanese of Equatoria.'

The Zanzibaris that were left at Bolobo were the weak, the sickly, and the worst characters whom Mr. Stanley picked out, a terrible-looking lot.

* The Soudanese did not carry loads; they were hired as soldiers, not as porters.

The Zanzibaris left at Yambuya, again, were the weak and most useless men.

The list of stores landed at Yambuya Camp per steamer *Stanley* from Bolobo numbered 493 loads ; Mr. Stanley left at Yambuya 167 loads. Zanzibari carriers 165 ; Soudanese soldiers 40.

Four times $165 = 660$, so that there were four times as many loads as carriers—and the worst carriers of the Expedition.]

' In the afternoon (of the 17th) the natives came in and said they would like us to go up to the Arab camp. I was anxious to obtain information about them. I let four Zanzibaris go, and kept a native as a hostage. I cannot eat much. If I could get more meat I should be all right.

' *Thursday, August* 18.—Early, one of the four Zanzibaris came back and said that the natives were afraid to go close to the Arabs, so he and the chief had come back, and the others had gone to the Arab camp. At 12 p.m. the other men returned with four Arab chiefs, the boss chief being Abdulla Korona and some followers. They told me they were not sent by Tippu-Tib, but that they belonged to him ; that Tippu-Tib had sent the 600 men, but, seeing the trees blazed, they turned back, supposing we had all gone on. These Arabs said they would take a letter to Tippu-Tib for us, and he would send the men.'

Proceedings of a Board held at the above camp, Yambuya village, August 18, 1887, for the purpose of considering the advisability of sending a European to Tippu-Tib at Stanley Falls, to inquire whether or no he will send the 600 men promised. President: Major Barttelot. Members: Mr. Jameson, Troup, Ward, Bonny. The Board having assembled, the under-mentioned circumstances were laid before it, viz. :

'Major Barttelot hearing that a party of Arabs were in the neighbourhood, and that five of these Arabs had come into the village opposite and fired shots on the morning of April 16, he determined to send a party to find out who they were. The native chief of the village opposite had come in the afternoon of the 16th, and said the Arab camp was a canoe's journey from here. Arrangements were accordingly made with him to convey a party of four Zanzibaris. They left on the 17th. At noon of the 18th they returned, bringing with them five Arab chiefs. On being interviewed, the information was elicited that the 600 men promised by Tippu-Tib had come, but had struck the river at the Upper Falls. Seeing the trees blazed there, they imagined that we had all gone on, and turned back. The principal Arab chief was of opinion that if a messenger was sent to Tippu-Tib he would send the men back. They further agreed to convey this messenger or letter across in safety, and promised to return with twenty men on the 3rd day, viz., the 20th.

'OPINION OF THE BOARD.

'The Board, having duly considered the matter, were of opinion that to send a letter might be useless, or would at any rate involve delay. To send a Zanzibari messenger would not be safe nor compatible with Tippu-Tib's dignity; so on due consideration it was determined that two white men should go, taking with them one Zanzibari and an interpreter, viz., Bartholomew.

'(*Signed*) President: Edmund M. Barttelot, Major.
Members: J. S. Jameson, Rose Troup,
Herbert Ward.'

'*August* 20.—I cannot eat the rice as I should. My opinion as to Bonny has considerably altered; though slow he is straight and brave, and I believe on one or two occasions he has shown tact, common-sense, and firmness. What work he has to do he does well.

'*August* 21.—At 12 p.m. some Arabs arrived, but not all; the rest are coming to-morrow. It is Jameson's birthday, so we had a box of sardines for dinner in consequence.

'*Monday, August* 22.—At 12 p.m. the Sheik Abdulla Korona, with a wife, and a huge fowl which he gave me, and another Sheik, Sulieman, whom I saw at the Falls and recognised at once, arrived with more Arabs and a whole host of slaves.

'I had a long palaver with them, and made an

agreement that they should carry Jameson's and Ward's loads to the Falls and back for three pieces of handkerchief. I was to give one piece to the canoes in advance, which I agreed to.

'I gave Abdulla a present of five pieces of handkerchief and Sulieman four pieces, and the four other chiefs two pieces apiece.

'Abdulla said it would only take four days. I hope it may.

'*Tuesday, August* 23.—Jameson and Ward, after much palaver, started at 7.15 a.m. I hope all may go well. I expect when I see Stanley, and hand in my report, he will drop into me right and left. In the first place, I have actually dared to give Ward, Troup, and Bonny some of their rights, by opening some of the food boxes, and giving them the same as all the others had, only not for six, but for three months.

'*Saturday, August* 27.—Jameson and Ward should arrive at the Falls to-day. The Soudanese came and said it was their Christmas Day, and they all came and kissed hands; they expected a present, so I gave them two metako each all round.

'*August* 29.—Our meat is finished again; we have one wretched hen left. To-day the Arabs came to visit us. I did not want to see them, for they only come to get what they can.

'*August* 30.—The Arabs left us. We gave the two head-men a present. Being Christmas Day for the Zanzibaris, they all had a holiday.

'*Thursday, September* 1.—I wonder what they did shooting at home to-day.

'*September* 2.—Bonny has fever.

'*September* 3.—Bonny and Troup both ill with fever. Arabs came in with reports. Gave them two canoes, some handkerchiefs, and cowries.

'*Sunday, September* 4.—The two canoes I gave the Arabs were anchored at the top of our path to the river. The sentry had orders to fire upon any-one trying to take them away. The natives tried to take them during the night; the sentry fired and wounded one man. About 8 a.m. the Arabs took their canoes away, but the natives captured one, and the Arabs came back and complained to me. I promised to get it back for them on condition they did not molest the natives till I had done so. A chief came in, so I made him a prisoner, and told him he would be a dead man if the canoe was not returned in twenty-four hours. The canoe was re-turned in the afternoon, and I let him go, cautioning him that if he and his men did not sell us fish as usual, I would no longer protect him from the Arabs.

'*Monday, September* 5.—During the night one of the sentries near the boats fired at a canoe full of Washengies; he said they were going to take the canoe, but my belief is they were only fishing. However, this morning they came to trade with us, and we bought an enormous fish as big as a cod.

'*Tuesday, September* 6.—Troup and Bonny are

better, but not well yet. The chief we tied up
yesterday came in to see us, and brought three
fowls, which we purchased. We opened a new box
of biscuits to-day and a fresh bag of rice. *Nearly
all the biscuits are bad.* A thunderstorm in the
afternoon.

' *Wednesday, September* 7.—The chief came in and
brought another fowl ; he wanted some canoes. I
told him I would sell him one for a goat, and he
could have the other six when we went away, provided he brought fish, honey, or palm-oil every
day.

' *September* 8.—Ward came back, arriving at
6 p.m. He brought a letter from Jameson. I am
afraid we shall not get the 600 men. He also
brought some sweet potatoes.

' *September* 9.—I commenced a new box of
matches, and finished my butter. Ward is sick.
The Sheik Abdulla brought me two fowls, one a big
one.

' *September* 10.—I walked to Stanley's first camp
to-day, a distance of seven miles. The chiefs have
been deceiving us, so Bonny caught eight women and
a baby to-day as their punishment. Ward is still
sick.

' *Sunday, September* 11.—Had a palaver with
natives about their women, but as they chose to
show independence no arrangement was come to.
The native chief came over, bringing the rifle the
natives had stolen from the Zanzibaris, seven fowls

and some fish. For them we let him take one woman.

'*Monday, September* 12.—Jameson returned with Salem Mohammed, and Salem and thirty Arabs ; he is in excellent spirits, and I was right glad to see him.

'*September* 13.— Bonny had a palaver with Ingungo the chief, but it resulted in nothing.

'To-day, the story of the stolen axe came out : it was stolen by the Soudanese, and not by the natives ; still, they are implicated. Morgan Radwan stole it, and Tuma Mohammed sold it. Salem Mohammed told me that the men (promised by Tippu) had started with Tippu-Tib, but that owing to fighting and losing men, and their hands getting sore from paddling, they turned back. He (Tippu-Tib) then sent them down to the Lomami River on the south bank of the Congo, to settle some disputes there. But he had sent to collect these and others to approach as near as possible the promised 600, who would arrive in ten days or so, with Tippu-Tib himself.

'*Wednesday, September* 14.—At 8 a.m. I formed up all the Zanzibaris and Soudanese on three sides of a square, made an address to them, and punished the five Soudanese publicly before them ; one, being a sergeant, was reduced to the ranks. It will have a salutary effect, I think. Ingungo brought us heaps of splendid fish, and we gave him back one woman. Ward no better. One of Jameson's men died to-day.

'*September* 15.— Abdulla's men attacked the village yesterday, and the Washengies are all gone.

'*September* 18. Ward better. Ingungo came to see us, and brought two huge pots of honey ; poor chaps ! the Arabs have treated them very badly ; the scene yesterday was disgraceful. They shot the poor fellows in the water. I remonstrated with Salem Mohammed ; he promised to stop it, and sent a canoe across for that purpose. There has been no shooting here to-day ; though early this morning there was a disturbance in the Arab camp. We have lost a lot of meat ; I suspect our boys.

'*September* 20.—Jameson's tortoises were stolen during the night ; our suspicion fixed on the Sou-danese. The boy who stole the meat was my boy Uledi, who was denounced by his companions ; he was flogged and upbraided. The Washengies came in, and we exchanged a woman for eight fowls and some fish.

'*September* 21.—The man who took the tortoises was denounced by his three friends ; he was publicly flogged, the others were made to do defaulters' drill. Ward is still weak and ill.

'*Sunday, September* 25.—The chief of Yambui came in and brought back Bartholomew and Msa bi Guma ; they are chained and padlocked in the guard-room. (These men had stolen a quantity of metako from Jameson when at the Falls, and he had left them in chains at Yambui.)

'*Monday, September* 26.—Salem Mohammed told

me Tippu-Tib could not collect the men, but had sent them to collect some Manyuema. His own Arabs think the loads too heavy.

'*September* 27.—There is a report from the natives that Stanley is coming back. Had had a fight and lost twenty men and one donkey. I tried to authenticate it. Bartholomew and Msa were flogged this morning.

'*Wednesday, September* 28.—Salem Mohammed is puzzled because I am going to the Falls. It may be our position is one of more danger than I think for; I shall fight it out. Had chicken for dinner. Ward is better.

'*Thursday, September* 29.—No confirmation of the report about Stanley. If I hear nothing fresh, I shall start for the Falls Saturday or Sunday.

'*September* 30.—Omar found Ingungo to-day, and bought a huge fish for us. Jameson and Troup went to see him, and brought the same information, that Stanley was at four days' distance. A wet night and morning. Fish for dinner.

'*Sunday, October* 2.—Fish for dinner. Salem Mohammed gave us a sheep and a goat. A heavy thunderstorm.

'*October* 3.—Salem Mohammed gave Jameson two fowls. We killed the sheep and had the brisket and liver for lunch. We heard from Ingungo that Abdulla had caught and tied up the supposed twenty men from Stanley. I determined to go to Abdulla's camp to see. We had soup and roast leg for dinner.

'*October* 4.—Jameson, two Soudanese, and self started at 2.30 a.m., and arrived at Abdulla's camp at 8.30 a.m.   No sign of any Zanzibaris, nor had the head Sheik (Abdulla was away) heard anything of Mr. Stanley's approach.   A terrible road and a tremendous lot of water.   Omar saw Ingungo, and told him he had lied ; but he still protested he had spoken nothing but the truth.   Jameson and I walked about twenty-five miles to-day.

'*October* 5.—We prepared for our journey to the Falls.

'*Thursday, October* 6.—Started from the camp with Troup, Salem Masudi, interpreter, and a boy called Ferani for Singatini.   We left at 8.30, and arrived at Yaraweko at 4 p.m.   The road was good, but there was much water to cross.   We had melafor, rice, and sardines for dinner.   We re-mained in camp to dry our clothes till 10 a.m., then marched till 4 p.m.   We halted in the forest, and could get no water.   On our way we met some natives, who told us Tippu would be at Yallasula to-morrow.

'*October* 8.—Left camp at 6 a.m. ; we marched to the nearest water, two hours, and had breakfast.   I got into Yallasula at 3.30 p.m.   Troup had bad feet, and came in two hours later.   Yallasula is on the Congo.   Said Mohammed treated us right well.

'*October* 9.—We are in a house here ; last night it rained hard, and came through.   About noon

Tippu appeared and a following. He told me that at Yarukombé were five Zanzibaris who had deserted from Stanley, and had brought money to him to seek his aid in flight; they had come from Abdulla's camp, where they had left five others, Abdulla having caught the lot and kept them; so what Ingungo said was partly true. Tippu, in compliance with my request, sent up to Yarukombé that afternoon for them. I began a new shaving squeeze of Burgess's.

' *October* 10.—I had a palaver with Tippu-Tib, but not about the men, as he seemed averse to broaching the subject by not mentioning anything about it himself. I arranged with him, however, that he should buy me twelve goats. In the afternoon the deserters came and told the usual untruthful story. They had, however, left Stanley well, and the others with plenty of food; but evidently Stanley had not got as far on his journey as he expected when they left him, which was twenty days down stream in a canoe. I am afraid he won't be back much before the New Year. Tippu-Tib told the men he would shoot them like dogs if they attempted to desert again, and that they were to remain quietly at Yallasula till my return.

' *October* 11.—Left Yallasula by canoe at 2 p.m.; a deluge — the canoe was nearly ,swamped, and everything drenched; at 6 p.m. we arrived at Yarukombé.

' *Wednesday, October* 12.—Paddled all day till

11 p.m. that night, when we reached Singatini and
the Falls; here we had a house given us. We
changed crews three times. I had christened the
canoe *Mabel*, and carved her name on her.

'*October* 13.—Tippu-Tib, before leaving, had
given Salem Mohammed orders to look after us,
and give us four meals a day, and whatever we
wanted. If we wished to go anywhere or see anything, Salem or Farran were to go with us.

EXTRACTS FROM LETTER TO MISS ——.

'Stanley Falls,
'*October* 14, 1887.

'I am on a visit to Tippu-Tib, partly for
pleasure, partly for business. We were disappointed
about getting the promised men from Tippu-Tib,
though, shortly after the *Stanley* left, I sent Jameson
and Ward on here from our camp at Yambuya to
see if Tippu could let us have them; this was on
September 23, and they came back on October 12,
saying that Tippu, when they left, was very busy
getting the men, and would follow them shortly.
He sent, however, only a head-man and his
interpreter, Salem, with but sixty men. After many
tales, they told us he could not get the men, and
had been obliged to send to Kasongo for them,
Kasongo being a month's journey, so I determined
to come and see him myself, and, if possible, to
arrive at the truth, which is a difficult matter with
the Oriental. Tippu has up till now caught, and

has promised that he will continue to catch, all
deserters, and send them back to us. Small lots
have come in from Stanley, and have gone to him
to request his aid to Zanzibar; but he sends them
always to me. The last lot brought very good
news, that they were all well, and in a well-
provisioned country. Troup and I left Yambuya
on October 6, and arrived at a place called Yallasula,
on the Congo, after three days' march through the
forest.

'The first day out we got to a village in the
forest called Yambui; shortly after we started it
came down in buckets, and we were wet to the
bone. We had no end of rivers to cross, the water
up to about our waists; Troup, who had long boots
on, had a lot of trouble, as his boots filled, and had
to be taken off and emptied every time we crossed.
The second day we camped in the forest, but away
from water, so we had only a cup of cold tea each
heated up and cold biscuit; the third day we got
into Yallasula. I was in about two hours before
Troup, as he had sore feet, and was always losing
the track and wandering away into the jungle, and I
had to go and get him, so at last, overtaking one
of our carriers (who were all supplied out of the
sixty men, and knew the road), I handed him over
to him, and cut on ahead. I hate going slowly;
besides, he nearly made me lose the road, by
continually questioning whether I was going right,
and causing me to doubt myself. The track is

11

simply a path through the brush, and is, in the first
case, generally made by elephants and deer going
from water to water, and of course there are many
divergent paths.   But the track used is generally
marked, first by blazing trees; secondly, by the
men's feet; and thirdly, by bits of grass or stick
placed across the roads you are not to go down.
Oftentimes it lies along the bed of a stream, and
then it is only by footmarks you can carry on, and
sometimes the dead grass gets carried away somehow from the debarred roads, which look, perhaps,
more likely than the actual track itself; then, again,
it is only by footmarks and the occasional blazing
you can tell, the blazings being few and far between,
and if at such time you are questioned, it is a bore,
because you perhaps imagine footmarks where they
are not.   However, I was only once at fault, and
soon found it out, and when I was by myself I
rattled along like anything.

' At Yallasula we heard T.-T. was coming down
himself the next day, so we waited for him ; and when
he came, which he did next morning, he told us he had
got five deserters from Stanley for me, who were at
the next village above us, called Yarukombé, and that
he would send them at once.   They had brought him
ivory, to bribe him to effect their escape to Zanzibar.
They arrived at Yallasula the following afternoon, and
I placed them under guard of T.-T.'s men, to await
my return.   The ivory I handed over to T.-T.   He
had to go down the river on business, and I had no

palaver with him then beyond giving him money to buy goats for me, which are easier bought down the river than here, and they will be collected at Yallasula against my return. On the morning of the 11th we left by canoe, and about noon it came down in torrents, and swamped the canoe, and I had stupidly left my coat behind, and was drenched to the skin; all our things got wet, too, and we were decidedly below par that evening. Next morning we started again at 8.30 a.m., and at 11.30 p.m. arrived here. We changed our crews three times—that was at every village we came to. T.-T., both here and at Yallasula, finds us in house and food, and they give us such a lot of the latter, and there is not much to do : I am getting quite fat.

'The canoe journey is not bad fun, but it is rather fatiguing sitting in such a constrained position for so long. T.-T. is not here yet, but is expected to-day or to-morrow. I shall stay here till the 21st. . . . As I do not expect the men from Kasongo for some time, if they ever come at all, I have made a real good place of our camp, though when we go it will all be handed over to T.-T., who is going to establish stations down from our camp to the Congo, and from here to Bangala, the last of the Free State stations. All the villages under his government are in most excellent order, and their services are always at his disposal; *e.g.*, when we came up by canoe, at every village we came to, Salem, his interpreter, told them we were on T.-T.'s business, and required

fresh men at once : they were immediately forthcoming.   All disputes are laid before Tippu ; all
villages are laid under a contribution to Tippu as
follows, namely, three out of every four tusks of
ivory they get.   Of course, this only refers to those
villages which acknowledge his supremacy ; those
which do not, he captures all their women and kills as
many of the men as he can, the women having to be
ransomed for ivory.   A short period of this treatment generally brings them into subjection, for
though they may move as fast as they like, they are
always in the end hunted down and killed. . . .
Whenever we have our meals, about twenty people
come and look on.   Troup is very amusing about
it : he cannot stand it, and the angrier he gets, the
more they come and laugh. . . . I have done all I
can now till Stanley puts in appearance, and, failing
that, I shall not take any decided step till February ;
it will be weary waiting, but it must be gone through
with. . . .

'*October* 21.—No sign of Tippu-Tib up to date,
though he was to have been here five days ago. . . .
To-night I heard that T.-T. could not come back, as
he was at war for some days, so I am going to return
to my camp on the 23rd.   Of course, his not being
able to return is a lie ; the truth is, he does not wish
to see me, as he never intended, or intends, to give
us the men at the price named in the contract.'

'*Saturday, October* 15.—Went to lunch with

Tippu's father-in-law, a most delightful old man, who gave us no end of a feed. It is nine months since leaving home ; wrote to father.

'*Sunday, October* 16.—Went over to the Old Falls Station, and had lunch with Nasoro, one of the men who came from Zanzibar with Tippu-Tib ; saw Salem Mohammed's new house, and got a knife he had promised me.

'*Wednesday, October* 19.—No signs of Tippu. I told Salem I should start on Saturday. Salem was inclined to be impertinent.

'*Friday, October* 21.—I had a row with Salem, who has been behaving badly to us all through, and lying like anything. I wrote to Mackinnon.

'*Saturday, October* 22.—We had news of Tippu, and Monday he arrived, and came to see me. From what he said, I see no chance, or at least very little chance, of getting any men.

'*Tuesday, October* 25.—I finished my letters home, and had lunch with Nasoro.

'*Wednesday, October* 26.—We left Singatini, homeward bound, in Tippu's canoes. At Singatini we had bought fifty odd fowls, rice, potatoes, and onions ; arrived at Yatakhana at 4 p.m. I bathed in the Congo. Here I received a letter from Jameson stating that Mswa had escaped.

'*October* 27.—We reached Yallasula, and found the twelve goats (purchased by Tippu for us), but most of them are very small.

'*Saturday, October* 29.—Spent Friday at Yalla-

sula, and marched to-day to Yaraweko.   I slept in a
native hut, and was horribly bitten.

' *Sunday, October* 30.—Arrived at Yambuya, found
all well ; a great improvement.

' *October* 31.—I saw Salem Mohammed, and told
him of Salem Masudi's lies and treatment.

' *November* 1. — Salem Masudi arrived in the
afternoon, and there was a row between him
and Salem Mohammed.   Troup came in late at
night.

' *November* 2.—Fish for lunch and dinner.   Uledi
was flogged for theft.

' *Friday, November* 4.—Mswa was caught to-day.
Salem Mohammed gave me a young antelope, and
told me he was going away, and all his men, from
Singatini.

' *November* 5.—I gave Salem Mohammed my old
mess jacket, as he was going away to-morrow.
Jameson killed the young antelope during the
night, as he cried so ; so we had him for dinner,
stewed.

' *November* 6.—A heavy rain last night.   Salem
Mohammed came to wish us good-bye.   Bonny
caught his and Troup's boy stealing while we were
at dinner last night.   They were flogged this
morning.

' *November* 7.—Mswa and Bartholomew were
flogged this morning.

' *November* 9.—I am laid up with fever.

' *Saturday, November* 12.—The fever left me.

'*November* 13.—Life is deadly slow. Fish for breakfast and lunch, fowls for dinner.

'*Monday, November* 14.—Been ten months in this country. Bought five more fowls. We are doing well with our live stock. Jameson and Troup are not well.

'*Tuesday, November* 15.—Nassiboo came to see me to-day, and talked the usual twaddle. It rained hard. Jameson is very unwell.

'*Wednesday, November* 16.—Assad Farran, who is suffering from ulcers, chiefly arising from want of cleanliness and a tendency to dropsy, says he will die soon, and I am of that opinion, if he does not wash himself. Jameson is no better. I saw the new moon this evening, and there was much firing off of guns in consequence among Tippu's men.

'*Thursday, November* 17.—Troup's birthday. We were to have had a feast to-day, but Jameson and Troup being so unwell, it was put off: both of them are better. I slept the whole morning between breakfast and luncheon. We killed a goat this afternoon.

'*Friday, November* 18.—Had fish and meat for breakfast, but we discovered that the goat was diseased. We killed it because it had a cold, but it turned out to be pleurisy. I had a palaver with Tippu-Tib's men about interfering with my men and the natives buying fish; in consequence, I am sending Ward to the Falls to complain to Tippu-Tib. We bought a lot of fish from a native, who gave us to understand that they dare not come and sell openly to us on account of Tippu-Tib's men. Some of our men have faded away to nothing.   It is surprising to me how uprightly and well they walk, though mere skeletons.   Troup and Jameson are still ill.

' *November* 19.—Ward left for Singatini early this morning.'

COPY OF LETTER TO MR. WARD, ON GOING TO SINGATINI.

' *November* 19, 1887.

' SIR,

' You will proceed to Singatini for the purpose of interviewing Tippu-Tib on the following subject, viz., the prevention of the natives selling fish, etc., to me by his men stationed here (Yambuya), though I have requested them to desist from it. You will explain to Tippu-Tib the facts of the case, and ask him if the men cannot be sent further away from our camp, with orders not to interfere with the traffic between me and the natives, or else send a responsible man as muniapara, with distinct orders not to allow his men to interfere between mine and the natives, or to tamper with the natives selling direct to us.   The muniapara here at present— Majato by name—has done all in his power to annoy me in this respect, though remonstrated with on several previous occasions.

' I have the honour, etc.,

' EDMUND M. BARTTELOT, Major.'

'*November* 20.—Troup is better ; Jameson ill.

'*November* 21.—Jameson is no better ; he has got jaundice. Troup is on the mend.

'*November* 22.— I got a letter from Salem Mohammed, and the present of a goat. He also sent Bonny 250 percussion-caps. We bought a fowl and eggs. All Tippu-Tib's men have cleared out except ten, for which I am very thankful. Jameson is as yellow as a guinea, and very ill.

'*November* 24.—Ingungo and people came over. I made blood-brotherhood with Ingungo's brother. Bonny and I talked about our probable action in the event of Stanley doing certain things. I expressed myself openly. Troup and Jameson ill.

'*Friday, November* 25.—I heard that Salem Mohammed and the Arabs are coming back. I hope it is not true. The Soudanese are very sick. Jameson is better ; Troup very seedy.

'*November* 26.—A native brought us a present of a fish. We have had plaintain puddings the last three or four days for dinner ; they are A1. Jameson is better ; Troup is a sad wreck.

'*Sunday, November* 27.—I am reading Pepys's Journal and Diary ; very interesting. Jameson is on the mend ; Troup a wreck.

'*November* 29.—Fish for breakfast and lunch. I went for a walk with Bonny, who told me Ward had told him Tippu-Tib hated me, but gave me no reason for it. Of course followers follow suit.

' *Wednesday, November* 30.—I resumed conversation of last night with Bonny, and he told me John Henry had told him that Tippu-Tib's men hated me. Assad Farran told me Salem Mohammed hated me, and only stayed here to get what presents he could out of us ; his hatred Assad Farran assigns to my refusing to land and shoot the natives on June 10 on the *Henry Reid*, and then, perhaps, my not allowing his men to come into camp may have something to say to it.

' *December* 1.—We killed a goat this morning.

' *Friday, December* 2.—Some party, at present unknown, went into Ward's house while he was asleep and stole the half-goat that was there.

' *Saturday, December* 3.—A soldier called Burgari and my boy stole the meat. They will both be flogged.

' *December* 4—Burgari was flogged and put in chains. Uledi was not flogged, but was to be banished from the camp.

' *Monday, December* 5.—Burgari acknowledged to-day that Uledi had nothing to do with stealing the meat, for which his fine has been increased to nine months' pay and another flogging later on.

' *December* 6.—After dinner Bonny and I walked again, and referred to our conversation of November 24. I made a determination never to partake of Stanley's hospitality while out here, as we have a private medicine chest. Jameson, in reference to our conversation of November 24, expressed his determination to act as I should, also to refuse Stanley's hospitality.

'Troup is better, but I think his illness has left him very weak.

'*December* 8.—Killed a goat. John Henry caught an immense cat-fish, about 30 lb. John Henry told Bonny that Tippu-Tib had sent a man to look after Stanley, but that he had returned unable to hear any news.

'One of the Soudanese died yesterday.

'*Friday, December* 9 —-Morgan Radwan, the thief, died to-day.

'*December* 14.—We have been eleven months away from England.

'*December* 18.—The thermometer showed 67° Fahr., the lowest it has yet registered. Killed the last of our fowls. Our rations are at a low ebb.

'*December* 19.—A lot of Tippu-Tib's men arrived yesterday.

'*December* 21.—No news of Stanley yet. One of our men, Doredi, got caught by the natives, as a reprisal for Tippu-Tib's men having made Ingungo prisoner ; but they released him, on my conveying to them that I would shoot Ingungo to-morrow if they did not return my man. A bit seedy.

'*December* 21.—Not very fit.

'*December* 23.—Better.

'*Saturday, December* 24.—Killed a goat. I reduced Munichandi ; gave all the men half a day off. It is a year since I first met Stanley.

' *Sunday and Christmas Day, December* 25.—We gave all hands two metako and twelve cowries ; the head-men three metako and eighteen cowries and a whole holiday. *Dear old Jameson gave me a very appropriate card.* A day of feasting. Fish for break-fast, cold ham and meat, pickles, sauce, and mustard (the last and ham given by Troup). For luncheon a pudding of chopped meat, ham, three pigeons and a chicken ; the crust of flour and suet excellent. A cold banana pudding. For dinner we had soup, grilled slices of mutton, roast leg of mutton, and a roly-poly pudding of flour, suet, five eggs, and a pot of raspberry jam, the flour and jam being given by Jameson and me. To finish up with we had some brandy and many songs. Considering the circum-stances and the place, we had not such a bad time of it. The flour for the meat pudding was given by Ward.

' *Monday, December* 26.—Gave the men another whole holiday.

' *Wednesday, December* 28.—The natives surprised five of Tippu-Tib's men in a canoe which they had stolen, stabbed one man in two places in the back and right side. They captured one man and four guns, the other three men escaped ; this was at 2 o'clock this morning. Bonny put back the man's inside and stitched up his three wounds, but I don't think he will live. We have been here six months to-day.

' *December* 29.—Tippu-Tib's man died to-day.

Wishing you a merry Christmas
A happy New Year

"I wonner when Maister Turnut all the summer home again"

'*Saturday, December* 31.—A dull monotonous year for me, and a disappointment for me.'

Thus ended the year 1887 for the five Englishmen and their poor followers, who had patiently waited for Mr. Stanley's return from the relief of Emin at Yambuya for six months without a message or communication of any kind from him.

CHAPTER VIII.

YAMBUYA CAMP.

RETROSPECT.

Gloom within and Danger without—Anxiety respecting Stanley—
Two Letters stated by Mr. Stanley to have been sent to Major
Barttelot, but which he never received, and which were sent
Home by Mr. Stanley himself immediately after Major
Barttelot's death.

THE knowledge of their position has not yet fully
dawned on the officers of the rear column. They
cannot yet realize it. They are full of foreboding
and doubt, scarcely balanced by the hope that
even yet all may be well. The mournful, heavy-
foliaged forest narrows their horizon on all sides ;
the dark river flows beside their camp. The
monotony of their weary life is only interrupted
by horrible scenes of savage warfare between the
cruel natives and their still more cruel and cunning
enemies, the Arabs. The daily routine of duties
grows unbearable ; the discipline seems unen-
durable, and the constant sight of the poor skeleton

Soudanese and Zanzibaris wasting to death, as they moved listlessly to and fro in that awful camp, was sorrow to the gaze and gall to the souls of those five patient men. With nothing to occupy their manly energies, the imagination would prey on the mind, and Arab craft began to try the effect of lies and dissimulation to create mischief between the camp and the natives, or between their own followers and the Zanzibaris; or even, if possible, amongst those in the very camp itself. With the wealth of stores in the camp the Arabs were well acquainted, and from the commencement of the year were drawing, in ever-increasing numbers, towards an attraction to them irresistible. Major Barttelot allowed no Arab into the camp unless it was to see him or the other officers. That rule, and the strict discipline enforced, undoubtedly preserved the rear column till their departure, and maintained the camp inviolate.

Again, the officers at Yambuya did not comprehend that they were deserted by the advance force, and that Stanley's promise to return in November would be broken and forgotten. They remembered that when Major Barttelot arrived at Yambuya with the steamer, only two days late, from Stanley Falls, Mr. Stanley was filled with anxiety and suspicion, and yet Mr. Stanley was to return in November. It is now the end of December; they are anxious, but they hear from stragglers of the difficulties of his march. They believe his word, and feel sure he will soon return. But it must have seemed very strange to them that as stragglers and deserters from the advance force could find their way back to them, not a message was received from Mr. Stanley, who had expected to reach Wadelai the end of July or beginning of August, to have made his arrangements with Emin, and to return to Yambuya about November. What steps does Mr. Stanley take to fulfil his promise to return in November, or, failing his ability to perform that duty, what attempt does he make to secure communications with his rear column? He *knew* the dangerous position of the rear column should it attempt to advance (see p. 179, vol. i., 'Darkest Africa') : ' If 389 *picked* men, such as we were when we left Yambuya, are unable to reach Lake Albert, how can Major Barttelot with 250 men make his way through this endless forest?' (Mr. Stanley omits to state that he had only some 300 loads, while Major Barttelot had 660.) 'We have travelled on an average eight hours per day for forty-four days since leaving Yambuya. At two miles per hour we ought by this date to have arrived on the Lake shore ; but instead of being there, we have just accomplished a third of the distance. August 18, 1887. Itiri.'

On September 17, when passing through Ugarrowwa's camp, Mr. Stanley says that he stipulated with Ugarrowwa that if he would deliver a letter to Major Barttelot, he should have an

order for three hundredweight of powder which
Major Barttelot was to give him (p. 199, vol. i.,
'Darkest Africa').

On p. 463, vol. i., 'Darkest Africa,' Mr. Stanley
recites how on his return journey to Yambuya on
August 11, 1888—eleven months later—his friend
Ugarrowwa handed him back this letter. Ugarrowwa,
who had been tent-boy to Captains Speke and Grant
in 1860-63, would probably know something of
English, and would be sure to find out the contents
of these letters and communicate with the other
Arabs. Between March and August 11, 1888,
Ugarrowwa had been travelling down the Aruwimi
River, laying waste the villages as far as Mugwye.
Ugarrowwa also handed to Mr. Stanley on
August 11, 1888, another letter for Major Barttelot,
dated February 14, 1888, and which is stated to
have been sent by twenty couriers, whom Stairs
took with him from Fort Bodo on February 16, and
reached Ugarrowwa's March 14, on the Ituri. On
the 16th Abdullah and his couriers were despatched
down the river (p. 342, vol. i., 'Darkest Africa'),
with Stairs' report (p. 429, vol. i., 'Darkest Africa').
Again, p. 464, vol. i., 'Darkest Africa,' Mr. Stanley
writes : 'Thus both efforts to communicate with
Major Barttelot had been unsuccessful, and could not
but deepen the impression that something exceedingly awry had occurred to the rear column.' In
the previous pages he gives a long account of the
thrilling tale told him by the remnants of his faithful

(but useless) couriers, whom he found in Ugarrowwa's camp not far from Mugwye on August 11, 1888, only six days from Banalya, and between fifteen and twenty* from Yambuya.

Mr. Stanley is full of compassion for the poor couriers, and of gratitude to Ugarrowwa for his kindness to them, and his impression is that something exceedingly awry has happened to the rear column —that is all.

He apparently does not question Ugarrowwa why he has not communicated with Major Barttelot—an easy matter by canoe. Oh no ; the fault is with Major Barttelot, not with the Arabs. The story of the efforts and sufferings of the couriers is dwelt on by Mr. Stanley at length ; their failure and Ugarrowwa's treachery in keeping the letters are not mentioned. And it is curious that the first we hear of these letters is that Mr. Stanley sends them home himself directly after Major Barttelot's death, and they were published in the newspapers. The only purpose he could have in doing so being to try and justify himself, and to attempt to meet the charge that would naturally suggest itself to his mind at Banalya, with the sad result before his eyes of his rear column deserted and his promise unfulfilled.

The character of the Arabs and Manyuema, in whose hands Mr. Stanley had placed the rear column, is powerfully sketched in the two letters appended, addressed to Major Barttelot.

* By land.

'Camp on S. Bank, Aruwimi River,
'Opposite Arab Settlement,
'*September* 18, 1887.

' MY DEAR MAJOR,

' You will, I am certain, be as glad to get news—definite and clear—of our movements, as I am to feel that I have at last an opportunity of presenting them to you.   As they will be of immense comfort to you and your assistants and followers, I shall confine myself to giving you the needful details. We have travelled 340 English miles to make only 192 geographical miles of our easterly course.   This has been performed in eighty-three days, which gives us a rate of four and one-tenth miles per day.   We have yet to make 130 geographical miles, or a winding course, perhaps, of 230 miles, which, at the same rate of march as hitherto, we may make in fifty-five days.   We started from Yambuya 389 souls, whites and blacks.   We have now 333, of whom fifty-six are so sick that we are obliged to leave them behind us at this Arab camp of Ugarrowwa.   We are fifty-six men short of the number with which we left Yambuya.   Of these, thirty men have died—four from poisoned arrows, six left in the bush or speared by the natives—twenty-six have deserted *en route*, thinking that they would be able to follow a caravan of Manyuema, which we met following the river downwards.   But this caravan, instead of going on, returned to this place, and our deserters, misled by this, will probably follow our track downwards until

they meet you, or are exterminated by the natives.
Be not deluded by any statements they may make.
Were I to send men to you, I, of course, would
send you a note ; but in no instance a verbal message, or any message at all by the scum of the camp.
Should you meet them, you will have to secure them
thoroughly.

'The first day we left you we made a good march,
which terminated in a fight, the foolish natives firing
their own village as they fled. Since that day we
have had, probably, thirty fights. The first view of
us the natives had inspired them to show fight. As
far as Panga Falls we did not lose a man or meet
with any serious obstacles to navigation. Panga is
a big cataract, with a decided fall. We cut a road
round it on the south bank, and dragged our canoes
and went on again.

'We had intended to follow a native path which
would take us toward our destination, with the usual
windings of the road. For ten days we searched
for a road, and then took an elephant track, which
led us into an interminable forest, totally uninhabited.
Fearing to lose ourselves altogether, we cut a road
to the river, and have followed the river ever since.
From the point where we struck the river to
Mugwye's country — four days' journey below
Panga—we fared very well. Food was abundant ;
we made long marches, and no halts whatever.
Beyond Mugwye's up to Engweddeh was a wilderness, eleven days' march, villages being inland, and

mostly foodless. From this date our strength
declined rapidly. People were lost in the bush as
they searched for food, or were slain by the natives.
Ulcers, dysentery, and grievous sickness, ending in
fatal debility, attacked the people. Hence our
enormous loss since leaving Panga — thirty dead
and twenty-six deserters. Besides which, we are
obliged to leave fifty-six behind, so used up that,
without a long rest, they would also die. Of the
Somalis, one is dead (Achmet); the other five are
at this camp until our return from the Lake. Of
the Soudanese, one is dead; we leave three behind
to-day. All the whites are in perfect condition to-
day—thinnish, but with plenty of go.

'Among our fights we have had over fifty
wounded, but they all recovered except four.
Stairs was severely wounded with an arrow,
which penetrated an inch and a half within a
little below the heart, in the left breast. He is
all right now.

'We have had one man shot dead by some person
unknown in the camp; another was shot in the foot,
resulting in amputation. This latter case, now in a
fair state of health, we leave behind to-day. The
number of hours we have marched ought to have
taken us back to you by this time, but we had to
daily hew our path through forest and jungle to
keep along the river, because the river banks were
populated. The forest inland contains no settlements that we know or have heard of. By means of

canoes we were able to help the caravan, carry the sick, and several loads. The boat helped us immensely. Were I to do the work over again, I should collect canoes as large as possible, man them with sufficient paddlers, and load up with goods and sick. On the river between Yambuya and Mugwye's country the canoes are numerous, and tolerably large. The misfortune is that the Zanzibaris are exceedingly poor boatmen. In my force there are only about fifty who can paddle or pull an oar; but even these have saved our caravan immense labour, and many lives which otherwise would have been sacrificed.

'Our plan has been to paddle from one rapid to another. On reaching strong water, or shoals, we have unloaded canoes and poled or dragged them up with long rattan or other creepers through the rapids, then loaded up again and pursued our way until we met another obstacle. The want of sufficient and proper food regularly pulls people down very fast, and they have not that strength to carry the loads which has distinguished them while with me in other parts of Africa. Therefore, any means to lighten the labour of the caravan is commendable.

'If Tippu-Tib's people have not yet joined you, I do not expect you will be very far from Yambuya. You can make two journeys by river for one that you can do on land. Slow as we have been coming up, and cutting our way through, I shall come down river like lightning. The river will be a friend indeed, for the current alone will take us twenty miles a day, and I will pick up as many canoes as possible to help us on our second journey up river. Follow the river closely, and do not lose sight of our track. When the caravan which takes this passes you, look out for your men, or they will run in a body, taking valuable goods with them.

'Give my best salaams and kind remembrances from us all to your fellows. Bid them cheer up ; so many miles a day will take you here in so many days. It depends on your own going, and your power, how many or how few you will be.

'I need not say that I wish you the best of health and luck and good fortune, because you are a part of myself ; therefore good-bye.

'Yours very truly,

(*Signed*) 'HENRY M. STANLEY.

'Major Barttelot.'

Written in pencil on the first corner of the above is the following :

'DEAR MAJOR,

'I send this on to you—the former attempt was a failure.

'W. E. STAIRS.'

This second letter was taken by Lieutenant Stairs on February 16 from Fort Bodo to Ugarrowwa's,

183 miles, in twenty-six days, arriving there March 14.
—'This letter remained in Ugarrowwa's hands
also'; at least, it was handed over to Mr. Stanley, so
he states, on arriving at Ugarrowwa's. August 11,
1888.

'Fort Bodo, Ibwiri District,
'*February* 14, 1888.
'My dear Major,

'After much deliberation with my officers
upon the expediency of the act, I have resolved to
send twenty couriers to you with this letter, which I
know will be welcome to you and your comrades, as
the briefest note, or even word from you, would be
to us.

'Fort Bodo is 120 English miles from Kavalli, on
the Albert Nyanza, or seventy-seven hours of
caravan marching (west), and is almost on the same
latitude. It is 527 English miles, almost direct east
from Yambuya, or 352 hours of caravan marching.
You can easily find out where it is by tracing on
your map a straight line from Yambuya to Kavalli,
and dividing that line into five equal parts : four-fifths
would be the distance from Yambuya, and one-fifth
from our post on the Nyanza. I send a little tracing
of our route, sufficiently exact for your use, and on
it I have marked the principal places where food
may be had between Yambuya and the Nyanza.

'First. Mugwye's villages on north bank of river,
184 English miles, or 124 hours' caravan marching
from Yambuya. The villages are five in number,

backed by extensive cultivations of manioc, bananas, and Indian corn.

'Second. Aveysheba villages, fifty-nine English miles, or thirty-six hours' marching. These villages are on south bank, near a lazy creek thirty-five yards wide. There were five villages here when we passed, and abundance of very large bananas. Ten miles higher up on north bank there is a settlement close to river, untouched by us. It is situate at the foot of a rapid. By sending forty guns across river from Aveysheba, you would gain better access to these.

'Third. Confluence of the Nepoko with the Aruwimi, villages on south bank, opposite the big cataract of the Nepoko, which tumbles into the Aruwimi in fine view of landing-place. Nepoko is almost as large as the Aruwimi, therefore you cannot mistake it. We found abundance at these villages, which are numerous and scattered. They are situate thirty-nine miles above Aveysheba, or twenty-six hours' caravan-marching.

'Fourth is Ugarrowwa's, an Arab settlement on north bank. Hospitality would be given, but food would be dear, and you would have to disburse cloth. It is ninety-three miles above the last place, or sixty-two hours' marching.

'Fifth. Fort Bodo is a place built by us in Ibwiri, after our return from the Albert Nyanza. We have abundance of food here. To-day, our stock inside the fort consists of four cows and a calf, ten goats, three of these being milk goats, six tons of Indian

corn.   Outside the fort we have four acres planted
in corn, and half an acre of beans.   We have bananas
for two miles west of us, and half a mile on either
side of the fort.   Our houses are comfortable, white-
washed within and without; the men mostly sleek
and glossy.   Stairs, Nelson, Parke, and Williams
are with me here.   Jephson is out foraging for live
stock, and I hope to see him to-morrow.   Our force
consists of 184 present, eleven at Ipolo, fifty-six at
Ugarrowwa's.   Total rank and file, 251 souls.   By
the new road we estimate Fort Bodo to be distant
from Ugarrowwa's 162 English miles, or 108 hours'
marching for caravan.

'Sixth is the brow of the plateau looking down on
the Albert Nyanza, and between it and Fort Bodo
we have experienced no want of provisions of all
kinds necessary.   The object of this letter is not
only to encourage and cheer you and your people up
with definite and exact information of your where-
abouts and the land ahead of you, but to save you
from a terrible wilderness, whence we all narrowly
escaped with our lives.   I wrote you from Ugarrowwa's a letter sufficiently detailed to enable you to
understand what our experience was between Yambuya and Ugarrowwa's; therefore I begin from
Ugarrowwa's and go east to the Nyanza.

'After leaving Ugarrowwa's on September 19, we
had 285 souls with us, and 56 sick at Ugarrowwa's;
total, 341.   By October 6 we had travelled along
south bank of river, amidst a country depopulated

and devastated by Arabs, and our condition was such,
from a constant pinching want, that we had eight
deaths and fifty-two sick—that is, sixty utterly used
up—in sixteen days.   I was forced to leave Captain
Nelson, lamed by ulcers, and fifty-two sick, and
eighty-two loads with him, at a camp near the river,
while we would explore ahead, find provisions, and
send back relief.

'Until October 18 we marched in the hope of
obtaining food, and on this day we entered a settlement of Manyuema ; but in the interval we had
travelled through uninhabited forest, where we lived
on wild fruit and fungi.   In those twelve days we
had lost twenty-two by desertion and death, but the
condition of the survivors was terrible.   We were
all emaciated and haggard, but the majority were
mere skeletons.   On the 29th Nelson's party was
relieved, but out of fifty-two there were only five
left.   Many had died, many had deserted ; about
twenty were out foraging, out of which party ulti-
mately only ten turned up.

'On October 28 we marched from the Manyuema
settlement for this place, Ibwiri.   Here we found
such an abundance that we halted to recuperate
until November 24.   On this day the advance
column mustered as follows :

Sick at Ugarrowwa's (Arab settlement)	56
Sick at Manyuema settlement . . .	38
Present in Ibwiri	174
Total	268

On September 19 we numbered .   .   .   341
On November 24 we numbered .   .   .   268
                                              ———
                    Dead and missing .   .   .   73

' Beyond this place I believe no Arab or Manyuema
had ever penetrated ; consequently we suffered no
scarcity, and on November 24 we marched from
Ibwiri for the Albert Lake, which we reached
December 13, having lost only one by death, the
result of wilderness miseries ; and we returned to this
place from the Albert Lake January 7, having lost
only four, two of whom died from cause of wilderness miseries ; one, Klamis Kaururu (chief), inflam-
mation of the lungs ; one, Ramaque Vin Kuru, fever
and ague, contracted near Lake. Thus, between
November 24 and January 7 we had lost but five ;
three of these deaths were the result of privations
undergone in the wilderness.

' We first met the Manyuema on the last day of
August, and parted from them January 6. In the interval we have lost one hundred and eighteen through
death and desertion.   In their camps it was as bad
as in the wilderness, for they ground us down by
extortion so extreme that we were naked in a short
time.   They tempted the Zanzibaris to sell their
rifles and ammunition, ramrods, officers' blankets, etc.,
and then gave food so sparingly that these crimes
were of no avail.   Finally, besides starving them,
tempting them to ruin the Expedition, they speared
them, scourged them, and tied them up, until in one

case death ended his miseries. Never were such abject slaves of slaves as our people had become under the influence of the Manyuema. Yet, withal, they preferred death by scourging, spearing, starvation, ill-treatment, to the duty of load-bearing and marching on to happier regions. Out of thirty-eight men left at the Manyuema camp, eleven had died, eleven others may turn up, but it is doubtful. However, we have only received sixteen—sixteen out of thirty-eight! Comment is unnecessary.

'When we left the Manyuema camp—October 28 —we were obliged to leave our boat and seventy loads behind, as it was absolutely impossible to carry them. Parke and Nelson were detailed to look after them. We hoped that we should find some tree out of which we could make a sizeable canoe, or buy or seize one ready made. Arriving at the Nyanza, we found neither tree nor canoe, therefore were obliged to retrace our steps here quickly, to send men back to the Manyuema settlement for the boat and loads. The boat and thirty-seven loads were brought here by Stairs and nearly one hundred men the day before yesterday.

'You will understand, then, that Emin Pasha not being found or relieved by us, made it as much necessary that we should devote ourselves to this work, as it was imperative when we set out June 28, 1887, from Yambuya. And you will also understand how anxious we are all about you. We dread your inexperience and your want of influence with your people. If, with me, people preferred the society of the Manyuema blackguards to me, who am known to them for twenty years, how much more so with you, a stranger to them and their language? Therefore, the cords of anxiety are strained to exceeding tension. I am pulled east to Emin Pasha, and drawn west to you, your comrades, people, and goods.

'Nearly eight months have elapsed, and perhaps you have not had a word from us, though I wrote a long letter from Ugarrowwa's. We were to have been back by December—it is now February, and no one can conjecture how far you may have reached. Did the *Stanley* arrive in due time? Did she arrive at all? Did Tippu-Tib join you? Are you alone with your party, or is Tippu-Tib with you? If the latter, why so slow that we have not a word? If alone, we understand that you are very far from us. These are questions daily agitating us.

'Therefore, we are agreed that while we bear the boat to the Albert Nyanza, to make a final finish with Emin Pasha, we should try to communicate with you. With that view, I have called for volunteers at £10 per head reward to bear this letter to you even as far as Yambuya, if (as it might chance, for all we know to the contrary) you have not started, and to return to me with your news. To us, who have gone over the ground, Yambuya seems about a month's distance only. Stairs escorts the twenty as far as Ugarrowwa's, and brings to me the

fifty-six men, who are all recovered (as we hear).
Stairs, on his return, will find me about five days
from the Lake, and we will then push on fast to the
Lake when he has joined us.

'According to my calculation, we shall be on the
Lake April 10; all about Emin Pasha will be settled
by April 25 ; on May 13 we shall be back here ; on
the 29th we shall be at Ugarrowwa's, if we have not
met you. We shall surely, I hope, meet with the
return messengers. *Re* these messengers, I should
advise your keeping two of them as guides—Ruga-
Rugu in front ; but they should be free of loads.
Send the eighteen and two others back to me as
soon as you can, because the sooner we hear from
you, the sooner we will join hands ; and after settling
the Emin Pasha question we shall have only one
anxiety, which will be to get you safely up here.

'Assuming that Tippu-Tib's people are with you,
our guides (two) will bring you quickly on here, and
we shall probably meet here or at Ugarrowwa's ;
and the *Stanley* steamer arrived within reasonable
time, you have arrived at some place about twenty-
two or twenty-four of our former journeys from
Yambuya, below Mugwye's, as I take it. Hence,
before you get near the Arab influence, where your
column will surely break up if you are alone, I order
you to go to the nearest place (Mugwye's, Aveysheba, or Nepoko confluence) that is to you, and
there to build a strong camp and wait us ; but whatever you decide upon, let me know. If you come

near Ugarrowwa's you will lose men, rifles, powder
—everything of value ; your own boys will betray
you, because they will sell food so dearly that your
people, from stress of hunger, will steal everything.

'At either of the three places above you will get
safety and food until we relieve you. So long as
you are stationary, there is no fear of desertion ;
but the daily task, added to constant insufficiency of
food, will sap the fidelity of your best men. (These
directions are only in case of your being alone, without Arab aid. If Tippu-Tib's people are with you,
I presume you are coming along slowly.)

'With everybody's best wishes to you, I send my
earnest prayer that you are, despite all unwholesome
and evil conjectures, where you ought to be, and
that this letter will reach you in time to save you
from that forest misery, and from the fangs of the
ruthless Manyuema blackguards. To every one of
your officers also these good wishes are given,
from

'Yours most sincerely,

(*Signed*)   'HENRY M. STANLEY.

'To Major Barttelot,
    'Commanding Rear Column, E.P.R.E.'

[It is a curious fact, and one so patent that it has
apparently escaped Mr. Stanley's notice, that if
Major Barttelot had received the two letters said to
be intended for him, and had carried them out, he
would have been in identically the same position as

he was without the letters. In fact, the second letter entirely justifies Major Barttelot's action of remaining at Yambuya until he got carriers under an Arab of superior authority to go with him. 'So long as you are stationary there is no fear of desertion.' 'Hence, before you get near the Arab influence, *where your column will surely break up if you are alone*, I order you to go to the nearest place to you (Mugwye's, Aveysheba, or Nepoko confluence), and there to build a strong fort and wait us.' If Major Barttelot had foolishly attempted to advance alone, and had received this letter, he would have been obliged to halt and form a camp at Mugwye's, 184 miles from Yambuya, on the Aruwimi, to wait for Mr. Stanley till he came, which he (Mr. Stanley) expected would be on May 29, whereas the Stanley calculations were again out by two and a half months, and he did not arrive at Mugwye's till August 10, when he found the whole country devastated by the Arabs, and the villages and plantations destroyed. Banalya was about half-way between Yambuya and Mugwye's, ninety miles, or seven days* down stream from either. Instead, too, of avoiding the Arabs, he would have found them on all sides. Ugarrowwa had come down river to Wasp Rapids between Banalya and Mugwye's, and Abdulla Korona was at Banalya. 'If you come near Ugarrowwa's you will lose men, rifles, powder, everything of value.' Major Barttelot

* By canoe.

13

dared not move from Yambuya without carriers and a responsible Arab chief, and by remaining stationary till he got carriers he saved the rear column from utter destruction, though in so doing he may have imperilled and lost his own life.

The whole country round Yambuya to the Congo, and to Banalya and beyond, was full of Arabs raiding the country. Mr. Stanley overlooks that fact, or he would know that 165 Zanzibaris could not carry 660 loads without being tempted to desert with the goods, to the certain ruin of the whole force. |

CHAPTER IX.

YAMBUYA CAMP: JANUARY 1—MARCH 17, 1888.

Bad News of Stanley—Arabs attack the Natives—Burgari shot -
Barttelot and Jameson go to the Falls—Shooting Expedition
—Letter of Instructions to Mr. Jameson on going to find
Tippu-Tib at Kasongo—Letters Home—Mortality in the
Camp from Want of Food.

'1888. *Sunday, January* 1.—We had meat for
breakfast. Had a palaver with the natives, about
three of Tippu-Tib's men, whom they have captured.
Went for a long walk, and began a new shirt and
collar.

'*Monday, January* 2.—I went over with Jameson
to Ingungo's village and released one man ; they
promised the other man and guns to-morrow : the
other man has escaped. We had heavy rain this
afternoon.

'*January* 3.—We opened our last tin of butter.

'*January* 4, 5, *and* 6.—Sick with an attack of
liver.

'*January* 7.—Better. Nasiboo from Yambui
arrived, and brought us a goat and rice. He gave

us bad news of Stanley as having progressed but slowly.

' *Monday, January* 9.—Salem Mohammed arrived to-day ; we did not get much news out of him.   He gave us a pot of ghee and a bag of barley-sugar, also some vermicelli.   Tippu-Tib sent Jameson a big goat, and we bought another.

' *Tuesday, January* 10.—I had a long palaver with Salem Mohammed, who told me of two men, deserters from Stanley, but I could get nothing out of him.

' *Wednesday, January* 11.—Ward's birthday.   We had soup, fish, meat, and jam roly-poly for dinner. Nasiboo sent in a buck antelope, but it died shortly after arriving, from exhaustion.

' *Friday, January* 13.—Cold antelope for luncheon and dinner.   We had some rain late in the evening. The river is very low, and there are no end of rocks cropping up.

' *January* 14.—I left England a year ago.   Am reading Shakespeare and Longfellow.

' *Tuesday, January* 17. — The thermometer is 126° in the sun, 80° in the shade, 76° night and morning.   We had heavy rain in the evening for an hour.

' *January* 19.—We have been ten months in this country.   Rain yesterday and to-day.   Mursah Topji, a Soudanese, died.

' *Tuesday, January* 24.—Salem Mohammed came into camp and told Jameson some news.

' *Friday, January* 27.—We lead the usual life day after day. Rain this morning and most days.

' *Saturday, January* 28.—Seven months since Stanley left.

' *Sunday, January* 29.—Very hot, the thermometer registering 136° in the sun at 2 p.m. We had slight rain in the evening. I issued a supply of tea, and we killed a goat.

' *January* 30 *and* 31.—Bought eight fowls.

' *Wednesday, February* 1.—The men whom we sent to buy oil at Yallasula came back with ten fowls and two pots of oil. Said, at Yallasula, sent me a present of a goat.

' *Friday, February* 3.—A Zanzibari died, making our loss by death forty-three.

' *Saturday, February* 4.—We killed the big goat, and had jam roly-poly for dinner, as it is Jameson's wedding-day.

' Salem Mohammed attacked the natives to-day ; successfully, I believe. Burgari deserted, taking Sergeant Abdul - ben - Hussein's rifle and sword. This happened about 8 p.m. I sent Omar and twenty-five men to catch him, and told Salem Mohammed, who promised to help.

' *Sunday, February* 5.—Burgari still at large. I went to visit the outposts this morning, and met two of Tippu-Tib's men, who told me that some natives had killed ten of their men and taken ten guns.

' Salem Mohammed has gone to see about it ; I

lent him a Remington rifle and 100 rounds of ammunition.   Msga Kabel died this afternoon.

'*Monday, February* 6.—Very hot day—85° in the shade, 137° in the sun.   The river lowest I have seen.

'*Tuesday, February* 7.—It rained all the morning. We bought four goats.   Bonny made good shooting at two geese on the rocks.

'*Wednesday, February* 8.—We bought five more goats.   No news ; the usual life.

'*Thursday, February* 9.—Burgari caught ; he had hidden in a native village to the eastward. Cooga, a Zanzibari, saw him and told one of Salem Mohammed's men, who captured him.   He was sentenced to death.'

'*Friday, February* 10.—At 7 a.m. the Soudanese Burgari was shot by eleven other Soudanese by my order.   Death was instantaneous.

'*Monday, February* 13.—We held a council, and determined on a course of action with Tippu-Tib as regards canoes.   It was determined that Jameson and I should go to the Falls and try to see Tippu-Tib.   It rained to-day.

'*Tuesday, February* 14.—Jameson, myself, and Salem Mohammed left for the Falls at 8.30 a.m., taking Assad Farran with us.

'We arrived at our old camping-ground, Yaraweko, at 4 p.m.   The bag containing our bedding got left behind with Assad Farran, who did not come in. A fine day.   I found a white frog.

' *Wednesday, February* 15.—Assad Farran and the boy turned up about 8.30 a.m., and at 10.30 a.m. we started. We halted about two hours later in the village of Yamima, and drank melafor; rested half an hour and started on. We lost our way in a cane-brake, the elephants having been there and played havoc with the path. We camped by a stream about 5 p.m. Assad Farran again got left behind, and did not come in that night. A fine day. We bought a fowl at Yamima, and so did well.

' *Thursday, February* 16.—Salem Mohammed sent out men to look for the road, and we sent men to search for Assad Farran, but they returned unsuccessful.

' Jameson and I then started, and had not gone far when we heard a shot near our camp. On sending to inquire, we found that the brave Assad Farran had returned. We came back to camp, and left again at 12 p.m., camping in the bush at 6 p.m. A fine day.

' *Friday, February* 17.—We left camp early, and got to Yallasula about 3.30 p.m. Said, the man in charge there, behaved right well to us, as usual. He gave us fish, rice, and a goat. About 4 p.m. there was a heavy shower, and we found that our house leaked.

' *Saturday, February* 18.—A wet night. I had to put up the fly of the tent to keep the rain off my bed.

'We left Yallasula at 12 p.m. by canoe, and got to Yarukombé at 6.30 p.m.

'On the way up we met 150 men from Kasongo for us, which looks better. Jameson shot a huge monkey, which he skinned. The natives who were paddling us were delighted. A fine day.

'*Sunday, February* 19.—We left Yarukombé at 8 a.m. and paddled all day till 4 p.m., when we arrived at the village of Yatakusè. Jameson shot three monkeys on the way. We slept in a native hut.

'*Monday, February* 20.—We left Yatakusè at 8 a.m. A terribly hot day. I felt unwell, and had a bad headache. We got to the Falls about 2 p.m. Nzigé, head-man under Tippu-Tib, greeted us, and told me that Tippu-Tib would not be back till the new moon, probably on March 12. He gave us the same house Troup and I had last October. It rained heavily in the evening.

'*Tuesday, February* 21.—A wet morning and a heavy thunderstorm. I gave Nzigé a big Thornhill pocket-knife, which delighted him. In the afternoon Jameson and I went to see old Nasiro, who gave us a feed. I presented him with a razor.

'*Wednesday, February* 22.—I was unwell all day, and kept indoors. Jameson went out after antelope, and got a monkey.

'*Friday, February* 24.—Jameson and I went out shooting. Salem Mohammed left.

' *Sunday, February* 26.—Nzigé told us he would make arrangements for us to shoot at a village called Batgambarri—chief, Muni Katoto, a Zanzibari.   A wettish day.

' *Tuesday, February* 28.—We left about 10 a.m. for Batgambarri, which lies to the north-east of Sin- gatini and across the river.   We arrived there at 1.30, and at 3.30 Muni Katoto gave us a splendid feast.   It rained heavily for two hours.'

On February 26 Mr. Troup wrote from Yambuya to Major Barttelot, telling him that seventy men had arrived from Kasongo, and that they were told that a large number would soon arrive from the Falls. He also said that a high death-rate still prevailed in the camp.   To this letter Major Barttelot replied as follows :

COPY OF A LETTER FROM MAJOR BARTTELOT, SINGATINI, TO MR. G. R. TROUP.

' Yambuya Camp,
' *March* 5, 1888.
' DEAR TROUP,

' We got your letter March 2 at midnight, and we both thought, " News of Stanley at last," or a mutiny in the camp, or some other very serious matter. But we were agreeably disappointed at finding nothing of importance in it.   I am afraid the arrival of seventy men, and their word that men are coming, is not of sufficient importance to prevent the necessity

of our carrying out the original plan of seeing Tippu-
Tib, for which purpose Jameson is on the point of
starting for Kasongo. I am sorry to hear the death-
rate continues high. Whatever men have arrived
are, I am given to understand, placed entirely under
the command of Salem Mohammed, and are not to
be utilized by us till we hear to that effect from
Tippu-Tib himself. It will be best, therefore, for you
to have nothing to do with them till you receive
definite instructions from me on the point. I have
had some trouble, and been put to some expense
concerning the departure of our messages, so please
do not send any letters except of real importance,
such as news of Stanley or any trouble in the camp.
I may be back any day after Jameson's departure,
or, on the other hand, I may require Ward's presence
here. That man, Suedi Wadi-Boresi, was sick when
he left Yallasula. Our treatment here, since our
arrival, has been that of favoured guests, and Nzigé
has done everything in his power for us, as regards
the Expedition, and our own personal comfort and
amusement. I hope you are all well. Jameson and
I unite in messages to all. Should I require Ward
I will send for him.

'Yours ever,

'EDMUND M. BARTTELOT.

'There are no men from Kasongo here, nor have
we seen any since our arrival here, though we are
told some are coming, but numbers and purpose

uncertain. Should a fresh issue of tea be required, please issue it from that open case of tea, and for two months, dating from February 29.

'E. M. B.'

'*Wednesday, February* 29.—We went out shooting with a native chief, Kayumbo. We got on elephant tracks about 8 a.m., and followed them till 2 p.m., when we found that some natives had taken them up, so we left them and went to look for chimpanzee or antelope, but unsuccessfully. We returned to camp about 5 p.m.

'*Thursday, March* 1.—We went out shooting with Kayumbo and Koko, two native chiefs, in a fine open forest. Jameson shot at a chimpanzee, but missed it. After a long walk we got back to camp at 5.30 p.m.

'*March* 2.—The natives turned up late, and having had no sport, we left Batgambarri at noon, and returned to Singatini, arriving about 2 p.m. There I heard news that determined me to send Jameson to Kasongo. I asked Nzigé about ways and means, and he agreed with me that it was the best thing to do, and promised to do all he could. He has helped us in every possible way during our stay, giving us milk, goats, etc. Before leaving Batgambarri, Muni Katoto gave me a big cock, who on our return fought another cock close to us and killed him.

'I got, by special messenger, a letter from Troup.

'*Saturday, March* 3.—Jameson wounded a lory.

'*Monday, March* 5.—About 10 a.m. we felt an earthquake—one shock severe. I sent Troup's special messenger away. Jameson and I went out shooting and got a squirrel, a weaver bird, and a parrot. I got badly bitten by an ant.

'*Tuesday, March* 6.—I went over the ground we shot yesterday and picked up the parrot, also, after a chase, the lory shot by Jameson on Saturday.

'*Friday, March* 9.—Unwell, from the amount of palm-oil they put in our food.

'*Saturday, March* 10.—Wet morning. Jameson had a bad attack of fever.

'*March* 13.—Jameson continues ill. We hear that men are coming.

'*Wednesday, March* 14.—A caravan arrived with a tremendous lot of men for us—about 200, I was told. I sent to find out, when it appeared there were only fifty, and that Tippu-Tib will not come till he has sent all our men. I am appalled, and determined to send a telegram to Mackinnon. No news of Stanley. Fourteen months away from England.

'*Thursday, March* 15.—I saw Nzigé, and asked him to purchase two canoes for me, which he promised to do. Rain fell this evening.

'*Friday, March* 16.—This evening I went to see a canoe at Nascros. Rained in the evening.

'*Saturday, March* 17.—I agreed to buy one canoe with Nzigé ; the other was too rotten.'

COPY OF LETTER OF INSTRUCTIONS TO MR. JAMESON
ON HIS PROCEEDING TO KASONGO.

'FROM MAJOR BARTTELOT,   'TO MR. J. S. JAMESON,
'SINGATINI.   'SINGATINI.

'*March* 17, 1888.

'SIR,

'You will proceed up river to Kasongo for purpose of interviewing Tippu-Tib.

'You will urge on him the necessity of expedition, and lay before him our propositions as regards obtaining 400 extra fighting men.

'You must obtain from him a definite answer as to the earliest date these men and the remaining 350 of the originally promised carriers can be obtained, and what sum he will undertake the business of providing these 1,000 men for from the time they leave Yambuya Camp, go to Albert Nyanza (Wadelai if necessary), following Stanley's route, and back to his territory. Also sufficient escort and carriers, if wanted, to take the remnant of the Emin Pasha Relief Expedition back to Zanzibar. Should we find Emin Pasha, and there be ivory with him and as in all probability certain loads will have to be left behind at Singatini under charge of an officer, should these loads on our return not be wanted, both they and the ivory, if Tippu-Tib is willing, can count towards the sum he proposes and you agree to.

'You will point out to him that the 600 carriers

are only to carry half-loads, which should make some difference as to their payment.

'Should Tippu-Tib be evasive in his answers as to dates and numbers of supply, tell him straight that unless the men are quickly forthcoming it will be no use our starting. Of course, if you cannot get 400 fighting men, get as near as you can—200, 300, or even 100 would be better than none. I cannot bind you down to any given sum to be paid him, nor to the exact lines of agreement, but I should think five dollars a head per month excessive ; and a contract worded something as follows should come into force the day a start is made from Yambuya Camp :

'" We, the undersigned, guarantee to Tippu-Tib the sum of £ s. d. for the time of 600 carriers and 400 fighting men as conveyance for and escort to the Emin Relief Expedition from Yambuya Camp to Wadelai and back to Tippu-Tib's territory. Furthermore, Tippu-Tib shall guarantee that these men, under the immediate command of their own chief, shall be subservient to my orders in every respect as regards marching and fighting ; and that he shall guarantee us his aid as regards purchasing and obtaining supplies, use of canoes, etc., so long and always as we may be in his territory, or where he has garrisons. For the above sum Tippu-Tib shall also provide escort and guides to coast on the return journey, providing, if necessary, sufficient carriers for the individual use of the officers—presumably five—through his territory to Zanzibar. All ivory found with Emin Pasha and loads left over to count as payment. That a headman shall be provided, who will be responsible for the men and their loyalty to us ; that this man will be entirely subservient to my commands, all orders from me concerning his men being given to him and from him to the men.

' " In case of desertion, so much for every ten men to be struck off from the sum ; if deserting with loads, the value of the loads to be struck off. Should the men be paid for at so much per head, then the amount for each deserter will be struck off. In case of death from illness, pay up to date of death."

' All this, of course, will be void should you hear news of Stanley's certain return.

' Till such news is heard and made good, or until we meet with Stanley, I am the head of the Expedition, and, in event of the second case, Mr. Stanley will assume command ; but the guarantee shall still stand good up to such date as the men may be used ; money to be paid on arrival at Zanzibar. If your stay at Kasongo be a lengthy one, send a messenger to me with news.

' Purchase twelve bags of rice, coffee, and ghee for the Expedition. Write to Mackinnon fully concerning the agreement.

' I have the honour to be, sir,

' Your most obedient servant,

(*Signed*) ' EDMUND M. BARTTELOT, Major.'

COPY OF A LETTER TO SIR W. B. BARTTELOT, BART.,
AND OTHERS, FROM MAJOR BARTTELOT.

'Stanley Falls,
'*March.*

' MY DEAREST OLD FATHER, MAMMA, AND OTHERS,

'I do not know whether you got my last
letter from here. We are still at Yambuya Camp,
and likely to be there for some time yet. Can get
no news of Stanley anyhow, and am in apprehension
about him. Tippu-Tib went to his capital, Kasongo,
about 356 miles from here, last November, and
up to date of writing has only got us 250 men,
so I have sent Jameson to Kasongo with instruc
tions to hasten him, and to tell him that 600
carriers shall only carry half-loads, and to give us, if
possible, 400 fighting-men extra. Of course, we
shall have to negotiate for these in our own name,
and if the Committee don't come down with the
money required I shall consider them a poor lot. I
am sending down Ward with these letters ; he is
carrying a telegram from me to Mackinnon at Banana
Point. He will have to go the whole way by canoe,
and through some baddish tribes. I came here on
February 20 on purpose to see Tippu-Tib, but of
course was told lies, and so have sent Jameson after
him.

'*March* 18.

' I go back to Yambuya March 20. Our death-
rate among the Soudanese and Zanzibaris is some-

thing awful ; they have only got manioc* to eat, poor
chaps! We are doing better, for we have meat four
times a week, plantains, corn, cakes, and rice every
day ; but it is a disgusting life—nothing to read, no
news, nothing to do. Jameson is the best fellow I
ever met : sound sense, bright and cheerful. We are
all well, suffering occasionally from liver attacks ; but
that is not to be wondered at, considering the climate
and the life we lead. I left the Falls the evening of
the 20th, and got to Yambuya at 4 p.m. on the 24th.
Ward leaves Yambuya to-morrow, the 28th, for
down river, and I hope will arrive safely, and that
you will get your letters. You must excuse a
meagre letter, but in a forest there is not much
news, as we see no one except the natives and
Arabs, who both eat human flesh. They are not,
properly speaking, Arabs, but men from Mangana,
nearer Zanzibar, and slaves to the Arabs. I have
enclosed an address for you, which, if you or any
of the others go and call at, you will see the sort of
people we live and dwell among. There may be
also some spears and knives from me ; you might ask
Mr. Hatton. The drawings, collections, etc., are
by Ward, who has been long out here, and is very
clever at such things.

'This should reach you in June. I cannot hope
to be home before March or April, 1889, at the
earliest. I hope I have missed no promotion or
advancement, or that nothing of importance has, or

* Manioc is a root from which a kind of sago is prepared.

14

will have, taken place by the time I get home.   As
I told you in October last, when I sent my letters to
Tippu-Tib, he was only awaiting his time, and he
has, with a vengeance.   Not a word can we get out
of him, except "presently," so I have sent Jameson
to Kasongo to try and run him to earth.   Jameson
and I, while at the Falls, went out elephant shooting,
but got nothing except monkeys.   Christmas Day,
New Year's Day, and Jameson's marriage-day we
kept by eating jam pudding, but we have no flour
or jam left now, and our clothes are rags.   My boots
and socks still hang out, and I still shave, but that is
all.   It is no good my writing a long letter to you,
for I cannot, simply.   There is nothing to tell.

'With my sincerest love to you all, ever your
loving son, brother, and uncle,

'EDMUND M. BARTTELOT.

'*Address of Ward's Collection :*
'*Care of Mr. Joseph Hatton,*
'14, *Titchfield Terrace,*
'*Regent's Park,*
'*N. W.*

CHAPTER X.

Jameson starts for Kasongo—Barttelot returns to Yambuya—Ill
with Fever—Ward goes to Banana with Letters and Cablegram
to Mackinnon—Death-rate—In the Hands of Tippu-Tib—
Surrounded by Arabs—Letter to Major Sclater—Alone with
Bonny—The Arabs mean Mischief—Instructions to Bonny
on Barttelot's Departure to the Falls—Return to Yambuya—
Proceeds to Yambu—Instructions to Bonny—Sala-Sala's
Camp—Report of Stanley.

'*Sunday, March* 18. — Jameson* started from
Kasongo. I was too ill to see him off. He took
Assad Farran, who is a little smarter than he was.
Fine day. A year to-day in Africa.

'*Tuesday, March* 20.—I left Singatini about 4.30
p.m., feeling very unwell. Nzigé gave me five
goats, and I bought one. I took my new canoe
with me and slept at Yatakusé. Owing to some
mistake, they tried to take my canoe, but a gun was
effectual.

* Some letters from Mr. Jameson, when in pursuit of Tippu-Tib,
are given in the Appendix.

' *Wednesday, March* 21.—Arrived at Yallasula at 12 p.m. Was prostrate with fever for about two hours. Raschid came in the evening and gave me a good dinner, which I could not eat. I made arrangements for Said to come with me to Yambuya, and also for a guide, as we cannot go the old road, it being obliterated by elephant-tracks.

' *Thursday, March* 22.—Went down river to a place called Yangambi, arriving there about noon, and stopped there all day.

' *Friday, March* 23.—Started at 7 p.m. and went up a terrible hill, which nearly killed me, for I was weak from fever, and had hardly eaten anything the last three days.

' We reached Yambu in the afternoon, completely worn out, and thought I should never reach camp. Could get nothing to eat. At 6 p.m. they brought me some melafor, and later on Said brought me a little dried fish and rice.

' *Saturday, March* 24.—A heavy thunderstorm early this morning. I ate a little raw manioc and drank some coffee. At 8 a.m. I started, shattered and weak, but got to camp at 3.30 p.m. They thought I was a ghost. I weighed about 8 st. 10 lb., I suppose. Rain.

' *Sunday, March* 25.—I was prostrate, and that opportunity was taken to play me false. Fine.

' *Monday,* 26.—Better. I find they have been playing the mischief since I have been away. I wrote hard business letters to Mackinnon, etc., all day. Fine.

'27.—Finished up business. Gave Ward his final instructions. Wrote to father, Evelyn, M. and Harry. *I am much upset at what I find.* . . . . . Fine day.

'*March* 28.—My birthday (29). Wet morning. Ward left for Banana and Troup for Lomami to buy goats.

' *Thursday, March* 29.—I was busy all the morning copying into book copies of letters sent. I feel tons better. Bonny and I left alone.'

INSTRUCTIONS TO WARD ON GOING TO BANANA POINT WITH TELEGRAM, MARCH 27, 1888.

'You will leave this camp, Yambuya, March 28, with thirty Zanzibaris and eight Soudanese, and march to Yangambi on the Congo. There you should find two canoes ready for you ; lash these together, embark your men and provisions, and start without delay down river to Bangala. At Bangala hand my letter to the chief of the station. Disarm the Zanzibaris, and hand their arms to the chief of the station, making arrangements for the immediate return of the Zanzibaris and Soudanese. Should this not be possible, they must remain at Bangala till you return, receiving (the Soudanese officer) two metako a day and the rest half a metako. On return the arms to be handed back to the Zanzibaris. You yourself, with the aid of the chief of the Bangala station, will obtain Bangalas and canoes to transport you to Leopoldville. Arriving there,

hand my letter to the chief of station, who will supply
you with couriers, and you will proceed to Matadi
and thence to Banana Point.   At Boma you will put
up at the English House and give my letter to the
Governor of the Free State.   At Banana ascertain
which is the nearest—St. Thomé or St. Paul de
Loanda—to send a cable from, and to the nearest
of these two you will proceed and send the cable
to Mr. W. Mackinnon.   You will await reply, on
receiving which proceed back with all despatch
to Leopoldville.   From Boma on your downward
journey to returning to that place you will receive
25s. allowance per diem.   You will give my letter
to Mons. Fontaine at Banana, who will find you
sufficient moneys for the telegram and other expenses,
You must remember despatch is to be used.   On
arrival at Leopoldville on your return journey,
proceed up river with all despatch, bringing Tippu-
Tib's loads with you to Njimbi on the Congo.
There you will learn if I have started for the Lakes
or not.   Should I have started, you will proceed to
the Falls, where you will find a letter of instructions awaiting you.   If I have not started, send a
messenger to me here, and await my arrival at
Njimbi with the steamer.

'An accurate account of your expenditure is to be
kept, one copy of which is to be sent to Mr. W.
Mackinnon, care of Gray, Dawes and Co., 14,
Austin Friars, London, E.C., and one for myself.
You will purchase while at Banana, on behalf of

the Expedition, two cases of champagne, four cases of tinned meat, each case to contain fifteen tins of 2 lb. weight, twenty-four axes and thirty matchetts.

'EDMUND M. BARTTELOT, Major.'

COPY OF LETTER TO MONS. FONTAINE.

'Yambuya, *March* 27, 1888.

'SIR,

'You may perhaps remember me on board the ss. *Madura* at Banana, March 18, 1887. I was introduced to you by Mr. Stanley as his second in command. Owing to circumstances, I am obliged to wire to Mr. Mackinnon, who is president of the Emin Pasha Relief Expedition. Your house is doing all our business for the Expedition, and, therefore, I wish you to find Ward, who is carrying above-mentioned wire, in all moneys which may be necessary.

'1st. For telegram.

'2nd. His personal expenses, viz., 25s. a day from Boma till his return to Boma.

'3rd. His return passage ticket, 1st class, either to St. Thomé or St. Paul de Loanda.

'4th. Seven sovereigns for extras (to buy outfit).

'5th. Twenty pounds cash (this has nothing to do with No. 2) to buy two cases champagne and a watch.

'Also on his return journey please have in readiness for him :

'(*a*) Twenty-four axes with handles.

' (*b*) Thirty matchetts.

' (*c*) Four cases of tinned meat, each case to contain fifteen tins of 2 lb. weight.

' (*d*) Thirty pounds of tobacco.*

' (*c*) Thirty pounds of tea in tins.

' Please send me by Mr. Ward an accurate account of money disbursed, and another to Mr. W. Mackinnon, care of Gray, Dawes and Co., 13, Austin Friars, London.

' I have, etc.,

' EDMUND M. BARTTELOT.'

COPY OF CABLEGRAM TO MR. MACKINNON.

' No news from Stanley since writing in October. Tippu-Tib went Kasongo November 16, but up to March 27 has only got us 250 men. More are coming, but in uncertain numbers and at uncertain times. Presuming Stanley in trouble, absurd for me to start with less men than he did, I carrying more loads than he did, and minus Maxim gun ; therefore have sent Jameson Kasongo to hasten T.-T. in regard to remainder of originally promised 600 men, and to obtain from him as many fighting men as possible up to 400 ; to make most advantageous terms he can as regards service and payment of men, he and I guaranteeing money in name of Expedition. Jameson will return about May 14, but earliest date to start will be June 1. When I start

---

* Major Barttelot never smoked at all himself.

I propose leaving officer with all loads not absolutely wanted at Stanley Falls. Ward carries this message. Please obtain wire from King Belgians to Administrator Free State to place carriers at his disposal, and have steamer in readiness to convey him Yambuya. If men come before his arrival start without him. Ward should return about July 1. Wire advice and opinion. Officers all well. Ward awaits reply.

'BARTTELOT.'

EXTRACTS FROM A LETTER TO MR. MACKINNON.

[The letter is a record of all events from October, and mostly of matter found in the diary, so I only quote extracts.]

'*March* 27, 1888.

'It is apparent to all of us that the Manyuema men could not carry full loads, and that as our *death-rate* up to March 27 is 67, and out of those left—155 Zanzibaris and 29 Soudanese—80 Zanzibaris only are fit to carry loads, and 30 of them are with Mr. Ward; and our ammunition loads alone are 240, and others *absolutely necessary* (85), making a total of 325 full loads, or 650 half-loads. This would absorb all Tippu-Tib's men and 50 of ours, leaving us only 30 Zanzibaris, should Ward's men have returned in time to come with us, for cutting roads, etc.; and about 14 Soudanese as escort, for these are all the Soudanese who are fit. Our death-rate is from June 28: Soudanese, 14; Zanzibaris, 50;

Somalis, 2; interpreter, 1. On February 13 attached propositions, marked X, were laid before the officers. On February 14 Mr. Jameson and I left for the Falls. I determined to send Jameson to Kasongo to lay propositions before Tippu-Tib; instructions to Mr. Jameson marked Y attached. I determined, as the delay would be too great for obtaining sufficient men to carry all the loads at half-loads (*the original number of loads being* 705), to obtain 600 carriers and 400 fighting men. Before he left, he (Jameson) and I agreed it would be best to telegram you. . . . Mr. Ward will proceed to Banana Point. I have selected him on account of his knowledge of the Bangala natives and their language, his intimacy with the State, and his energy.

'The reason for my taking 400 fighting men is that I consider it useless to try and relieve Mr. Stanley, if he be in a fix, with a force as small as he started with, supposing him in a fix; and we cannot help thinking otherwise, as we can get no news of him either from Tippu-Tib or other sources, and Tippu-Tib would certainly have it if there is any. He may have it, and be keeping it from us. There is no doubt in my mind that he could have let us have the men long ago had he wished, and I cannot understand his motive in delaying thus long; but I hope Mr. Jameson will be able to effect something. But, at any rate, June 1 is the very earliest a start can be made, as far as I am able to calculate.

He pleads shortness of canoes ; but he has had 250
men sent to him at the Falls at one time, since he
has been at Kasongo. I see no good in attempting
to take all the loads, as if full loads were given to
the Manyuema they would not carry them. Ammunition is necessary, brass-wire, beads, metako. *a
certain amount of provisions*, and *clothes for Mr.
Stanley* and the officers with him. The rest of the
loads I propose transporting to the Falls, and
leaving with an officer there.

‘ I am afraid you will think I have been strangely
dilatory at Yambuya, but, believe me, I have done
all in my power for the Expedition. I cannot arrest
the death-rate nor force Tippu, as I am entirely in
his hands, and he knows it. Even the men already
sent—viz., 250—I cannot use, as they are not to be
handed over till Tippu himself arrives. To have
sent a small force to reconnoitre would have been
uselessly to send them into danger, and needlessly
weakened our position. Attached is a précis, marked
B, of all events from the time Mr. Stanley left to the
time of sending this. Mr. Jameson and I thought
it advisable to telegram to you, as affairs wear a
serious aspect ; and should we not have started
before Ward arrives, you may have orders which
may alter my plans. The question of expenses is
a serious one, and Mr. Jameson and I have been
obliged to use our names on behalf of the Committee,
as a *personal guarantee* is the only means of satisfying
Tippu-Tib.

'It should be remembered that Tippu is an officer of the "State," but that up to the present no notice has been taken of him at all, and he feels justly aggrieved; besides, there being certain loads of his left by him at the Pool to be forwarded by the "State," which have never been forwarded, I have directed Mr. Ward to bring these last up.

'The natives round us, though constantly killing Tippu-Tib's men, have never touched ours. They have captured them sometimes, but have always returned them unhurt the next day, and any of the officers can walk with perfect safety among them. They do all they can for us, and would do more if they were not interfered with by Tippu-Tib's men. We are completely surrounded by his stations, which extend eastward up river some distance.

'I have, etc.,

'EDMUND M. BARTTELOT.'

FROM A LETTER TO MAJOR SCLATER.

'March 28, 1890.

'The Zanzibaris will not lift a hand against Tippu-Tib's men, of course, for they are of the same race. Not that it would avail much if they would, for we are completely surrounded by Arabs, and they could swamp us any day. I have taken away their rifles long ago for fear they should hand them over. The Soudanese, who hate the Arabs, keep theirs, but I have only twenty of them available for duty. I was badly ill in July, and again in August, and suffer from liver now, but that is from worry and want of sleep. Stanley should never have left without his whole force, nor without T.-T.'s men. Of course, if he returns all the blame will be mine; should I be alive, however, I can defend myself: if dead, please let Mackinnon read this letter. Many, many times have I averted war with the Arabs by eating simple dirt; and I can tell you it is not pleasant for me. By constant and petty annoyances and insolences they forced Dean into a row, and burnt the Falls Station, September, 1886, and they have all got their eye on the spoil at Yambuya. I never allow a single Arab into camp without my leave, or even sale and barter to go on. Jameson is a dear good chap; you would like him much. Don't show this letter to anyone, but keep it; I may want it some day. . . . Good-bye, dear old Harry, and God bless you! I hope I will see you once again on this earth. Love to dearest little E.

'E. M. B.'

ALONE WITH BONNY AT YAMBUYA.

'*Friday, March* 30.—Heavy rain and wind. During the early morning all the Soudanese houses were blown down. More disclosures* were made to me. . . .

'*March* 31.—Rain fell; cloudy, windy day; took a long walk.

'*Easter Sunday, April* 1.—I put on a new shirt,

---

* Presumably by Bonny.

new collar, and new socks. Wet weather set in, I am afraid.

'*April* 2.—One of the Manyuema offered a knife for sale for fourteen metako ; one of my men bought it for thirteen, and sent the metako up by another man. The Manyuema refused to let it go, or give the metako back, saying he would knife the man if he came again. I sent for Salem Mohammed, and told him about it ; he was furious at having to act, but the metako were returned. As an offset Salem Mohammed brought some natives who said a paddle had been taken from them, but I dismissed the palaver, saying I had nothing to do with natives. (Salem Mohammed is, in my opinion, egging on his men to a row with mine, in order to have a shy at the stores.) While I was at the Falls there was a woman palaver here at Yambuya. The Manyuema complained that our men molested their women whenever they went away. A trap was set for a man of mine, Munichandi, and they took all his clothes from him. The affair was settled, but Salem Mohammed was heard to say, " This will be a second* Stanley Falls palaver." Subsequently our men chaffed the Manyuema, because they found them eating human flesh. This embittered the already bad feeling between them all the more. Salem means mischief. Fine day, though thunder about in the afternoon.

* A woman having sought Mr. Dean's protection, the Arabs attacked and drove him out of the station, 1886.

'*Tuesday, April* 3.—Things look black. Salem Mohammed is drawing the string tighter. He told one of my men he was going to the Falls to-morrow to tell Nzigé to stop all white men going there, and to prevent me from forming my camp* there ; his pretext being that the Zanzibaris fall out with the Manyuema, it being the other way in reality.

'*Perhaps my days are numbered.*

'I had a palaver with Salem Mohammed this evening, and of course I had to eat dirt. We parted, he with many professions of friendship, but evil in his heart. I shall go to the Falls unless stopped, and try to get Nzigé's aid. It was only the fear of headquarters which had kept Salem Mohammed in check at all, and if our communication had been cut off Salem could have done what he liked. To stop this was my aim. I asked Salem Mohammed could he send a messenger to the Falls about the loads, as I heard he was sending ; he told me his messenger was gone : I said, " It does not matter." Next day—

'*Wednesday, April* 4—I consulted with Bonny, who was alone with me in camp, and we both thought I had better go to the Falls and explain our position to Tippu-Tib's representative there. I saw Salem Mohammed early, and gave him a present : he took the present, and returned nearly the whole of it later on. A chief called Nasiboo came and

---

* Major Barttelot had intended to send the stores he could not carry to the Falls Station under a white officer.

saw me, and as he is going to the Falls to-morrow, I shall go under his escort. Rain fell in the afternoon.'

COPY OF INSTRUCTIONS TO MR. BONNY ON MY PROCEEDING TO THE FALLS, APRIL 5, 1888.

'SIR,

'During my absence you will take over command of Yambuya Camp, the Soudanese and Zanzibari companies. You will retain this command till my return, for though Mr. Troup may return before I return, yet it will be such a short period before, that it will be best for you to retain the command. It is my especial desire that for the period I am away you will do all in your power to keep the peace between the Arabs and ourselves, for which purpose it will be best to prohibit your men their camp entirely; and in case of disobedience on our men's part, severe punishment. Till I return do not allow the European provision boxes to be touched on any pretence whatever, nor open a fresh bale of cloth for the purpose of purchasing provisions.

'Should the natives prove aggressive, inform and place yourself in the hands of Salem Mohammed.

'I have the honour to be, sir,

'Your obedient servant,

'EDMUND M. BARTTELOT, Major.'

'Started myself at 8 a.m., and got to our camping-ground at Yarilua at 4 p.m. The men carried well.

Nasiboo met me on the road, and gave me a guide, and told me he would be at Njimbi* the day after me. I told him I would wait one day longer for him there. Fine day; gave men melafor, rice and meat.

'*April* 6.—Left Yarilua at 6 a.m., arrived Njimbi at 5 p.m. Men carried well on the road. Got a letter from Ward and Troup. It rained in torrents.

'*April* 7.—Njimbi; rain early morning; dried my things.

'*April* 8.—Left Njimbi at 7 a.m., and made a good journey to Yatuka, getting there at 7 p.m. Good paddlers the whole way. Abdulla fed my men.

'*April* 9.—Yatuka to Yatakusé lower; here the Zanzibari Asenia gave me a big feed; then to Yatakusé upper.

'*April* 10.—Left Yatakusé at 6 a.m., and arrived at the Falls at 11 a.m. I had a palaver with Nzigé, and told him what had been happening at the camp, and that if he wished the loads to be safe, Salem Mohammed had better move his camp a mile, or else all the loads be removed to the Falls.

'*Wednesday, April* 11.—About 11 a.m. Nzigé and Naribo ben Sulieman came, and told me their decision, that Salem Mohammed be recalled. The 250 Manyuema intended for us to be placed entirely under my control. The loads not to be shifted till Tippu-Tib arrives.

'*April* 12.—Left for Yarukombé, by Yatakusé.

'*April* 13. — Left Yarukombé with splendid

* Njimbi must, I think, be the same as Yangambi.

15

paddlers as far as Nasiboo's village, where I changed crews; got to Njimbi at 12 p.m., and found Abdulla of Yatuka there. He tried to draw me out about Salem Mohammed, and told me he was very bad to white men, and would do nothing for them except mischief.

'At 2 p.m. Troup turned up ill, and with no goats.

'*Saturday, April* 14.—Left Njimbi at 6 a.m.; it came on to rain hard; got to Yarilua at 5 p.m. An Arab turned out of his house for us, but in the middle of the night we had to leave, as the place became infested with ants.

'*April* 15.—Left Yarilua at 6 a.m., and reached Yambuya at 3.30 p.m.—about twenty-five miles. On arrival in camp a tale of woe greeted me. I found Bonny well. He gave me a bad account of Salem Mohammed, who has been trying to turn the natives on to us, but Bonny has frustrated him for the time.

'One of the native chiefs during my absence had come to where our canoes were tied, and the watchman, not dreaming of mischief, allowed him to approach; he commenced breaking up one of the canoes, an old one, when the watchman called out, and the Soudanese guard rushed down and stopped him.

'Being brought up before Bonny, he said in reply, when asked why he had done this, that Salem Mohammed had told him to do it. Salem Mohammed, being confronted with him, and asked if this was true, said : "Cut the white men down when they go to the jungle." Bonny turned to Salem, and said : " Look here, Salem Mohammed, there is only one white man here, and he is not afraid to lose his life ; but rest assured if he loses his, yours goes before." Salem Mohammed slunk off with the native. Next day the natives came and shouted out, " The white men are bad." Being asked who told them so, they said, "Salem Mohammed." That evening a crowd of natives and the chief met Bonny and made impertinent gestures at him. He sent for his revolver, and they dispersed.

'Before this the natives were always most friendly to us. Before leaving for the Falls I had extracted a promise from Salem Mohammed that he would allow no harm to happen to Bonny, the camp, or stores.

'I saw Salem the evening of my return. He was anxious to know why I had gone to the Falls, but I baffled him. I thanked him effusively, however, for keeping his promise, which drew him right well. Fine, slight rain at night.

'*Monday*, *April* 16. — I slept like a top. At 11 a.m. Troup and some of the carriers turned up, and after lunch, at Troup's wish, I had an explanation of his conduct while in command of the camp.

. . . .

About 4 p.m. all the carriers but three turned up ; one of them, John Henry, has bolted with my revolver. A maniapara brought in his load. One of the men, Msa, knows where he is, so I despatched him and three soldiers to bring him back.

'*April* 17.—Rain fell in the early morning; all things look pretty quiet. I got my padlock from Salem Mohammed, and asked him to remove all his canoes, which he did. I had a palaver with him.

'*April* 18.—I was ill all day. Salem Mohammed came to see me, and told me he was going away down river. This may be a blind. I have sent men out to watch him.

'*April* 19.—Rain fell during night. Have been thirteen months in this country. Salem Mohammed started at noon with seven canoes, 120 Manyuema, 50 natives, and 30 women, down country. The natives showed insolence to Bonny and Troup.

'*Friday, April* 20.—I felt far from well. I took over our stores from Troup.

'The party I had sent turned up with John Henry. He had sold my revolver, but they recovered it.

'*Saturday, April* 21.—I shifted all stores from Jameson's house. . . . . My temper, with all these worries and vexations, is none of the best.

'*April* 22.—Shortly after getting into bed last night it came on to rain and to blow hard, and came into my bed. I shoved up an umbrella, and put on my waterproof sheet, and was snug.

'This morning, after breakfast, John Henry was

brought out before all the Zanzibaris to make them acquainted with his punishment. I told them after a short palaver that he would be shot to-morrow, at sunrise.

'The prisoner and escort returned to the guard-room directly I left. They burst out to Bonny that if John Henry was shot they would desert in a body. I had them fallen in, and told them that, of course, if they deserted they could never expect to see Zanzibar again, and their money would be lost to them, as also their freedom, for they would become slaves to Tippu-Tib, but that, whatever they might threaten to do, I could not depart from my decision. They broke up quite quietly, and went away. However, in the afternoon Bonny persuaded me not to shoot him, so I suppose I will have to let him off.

'*Monday, April* 23.—John Henry was flogged. The sun has gone round to the north again; short days; it sets between 5.30 and 5.45 p.m. I should hear from old Jameson soon. He must have been at Kasongo five days now. If fine to-morrow, I go to Yambu to see the Sheik there.

'COPY OF INSTRUCTIONS TO MR. BONNY ON MY PROCEEDING TO YAMBU, APRIL 24, 1888.

' SIR,

'You will follow the instructions of the pre-ceding letter, dated April 5, 1888, with the excep-

tion that you will not hand over the command to
Mr. Troup,* but maintain it, and that you will sleep
in the store-house.

> ' I have the honour to be, sir, etc.,
>
> ' EDMUND M. BARTTELOT, Major.

' I left camp early, but did not feel like going,
and got to Yaraweko proper, which I had always
supposed to be Yambu, at 2.30 p.m. ; very tired.
The head-man, Kasima, a Manyuema by birth, gave
me a thundering feed of fowl and rice. He told me
Yambu proper was further west. He gave me a
small house to live in.

' *Wednesday*, *April* 25.—I told Kasima I wished
to leave to-day, but he made me stay. He told me
many things. All Englishmen were bad ; French
good. English in too big a hurry, always driving
and beating. He said he would catch any deserter
for me. He told me of Imsa's (the Zanzibari's)
roguery : how he stole Troup's looking-glass, and
wanted to open my box, but had no key ; of the
monstrous lies John Henry had told him about us
and Salem Mohammed, and that my revolver was
his own. But Kasima told me many lies himself ;
amongst others, that he was sixteen years old, and
that he could walk from his camp to ours in about
six hours, which is impossible. He promised to
catch deserters, and to send fowls, etc. Yaraweko
is a big village ; he told me he had 100 Manyuema

* Mr. Troup was very ill at this time.

there. There were six large adobe houses built,
and four more building, besides many smaller ones.
Towards evening a light rain. Kasima has fed and
housed a sick Zanzibari whom Ward left behind at
Yarilua, called Ali Mohammed.

'*April* 26.—I meant to have left early, but there
was such a thick fog I mistook the time, and left at
7.30, arriving at Yambuya in a heavy thunderstorm.
I heard on arrival that John Henry had died yesterday; but I am certain he must have been shot or
hung, sooner or later, for he was a monstrous bad
character. I found Bonny had bought ten goats
and a kid, making our number twenty-two. The
prevalent idea among the Arabs is that Mr. Stanley
had gone to Uganda. He may have been taken
there by force—otherwise, no.

'*April* 27.—A very hot day, and we have great
trouble in keeping our meat after the second day.
The thermometer registers 87° in the house, and 119°
in the sun, at 4 p.m. If fine I am going to see
Sheik Sala to-morrow. Raschid sent us some goats.

'*Saturday*, *April* 28.—I left camp at 8.30 a.m.,
arrived at Sala's camp at 12.30, and found a most
sumptuous fare awaiting me. Fowl and rice stews,
a sort of rice pudding, and stewed plantains, which
tasted exactly like prunes. He promised to stop
deserters for me; he has a large camp there of about
1,000 men, and the road to it from here has been
made as good as the country will permit, with the
object, no doubt, of concentrating men on us quickly

should the occasion arise. All the villages between us and Sala's camp are occupied, three-quarters of the way by Salem Mohammed and natives, and the rest by Sala's. Sala told me he thought Stanley had gone to Uganda. I stayed an hour and a half, and received a present of a cock, plantains, and some Indian corn, and got back to camp at 6 p.m. On my way back I found all Salem Mohammed's natives sitting at their doors with their spears by their sides. A hot, fine day.

'*Sunday, April* 29.—Thunderstorm.

'*Monday, April* 30.—Light rain in the early morning. After breakfast we fought Sala's cock against Muni Katoto, but it was no good; Muni Katoto game, but out of condition. Bonny got a dinner out of me thereby. Bonny told me tales of Troup and Ward.

'*Tuesday, May* 1.—Sala sent in last night two fowls and a lot of plantains, very fine ones. I sent his men and a present back this morning. Bonny told me, by way of a refresher, that Ward had told him that Stanley had told him (Ward) that he (Stanley) had left me behind because I was of no use to him. Certainly, I don't think I am much, but, then, it is because Stanley does not attempt to utilize me, and hates me like poison.

'*Wednesday, May* 2.—Showery. Troup has something wrong with him, which Bonny says may be serious. Clothes and boots wearing out fast; have entered on my last pair of pyjamas. The cocks, Muni Katoto and Sala's, fight all day, and have to be continually separated.

'*May* 3.—Took the bearings of the sun last night, and found it set north-west exactly, by magnetic compass, the variation being 18° east. I took a walk round to where Nasiboo has established a village, but could learn no news. Fine day.

'*Friday, May* 4.—Rained last night. Bonny and I measured to-day. I am a smaller man altogether than he is; round the chest I measure 34 inches; I used to measure 36. I must have shrunk. Round the arm 9 inches—very small; round the forearm 10 inches, round the waist 31 inches, round the calf 12 inches.

'*Saturday, May* 5.—I started after breakfast for a walk down river. Roads tremendously overgrown, as all traffic is done by canoe. I found the old village in ruins, and natives all in one village. On my return at 4 p.m. Bonny told me two natives had come in, who reported Stanley on his way down; they had seen him two and a half months ago at the village of Barifua. Later on two of Sala's men brought plantains, and said that Stanley was only four days off.

CHAPTER XI.

Report of Stanley's Approach.—Arrival of the *A.I.A.*—Insolence of Natives—An Awkward Moment—Natives told to take Barttelot's Life—Instructions to Bonny—To the Falls-- Meeting with Jameson and Tippu-Tib — Four Hundred Carriers—They guarantee £1,000 to Muni Somai—Van Kerkhoven and Tippu—The River Ubangi--*Kapeppo--Mikalee*—Yambuya—Troup ill--Arrival of Tippu—Terms-- Mr. Werner's Visit to Yambuya—Stanley's Baggage—List of Stores—Loads refused—Tippu-Tib gives Orders to shoot Major Barttelot.—Loads to be re-adjusted.—What Mr. Troup said.

'*Sunday, May* 6.—Much beating of drums, in consequence of Salem Mohammed having returned. Bonny told me yesterday that small-pox was very rife among the Manyuema. Salem Mohammed came down to see me in the afternoon, and told me it was reported* Stanley was returning, but without

* These reports of Mr. Stanley's returning might have been due to the second letter from Mr. Stanley to Major Barttelot, brought by Mr. Stairs to Ugarrowwa, in which Stanley said he would be at Ugarrowwa on May 29—of course Ugarrowwa would spread the report.

the white man he had gone to relieve. This looks
doubtful. I sent a Zanzibari "Hamadi" up to
Sala's camp to ascertain the truth. No Arabs or
Manyuema have seen him, or know anything about
him.

'*May* 7.—Doweli returned, and said Stanley is
reported two days from Sala's camp. I shall go up
myself to-morrow and see.

'*Tuesday*, *May* 8.—At 11 a.m. a steamer is reported in sight. At 11.30 she arrived—the *A.I.A.*,
with Mr. Van Kerkhoven, the engineer, Mr. Werner,
and our thirty-five men, less Abou Bek, my Soudanese
officer, who died at Bangala. Ward got down per
the Lomami in five days to Bangala, and twenty-
four hours to the equator, where he caught the
Stanley. They gave me a box of sardines, a tin of
coffee, a tin of butter, and two pots of Liebig. At
1 p.m. I started for Sala's camp, and got there at
sunset. He told me about Stanley, but in such a
manner, and with such variations, I knew it was in-
correct.

'*May* 9.—Wet last night. Sala let out that a
letter* had come for me from the Falls ; but Salem
must have taken it, as I have not got it. A
8.30 a.m. I started up river by land. After two
hours' march I got to a village ; asked news of
Stanley, but they knew nothing about him. I returned to Sala's at noon, had luncheon, and returned
to camp at sunset. Van Kerkhoven gave me a tin

---

* This was a letter from Jameson to Barttelot from Kasongo.

of tea, a box of biscuits, a pot of jam, and a box of sardines. Werner gave me a cake of soap.

'*Thursday, May* 10.—I sent to Salem Mohammed for my letter. He sent to say there was not one. Later on he came down to see me. I told him the rumour about Stanley was a lie. Kerkhoven gave me some petroleum to blow up my stores if necessary.

'*Friday, May* 11.—The Belgians left this morning at 5 a.m. for Stanley Falls; and in the evening the natives were insolent to me, and one man tried to knock me off the path as I was walking up and down our promenade. I knocked him flat with my stick—wrong on my part, perhaps, but almost unavoidable. This man went straight to Salem Mohammed, and came back escorted by about twenty Manyuema armed with sticks, spears, and guns. They met me on the road. I stood still in the centre of the road; I had only my stick; but for some reason they sheered off on one side and left me clear. They made a great noise, and no doubt cursed me. Close to the Fort-gate, but of course outside it, stood Salem Mohammed with a man whom I swear had a gun under his clothes. They were talking to Bonny, who happened to come out just at that moment. This evening we heard that Tippu-Tib had come to the Falls; also that the natives had been told to take my life. I expect Jameson back about the 14th.

'*Saturday, May* 12.—Wet all forenoon. I go to the Falls on Monday.

' *Sunday, May* 13.—I read the English papers ;[*]
see several accounts of Stanley. The nights have
begun to get much cooler again. I leave to-morrow
for the Falls.

' Letter of instructions to Mr. Bonny on my proceeding to the Falls, same as letters of April 5
and 24.

' E. M. BARTTELOT, Major.

' *May* 13, 1888.'

' *Monday, May* 14.—I left camp at daybreak, and
got to Yarina at 4.30 p.m. I met many natives on
the road coming to fetch manioc from our plantations, from Yaraweko, Yambu, and Yarilua. I put
up in the same house where Troup and I were
formerly attacked by ants. The Manyuema in
charge is a civil man.

' I have been sixteen months away from home,
and done nothing.

' *May* 15.—I left Yarina at daybreak. I woke up
in the middle of the night, and my boy told me it
was dawning ; so I got up and had breakfast, and
packed. In reality it was only 2 a.m. I got to
Yarukombé at 4 p.m. ; the *A.I.A.* had only gone
two hours. I received a letter from Jameson from
Riba Riba, dated April 3 ; no news of Stanley
in it.

' *May* 16.—Left at daybreak, and reached Yallasula at 9.30 a.m. ; found the steamer, and got on

* Brought by the steamer *A.I.A.*

board. I am suffering terribly with my hands, which are covered with small suppurating ulcers, which make my fingers and joints quite stiff. We lay the night at Yarukombé, and Abdulla gave us a feed. The Belgians spend an enormous amount of cloth in . . . . [*illegible*] . . . . Fine day.

' *May* 17.—Dense fog ; could not leave till 8 a.m. We put in at Yatakusé, and lay the night at a fishing-village below the Falls.

' *May* 18.—We reached the Falls. Nzigé came over, and was much puzzled at the Belgians coming. A vague report that Stanley was dead.

' *May* 19.—I went with Kerkhoven to see Nzigé. He gave us stewed fowl, tea, and sugar. In the evening Werner and I went for a walk.

' *Sunday*, *May* 20.—I loafed around and explored the island.

' *Monday*, *May* 21.—I wrote to Bonny.

' *Tuesday*, *May* 22.—I am not feeling well ; this place always unfits me. At 4 p.m. I heard that Tippu-Tib and Jameson had come, and canoed over to see them, and found it true. Dear old Jameson, whom I was right glad to see, and was very fit, told me Tippu had promised him about 800 men. I made my salaams to Tippu-Tib, and we came over and dined, and Van Kerkhoven gave us champagne, the first I have tasted for fourteen months. Jameson told me that Tippu hated Stanley, because he had broken his word to him about presents he had pro- mised him when he crossed Africa, which he had

never sent , also because the powder was not at
Yambuya in the first instance, and because he said
that in June last, acting under Mr. Stanley's orders,
I had refused aid to him by not allowing my men to
fire on the natives after the burning of the village of
Mbunga. He absolved me from all blame, but he
had said that if he had not been hurried up by
Holmwood, the Consul at Zanzibar, and by the fear
of losing his good name with the English, he would
never have sent the men at all. My firm belief is
that he (Tippu) knows about Stanley, and I suspect
he is acting a double part.

' *May* 23.—Next day I had a palaver with Tippu.
He then said he had got 400 men for me, but no
more; that out of these 300 were to carry 40 lb.,
the others only 20 lb. Jameson reminded him of
what he had said at Kasongo about the 800 men,
and he said it was nothing of the sort—that 400
men were all he could spare us; every available
man he had was wanted. Concerning payment, he
wanted none; he trusted to the Committee, whom
I trust will give him nothing. We have to pay,
or, rather, guarantee, £1,000 to a big Arab (Muni
Somai), who is to come as the commander of the
400 Manyuema, and is to see us through this
business, being responsible for all loads and men

' *May* 24.—The Queen's birthday : we drank her
health in champagne. Tippu came over early to
see us, and after a palaver Van Kerkhoven asked
Jameson and self to leave the room, and he had

a tremendous palaver with Tippu. After that we knew why we had only got 400 instead of 800 men; for Van Kerkhoven had told Tippu of the Ubangi River, and asked him to send men there, for the double purpose of diverting him from Bangala, and of preventing anybody else getting possession. Van Kerkhoven had told Tippu of this river the evening he arrived, and while I went over to meet Jameson. This is why Salem Mohammed came over early to see Van Kerkhoven.

'*Friday, May* 25.—I had a final palaver with Tippu-Tib, and signed the contract with Muni Somai for the sum of £1,000; £120 to be paid in goods at the camp. I trust our trip, if we ever start, may be a success, but I cannot help thinking Tippu is acting treacherously. But though with only 400 men, I must start, and will send all the loads I do not want to Bangala, Mr. Van Kerkhoven having placed the ss. *Stanley* at my disposal.

EXTRACTED FROM A LETTER TO MAJOR SCLATER, R.A., JUNE 1.

'The river Ubangi,* which enters the Congo below Equator Station on the north bank, up which Van Gèle has been exploring, does not belong to the Free State territory. There is plenty

---

* The Ubangi River or Mobangi Welle rises in the north-east corner of the Congo Free State in Monbuttu, and flowing west, forms the northern boundary of the State, till it turns south and joins the Congo.

of ivory up it, and many villages, with a plentiful supply of food. The Belgians are afraid Tippu meditates taking all the country down to Bangala. To stop this, Van Kerkhoven, without a word to us, told Tippu of the necessity of someone taking it before the French or some other big Power or trading association take possession of it; of the easiness of access to it from our camp. Salem Mohammed had sent a party of men from our camp to the northward, who had actually touched this river, had met a steamer with white men on board, and had turned back, fearing hostilities. We did not have our palaver with Tippu till 4 p.m., after Kerkhoven had asked Jameson and myself to leave the room, and Tippu told us we could have only 400 men instead of 800. When Van Kerkhoven told me what he had done, the change of front in Tippu was perfectly open to me. It is crushing luck. I don't think Van Kerkhoven meant us harm, but he has certainly done it. Tippu wishes for a new outlet to the sea; this he will obtain under the Belgian flag as an officer of that State; but when he has accomplished that object, he will take the whole of the Congo down to Stanley Pool, and fling off the Belgian suzerainty, should it suit his purpose. Tippu thinks the Sultan of Zanzibar has entirely lost his power. He is also afraid of German influence on his neighbours on the east of his territory. I am writing a long letter to you, but it does me good to unburthen myself. . . . .

16

'The Arabs dislike me because I am connected with Stanley, and because I am continually worrying them about the men, and don't give them as large presents as they expect, or allow them and their followers the freedom of my camp. They call me " Kapeppo," signifying " whirlwind," because I speak so fast, and am impetuous ; and also on account of my fast-walking capabilities. *They say I do not walk, but run.* " Mikalee," or " him of the strong mind," because I am not easily diverted from my purpose.

'The Belgians are jealous of me because I am of superior rank to all of them, though much younger, and because I happen to have the command of this rear-guard, and none of them have been employed on this Expedition, which they regard as a tremendous grievance. The abscesses on my hands are breaking out again, and I am getting a bubo on my right arm from them.'

'*Saturday, May* 26.—I left Singatini with 320 men at 3 p.m., and lay at Yatakusé for the night in a canoe.

'*May* 27.—Got to Njimbi at 3, and waited for Muni Somai.

'*May* 28.—Muni Somai begged me to walk slowly, saying it was known all over the country how I walked, but if I walked like that I would soon lose all the men. We camped in the bush.

'*May* 29.—To Yarilua.

'*May* 30.—Left Yarilua at 6 a.m. in boots, the felts of which (for they had no soles) came off directly I started, and had to be tied on with string. We met Karema, Chief of Yambu, on the road; he gave me melafor. Reached Yambuya at 4.30 p.m. with sore heels and feet. Bonny told me there had been trouble with the Manyuema stealing manioc, cowries and clothes from our men, but Salem Mohammed had settled it. But had he not encouraged them, I am sure they would never have done it. I trust his day of reckoning is coming.'

EXTRACTED FROM A LETTER TO MAJOR SCLATER, R.A., JUNE 1.

'I got back here May 30, and am now laid up with swollen fetlocks, caused by abscesses, the same as on my hands. Rest will cure them, I think. On arrival here I found Troup in a dying state, and he will have to go home. We are all very busy, myself directing, and Jameson and Bonny doing the work, packing up and weighing the stores. I can't get out of my mind that something will happen to prevent us starting. What a fiasco it has all been! and what a waste of time for me! Stanley should never have gone till Tippu's men had been forthcoming. He had got what the Arabs call " the big head," and I fancy he is suffering for it. Please give my very best salaams to Sir Francis Grenfell, and tell him I am having a rare time of it with

Zanzibaris, Arabs, natives, Soudanese, and other scoundrels. My head-man, Muni Somai, of whom I have told you, is a ripper at begging. He asks me for everything that he sees. They have no idea of exhaustion, these Arabs, but think every white man, no matter how or where he is situated, has an unlimited supply of stuff, and that he is fair game for all comers. I tell you, Harry, it requires all my strength to prevent me from breaking out at him. I think he is put up to it by Salem Mohammed, who is doing all he can to make a rupture. I hope, however, to get clean away, and frustrate them all. Anything is preferable to sitting in this misery, where I have already worn out two seats to my trousers, besides my temper, and somewhat of my health, doing nothing. I am sending a terrible lot of stores to Bangala, which I cannot carry ; amongst other stuff a lot of food, like jam, herrings, etc. I could eat them here, of course, but knowing Stanley as I do, I prefer to be quit of them, and jam, herrings, and soap ain't going to keep us alive. They weigh a lot and are bulky, and for light there is always palm-oil, and for soap native soap. I have written to Sir R. Buller this mail ; I thought he might like it. Whenever you write or see Colonel Grove, remember me most kindly to him.'

' *Sunday*, *June* 3.—Muni Somai demands metako ; he intends cheating me if he can. Abed Saida also came. I wrote to father, M., and Harry.

'*June* 4.—I gave a goat to Muni Somai and Sala, who said Salem Mohammed refused them food. The *Stanley* steamer, with Captain Van Gèle, Captain Shackerström, Lieutenant Baert, and two other engineer officers, and the engineer De Mann, came to-day at 4 p.m. Also the *A.I.A.*, with Tippu-Tib, Van Kerkhoven, and Werner. The *Stanley* brought us letters.

' *Tuesday, June* 5.—I had a palaver with Tippu-Tib; he gave me thirty more men. Settled up advance pay; wrote many letters; a heavy thunderstorm in afternoon. The thirty men belong to Muni Somai, to whom we have to pay seven dollars a month each to-day.

' *Wednesday, June* 6. — Another palaver with Tippu; he wishes an advance of money, and a guarantee that his men shall be paid. I agreed to make terms.

' *Thursday, June* 7.—I signed agreement with Tippu and Muni Somai. Captain Van Gèle and Mr. Boton witnessed signature. Tippu requests a guarantee that the money shall be paid him when the Expedition is completed. This I have acceded to. He also asked for an advance in cloth and powder; this I gave him to the value of £836. I have had to write to father about paying the half of the £1,000 to Muni Somai, because if the Committee think it too much, they may refuse, and I don't want to be like Stanley when he crossed Africa. I am afraid father will think it a blister if he has to pay, but it cannot be helped. Englishmen's names must not be disgraced for a paltry £500.

'Van Kerkhoven and Tippu have just had a tremendous row. Tippu says he will send men to Bangala. Van Kerkhoven says he will shoot every man of Tippu's who goes near the place. Tippu - Tib means to have Bangala. Finished letters to M. J., father, and Harry, and wrote to Evelyn and Galfrid.'

[Mr. Werner, in his most interesting book, ' River Life on the Congo,' being present, as engineer of the steamer *A.I.A.*, at Yambuya at this date, writes, p. 270: 'A note arrived from Major Barttelot asking that two carpenters (natives of Lagos) might be sent to assist him. Having obtained the two men. I took a canoe and went up to the camp, where I found Jameson hard at work with a screwdriver, singing all the time. . . . In a few minutes we were all busy among the ammunition cases (p. 269). Tippu stipulated that none of the loads carried were to exceed 40 lb. ; it became necessary to reduce 400 loads from 60 lb. to 40 lb. This meant unscrewing the lid of each case of ammunition, removing a portion of the contents, filling up the empty space with dried grass, and screwing on the lids again. Troup and Bonny being laid up, the Major writing despatches, there was only Jameson. Among these loads were a number containing Stanley's private stores. Finding, when all was done, that the carriers would be insufficient, the Major decided to open such of

them as he could, and sort out the contents, only
sending on such things as were necessary. As we
could get no keys to fit the locks, I cut the hinges
of several tin uniform-cases ; and the Major and Mr.
Jameson, having divided the *contents into two lots,*
repacked the cases, and I soldered them up again.'

Mr. Werner is the only one living of the three who
opened Mr. Stanley's boxes and saw the contents,
and his testimony, with that which is found written
by Major Barttelot, is sufficient proof that the officers
did take on clothing, etc., for Mr. Stanley.   Mr.
Bonny ought to know absolutely what was taken,
but he was ill at the time of arranging Mr. Stanley's
loads.

Major Barttelot writes to Miss —— : ' To-day
we had to open Mr. Stanley's boxes. I
expect he will make a stir about our opening his
boxes, he is so suspicious of anything of that kind ;
but as some of them are more like Noah's arks
than boxes, I cannot carry them ; and they must
be opened to get out anything we may think he
wants.'

We find, therefore, that Mr. Stanley's boxes
were opened by three officers—Major Barttelot,
Mr. Jameson and Mr. Werner.   The things were
divided into two lots, we may venture to presume,
the one lot to be taken on, and the other sent back,
and the object, Major Barttelot says, in opening the
boxes was ' to get out anything we may think Mr.
Stanley wants.'   ' As some of the boxes are more

like Noah's arks, I cannot carry them.'   In the letter
to Mr. Mackinnon, of March 27, already quoted,
Major Barttelot writes of the loads : ' I see no use
in attempting to take all the loads, as if full loads
were given to the Manyuema they would not carry
them. . . . Ammunition is necessary, brass wire,
beads, and metako, a certain amount of provisions
and clothes for Mr. Stanley and the officers with
him.'

Of course, when it came to be simply a question
of carrying the luxuries of Mr. Stanley's African
toilet or the ammunition and powder for the relief
of Emin Pasha, and perhaps for the relief of Mr.
Stanley himself, the officers of the rear column,
however delicate they may have felt the situation
to be, could hardly do otherwise than elect to take
the ammunition in preference to the articles of
toilet, and gunpowder and necessary clothes rather
than candles, jam and soap (I refer to Mr. Stanley's
remarks here rather than later on, as being more
convenient).   On August 28 Mr. Stanley writes to
Mr. Mackinnon a letter of questionable taste, giving
an account of his finding of the rear column at
Banalya, of Barttelot's death, and then concerning
his clothes : ' There are still far more loads than
I can carry ; at the same time articles needful are
missing. For instance, I left Yambuya with only
a short campaigning kit, leaving my reserve of
clothing and personal effects in charge of the officers.
In December some deserters from the advance

column reached Yambuya to spread the report that
I was dead. They had no papers with them, but
the officers seemed to accept the report of these
deserters as a fact, and in January Mr. Ward, at
an officers' mess meeting, proposed that my instructions be cancelled. The only one who appears to
have dissented was Mr. Bonny. Accordingly, my
personal kit, medicines, soap, candles and provisions
were sent down the Congo as "superfluities."
Thus, after making this immense personal sacrifice
to relieve them and cheer them up, I find myself
naked and deprived of even the necessaries of life
in Africa. But, strange to say, they have kept two
hats, four pairs of boots and a flannel jacket ; and I
propose to go back to Emin Pasha and across Africa
in this truly African kit.'

Mr. Stanley is quite wrong in attributing to his
officers of the rear column the general belief that
he was dead. It is true the officers thought that
something serious must have happened to prevent
the man of punctual performance from keeping his
promise to return in November. Major Barttelot's
writings show he did *not* trust the reports of deserters,
or believe that Stanley was dead. Mr. Stanley's
instructions were never cancelled, but were carried
out to the letter. Mr. Stanley, in writing of his
clothes, overlooks or suppresses the fact that Major
Barttelot could not be responsible for the Expedition after his death ; while at the time of the
murder there was a general panic, during which

a number of loads were stolen, and Mr. Stanley's things were probably lost.

Mr. Stanley, if possible, exceeds himself in unkind sophistry when he thus attempts to blame for the loss of his clothes a man who had actually been murdered while in the very act of trying to convey the wretched things to him, and who, but for his death, would doubtless have handed them over safely.

The immense personal sacrifice Mr. Stanley says he had made to relieve and cheer them up consists of a sixty-one days' easy journey, a great part of the way in canoes down stream from Fort Bodo, leaving in June and arriving in August ; a broken promise to be at Yambuya in November ; and a complete desertion of his rear column from June, 1887, to August, 1888, when he knew them to be surrounded by Arabs and Manyuema.   For Tippu-Tib was at Stanley Falls with a full knowledge of the circumstances and wealth of the camp, and of the character of the officers and men with whom he had travelled from Zanzibar.   And Ugarrowwa, to whom Mr. Stanley had in September, 1887, gladly confided the fact that Major Barttelot had two and a half tons of powder, was advancing towards Yambuya. Mr. Stanley says (see p. 199, vol. i., ' Darkest Africa ') : ' It was Ugarrowwa's wish to obtain gunpowder, as his supply was nearly exhausted.' So Mr. Stanley gave the rogue an order for 3 cwt. of powder, and passed him on towards the rear column.

Such was the immense personal sacrifice to which Mr. Stanley plausibly calls our attention while writing his first account home of the murder of Major Barttelot, and from the immediate neighbourhood of the poor fellow's grave.

From this list the careful way the stores were looked after may be judged :

A LIST OF STORES IN CAMP, MAY 6, 1888 (FOUND IN MAJOR BARTTELOT'S NOTE-BOOK*).

No.	Class of Store.	Description.	How Packed.	No. of Loads.	No. of Loads in each Class.
I.	Money	Wire, brass } „ iron }	Bales	27	194¼
		Metako	Boxes	9	
		„	Bales	7	
		Beads	Bags	33	
		Cowries	Boxes	3¼	
		„	Sacks	13	
		Cloth, Zanzibar	Bales	88	101
		Handkerchiefs	„	10	
		Assorted	„	3	
		Savelist	Bale	1	
II.	Ammunition	Winchester	Boxes	38	338
		Remington	Special boxes	34	160
		„	Tin-lined boxes	65	
		„	Wood boxes	61	
		Maxim	Boxes, small	25	30
		„	„ big	5	
		Powder	Boxes	100	
		Percussion-caps	„	10	

* This book was brought home among Mr. Jameson's papers by Mr. Ward to Mrs. Jameson, who gave it to me. This list is in his own handwriting.

No.	Class of Store.	Description.	How Packed.	No. of Loads.	No. of Loads in each Class.
III.	Private Baggage	Mr. Stanley	—	15	
		Mr. Stairs	—	1	
		Dr. Parke	—	2	21
		Mr. Jephson	—	2	
		Mr. Nelson	—	1	
IV.	Provisions	European	Boxes	24	
		Salt	Sacks	7	
		Rice	,,	13	$50\frac{1}{2}$
		Beans	,,	$1\frac{1}{2}$	
		Biscuits	Boxes	5	
V.	Various	Rope	Coil	1	
		Paulins	—	3	
		Tobacco	Box	1	
		Tool-chest	Chest	1	
		Tools for Emin Pasha	Bag	1	
		Clothes, Somalis'	Package	1	10
		Clothes, deserters'	,,	1	
		Tin ware	Box	1	
		Total number of loads	...		$613\frac{3}{4}$

Loads.

Page 519, vol. i., 'Darkest Africa,' Mr. Stanley gives a list of stores landed at Yambuya per ss. *Stanley*, August 14, 1887 493
Also a list of stores left at Yambuya June 28, 1887 ... 167

Total number of loads left by Mr. Stanley in charge of Major Barttelot 660
Total number of loads in camp May 6, 1888 ... $613\frac{3}{4}$

Number of loads less being ... ... $47\frac{3}{4}$

—consisting, as far as I can compare the lists, of cloth, metako, provisions, etc., that would necessarily be consumed during the twelve months that had elapsed since Mr. Stanley deserted Yambuya, in buying necessaries and giving presents, etc.

Of the 613¾ loads at Yambuya, May 6, 1888, it was decided to carry 470 loads to the front, leaving 143¾ loads to be disposed of. One hundred and thirty loads were sent to Bangala, to remain under the charge of Mr. Ward, leaving 13¾ loads to account for. Tippu-Tib and Muni Somai had both to receive an advance payment in cloth, powder, beads, and cowries, the latter to the value of £120, the former to the value of some £836, which would probably account for these 13¾ loads, and the cloth powder, and the ammunition taken out of the loads in reducing them from 60 to 40 lb. If Major Barttelot had had sufficient carriers. the loads would not have been sent to Bangala at all.

Bangala was evidently chosen to send the stores to, rather than Stanley Falls, owing to the danger Major Barttelot apprehended from the Arabs. Of the 130 loads sent to Bangala, there were eight loads of Mr. Stanley's private baggage only, leaving seven to be taken to the front out of the fifteen on Major Barttelot's list of May 6 of his stores.

I have written to ask the Committee for the details of the loads as supplied them by Major Barttelot, but up to date have not received them.]

'*Friday, June* 8.—I handed over the loads to Tippu-Tib; but he refused them, because they were a pound or two overweight—in reality, because the cloth he bought of me was not up to much. Troup left for home. Showery in the afternoon and evening.'

Mr. Werner, in 'River Life on the Congo,' p. 271, writes: 'On the morning of the 8th I went up to see Tippu-Tib muster the caravan. There were 130 surplus loads, and the Major decided that, as he could not get men to carry them, they would be safest at Bangala. Accordingly, Captain Shackerström took them down to the *Stanley*, as well as two donkeys, the country through which the Expedition had to go being so bad that a donkey would have been of no use.

'About 9 a.m. Tippu-Tib and the Manyuemas came for the loads, which were all ready, laid out in rows just outside the camp gate. I was talking to Troup inside his hut, when I heard a noise, something between a yell and the howling of hyenas, and, rushing out, found that the 400 men brought by Tippu-Tib had refused their loads, because they said some of them were a pound or two overweight. . . . The loads could not be reduced to the required weight without an immense amount of trouble, as the powder and cartridges were in air-tight, soldered tins, weighing about 15 lb. each. Three of these tins, packed in a wooden case of from 10 to 12 lb. weight, formed a load. Thus, when one tin was taken out, each load, including the case, would weigh 41 or 42 lb. To reduce this, the tins would have to be opened and soldered up again. . . . In the evening I heard that Tippu-Tib had been persuaded to pass all the loads containing powder and cartridges in air-tight tins.' Mr. Werner goes on to recount his start in the *A.I.A.*, on June 9, from Yambuya, and then, 'Before we had gone very far the Belgian officer in command* of the *A.I.A.* came and told me that Tippu-Tib had told the Manyuemas that if the Major did not treat them well they were to shoot him. This was such an astonishing statement I could hardly believe it; but it was confirmed by one of my men (a Zanzibari), and also by several of Tippu's own men, then on board, and, some days later, by Salim bin Soudi, the interpreter.' Mr. Troup left with the steamers, and came home. On his arrival at Charing Cross I went to see him, and had a long conversation with him (September 20, 1888), which I noted down immediately afterwards. With reference to the conduct of Tippu-Tib on June 8, Mr. Troup told me a short time before they started, on the break-up of the camp, when Tippu-Tib had come to palaver about the loads, 'I was ill in bed, and I heard a tremendous row going on. I thought the Arabs were going to rush the camp and take it. I sent my servant-boy to find out what it was. He came back and said the loads had been made up to more weight than the agreement with Tippu allowed; that the Manyuema asked Tippu what they should do if Barttelot made them carry more than the amount agreed, and Tippu had said in reply, " Shoot him."

* Van Kerkhoven.

'After that there was a palaver between your brother and Tippu, and the matter was settled. I don't know any more about it, because I was too ill in my tent to move.' About Major Barttelot Mr. Troup said : ' Your brother was a bit hasty at times, and if his temper was upset he let us have it ; and, being a soldier, he expected to be obeyed. His discipline was very strict, and the men complained a great deal of it. He was a wonderfully cheery fellow, and used to keep us alive with his tales. He used to tell us stories about old Shepherd, Lord Leconfield's huntsman, and would imitate his voice : and he could take off Stanley splendidly. In these degenerate times it was quite a pleasure to meet a man so devoted to his father as he was; he generally had his Bible and a photograph of his father with him. He would often in the middle of something he was doing say, " Ah, my poor old father! I know he is worrying about me—that he is terribly anxious over all this business." Your brother was a great walker. I never saw anybody walk like him ; he could walk what it would take the best native a day and a half to do in a day, and come in just as fit and fresh at the end of it as when he started. No one in the place could touch him walking. But he was very careless about himself, and would constantly go out of the camp unarmed. I warned him several times of the danger.'

CHAPTER XII.

Worthlessness of Mr. Stanley's Stores—Caps—A Short Review—
Barttelot's Last Report to Mackinnon—Agreements with
Muni Somai—Business Letters—Instructions to Mr. Ward—
Reasons for sending Cablegram to the Committee.

'*Saturday, June* 9. — The steamers left this
morning, but Mr. Baert (of Matadi) stops with
Tippu-Tib to act as his secretary. Van Kerkhoven
sent me two carpenters' (these are the men referred
to by Mr. Werner, who was acting under Van
Kerkhoven). 'Very good of him. One of our cases
of brandy went off by mistake in the *Stanley*. Fine
day.

'*Sunday, June* 10.—I looked into the loads : all
satisfactory till the issue of caps, when 80 per cent.
of them were found to be bad, and I had to
purchase fresh ones from Tippu-Tib. All Stanley's
stores are the same. Wet afternoon.'

Mr. Jameson states in his diary that he had

17

pointed out the worthlessness of these goods to Mr.
Stanley at Zanzibar.*

With regard to these caps and other stores, Mr.
Stanley, while he insinuates that they have disappeared in an unaccountable manner, fails to state
the whole facts.   On this matter I wrote the following letter, which most of the morning papers were
kind enough to publish :

‘ SIR,
        ‘ Mr. Stanley, in his book “ In Darkest
Africa,” professes to give a true account of the
situation of his rear column, and of the actions of his
officers in command.   When the diaries and letters
of Major Barttelot and Mr. Jameson are published,
it will be seen that Mr. Stanley's defence of his
conduct and arrangements in connection with the
rear column is quite inadequate, besides being in-
accurate, misleading, and ungenerous.   As an instance
of the *suppressio veri* and the *suggestio falsi* which
characterize the work, take the following (p. 475,
vol. i.) :
        ‘ “ On August 14 Mr. Troup delivered to Major
Barttelot 129 cases of Remington cartridges, in
addition to 29 left by me.   These cases contain

---

* Extract from Mr. Jameson's diary, June 10, 1888 : ‘ Nearly
all the caps turn out to be bad.   When passing them on board
the ss. *Madura*, I tried some of them, and told Mr. Stanley that
they were bad, but he would not listen to me ; the consequence
is we have had to buy from Tippu-Tib.’

80,000 rounds. By June 9 (see Barttelot's report)
this supply has dwindled down to 35,580 rounds.
There has been no marching, no fighting. They
have decreased during a camp life of eleven months
in the most unaccountable manner. . . . Half of
the gunpowder and more than two thirds of the
bales of cloth have disappeared. Though Yambuya
originally contained a store of 300,000 percussion-
caps, it has been found necessary to purchase £48
worth from Tippu-Tib."

'The answer to the first part of this outrageous
insinuation is to be found in Major Barttelot's report
(p. 504, vol. i.) :

'"*June* 9.—We shall easily be able to start by the
11th ; but I am sorry to say our loss of ammunition,
by the lightening of the loads—for it was the ammunition they particularly took notice of—is something enormous."

'As to the 300,000 percussion-caps, when Major
Barttelot came to issue them he found 80 per cent.
useless and bad—" the same as all Stanley's stores "
—and out of necessity had to buy of Tippu-Tib.
There is no excuse for Mr. Stanley, as his officers
had pointed out to him the worthlessness of the
goods at Zanzibar. The public may judge of the
whole of Mr. Stanley's reports by this scandalous
misrepresentation of facts concerning officers who
died in his service. It is the same thing with the
story of Mr. Stanley's clothes and articles of toilet ;
the same with the doubtful repetition of conversa-

tion between Mr. Stanley and Major Barttelot ; the same with the account of the journey up the Congo. It is very difficult to follow the truth in and out of this maze of journalistic narration, which is arranged so as to show one figure alone in a good light.

' Mr. Stanley attributes the fate of the rear column to malign influences. He certainly ought to know best what adjectives to apply, for the influences were none other than those arising from his own arrangements and actions, and were entirely of his own making. The rear column was powerless to move from Yambuya without carriers. Their position was as follows : Some 600 loads to carry, 160 to 170 men to carry them ; some 40 sick men to carry. To effect this in marches of six miles, each man would have to carry loads four times over the six miles. Thus, to advance six miles each man would have to travel forty-two miles, being three double and one single journey, and a camp would have to be guarded at either end of the march. So long as the stores were in camp they were easily guarded by the few men. On the march this would have been impossible, especially as the Zanzibaris left at Yambuya were the scum of the Expedition, and had to be disarmed, and were even ready to desert to the Arabs. Also, in the face of Mr. Stanley's promise to return in November, it would seem utter folly to attempt such a hazardous advance, when at the most eighty or one hundred miles might be

covered, at very great risk to the whole column, and
to little purpose.

'Moreover, Mr. Stanley had always intended the
rear column to await his return at Yambuya, and it
was only at Major Barttelot's earnest entreaty that
he gave him permission to advance if he could, and
if he preferred to do so. And even if he had been
able to advance (which Mr. Stanley in his letters to
Major Barttelot from the front doubted), Mr. Stanley
had sent to order him not to advance beyond
Mugwye's in the forest.

'The rear column was in a trap. Major Barttelot
was not deceived by Tippu-Tib, but, to his horror,
found himself placed by Mr. Stanley completely in
the power of this unscrupulous slave-trader, for what
purpose remains to be explained. Mr. Stanley's
grave errors are not lessened by casting blame
wrongfully, and in a manner so unworthy of a man,
upon those who are dead in order to shield himself.

'Yours, etc.,

'WALTER G. BARTTELOT.'

Sir W. Mackinnon and the Committee received a
letter from Major Barttelot, dated June 10, 1888, in
which he states that he found that 80 per cent. of
the caps are unfit for use, and the Zanzibar bales of
cloth the same.

The Committee never published this letter, and
took no trouble to defend the memory of the officers
who were sacrificed in their interests.

As Mr. Stanley has not replied to this letter comment is unnecessary. To show the absolute pettiness of these insinuations concerning the loads and the value he set on them, the first thing Mr. Stanley did almost after meeting the rear column was to take £1,000 worth of loads and distribute them among the Zanzibaris and Soudanese. These were the loads the poor officers had so zealously guarded, according to instructions, for the relief of Emin Pasha (p. 13, vol. ii., 'Darkest Africa': £760 to the Nyanza force, and £283 to the Banalya men).

If the camp at Yambuya was maintained without any overt action of war, and without a single shot being fired in its defence, it was not because there were no enemies to its peace. As soon as possible after Mr. Stanley's departure, the Arabs began to arrive, coming on continually towards Yambuya in ever-increasing numbers. From Yangambi on the Congo to Banalya on the Aruwimi, north-east of Yambuya, a complete cordon of Arab camps was formed, closing every track into the forest, and barring any advance of the rear column to the east.

A glance at the map I have prepared will sufficiently show the position. The number of men in the Arab camps varied from time to time, as they went on their merciless errands, raiding the native villages for ivory, capturing slaves, killing their victims, and practising their inhuman cannibal achievements.

Salem Mohammed's camp was placed close to Major Barttelot's.

The number of men there would be two or three hundred ; sometimes more, sometimes less. Kasima of Yaraweko had at least 100. Sala Sala told Major Barttelot that he had 1,000 men ; that would probably be an exaggeration, though, if he included the native slaves, it was possible.

Abdulla Korona had a large force at Banalya, Nasiboo a small number of men at Yambu.

All these were in communication with Singatini, Tippu-Tib's headquarters at the Falls, where large bodies of men were continually being collected, to be sent raiding down the various rivers, from which favourable reports had been received by Tippu, as to value likely to be obtained in slaves and ivory.

Ugarrowwa was also moving down the Aruwimi with some 800 men towards Yambuya, having heard of the rear column and its stores of powder from Mr. Stanley : at the time of Major Barttelot's death he had arrived at Mugwye's.

The Arabs would not commit an open act of war, but they tried by every provocation to drive the garrison to exasperation—as Major Barttlelot has thoroughly explained. There was every reason to make an impetuous man rush into open conflict, and do or die, rather than suffer the tortures the officers at Yambuya had to undergo, and the miseries they had to witness and endure ; as Mr. Stanley says : ' I would have wagered he (Barttelot) would have seized that flowing gray beard of Tippu-Tib and pounded the face to pulp, even in the midst of his power, rather than allow himself to be thus cajoled time and time again' (p. 494, vol. i., 'Darkest Africa'). Yes ; that, no doubt, is what was expected. But Major Barttelot did not allow himself to do any-thing of the kind : he preferred to carry out Mr. Stanley's instructions, although at times his powers of self-restraint, from this persecution and provocation, were tried almost beyond the limit of endurance, and the severity of the camp discipline became almost intolerable.

It was that discipline—so irksome, so miserable, so cruel—that alone saved the camp and the stores. The fear of the dire punishment by flogging and the death penalty alone prevented the wholesale deser-tion of the men from this starving camp. If the commander for a moment had allowed the gentler feelings of his nature to outweigh his knowledge of the military necessities of his position, his men would have been utterly demoralized by the Arabs who surrounded him. Of this Mr. Stanley had bitter experience at Ugarrowwa's and Kilonga Longa's, and his camp would have been deserted and looted. Twice Major Barttelot had to make examples, and use the death penalty ; in one case it was unfortu-nately remitted at the request of the officers, and the man was flogged instead ; and he eventually died.

The camp was, as a matter of fact, in a state of siege, and discipline alone saved it. No Arab was allowed into the camp unless specially permitted, and barter and sale were forbidden between the Arabs and the garrison. According to the instructions, Mr. Stanley says : ' I associate Mr. J. S. Jameson with you at present ; Messrs. Troup, Ward, and Bonny will submit to your authority. In the ordinary duties of the defence and the conduct of the camp or march, there is only one chief—which is yourself.' This was Major Barttelot's authority from Mr. Stanley to take command. He accepted it, and the responsibility of it. ' But should any vital step be proposed to be taken, I beg you will take the voice of Mr. Jameson also.' I believe Mr. Jameson's journals show that Major Barttelot acted fully on this instruction in letter and spirit. ' And when Messrs. Ward and Troup are here, pray admit them to your confidence, and let them speak freely their opinions.' Mr. Ward and Mr. Troup did give their opinions, and often constituted a Board for the decision of some important question, though Major Barttelot was not bound in any way by the instructions to carry out their views if opposed to his own and Mr. Jameson's.

Major Barttelot was not instructed to consult Mr. Bonny at all, but I find that he did take his opinion a good deal, being alone with him for some time. And when Mr. Troup returned to camp, so ill, in April, Bonny had to take over the charge of the stores, as well as look after the Zanzibari company. Ward was then away on his journey to St. Paul de

Loanda, and Jameson at Kasongo. As Mr. Bonny was the only white man present at the time of Major Barttelot's death—and as my brother in his letter had spoken so kindly of him—I called on him when he arrived in England, and had two interviews with him, when he gave me startling items of information, and seemed to have no regard for any single officer of the Expedition except himself.

With regard to the disposition of Mr. Stanley's forces, from a military standpoint, a glance at the map will show the folly of Mr. Stanley's arrangements.

He forms a camp at Yambuya, where he places the powder and goods for Emin's relief, and advances 600 miles to the Lake Albert without providing stations or means of communication with the rear, and without taking anything to relieve Emin with, so that when he sees Emin, it is only to shake hands with him and then leave him to be captured by the rebels. In this long tract of 600 miles between himself and his gunpowder are two great caravans of Arabs, devastating the country, Ugarrowwa and Kilonga Longa ; and for miles round Yambuya the Arabs are in force. Imagine Major Barttelot to advance, trying to transport these 660 loads with the men he had fit to carry, some 160 or 170. How would he have passed through or by these Arab camps ? He would have lost every man and every load. The proof is before us ; as soon as he *did* march the Zanzibaris deserted, and

he had to go again to Tippu-Tib to get chains to
punish them. Supposing he had managed, however,
to avoid the first line of Arab camps, and to have
reached Mugwye's. They would have had the Arabs
following on their track, and Ugarrowwa advancing
on them from the front ; and they would have had
the same difficulties to encounter at Mugwye's as at
Yambuya, only in a more difficult and out-of-the-way
situation. Had they gone there and perished, no
diaries or papers would ever have come forth to
throw a light on the doings in ' Darkest Africa.'
They would have been blamed for not waiting for
Tippu-Tib's men, and the absurdity of their advancing under such circumstances would have been
trumpeted forth to the world.

There is only one excuse for the arrangements
made ; viz., that there were other objects in view,
and that the rear column was intended for some
other purpose than the relief of Emin Pasha.*

If Tippu-Tib had not been brought further than
Bolobo, and if the steamer used for his people had
brought up the whole rear column, they could all
have advanced either together, or in two columns
parallel, or one behind the other.

---

* According to the papers laid before Parliament, of which see
copies in the Appendix, there was an idea of bringing Emin's
women and refugees home by the Congo ; but nothing of this is
mentioned to Major Barttelot as far as we know ; nor does it
appear that the Committee did make any arrangements for that
purpose, although that was De Winton's chief argument for taking
the Congo route.

There is only one difficulty in African travel,
viz., to obtain food and porters. That difficulty
is forced upon Major Barttelot without any sufficient reason.

Mr. Stanley says (vol. ii., p. 13, 'Darkest Africa')
that a caravan such as Major Barttelot started with
from Yambuya could only be conducted by a head
Arab whom the others would obey, such as Tippu-
Tib. Then why, as Tippu was brought by Mr.
Stanley so far, did he not take him on with him?

But as Mr. Stanley thoroughly knew and understood Tippu-Tib, and was on most amicable terms
with him, and seeing that the arrangements he had
made precluded an advance of the rear column, the
solution of this question can only be found from a
knowledge of the objects and aims of the Expedition
other than that of the relief, pure and simple, of
Emin Pasha.

That the camp, with its wealth, was a centre of
attraction, drawing upon itself the swarms of dusky
beings who, under Arab guidance, were haunting
the shades of that vast forest by the Aruwimi, just
as a lamp attracts moths, and so enabled Mr. Stanley,
once out of the forest, to feel that he was secured
from their hated presence, is a fact of no slight
significance. For instance, how different the life
in camp at Fort Bodo to the life in the camp at
Yambuya! The one surrounded by pleasant fields
of corn, fruit, and tobacco; the other always
shadowed by the illimitable forest. At Fort Bodo

there were no annoyances but those caused by a few elephants and natives, who were easily chased away, until not one remained within eight miles of the camp; at Yambuya they endured a siege of eleven months' duration, and were completely in the hands of the minions of Tippu-Tib. At Fort Bodo the officers were at rest, having seen Emin and the Lake, their mission partly accomplished; at Yambuya the officers were in torment, deceived, deserted, and hope so long deferred had made the heart sick. If the officers at the camp at Yambuya had blundered a thousand times, and if they had committed the greatest follies, the life they had led would have atoned for all in the eyes of a generous English commander. But having loyally carried out their instructions; having maintained the camp in spite of Mr. Stanley's arrangements, and kept their patience in spite of his expectations; and having obtained, no thanks to Mr. Stanley, the carriers they did; having pledged their credit for payment, and having lost their lives or their health in his service, Mr. Stanley turns upon the victims of his will, and treats the living and the dead with contumely and base ingratitude.

MAJOR BARTTELOT's LAST REPORT.

On September 20, 1888, I had an interview with Mr. Burdett Coutts, of the Relief Committee, at Holly Lodge, when, among other things, he told me that Sir Francis de Winton, who was Acting

Secretary to the Committee, had actually suggested
to leave out of the published report of this, my
brother's last despatch, all remarks as to Tippu-
Tib's treachery, and that he (Mr. Burdett Coutts)
had pointed out what a very unfair thing that would
be ; so they were published.   But I do not think
the whole of the report is published even now ;
certainly none of the lists of loads, etc., so carefully
sent home, have been.   It was to the interest of the
Committee not to divulge much.   They were far
too nearly concerned : they were in Mr. Stanley's
hands.

To Mr. WILLIAM MACKINNON, PRESIDENT OF THE
EMIN PASHA RELIEF EXPEDITION.

'Yambuya Camp, *June* 4, 1888.

'SIR,

'I have the honour to report to you that
we are about to make a move, though with far less
numbers than I originally intended.   Tippu-Tib has
at last, but with great reluctance, given us 400 men.
I have also obtained from another Arab called Muni
Somai 30 more carriers.   We shall move not earlier
than June 9, and our forces will be as follows :
Soudanese 22, rifles 22 ; Zanzibaris 110, rifles 110,
loads 90 ; Manyuema 430, muskets 300, loads 380.
The officers who are going are Major Barttelot, in
command ; Mr. J. S. Jameson, second in command ;
Mr. W. Bonny ; Sheik Muni Somai, in command of
the Manyuema force.

'Sheik Muni Somai is an Arab of Kibuyeh, who volunteered to accompany the Expedition as commander under me of the native contingent.

'On May 8 the Belgian steamer *A.I.A.*, with M. Van Kerkhoven, the chief of Bangala, arrived here, having on board Mr. Ward's escort of thirty Zanzibaris and four Soudanese, one Soudanese dying at Bangala.

'*May* 11.—They left us to go to Stanley Falls.

'*May* 14.—I left for Stanley Falls, going overland, and catching the steamer at Yallasula, on the Congo. I proceeded with the Belgians to the Falls on May 22.

'Mr. Jameson and Tippu-Tib, with 400 men, returned from Kasongo.

'Mr. Jameson wrote to you while at Kasongo of his proceedings there. He told me on arrival that Tippu-Tib had promised him 800 men, but would make no written agreement with him.

'*May* 23.—I had my palaver with Tippu-Tib. He then told me he could only let me have 400 men, 300 of whom were to carry 40-lb. loads, and 100 20-lb. loads. He said the men were present, and ready to start as soon as I had my loads ready. I told him of what he had promised Mr. Jameson at Kasongo, but he said never had any mention of 800 men been made, only of the 400; that it was quite impossible he could give us more men, as he was short of men at Kasongo and Nyangwe, as he was at present engaged in so many wars that he had completely drained the country. I was forced to submit, but hoped that he might be able to collect another hundred or so at and around Yambuya.

'Tippu then asked me if I wanted a head-man, stating that in the former agreement Mr. Stanley had said that if a head-man was taken he should be paid. I replied, "Certainly I want a head-man." He then presented me to the Arab, Muni Somai. This man agreed to come, and I send you the terms I settled with him. I got back to Camp Yambuya May 30.

'*June* 4.—The *Stanley* steamer arrived, and the *A.I.A.*, the former bringing Belgian officers for the Falls station, the latter Tippu-Tib himself.

'*June* 5.—I had another palaver with Tippu-Tib, asking him where were the 250 men already sent. He explained to me that they had been dispersed, and on trying to collect them they refused to come, owing to the bad reports brought in by the deserters, and that as they were subjects, and not slaves, he could not force them. That was the reason why he had brought 400 entirely fresh men from Kasongo for us.

'However, Tippu said he could let me have 30 more men of Muni Somai. This, as I was so terribly short of men, I agreed to.

'Muni Somai himself appears a willing man, and very anxious to do his best. He volunteered for the business. I trust you will not think his payment excessive; but the anxiety it takes away as regards his men and the safety of the loads is enormous for he is responsible for all the Manyuema and the loads they carry, and thus saves the white officers an amount of work and responsibility which they can now devote to other purposes.

'The loads we do not take are to be sent to Bangala. They will be loaded up in the *A.I.A.* or *Stanley* on June 8, a receipt being given for them by Mr. Van Kerkhoven, which is marked B and forwarded to you, also a letter of instructions to him and to Mr. Ward. Perhaps you would kindly give the requisite order concerning the loads and the two canoes purchased in March for Mr. Ward's transport, also for those stores purchased by Mr. Ward on behalf of the Expedition, as it is nearly certain I shall not return this way, and shall therefore have no further need of them or him. Mr. Troup, who is in a terrible condition of debility and internal disarrangement, is proceeding home at his own request. Mr. Bonny's certificate of his unfitness is attached, and his application marked E, also letters concerning passage, etc., to M. Fontaine, marked F. I have given him a passage home at the expense of the Expedition, as I am sure it would be your and their wish.

'The interpreter Assad Farran I am also sending home. He has been, and is, utterly useless to me, and is in failing health; and if I took him with me I would only, after a few marches, have either to carry or leave him, and I am terribly short of carriers.

18

So I have ventured to send him home with a steerage passage to Cairo, and have sent a letter to the Consul-General, Cairo, concerning him; also a copy of agreement made by Assad Farran with me on his proceeding home, also papers of interpreter Alexander Hadad, who died June 24, 1887, both marked G. These two interpreters made no sort of agreement concerning pay, terms of service, etc., when they agreed to come on this Expedition in February, 1887, so perhaps you would kindly inform the proper authorities on that subject. With British troops in Egypt, as interpreters, they would have received not more than £6 a month and their rations, for as interpreters they were both very inferior.

'A Soudanese soldier with a diseased leg is also proceeding down country. Besides these there are four other Soudanese and twenty-nine Zanzibaris who are unable to proceed with us. Tippu-Tib has kindly consented to get these to Zanzibar as best he can. A complete list of them, their payments, etc., will be forwarded to the Consul at Zanzibar, and I have requested him to forward on the Soudanese to Egypt.

'My intentions on leaving this camp are to make the best of my way along the same route taken by Mr. Stanley; should I get no tidings of him along the road, to proceed as far as Kavalli, and then, if I hear nothing there, to proceed to Kibero. If I can ascertain either at Kavalli or Kibero his where-

abouts, no matter how far it may be, I will endeavour to reach him. Should he be in a fix, I will do
my utmost to relieve him. If neither at Kavalli nor
Kibero I can obtain tidings of him, I shall go on to
Wadelai and ascertain from Emin Pasha, if he be
there still, if he has any news of Mr. Stanley, also
of his own intentions as regards staying or leaving.
I will persuade him, if possible, to come out with
me, and, if necessary, aid me in my search for Mr.
Stanley. Should it for sundry reasons be unnecessary to look further for Mr. Stanley, I will place
myself and force at his disposal to act as his escort,
proceeding by whichever route is most feasible, so
long as it is not through Uganda, as in that event
the Manyuemas would leave me, and I have
promised Tippu-Tib they shall not go there, and
that I will bring them back or send a white officer
with them back to their own country by the shortest
and quickest route on completion of my object.
This is always supposing Emin Pasha to be there
and willing to come away. It may be he only needs
ammunition to get away by himself, in which case
I would in all probability be able to supply him,
and would send three-fourths of my Zanzibar force
and my two officers with him, and would myself with
the other Zanzibaris accompany the Manyuemas
back to Tippu-Tib's country, and so to the coast
by the shortest route, viz., by the Mwueta-Nzigi,
Tanganyika and Ugigi. This is also the route I
should take should we be unable to find Stanley, or,

from the reasons either that he is not there or does not wish to come, relieve Emin Pasha.

' I need not tell you that all our endeavours will be most strenuous to make the quest in which we are going a success, and I hope that my actions may meet with the approval of the Committee, and that they will suspend all judgment concerning those actions, either in the present, past or future, till I or Mr. Jameson return home.

' Rumour is always rife, and is seldom correct, concerning Mr. Stanley. I can hear no news whatever, though my labours in that direction have been most strenuous. He is not dead, to the best of my belief nor of the Arabs here or at Kasongo. I have been obliged to open Mr. Stanley's boxes, as I cannot carry all his stuff, and I had no other means of ascertaining what was in them. Two cases of Madeira were also sent him. One case I am sending back ; the other has been half given to Mr. Troup, the other half we take as medical comforts. Concerning Tippu-Tib I have nothing to say beyond that he has broken faith with us, and can only conjecture from surrounding events and circumstances the cause of his unreasonable delay in supplying men, and the paucity of that supply.

' I deem it my bounden duty to proceed on this business, in which I am fully upheld by both Mr. Jameson and Mr. Bonny ; to wait longer would be both useless and culpable, as Tippu-Tib has not the remotest intention of helping us any more, and to withdraw would be pusillanimous, and, I am certain, entirely contrary to your wishes and those of the Committee.

' I calculate it will take me from three to four months to reach the lakes, and from seven to nine more to reach the coast.

' Should you think and the Committee agree that the sum is excessive to give Muni Somai, and are not prepared to meet it, or, maybe, are prepared to place only a portion of that at my disposal for that purpose, both Mr. Jameson and I are fully prepared to meet it, or the remaining portion of it, as it is entirely for our benefit he is coming ; though, of course, it must be remembered that our object is to reach our destination with as many of our loads as possible, and that our individual hold over the Manyuema without outside aid would be nil. Should you agree to place the sum at my disposal, please arrange accordingly ; if only a portion, that portion, for he has received an advance in powder, cloth, beads and cowries to the value of £128. In case of not meeting it, or only a portion of it, please inform Sir Walter Barttelot, Carlton Club. I insert this as it is most necessary the money should be there when wanted, as Arabs and all Orientals are most punctilious in pecuniary transactions.

' I have much pleasure in stating that from all the officers of the State with whom I have come in contact, or from whom I have solicited aid, I have met with a most willing and ready response, which is highly gratifying. I would particularly mention Captain Van Kerkhoven, chief of Bangala, and Lieutenant Liebriechts, chief of Stanley Pool, and I trust that they may meet with the reward and merit they deserve.

'*June* 6.—This morning Tippu-Tib sent for me and asked me if I thought he would get his money* for the men. I told him I could give no assurance of that. He then said he must have a guarantee, which I and Mr. Jameson have given; terms of agreement and guarantee are attached. All receipts, agreements, etc., made between Arabs and myself, and signed by them, I have sent to Mr. Holmwood, and the copies of same to you.

'*June* 8.—This morning I had the loads for Tippu-Tib's and Muni Somai's men stacked; and Tippu-Tib himself came down to see them prior to issuing. However, he took exception to the loads, said they were too heavy (the heaviest was 45 lb.), and his men could not carry them. Two days before he had expressed his approbation of the weight of the very same loads he refused to-day. I pointed out to him that he, as well as I, knew the difficulty of getting any load other than a bale to scale the exact weight, and that the loads his men carried were far above the prescribed weight of 60 lb. We were to have started to-morrow, so we shall not now start till June 11 or 12, as I am going to make all his loads

---

* The original contract Mr. Stanley said he made with Tippu-Tib cannot have been very explicit.

weigh exactly 40 lb. It is partly our fault, as we should have been more particular to get the exact weight. The average weight over due was about 2 lb., some loads being 2 lb. under. But it is not the weight of the loads he takes exception to —in reality, it is having to perform the business at all. He has been almost forced to it by letters received from Mr. Holmwood against his own, and more than against the wish of his fellow Arabs ; and, filled with aspirations and ambitions of a very large nature, the whole business has become thoroughly distasteful to him, which even his professed friendship for Stanley cannot overcome. His treatment of us this morning showed that most thoroughly. But should he not act up to his contract, I hope it will be taken most serious notice of when it comes to the day of settling up. He has got us tight fixed at present, but it should not always be so.

'On our road lie many Arab settlements to within a month of Lake Albert Nyanza, though the distance between some of them is bad, and the inhabitants of that distance warlike. I shall, whenever opportunity offers, hire carriers, if not for the whole time, at any rate from station to station, for, of course, death, sickness and desertions must be looked for, and I must get my loads in as intact as possible to my destination.

' This is when Muni Somai will be so useful. We seem to have paid a big price for his services, but

then he is a big Arab, and in proportion to his big-
ness is his influence over the Manyuema to keep them
together, to stop desertions, thefts, etc. A lesser
Arab would have been cheaper, but his influence
would have been less, and in consequence our loads
gradually less ; and loads mean health, and life, and
success, and therefore cannot be estimated at too
high a value. We are carrying light loads, and
intend to do at first very easy marches, and, when I
get into the open country by Uganda, to push
on.

'We weighed all the loads before one of Tippu-
Tib's head-men, and he passed loads which had been
condemned shortly before in the morning, which
fully shows that for some reason or other he wishes
to delay us here, but for what purpose I cannot
say.

'*June* 9.—We shall easily be able to start by the
11th, but I am sorry to say our loss of ammunition
by the lightening of the loads—for it was the ammunition they particularly took notice of—is something
enormous.

' Both the *A.I.A.* and the *Stanley* left this morning
for Stanley Falls, but Tippu-Tib and his Belgian
secretary remain behind, also four ships' carpenters,
whom Captain Van Gèle and M. Van Kirkhoven left
with us to help us. The Belgians have behaved
with very great kindness to us, and helped us on
our way enormously.

' Before I close I would wish to add that the

services of Mr. J. S. Jameson have been, are, and
will be, invaluable to me. Never during his period
of service with me have I had one word of com-
plaint from him. His alacrity, capacity, and willingness to work are unbounded, while his cheeriness
and kindly disposition have endeared him to all.
I have given Ward orders about any telegram
you may send, and Tippu-Tib has promised he
will send a messenger after me should it be necessary, provided I have not started more than a
month.

'Tippu-Tib waits here to see me off.

'I am sending a telegram to you to announce our
departure, and I will endeavour, through the State,
to send you news whenever I can. But it would
not surprise me if the Congo route was not blocked
later on.

'I have not sent you a copy of Mr. Holmwood's
letter, as it was not official, but of all others I have.
I think I told you of everything of which I can
write. There are many things I would wish to
speak of, and no doubt I will do so should I be
permitted to return home.

'Our ammunition (Remington) is as follows:
Rifles, 128; reserve rounds, per rifle, 279; rounds
with rifle, 20 = 35,580.

'*June* 10.—The loads have been weighed and
handed over—powder and caps issued to the
Manyuema force; and we are all ready to start, which
we shall do to-morrow morning. I have told you of

all now I can think of, but I would bring finally to
your notice that Tippu-Tib has broken his faith and
contract with us. The man Muni Somai, I think,
means business, and therefore I trust all will be
well.

        ' I have, etc.,

           ' EDMUND M. BARTTELOT, Major.

' AGREEMENTS BETWEEN MUNI SOMAI AND MAJOR
    BARTTELOT AND MR. JAMESON.

I.

'Stanley Falls, May 24, 1888.

' I, the undersigned, Muni Somai, hereby agree
for the sum of £1,000 (one thousand pounds sterling),
to be paid to me in goods of that value before our
departure from Yambuya Camp, to faithfully serve
and obey Major Barttelot in my capacity of commander of the 400 men supplied to the Emin Pasha
Relief Expedition by Sheik Hamed bin Mohammed,
and to accompany him with these men as far as
Wadelai, or whatever place short of that it may be
necessary for Major Barttelot to go to in his quest
of Emin Pasha and Mr. Stanley, and to return from
thence with the aforesaid men, with him (Major
Barttelot), or whatever white officer he may appoint,
by the nearest route to the territory of Sheik Hamed
bin Mohammed, after he (Major Barttelot) considers
his relief of Emin Pasha, or Mr. Stanley, or both, to
have been accomplished. And I also agree in case

of Major Barttelot being rendered incapable of continuing his command to fulfil all the above conditions
under whatever white officer he (Major Barttelot)
may appoint.

'Signed   { HAMED BIN MOHAMMED
           { MUNI SOMAI.

'Witnessed { EDMUND M. BARTTELOT.
           { JAMES S. JAMESON.'

II.

'Stanley Falls, *May* 24, 1888.

'We, the undersigned, Major Barttelot, commanding the rear-guard of the Emin Pasha Relief Expedition, and Mr. James S. Jameson, officer of the
same, hereby agree to pay to Muni Somai the sum
of £1,000, 600 dollars of which sum to be paid to
him in goods of that value before our departure
from Yambuya Camp, under the following conditions :

'That he (Muni Somai) faithfully serves and
obeys Major Barttelot in his capacity of leader of the
400 men supplied by Sheik Hamed bin Mohammed
to the Emin Pasha Relief Expedition, and to accompany him with those men to Wadelai, or whatever
place short of that he (Major Barttelot) may have to
go in his quest of Emin Pasha or Mr. Stanley ; and
that he (Muni Somai) returns with these men under
Major Barttelot, or whatever white officer he may
appoint, by the shortest route to the territory of

Sheik Hamed bin Mohammed at whatsoever time he (Major Barttelot) may consider his relief of Emin Pasha, or Mr. Stanley, or both, to have been accomplished ; and that he (Muni Somai) also agrees, in case of Major Barttelot being rendered incapable of continuing his command, to fulfil all the above conditions under whatever white officer he (Major Barttelot) may appoint. The said Muni Somai having fulfilled all the above conditions, we, the undersigned, agree to pay him the remaining sum as soon as possible after our return to Zanzibar or Banana Point.

'Signed { EDMUND M. BARTTELOT.
          { J. S. JAMESON.

'Witnessed { TIPPU-TIB.
           { MUNI SOMAI.'

At this date (June 1888, Yambuya) Major Barttelot wrote letters to the following, mostly in duplicate, and copied in his letter-book :

To Mons. Fontaine, chief of the Dutch House, Banana, concerning Mr. Troup's going home, and making necessary arrangements for his passage, etc. One copy to M. Fontaine, and one to Mr. Mackinnon.

To Mons. Liebriechts, Commissaire de District de Stanley Pool, for Mr. Troup's transport from Leopoldville to Banana. One copy to Liebriechts, and one to Mackinnon.

To Mr. Van Kerkhoven, Commissaire de District

de Bangala, requesting him to take charge of the
stores sent to Bangala, and to hand them over to
Mr. Ward on his arrival. One copy of letter to
Mr. Van Kerkhoven, and one to Mackinnon.

To Mr. Van Gèle, Commissaire de District de
Stanley Pool, to arrange passages and pay for Mr.
Troup, Assad Farran, and two others as far as
Leopoldville. Also to arrange as follows : ' Mr.
Ward, when he returns to Bangala, is bringing up
four guns as payment for the canoes which brought
him down from the Falls last March, for which we
have to pay Tippu-Tib at the rate of two guns per
canoe. Please get these guns from Mr. Ward, and
kindly pay Tippu-Tib.' One copy to Mr. Van Gèle,
and one to Mr. Mackinnon.

Letter to Frederick Holmwood, Esq., Consul,
Zanzibar, detailing all arrangements with Tippu-Tib,
and enclosing copies of agreements with Muni
Somai and with Tippu-Tib ; also an agreement with
Muni Somai for thirty men to carry 40 lb. at seven
dollars a month, an advance of four months' pay
being given in powder here. Also to arrange for
payment of sick men, Zanzibaris and Soudanese,
left in charge of Tippu to convey to Zanzibar, and
passage for the Soudanese to Cairo. ' I am not very
sanguine of this business, after Tippu's base treatment of us. . . . Each man bears a paper with
the word " Wangwarra " written on it, and my name
underneath.' The number and names were enclosed
in a list.

' To Her Britannic Majesty's Consul-General,
Cairo.

' Sir,

' I have the honour to inform you, on behalf
of the Commander of the Emin Pasha Expedition,
that I am sending home an interpreter called
Assad Farran, engaged by Mr. Stanley in Cairo in
February, 1887. No agreement of pay was made
between this man and Mr. Stanley; it must therefore be settled by the Committee, concerning which
I have written to them. Please, therefore, give
no advance of pay till such information be forthcoming.

' I am also sending home six sick Soudanese,
whose names are on a list attached, and whose
monthly pay is 150 piastres, less two months' advance
and fines for loss of kit, all attached. The terms of
agreement under which Assad Farran goes home
are attached, which, if he breaks, he forfeits pay and
character.

' I have the honour to be, etc.,

' Edmund M. Barttelot.'

One copy to Sir E. Baring, and one to Mr. Mackinnon.

Terms of Agreement with Assad Farran.

' I, Assad Farran, interpreter to the Soudanese
Company of the Emin Pasha Relief Expedition, on

being permitted to return home at my own request, do hereby state that through my own negligence no terms of agreement concerning pay, service, or rations were entered into between Mr. Stanley and myself when I volunteered to accompany the Expedition, offering my services to Mr. Stanley personally at Shepherd's Hotel, Cairo, in February, 1887. I do further swear on oath that I will not divulge, or cause to be divulged, any information concerning the Expedition, its movements, the movements of any individual of the Expedition, during my period of service with it, till six months after the official report has been published in England, on pain of forfeiting all claims to pay and character. I do further faithfully promise to proceed straight to Cairo on leaving the Expedition, or be subject to same penalty as above.

(*Signed*)   'ASSAD FARRAN.'

One copy to Sir E. Baring and one to Mr. Mackinnon.

INSTRUCTIONS TO MR. WARD, WHO HAD GONE TO THE COAST WITH A TELEGRAM, SENT BY THE STEAMER TO AWAIT HIM AT BANGALA, DATED JUNE 4.

' SIR,

' On arrival at Bangala you will report yourself to the chief of the station, and take over the stores from him belonging to the Expedition. You

will remain at Bangala till you receive orders from
the Committee concerning yourself and the loads
. . . . On receiving your orders you will inform
the Committee of your proceedings.

'I have the honour to be, etc.,

(*Signed*) 'EDMUND M. BARTTELOT, Major.

'P.S.—All the stores ordered for the Expedition
which you may have brought up with you will be
included in the list of stores handed over by Mr.
Van Kerkhoven to you. You will hand over to
Mr. Van Kerkhoven one box of pressed meat. Any
private stores you may have brought up for me
personally hand over to Mr. Van Gèle, and four
guns. [The guns were to be given to Tippu as
payment for some canoes.]

'Should you bring a telegram of recall, you will
make arrangements with the chief of the station to
forward it to the Falls, where a messenger awaits it.
You will not, however, send any other message after
me, nor will you on any account leave Bangala till
you receive orders from home.'

[Mr. Stanley finds it difficult to understand why
Mr. Ward was sent with a telegram to the Committee at home. The reason is simple. There are
two sides to the African Continent, and Major
Barttelot expected the Committee might have news
of Mr. Stanley from Zanzibar. Major Barttelot was
quite prepared to hear that the relief had been

effected, and to receive a telegram of recall. The Committee might also be reasonably supposed to have a wish to know what was going on.

Mr. Stanley then wonders why Mr. Ward had orders to remain at Bangala. He was to remain there to look after the goods, as Tippu-Tib's behaviour had made Major Barttelot doubt the policy of leaving them at the Falls Station, as originally intended.

Mr. Stanley, in his letter of May 2, 1890, to Sir Walter Barttelot, blames Major Barttelot for sending rations to the Belgians of Bangala. This letter to Mr. Ward shows that the ' rations ' consisted of one box of pressed meat and Major Barttelot's own private stores.]

CHAPTER XIII.

Important Letters and Extracts from Letters written on Departure from Yambuya to Sir Redvers Buller, V.C., Sir Walter Barttelot and others—Letter from Sir Redvers Buller.

ON this, the eve of his departure from Yambuya, Major Barttelot wrote several letters home, and sent them off by the steamers. I give the following extracts :

To Major Sclater, R.A. : ' I was very much amused to-day. I asked Tippu-Tib what excuse I shall give the Committee, and the reason why the 250 men sent for us last February were not forth-coming. He said they were dispersed while waiting, and were impregnated with distaste for the business by reports which deserters circulated, and refused to come ; that they were free men and subjects, and he could not force them. Humbug, pure and simple. It is true the Manyuema are not slaves in the accept-ance of the word; but they are this much under him,

that he can order so many men, or as many as he
likes, from any district in his territory, to go anywhere for any purpose ; and if the men bolt or
refuse, he chains them, and the courbash is not
wanting. . . . . Doubtless you have much better
information than we have as regards both Stanley
and Emin, and we are entirely dependent on the
Arabs, who are born liars and actors.'

To Miss ——— : 'I shall be sorry and glad to
leave Yambuya : sorry, because the place has been
our home for so long, and because there I made one
of the firmest friendships I shall ever make in this
world—viz., with Jameson ; he and I were thrown
together in the first instance, and suffered real hard-
ships during the first two months of our stay. Such
a man is met with but once in a lifetime.

' I shall be glad to leave because I am surrounded
by hatred and treachery. Living among Arabs is
not a bed of roses. If we were not a relief party,
our force would be ample ; but it is the stores which
trouble me ; but I hope, somehow or another, it may
turn out good for us. Bonny is a mixture of con-
ceit, bravery and ignorance ; he is most useful with
the natives and Arabs ; of a slow temperament, he
is just suited to them. He purchases all supplies
for us, and doctors the sick, for he was a non-com-
missioned officer in the Army Medical Department.
His continual cry is that he is every bit as good as
we are, and must be treated the same. Stanley
was very down on him, and he was very bitter

about it. Since he has been with me I have done all I can for him. I am writing this by the light of palm-oil lamps. Palm-oil is also constantly used in our food: it is the stuff they grease the railway-carriage wheels with at home! My house all day is full of Arabs, come to say "Good-bye," and to see what they can get. Luckily it is the feast of Ramadan now, and a good deal of their time, especially towards evening, is taken up with prayer, which is fortunate for me. Two of our number are going home. Troup goes home at once: poor fellow! he is very ill; and Ward will, I expect, be ordered to return home.

'Three-quarters of our men are slaves; and when they get to Zanzibar, poor fellows! they only receive one-fourth of their money; the rest goes to their masters.

'My little boy, called Sudi bin Bohati, is a slave, but I shall purchase his discharge, for, though a wooden-headed little beggar, he is honest and willing, and will do anything for me. He is the queerest little mite you ever saw, and, when he has his long clothes on, looks like a baby in its night-dress. He cannot be more than ten years old, yet he can walk twenty-five miles in the day, carrying an axe, my food and tea, and will sit up half the night drying my clothes, and be fit to start again next morning.

'To the best of my belief Stanley is *not* dead: that he may be in a fix I don't deny; and I hope

out of that fix I may get him—a move out of this
camp means a move homewards.

'It was rather amusing this evening (June 4).
When at dinner, an Arab called Sala came down
and said, would I go and read some English letters
Tippu had got to him. I started off: there were
two letters; one was about centrifugal pumps, and
the other about reclaiming slaves, from some
religious society in America! Tippu and I both
roared over it. The simple idea of the biggest
slave-dealer in Central Africa having anything to do
with reclamation is too absurd.

'Tippu said to me to-night, "You look happy,
Major!" I said, "Yes; I have heard from home."
He asked me all about it, and took a keen interest
in all I told him.

'I have no end of letters for Emin Pasha; I
wonder if I shall ever be able to give them to him.
At night here it is very cold, with dense fogs, which
last till the early morning; but it must be a healthy
spot, or else we five could never have survived as we
have done. Tippu's admiration of the camp and its
defences is very great. Certainly it is a strong
place, and would be very hard to take.'

LETTER TO G. A. C. DE TRAFFORD, ESQ.,

'Yambuya, *June* 7, 1888.

'DEAR OLD GALFRID,

'I hope you are well and married by this. I
can only write you a few lines, as I am terribly busy

and short of time. We leave this June 9, and I
have had a bad time of it—what with fevers, Arabs,
natives, and my own men. I hope to be home by
June, '89, but who can tell? Will you kindly do
this for me : there are two Belgian officers here, and
I have ordered them about right and left, and they
have done everything we wanted. So Jameson and
I want to make them a present. We think two
goblets would be the thing—two silver ones, nicely
embossed, with the following inscriptions. For
one :

'PRESENTED TO LIEUTENANT LIEBRIECHTS,
Commissaire de District de Stanley Pool,
'In remembrance of many kindnesses and aid rendered to the
Emin Pasha Relief Expedition,
'By MAJOR EDMUND M. BARTTELOT and
'MR. J. S. JAMESON.
'June, 1888.

'The other cup :

'PRESENTED TO CAPTAIN VAN KERKHOVEN,
'Commissaire de District de Bangala,
'In remembrance of many kindnesses and aid rendered to the
Emin Pasha Relief Expedition,
'By MAJOR EDMUND M. BARTTELOT and
'MR. J. S. JAMESON.
'June, 1888.

'This is what I want put on. The goblets should
be about 18 inches high. You know the sort of
thing. You had best go to Ortner and Houle for
them. . . . I should think £15 apiece ought to do it.
When finished, please tell Ortner and Houle to send

them out, with a card with Jameson's and my compli-
ments, to the following addresses . . . .
This is not much of a letter, but I know you will see
to this for me. Good-bye, dear old chap, and my
best wishes with you.

'E. M. B.

FROM MAJOR BARTTELOT TO HIS SISTER, MRS.
SANDHAM.

'Yambuya, *June* 7, 1888.

'MY DEAREST E.,

'After many disappointments and grievous
vexations, we are going to move, and should leave
this on the 9th—new moon ; perhaps luck. I have
only got 400 men instead of 1,000 ; but that is better
than a poke in the eye with a blunt stick. I
drew a cheque for £5 (June 5) in favour of Troup
at Cox's. You will see it is met, won't you ? Troup
is going home deadly sick. He often lives with
some people near Lancing ; if Charlie went over he
could see him. It would be a kindness if you asked
him to Rowdell. I long to be home, but I must
finish this first. I cannot write much, as I am
terribly busy, for I have so few and such small
carriers I have to alter all the loads. The Belgian
officers have been very good to us. . . . .

. . . .

'P.S.—We leave this June 11, 1888, for abomin-
ation, desolation, and vexation, but I hope in the end

success. Perhaps I may not come back, perhaps I may ; but while there is life there is hope, and God rules all.

'Good-bye, dearest.

'Your affectionate brother,

'E. M. B.

Don't forget Troup at Lancing.'

COPY OF A LETTER FROM MAJOR BARTTELOT TO SIR WALTER BARTTELOT.

'Yambuya Camp, *June* 1, 1888.

'MY DEAREST FATHER,

'I really believe there is some chance of our moving at last. Tippu-Tib has been graciously pleased to give us 400 out of 1,000 men ; says he cannot spare more, as he has much fighting to do ; and as we are entirely in his hands it is no use demurring. Since writing to you in March last I have been very busy going all over the country. I have been twice to the Falls, and a considerable distance up river.

'Jameson has returned from Kasongo, very fit and well. The Belgians came here, bringing back Ward's escort on May 8 in the State steamer the *A.I.A.* They left again on the 11th. They brought us a few papers, but I did not see much news.

'On May 14, this being the date I expected Jameson back, I sent to the Falls, and on May 22

he came. I can get no news of Stanley anyhow ;
—the Arabs know nothing of him ; but he is such
a peculiar man that perhaps even now he may be in
England, and has left us here to moulder. One
thing is, that, with the exception of Troup, we are
all in pretty good health considering our food,
entire want of stimulants, and the solitary lives we
have led. However, when the Belgians came they
fed us up and gave us wine, and I feel quite another
man for it. I am a good deal shrunk, my arms and
legs resembling pipe-stems ; but I don't think I
have lost any of my powers of endurance, and I can
out-walk anybody in this country—native, Arab, or
Zanzibari. I hope you and all are well at home. I
am continually thinking of you, and I do hope and
trust we may both be spared to meet again in this
world. I long to be with you in the quietness of
home. I shall be proud to introduce Jameson to
you. I have seldom met a man like him—sweet-
tempered as a woman, courageous, honest, and a
friend of all.

' Doubtless you will see many hard things about
me in the papers, and blame attached. But this
you must not mind or take the slightest notice of,
because I am fully prepared to meet all foes and
questions, and I undertake to say I will make some
of the Committee jump when I get home.

' Stanley, when he left me here, knew what he
was leaving me to, and partly warned me ; he also
knew how all the Arabs regarded him, but in me he

saw an excellent scapegoat, and gave me a work to perform which he knew perfectly to be well-nigh impossible. That we are going to perform it, with but scant material, is no thanks to him; and had it not been for an untoward event, we should have had our full complement of men. That for the last three months we have been virtually prisoners is, I should think, by now a well-known fact. Every inducement has been offered, every means tried by the Arabs to break the peace; but I have been able to ward it off. Whether Tippu is really in earnest now, and our start a consummated fact, I cannot say. The men are here, the agreement signed, but the fact remains that we are in their hands, with whom no contracts or oaths are binding, and who, if it suits their purpose, will scatter us to the winds.

'Stanley, if he gets home, will no doubt twist events so as to make it appear that all the failure was due to me; but if I come back, too, I can show him up in his true light, for I have not been round these villages and all the Arab stations hereabouts for nothing.

'Of course, we may be successful to a certain extent, but I am not over-sanguine about it. It will take me ten months to go to my extreme point and return to Zanzibar, and heartily glad I shall be to quit this land of lies and treachery.

'To deal with Arabs, you require an urbane disposition, a rare facility for lying, an impassible face, a suave and gentle manner, and a limitless purse. None of these I possess, though they think I possess the latter, because they are told of the vast amount of stores I have, and think they must be mine ; and because I don't give according to their ideas they hate me.

'Tippu is expected here to-day in the Belgian steamer *A.I.A.*

'The Belgian officers wear their hair as long as women, and pointed boots and finikin coats. They have behaved really well to us, and given us no end of stores.

'Van Kerkhoven, their chief, gave me a parrot. They certainly prolonged Troup's life, but I am afraid he won't live to get home ; he is in a shocking state—cannot stand or walk ; if he did it would kill him ; and he is terribly emaciated.

'In case I may not write again, would you kindly have a sum of £25 placed to my credit at Gray, Dawes, and Co., with instructions that I can draw on their house at Zanzibar for that amount, for I shall be almost naked when I get there, though at present I can turn out pretty respectable, with a clean collar, shirt, ... and coat.

'I ought to have grown a beard, as they are much reverenced by all people of colour ; but I have not come to that yet.

'I am expecting the big steamer *Stanley* up daily, though, of course, Ward cannot be here for some time ; and when he does come, he will have to go back again with the loads we do not require to Bangala.

'I am very busy getting our stores ready for the road.

'The next time you ride through Pulborough, please tell Sellers that the two pairs of flannel trousers he made me in '82 are the most serviceable things I have with me, and have worn uncommonly well.

'I wish all my other things had done the same.

'*June* 7.—The steamers *A.I.A.* and *Stanley* came here June 4—the *A.I.A.* bringing Tippu-Tib. We have been terribly busy; I have not written so much for years, and I am not done yet.

'We start (D.V.) on Saturday, June 9.

'There is one thing I must ask of you, but I do not think it will ever be necessary, and you are not to act unless you hear from Mr. William Mackinnon. I am taking a big Arab chief with me, called Muni Somai, and he of course won't come for nothing.

'His price was £1,000, and Jameson and I have guaranteed it, which sum, if the Committee refuse to pay, of course we must.

'I am sure they will pay, but if they do not, Mackinnon is to acquaint you, in which case would you, to save my name, give orders to Gray, Dawes, and Co. that I can draw on their house at Zanzibar for the sum of £500?

'I am terribly vexed to ask for this; but, dear father, who am I to ask if not you? And it should

be paid to my detriment hereafter, for it is a large
sum, and I know how bothered you are about rents,
etc. In any case, I should not require it before
another year, and I shall be more than surprised if
I do then ; but on no account take notice of this till
you hear from Mackinnon.

'What I have written him is this :

'"Should you and the Committee refuse to pay
this, or only pay a portion of it, please inform Sir
Walter Barttelot, Carlton Club, accordingly."

'If they pay a portion of it, you have only to pay
half of the remaining portion.

'Of course I could have got a cheaper man, but
then he would not have had the power or influence
over the Manyuema that a man like this Muni
Somai has, and they would desert with the loads
right and left.

'Our lives, our well-being, the success of our
business, depend on our loads ; and they, again,
depend on the influence brought to bear on the
Manyuema, which, with a small man as chief,
would be nil—with a big Arab, enormous. We
may be successful, and then you will be proud and
glad; and our success depends on these Manyuema
and how they behave, for our own carriers are
very few.

'Good-bye, dear father and mamma, and all others.
It will be months, perhaps, before you hear of us
again, probably not till we arrive at the coast, which
I hope will be in ten months. We are starting in

the cool season, luckily, though rain is rather more plentiful than I care about.

'Our first four days' march will be one of weariness, I expect. in a composite caravan like ours— they always are ; but men and officers will soon fall into their loads and duties, and all will, I hope, go smoothly.   My sincerest love to you all.

  ' Ever your very affectionate son,

    (Signed)   ' EDMUND M. BARTTELOT.'

'P.S. Stanley is not dead to the best of my belief. I can hear nothing about that.

'That he may be in a fix I think possible, but we will (D.V.) get him out. We leave to-morrow, June 11.

'Good-bye to you both, and God bless you !'

LETTER FROM MAJOR E. M. BARTTELOT TO SIR REDVERS BULLER.

    ' Yambuya Camp, Aruwimi Falls,
      ' *June* 1, 1888.

' DEAR SIR REDVERS BULLER,

  ' I thought perhaps you might like to have a short account of our Expedition, which, as far as the rear-guard is concerned, and we can judge, has turned out a fiasco and a delusion.

' We started on our march up country from the Lower Congo on March 25, 1887, and reached Stanley Pool April 21, 1887.

' During the march Stanley found out that I was

not suited to him, and he hated me accordingly, and
took no pains to conceal it. He threatened me by
saying he would assail my reputation in the papers.
I laughed at him. The cause of it was that he
wished the Soudanese to carry loads, and they
refused, and I said they had not come for that
purpose. However, on arrival at Leopoldville,
after I had helped him to take the steamers, he
sent me off with the Soudanese and 150 Zanzibaris
to march to Kwamouth, which is at the junction of
the Kassai and Congo on the south bank. I was
picked up then by the steamer *Stanley*, and taken to
Bolobo, where Stanley had made a camp, which he
intended leaving me in command of. From this,
however, he was dissuaded by Tippu-Tib, who said
that an officer and the Soudanese should be left at
the entrenched camp here, as the natives were very
wild and warlike ; so on I came. We reached
Bangala May 30, 1887. This is the last of the
Belgian stations on the Congo. Here I was transferred to the *Henry Reid* steamer, to escort Tippu-
Tib to the Falls, which we reached June 17, 1887.

'Stanley has made an agreement with Tippu-Tib
for 600 men, Stanley supplying him with powder and
caps. These men were to carry loads for us, and if
they did not reach the camp before Stanley had
started, they were to remain with me at our camp
here till such time as I started, which was to be
when the steamer *Stanley* arrived with the men
from Bolobo, and the loads from Stanley Pool,

among which were the powder and caps. Tippu asked me, " Is the powder at the camp ?" I said, " No," but that it would come with the *Stanley.* Then he said, " The men shall not come—Stanley has deceived me."

'On June 19 I left the Falls, and got to this place on the 22nd. I told Stanley what Tippu had said ; he got furious, and said he did not want the men, he could do the work by himself.

'On June 28 Stanley left, and from that day to this I have never heard a word of him, and Tippu says he has not, either ; but I think that is far from the truth.

'On August 14 the *Stanley* returned. Up till then no sign of Tippu, though natives had come to us for protection, saying the Arabs were on the move.

'On the 17th the Arabs attacked a village on the opposite side of the river to us, and a little above us.

'I sent over to find out who they were, but they all disappeared ; the natives, however, told us they had a camp one day up river from us, and on the same side.

'On August 18 I sent a party to their camp, who returned on the 20th with some of the Arabs. They said they had been sent to get ivory, and on being further questioned they said there was a good road to Stanley Falls, Tippu's head-quarters.

'I agreed with them for an escort and guides for

two officers, viz., Jameson and Ward. Jameson is a splendid officer; I wish they were all like him.

'On August 22 they started, and on September 12 they returned with the good news that Tippu was coming with 600 men. On October 1 Salem Mohammed, a chief who had come with Jameson, said, "Tippu very much ashamed, but the men refused to come, as the loads were too heavy and the road bad, with scarcity of food." On October 4 I started for the Falls, taking with me Troup, son of the old Indian General, and reached there on October 12. Tippu was away, but returned on the 22nd. I had a palaver with him about the men, and he said he would go to Kasongo, his chief town, situated on the Congo in Unyamente, and get the men. I got back to the camp on the 30th. Stanley, on leaving in June, had said to me, "Good-bye, Major; I shall find you here when I return in November." All November I looked for him, and December and January passed by, and no news.

'I had no means of moving, for my men were dying fast from want of proper food and medicine; they have nothing but makago or manioc. Our number of loads trebled the men who were fit to carry. Deserters had come in and stated that Stanley had had great trouble on the road; so I expected he would be late, but not so late as this.

'In the meantime, on November 15, Tippu had gone to Kasongo, and was expected back on February 1, 1888. But on February 1 we heard that men were scarce, and that Tippu would not return for several months.

'About fifty men had been sent, ostensibly for us, to Salem Mohammed, but we were not to use them till Tippu came.

'From October, 1887, to March, 1888, about 800 Arabs were sent up eastward on Stanley's track, and we are completely surrounded by their camps. The paucity of men, and Tippu's protracted absence, determined me to hunt him, and on February 14, 1888, Jameson and I started for the Falls for that purpose. We got to the Falls February 20, and we were told Tippu would come in ten days; however, he did not. Then, that a big caravan entirely for us would arrive with Tippu on the new moon, March 12. A caravan of 300 came on the 14th, but only fifty small-poxed men for us. Sick and disheartened at this, I sent Jameson to Kasongo, March 18, with full instructions to offer Tippu money for 1,000 men — 600 carriers and 400 fighting men. And I hastened back to camp, got there on March 24, and sent Ward down river to Banana Point with a telegram to Mackinnon. Salem Mohammed, meanwhile, had got troublesome, and had undoubted designs on our camp and the stores, but I frustrated him.

'The natives I have found quite peaceful, and willing to trade, till they were stopped by the Arabs. The Arabs are the danger here, not the natives.

'On May 8 the Belgian steamer *A.I.A.*, with two officers on board, arrived here, bringing back Ward's escort. They stayed three days, and then went round to the Falls.

'Three days later I went to the Falls overland, and caught them up—we both arriving together on May 18.

'No news of Jameson, Tippu, or Stanley, beyond a vague report that the latter was dead, which is not true. I came to the Falls to watch the Belgians and the head Arab, Nzigé, and because I heard from up river of a large caravan coming to the Falls ; also I reckoned that Jameson should return about the 14th.

'On May 22, unexpectedly, Jameson and Tippu came back with 400 men, all for us. And Tippu told Jameson that 800 men would be forthcoming, which Jameson told me. But on the 23rd, when I had my palaver with Tippu, he said he could only let us have 400 men, and these were only to came on condition they only carried 40 lb., our original weight being 60 lb. He said he knew nothing about the 800 men, and that as he had much fighting to do he could give us no more. He would enter into no written agreement with me.

'The truth came out in a few days. It has been apparent to me for the last eight months that Tippu had designs on Bangala : it is a country rich in ivory and slaves. The Belgians became aware of it on its being pointed out to them, and to avert it asked Tippu to send a strong force to the Mobangi River, before anyone else took it. It abounds in ivory, slaves, and food, lying north of the Free State territory, and entering the Congo west of Bangala, on the north bank, at Equator Station.

'Tippu's ambition aroused, his promises of help to us were immediately placed on one side. Seeing how matters stood, I said nothing, but took the 400 men and came on here with all speed.

'Tippu should be here to-morrow, and then I will tackle him, and, I hope, get another 200 out of him. I am very busy now rearranging stores, etc.

'Tippu, of course, could have let us have the men long ago if he had wished, and if it had not been for Holmwood, the Consul at Zanzibar, we should not have got them now.

'All the Arabs are dead against Tippu helping us—Tippu and all hating Stanley for his mean treatment of them when he crossed Africa.

'I hope to start not later than June 12, to look for Stanley and find out about Emin Pasha. During my long stay here, I have never been idle ; the village chiefs, etc., for miles round I know, and I know more of the Arab movements than they dream of.

'The camp is a healthy one, our men dying chiefly from debility caused by the food ; out of 240 I have lost eighty-seven since June 28, 1887.

'The English officers are all well but Troup, and he is in a dying state, and is going home as soon as the steamer *Stanley* arrives, which she should do in a few days.

'The officers are Jameson; Troup, son of the late General Troup; Bonny, an ex-sergeant of A.M.D., and who got the D.S. order at Sekokuni's stronghold; and Ward, nephew of the naturalist.

'Jameson, Bonny, and self will be the three to go up. Ward goes to Bangala with the stores I cannot carry.

'A better officer than Jameson I could not have; and Bonny, though rough and slow, is steady, honest, and sure.

'I hope to be in England this time next year; but time in Africa is uncertain.

'The country for miles is a dense jungle, only clearings on the waterway; food scarce, the roads execrable. I would far sooner be in the desert again; I am looking forward with the keenest pleasure to this trip, though I am afraid it may not be productive of anything, for Stanley is such a funny fellow, that very likely he may be in England now. At the same time he may be in a scrape, out of which I may perchance rescue him, though, if ever I do get to him, I shall catch it.

'I trust you are well, and that all fighting may be postponed until I arrive home.

'I will put in below if I get more men, and the day I start. With kind regards,

'Believe me, yours sincerely,
(*Signed*) 'EDMUND M. BARTTELOT.

'We leave this to-morrow, June 11, 1888. So good-bye, sir.'

COPY OF A LETTER FROM SIR REDVERS BULLER, V.C., ETC., TO MAJOR SCLATER, R.A.:

> 'Hurstbourne Park, Whitchurch, Hants,
> '*September* 25, 1888.

'MY DEAR SCLATER,

'I had quite forgotten that you were poor Barttelot's brother-in-law. I received a few days ago the enclosed letter, and I was waiting till I returned to London and could find out Sir Walter's address, when I meant to send it to him. It is typical of the lad, full of go and hard work, and withal so honest and unassuming. His family, I know, must have received many letters of sympathy; indeed, I am sure that all who knew the poor fellow would feel his loss deeply, even if they did not write and say so.

'Personally I much regret him, and perhaps the more so as I feel I had some hand in sending him out, though certainly much against my will.

'You can make any use you or the family think fit of the letter. If I could have had five minutes alone with Assad Farran, or whatever his name is, I should be glad.

> 'Very truly yours,
> (*Signed*)   'REDVERS BULLER.'

CHAPTER XIV.

JUNE 10, 1888.

Last Night at Yambuya—Tippu-Tib's Agreement—Imperial
British East Africa Company—Mr. Stanley's Objects—Major
Barttelot's Misgivings.

SUNDAY, June 10, 1888, is passing away, and the
sun has set for the last time on the rear column
in the camp at Yambuya. To-morrow, at last, the
start is to be made ; the almost impossible task has
at length been accomplished. The carriers have
been fetched from far Kasongo, over 500 miles away,
by Mr. Jameson, and the wily Tippu has been brought
to fulfil his contract, as the rear column understand
it, in a partial, half-hearted and suspicious manner.

With what care all possible arrangements have
been made to acquaint the Committee at home of
the exact position of affairs! How Major Barttelot
in his report appeals to them to guard his and his
officers' reputations! What thoughtful provision he
has made for the return home of those who are
unable to proceed! How jealously he safeguards

the interests of the Committee in his agreements with Tippu and Muni Somai—Mr. Jameson and himself pledging their credit in fulfilment, should the Committee not approve the terms! The loads have all been reduced by one-third—each load from 60 lb. to 40 lb—to suit the small Manyuema porters, to whom they have been distributed, and the surplus has gone as part payment in advance to Tippu-Tib and Muni Somai.

The weight on Major Barttelot's mind was very great; Mr. Stanley had told him nothing that could explain in any way his prolonged absence, or that could account for the double-faced dealings of Tippu-Tib and the Arabs who had invested his camp. If Mr. Stanley had openly informed Major Barttelot that the carriers were not wanted from Tippu-Tib unless and until he had secured Emin Pasha's £60,000 worth of ivory, when they might be required to carry it to the Congo for transport home to the Committee, and that Major Barttelot's ammunition and men might be required to protect it, Major Barttelot would have been relieved of immense anxiety; but the understanding between Mr. Stanley and Tippu-Tib was, it seems, not mentioned to him, or he might have understood that Tippu would naturally not be such a fool as to give the men until he knew that the ivory was really there.

That he did give a few men at last, when he had absolutely exhausted his stock of lies and prevarications, is still further proof of there being arrangements, the full scope of which was not made known to Major Barttelot. This is very evident, for out of the 430 Manyuema accompanying Major Barttelot from Yambuya, 380 carried loads. Mr. Stanley, on taking over the rear column at Banalya, quickly reduced the number to sixty-one carriers (pp. 13, 14, vol. ii., 'Darkest Africa'), saying to them : ' I do not need you, but if you like to follow me, I can make use of you.' There was, perhaps, no ivory to bring away ; he did not, therefore, want them or the loads. As to the latter, a good present to the Zanzibaris would make them think Stanley a right good fellow in comparison with Barttelot, who could give them nothing ; so he divided a thousand pounds' worth of goods between them.

In the first letter Mr. Stanley writes to the Committee, reporting how he had found the rear column, Mr. Stanley censures the officers of the rear column in a most unsparing manner, but does not say a word or give a hint that he has any fault to find with Tippu-Tib.* Another curious fact is that Ugarrowwa could send a sick man of Stanley's force to the Falls Station, and send Mr. Stanley's letters safely there also ; but the two notes supposed to have been forwarded to Major Barttelot from Mr. Stanley are

* It is not till Mr. Stanley arrives at Msalala, south of the Victoria Nyanza, on his homeward march, and receives a packet of newspaper-cuttings, in which he reads that more is known of Major Barttelot's death than he supposed, and more interest taken in it than he expected, that then for the first time he allows himself to say a word against Tippu-Tib, and that is apologetic.

said to have remained in his hands for months. The Arabs and Mr. Stanley thoroughly understood one another. Tippu-Tib had not come round all the way from Zanzibar, as the highly-favoured guest of Mr. Stanley, for nothing; nor was Mr. Stanley's personal dislike and treatment of Major Barttelot unknown to him and his companions. That portion of Tippu-Tib's contract concerning the ivory had apparently fallen through, or been carried out some other way, and the rear column became evidently of very secondary importance in the eyes of the slave-trader and his friend Stanley ; still, the powder was there, and was valuable.

This little matter of the ivory and treasures of Emin may partially account perhaps for Mr. Stanley's long delay. The contract with Tippu-Tib was for 600 carriers at £6 per loaded head each round trip from Stanley Falls to Lake Albert and back, and to carry ammunition to Emin and bring ivory back—of course, if the heads were not loaded, I suppose the £6 would not be forthcoming. Major Barttelot only seems to have known of the half-truth of the contract, of carriers to take loads to Emin.

Major Barttelot complained many a time to Mr. Stanley that he did not give him any information— a proof that Mr. Stanley either did not trust his officers, or was carrying out plans which he would not divulge.

Major Barttelot was also probably quite unaware that while they were all so busily engaged transhipping

the men and loads at Zanzibar, the basis of a future
empire had been laid, and Mr. Stanley had wheedled
out of the dying Sultan a concession of territory for
Mr. Mackinnon, the Chairman of the Emin Pasha
Relief Expedition. So also Mr. Stanley had arrangements to make for relieving Emin Pasha of his
territory, and the various offers with which he puzzled
Emin Pasha no doubt required time for consideration :
whether he would like to become an English subject
and rule an empire, with a capital on the Victoria
Nyanza ; or a Belgian subject, and hand his province
over to the King of the Belgians ; or an Egyptian
subject ; whether he would remain or come away ;
whether he would let Stanley have his ivory and
goods, or whether he preferred to keep them ? In
all this Mr. Stanley, no doubt, had some reason for
keeping a part of his force at Yambuya. If there
was ivory to be sent home, the camp would be a
good place to store it ready for shipment down the
Congo ; but why not have explained the matter to
the officers of the rear column, or at least to the
commander ? Mr. Stanley made an offer to Emin
Pasha for the King of the Belgians (p. 387, vol. i.,
' Darkest Africa') : ' He has requested me to inform
you that, in order to prevent the lapse of the
Equatorial Provinces to barbarism, and provided they
can yield a *reasonable revenue*, the Congo State might
undertake the government of them, if it could be
done by an expenditure of about £10,000 or
£12,000 per annum ; and, further, that his Majesty

King Leopold was willing to pay a sufficient salary to you, £1,500 as Governor, with the rank of General. . . . . Your duty would be to keep open the communications between the Nile and the Congo, and to maintain law and order in the Equatorial Provinces.' Again, and this is very important, Mr. Stanley says to Emin : 'The revenue, with this additional sum, must be sufficient to maintain about twenty stations between him (Emin) and Yambuya ' (p. 391, vol. i., ' Darkest Africa '). So Yambuya was to be the basis of communication.

If Emin's province was to be joined to the Congo State, and communications kept open between the Nile and the Congo, Emin, Governor of Equatoria, must join hands with Tippu-Tib, Governor of the Falls Station, and Tippu-Tib and Major Barttelot at Yambuya would be pieces in reserve in this game should the player require to make use of them in the development of this scheme for the benefit of Leopold, King of the Belgians. Tippu-Tib, the slave-trader, had already been established at the Falls for the benefit of King Leopold at the expense of the Expedition, and King Leopold wanted to get Equatoria as well without paying for it.

But others wanted Equatoria also, and also without paying much for it. Seated comfortably in London in June, 1888, just at the time the rear column was leaving Yambuya, six of the members of the Emin Pasha Relief Committee enrolled themselves as president and directors of a company called the Imperial British East Africa Company, to take over the possessions on the coast of East Africa, which Mr. Stanley has told us he obtained for Mackinnon by promise from the Sultan of Zanzibar.

List of Members of the Emin Pasha Relief Committee.

SUBSCRIPTIONS TO THE EMIN RELIEF FUND.

	£
Hon. G. Dawnay . . .	0
P. Denny.	1,500
Colonel Grant . . .	100
Lord Kinnaird	100
Mr. Hutton	250

The Court of Directors of the Imperial British East Africa Company.

SUBSCRIPTIONS TO THE EMIN RELIEF FUND.

	£
The Marquis of Lorne . .	0
Sir Arnold Kemball . . .	0
Sir Robert Harding . . .	0
W. P. Alexander . .	100
James M. Hall	375
Sir Donald Stewart . .	0
Sir T. Fowell Buxton . .	250
Lord Brassey	0

(MEMBERS OF EMIN RELIEF COMMITTEE AND DIRECTORS OF EAST AFRICA COMPANY.)

	£
Sir W. Mackinnon . . .	3,000
Sir John Kirk	0
Sir Lewis Pelly.	0
W. Burdett Coutts . . .	400
A. L. Bruce	750
Sir Francis de Winton . .	0

The total amount subscribed to the Emin Pasha Relief Fund by the directors of the East Africa Company was £4,875.

The Committee of the Relief Fund and the Court of Directors use the same offices, and always have done, and the same clerks. Sir Francis de Winton, who in 1887, 1888, and 1889, was at the War Office as Assistant-Quartermaster-General, was the Secretary to the Relief Committee, and is now Administrator-General of the empire won for the Imperial British East Africa Company by the Emin Pasha Relief Committee.*

This company obtained all Emin Pasha's territory, the territories of all the chiefs round the south of Albert Nyanza, between the Albert Edward Nyanza, the Belgian Free State, and the Victoria Nyanza, owing to the work done by the Emin Pasha Relief Expedition, sent out for the sole purpose of relieving Emin. In the report to the shareholders of this company, July, 1890, it is stated : 'In May, 1889, Mr. H. M. Stanley, on his way to the coast, came into communication with chiefs of many States through which he passed, and obtained from them the cession of their sovereign rights respectively, in consideration of the protection he afforded them against the attacks of the King of Unyoro. All

---

* Mr. Burdett Coutts told me that it was Sir Francis de Winton who so strongly advocated the Congo route, instead of the more direct one from the east coast. This is also apparent in the correspondence presented to Parliament. See Appendix.

these rights Mr. Stanley has patriotically transferred to the company, and your directors deem this a fitting opportunity to acknowledge with gratitude the valuable services rendered to them on all occasions by the illustrious explorer. The States and territories thus brought into affinity with the company are Mpororo, Ankori, Kitagwend, Unyampakado, Ukonju, Undussuma, Usongora, the Semliki Valley, and the valley between the Albert Nyanza and the Ituri River.'

Why the directors do not count in Emin Pasha's province I don't know. Mr. Stanley offered to hand it over to the King of the Belgians with Emin as Governor, and if Emin had relished the proposal I suppose it would not have been joined to the possessions of the English merchants, but would have been added to the Belgian Free State.

One great result of the Expedition has been, therefore, to obtain possession of large countries for the East Africa Company at the expense of the public contributors to the relief of Emin, and at the sacrifice of the time and laborious exertions of those who volunteered to go out and shared the dangers and trials of the Expedition for his relief. Mr. Stanley received the thanks of the directors for the magnificent possessions acquired for them by him and his Expedition. The other officers are not noticed, nor are the subscribers to the Relief Fund thanked, at whose expense they virtually have gained the territory.

(For well-told and interesting description of the scenery, soil, products, and inhabitants of the countries bordering the great African lakes now owned by the company, read 'Emin Pasha in Central Africa,' being a collection of his letters.)

The total amount subscribed to the Relief Fund was £33,268 12s., of which the Egyptian Government subscribed £14,000, and gave up a province, its revenue and its Governor, Emin—a costly work for Egypt—and £4,875 only was subscribed by directors of the Imperial British East Africa Company (p. 461, vol. ii., 'Darkest Africa').

The concession of territory on the east coast of Africa to Sir W. Mackinnon cost the sum of £4,436 6s. 7d., and has been taken over by the company at that price (see report of the Court of Directors, June, 1889). As the net outcome of the Anglo-German agreement, and the agreement with the Italian Government, the limits of the sphere in which the company operates embrace some 750,000 square miles, with 400 miles of sea-coast, and a fine harbour at Mombasa (see company's report, 1890). The total cost of this empire to the company has therefore been :

	£	s.	d.
Emin Relief subscriptions .	4,875	0	0
The concession from the Sultan of Zanzibar . . .	4,436	6	7
Total, about . . .	9,311	6	7

Besides this sum, £16,000 has been spent by the company in sending caravans into the interior from the east coast, and in making treaties with the tribes of the interior, bringing the total cost of sovereignty to some £25,000.

One or more caravans were sent into Uganda from the east, and it is stated in the company's prospectus, dated August 14, 1889, that 'it is probable that the company's exploring caravans have already joined hands with Emin Pasha and Mr. Stanley, and it may be expected that the products of the Equatorial and Bahr el Ghazal provinces will eventually find their way by the company's roads to this port ' (Mombasa).

The arrangements were well made : Mr. Stanley advances from the west, another caravan from the east.   It was hoped they would meet, and that the products of Equatoria would fall into the hands of the company.   These arrangements would probably also occupy Mr. Stanley's time and attention to no little extent, especially if any of Emin's ivory was to be sent to the east.

No one grudges the company the empire they possess ; but why invite men to go on an expedition without telling them the purposes and scope of it, and with a gag on their mouths, and in absolute ignorance of the meaning or bearing of their own doings and actions as they carried out the instructions of Mr. Stanley ?

All these great schemes in Mr. Stanley's head

must have tended to divert his thoughts from the object for which Major Barttelot had gone out— viz., to relieve Emin by handing him gunpowder. And in the ambition to grasp the tempting prizes* that lay scattered around him on the borders of the Nyanzas, in his haste to accomplish at any cost the projects of empire, and dazzled by the splendid possibilities of wealth and position which the occasion offered, he neglects the rear column of his Expedition, who know nothing of all these vain things, and are deserted and without proper food, and without carriers. He forgets they are looking out for him. How eagerly day after day they watched that road from Yambuya to the east, looking for their leader! But his promise to return is forgotten, laid on one side; it is an inconvenience, or it is a pre-arrangement. He heeds it not, and the faithful at Yambuya are to suffer for the unfaithful, and the just are to be sacrificed for the unjust.

It is unsatisfactory to find that Mr. Stanley had all through the Expedition been over-anxious to figure as one who never failed to keep his promise. When Major Barttelot was two days late in steaming up the Aruwimi to Yambuya from the Falls Station, Mr. Stanley was quite passionate with rage and sus-

* In a letter to Mr. A. L. Bruce, dated S. Mupe, Ituri River, September 4, 1888, Mr. Stanley writes: 'All the land round about from the Forest to the Lake the chiefs made formal tender of to me.' Also, 'The sharp punishment the natives of the grass-land had received on our first visit had so tamed them, they all made peace and paid indemnities.'

picion. Again, when in August, 1888, Mr. Stanley leaves Banalya (p. 15, vol. ii., ' Darkest Africa'), he says : ' I had given my word to the officers at Fort Bodo that on December 22, or thereabouts, I should be in the neighbourhood of Fort Bodo ; and no inducement would tempt me to remain in the neighbourhood of Banalya.' So he deserted Mr. Jameson and Mr. Ward, and left them behind.

Mr. Stanley takes care to be back at Fort Bodo to date, being two days before his time, and compares his happy return then with the finding his rear column shattered at Banalya.

The comparison is unjust in the extreme. Mr. Stanley had kept his promise to the officers at Fort Bodo, and had returned to them to date ; but he had broken his promise to the rear column, and had not returned to them. As Mr. Stanley truly observes, (p. 21, vol. ii., ' Darkest Africa') : ' Any person who has travelled with the writer thus far will have observed that almost every fatal accident hitherto in this Expedition has been the consequence of a breach of promise.'

Major Barttelot and his officers were quite unaware of all the projects and pent-up secrets of the leader of the Expedition. They had come out for a simple purpose, and could not see through the cloud of suspicious circumstances by which they were surrounded, or fathom the designs of him who had deceived them.

All that Major Barttelot knew on this his last

night at Yambuya was that the road towards Emin
Pasha and Stanley's track lay ahead to the east,
through the terrible forest, and that he would carry
out the instructions given him in the letter and in
the spirit to the end, and, please God, he might find
Emin and Stanley and the other officers, and succour
them.

He had grave misgivings: his life had been
threatened by the Arabs; nay more, his very
reputation had been threatened by Mr. Stanley.
To Mr. Stanley 'kudos' is incomprehensible, and
a thing not understood—to quote his own unpleasant
words: 'The kudos impulse is like the pop of a
gingerbeer bottle, good for a V.C. or an Albert
Medal, but it effervesces in a month in Africa'
(p. 126, vol. i., 'Darkest Africa').

With Major Barttelot it was otherwise; honour
to him was more than life, and he could say in
Shakespeare's words :

> ' Mine honour is my life : both grow in one.
> Take honour from me, and my life is done.'

He knew that Mr. Stanley's promise was unfulfilled; he knew of the white-robed Arab's base
treatment of him; he knew that Mr. Stanley and
Tippu were on most friendly terms from Zanzibar
till they parted on the Congo; he knew that then
Tippu complained to him (Barttelot) about Stanley;
he knew that then Stanley depreciated Tippu-Tib
to him (Barttelot).

He may have had suspicions, but his honourable nature would not allow him to draw the only conclusion, that these two men were playing a deep game, whose secret he must not share, and that he was being blinded by both mutually for some purpose other than the noble object of the Expedition.

For honour Edmund Barttelot had gone out to the relief of Gordon, and was many times thanked by his leaders for his work; for honour he had come out to the relief of Emin Pasha, Gordon's lieutenant, and fell a victim to the cruel circumstances of his position.

To-day all is clear, but on that last night at Yambuya all was dark; the miseries of the past year alone were truly known; all else was vague and mysterious as the shifty ways of the Arabs who for so many months in their neighbouring camps had kept the little force at Yambuya in a state of siege. To-morrow, please God, they would leave this place and these surroundings for ever.

CHAPTER XV.

THE MARCH TO BANALYA.

The Start—The Zanzibaris desert—Instructions to Mr. Bonny—
Mr. Stanley with Mr. Bonny after Major Barttelot's death—
Malignity.

'*Monday, June* 11.—We left camp at 7 a.m.; all glad to start—I hope never to return. We got to camp at Suedi's village at noon. Fine day.

'*Tuesday, June* 12.—It rained in the early morning. We left camp at 10 a.m., and arrived at Sala's camp at sunset. I was rear-guard. The road was shocking; the men carried well.

'*Wednesday, June* 13.—We halted this day at Sala's; he gave me some meat and seven eggs.

'*Thursday, June* 14.—We left Sala's village at 6.30 a.m., and got into camp at 6 p.m. This is the last village between the wilderness of four days' march and Nasoro bi Sofia.

'Muni Somai's men are all over the place; they won't be in till to-morrow, so I shall leave Jameson with him, and march myself with the Zanzibaris. Fine day, but hot.

'The next day, June 15, we left at 5.30, through
a fine forest. I took a wrong turn, and got too
much to the north. However, after an hour's delay
the right road was discovered, and that night Bonny
and I camped in the bush. We found that fourteen
men had deserted with twelve loads. Most of the
men I suspect. Salem Mohammed and Sala Sala
are at the bottom of this. The latter's two sons
have deserted—of course at the instigation of their
father. We had a thunderstorm in the afternoon.
A cock was given me yesterday.

'We halted the next day in camp, and could get
no news of deserters. Jameson is not yet returned
from Salem Mohammed's camp, where he has gone
to look for them.

'*Sunday, June* 17.—Jameson is come back. He
is a good fellow ; I wish I had more like him. A
heavy thunderstorm came on and flooded his tent
out. I found him terribly short of food, so sent him
over some.

'*June* 18.—Munichandi bolted, taking his rifle and
the fly of my tent ; also a man named Beni Sua.
We had got too far to the south, so I sent for a
guide. We marched from 7 a.m. till noon.

'*June* 19.—A guide turned up at 8 a.m., but
proved a fool, so I steered a course of my own down
a stream north-east. The Zanzibaris came out in their
true colours : the road was a little bad, so they said
they could not carry. About mid-day we halted and
hit off the road, or what I presume to be the road.

'We have been fifteen months in Africa to-day.

'We made a good march next day, the 20th, and camped close to a native village. About 1 o'clock it came on to rain hard, and thundered. Everything most wretched.

'The next day we marched on to a deserted village, and I put up in an Arab house, and sent men on to look for a road, but they returned, saying they could find none. I quickly found one myself.

'*Friday, June* 22.—We marched at 6.30, and arrived in camp at 11.30 a m. The road north-west, and is apparently made by the Arabs. During the march three men and a boy, with three loads and four rifles, deserted, so we sent a party to look for them.

'The next day, Saturday, we halted to try and catch the deserters, and to look for a road. I punished my boy Sudi for idiocy in the morning, and when I returned towards evening found he had deserted, and no news of the other deserters. My revolver and seventy-five rounds of ammunition were gone, also my table-knife. The poor little beggar only took what he considered absolutely necessary, and was advised to it by the men. On being informed that they all knew where he was, I offered a reward for him, but no one responded. I was told that many others intended to desert. I fell them all in, and took away all the arms from the Zanzibaris, and their ammunition.

'The Soudanese are faithful.

'I told Bonny I should go to the Falls the next day and get some chains, and that I would not return the rifles to the Zanzibaris for some lengthened period. He thought it good. It has been showery to-day. I ran a thorn into my foot.'

EXTRACT FROM LOG OF THE REAR COLUMN, SUNDAY, JUNE 24 :

'Major Barttelot, with 14 Zanzibaris and 3 Soudanese and boys, left here this morning for Stanley Falls.'

COPY OF ORDERS TO MR. BONNY, JUNE 23, 1888.

'1. Take over charge of the camp, remaining till Mr. Jameson's arrival.

'2. To have a special care of all Zanzibari rifles and ammunition.

'3. When move is made, to see that all loads, such as ammunition, are under Soudanese escort.

'4. Any attempt at mutiny to be punished with death.

'5. To try to obtain information of where-abouts.

'6. To hand over command to Mr. Jameson when he arrives, and not to proceed further than Abdulla Kihamira's (Banalya).

'EDMUND M. BARTTELOT.'

(See p. 506, vol. i., 'Darkest Africa.')
These orders of Major Barttelot are to be particu-

larly noticed ; they are the last orders he gave, and
by these orders Mr. Jameson was put in command
of the rear column during Major Barttelot's absence.
No. 6 is a positive instruction to Mr. Bonny to hand
over the command to Mr. Jameson.

ANNEX TO CHAPTER XV.

MR. STANLEY AND MR. BONNY.

In order to deal with the following matter as lucidly
as possible, I must apologize for breaking the narrative at this point, and ask the reader to be witness
to a scene which occurred after Major Barttelot's
death (which was known to the actors in the scene,
Mr. Stanley and Mr. Bonny), and about the same
time as, or within a few days of, Mr. Jameson's death,
which was not known to them. Mr. Stanley arrived
at Banalya on August 17, received his reports from
Bonny, and the explanations he had to give of all
that had happened during the fourteen months since
Mr. Stanley had left them ; he had the log-book
given him, to which he could refer for every event.
Mr. Bonny told Mr. Stanley how well he had done
(p. 2, vol. ii., ' Darkest Africa ') : ' By his written
report and his oral accounts ; by the brave deliberation of his conduct during the terrible hours of
July 19, and by the touching fidelity to his duties,
*as though every circumstance of his life was precisely
what it ought to be,* Mr. Bonny had leaped in a
bound, in my estimation, to a most admiring
height. . . . But no sooner had permission been
given to the men to speak, than I was amazed at
finding himself (Bonny) listening to a confession that
the first day's march to the eastward, under Mr.
Bonny, was to be the signal for his total abandon-

ment by the Zanzibaris.' Mr. Bonny* does not
say much that is good concerning the officers of the
rear column ; in fact, he writes a report to Mr.
Stanley which, as soon as he has done it, he bitterly
repents, and asks to have it returned to him. He
says many things he now regrets having uttered.
Nothing was right but what Bonny had done.
Every little tale and every petty incident of the
camp-life at Yambuya is served up to Mr. Stanley
with the bitter sauce of a mind chafing against the
subordinate position he occupied in the camp with
the other officers, and on the journey up the Congo,
and now finds itself at last freed from all restraint.
Mr. Jameson is alone left of the officers, and he
has gone to Stanley Falls ; and Mr. Bonny aspires
to the command of the second column of the Emin
Pasha Relief Expedition. (This was before the
arrival of Mr. Stanley.) Bear in mind the last order
Major Barttelot gave to Mr. Bonny, on June 24,
*to hand over the command to Mr. Jameson when he
arrives*, and which is before Mr. Stanley's eyes, and
incorporated in his book. Mr. Stanley now narrates
(p. 479, vol. i., ' Darkest Africa ') how Mr. William
Bonny, 'whose capacity to undertake serious responsi-
bilities is unknown to me . . . hands me the following order, written by Major Barttelot :

' " Yambuya Camp,
' " April 22, 1888.

' " SIR,

    ' " In event of my death, detention by Arabs,
absence from any cause from Yambuya Camp, you
will assume charge of the Soudanese company, the
Zanzibar company, and take charge of the stores,
sleeping in the house where they are placed. All

---

* Mr. Bonny, I find, on looking through my brother's diary,
was continually repeating to him tales about the other officers, and
what they said and did. The reader may have noticed it also.

orders to Zanzibaris, Somalis, and Soudanese will
be issued by you, and to them only. All issues of
cloth, matako (brass rods), etc., will be at your discretion, but expenditure of all kinds must, as much
as possible, be kept under. Relief to Mr. Stanley,
care of the loads and men, good understanding
between yourself and the Arabs, must be your earnest
care ; anything or anybody attempting to interfere
between you and these matters must be instantly
removed.

  ' " I have the honour to be, sir, etc.,
   ' " EDMUND M. BARTTELOT, Major."

 ' What remains for the faithful Jameson, " whose
alacrity, capacity, and willingness to work are unbounded," to do ? Where is the promising, intelligent, and capable Ward ? What position remains
for the methodical, business-like, and zealous Mr.
John Rose Troup? Mr. Bonny has been suddenly
elevated to the command of the rear column in the
event of any unhappy accident to Major Barttelot.

 ' My first fear was that I had become insane.
When I alone of all men attempt to reconcile these
inexplicable contrarinesses with what I know animated
each officer of the rear column, I find that all the
wise editors of London differ from me.'

 Yes, indeed, that is the proof of condemnation :
everyone will differ from Mr. Stanley. In the first
place, it is curious that Mr. Bonny should have
placed this letter, particularly, before Mr. Stanley,
and that in Mr. Bonny's official report, which Mr.
Stanley ' permits to detail ' what occurred at
Banalya in a revised form, Mr. Bonny, on the very
day of Major Barttelot's death—July 19—makes this
entry :

 ' The Major wrote and handed me the official
order appointing me in command of the Zanzibari

and Soudanese when the camp at Yambuya was in great danger, and his own life especially. I therefore take command of this second column of the Emin Pasha Relief Expedition until I see Mr. Stanley or return to the coast. Mr. Jameson will occupy the same position as shown in Mr. Stanley's instructions to Major Barttelot on his going to Stanley Falls to settle with Tippu-Tib for another head-man of the Manyuema. He has free hands, believing himself to be in command. I did not undeceive him. On his return here I will show him the document, a copy of which is given above.'

Then this curious entry, which is apparently a portion of Mr. Bonny's log, is signed:

'I have the honour to be, etc.,

'WILLIAM BONNY.'

It will be noted that the date of this order to Mr. Bonny is April 22, is three months old when Mr. Bonny produces it, and that it referred alone to Yambuya Camp. Major Barttelot never mentions it, hints at it, or refers to it in any way. Major Barttelot gave special orders to Mr. Bonny on April 5, on April 24, on May 13, and on June 23— three special orders since April 22, so that, assuming the order of April 22 is correct, it is rendered absolutely void by the later orders. I will note them down (though they have been already given in the diaries), the better to compare them. They are taken from Major Barttelot's letter-book.

'COPY OF INSTRUCTIONS TO MR. BONNY ON MY
PROCEEDING TO THE FALLS.

'*April* 5, 1888.

' SIR,

' During my absence you will take over command of Yambuya Camp, the Soudanese and Zanzibari companies. You will retain the command till my return, for though Mr. Troup may return before I return, yet it will be such a short period before, that it will be best for you to retain this command. It is my especial desire that for the period I am away you will do all in your power to keep the peace between the Arabs and ourselves, for which purpose it will be best to prohibit your men their camp entirely, and in case of disobedience on our men's part severe punishment. Till I return do not allow the European provision-boxes to be touched on any pretext whatever, nor open a fresh bale of cloth for the purpose of purchasing provisions. Should the natives prove aggressive, inform, and place yourself in the hands of, Salem Mohammed.

'I have the honour, etc.,
'EDMUND M. BARTTELOT, Major.'

'To MR. BONNY, ON MY PROCEEDING TO YAMBU.

'SIR,   '*April* 24, 1888.
'You will follow the instructions of the preceding letter, dated April 5, 1888, with the exception that you will not hand over the command to Mr. Troup, but maintain it, and that you will sleep in the storehouse.

'I have the honour, etc.,
'EDMUND M. BARTTELOT.'

'LETTER OF INSTRUCTIONS TO MR. BONNY ON MY PROCEEDING TO THE FALLS.

'*May* 13, 1888.
'Same as letters of April 5 and April 24.
'E. M. BARTTELOT, Major.'

It is very remarkable how similar the letter of April 5 is to the one produced by Mr. Bonny, but it

is not identical; and the letter of April 5 seems to
cover the ground, so as to render the letter of
April 22 unnecessary; and then the letters of
April 24 and May 13 refer to the letter of the 5th,
and not to Mr. Bonny's production, and the order of
June 23, No. 6, 'To hand over the command to Mr.
Jameson,' is absolute. The object of Mr. Bonny is
plain: 'I therefore take command of this second
column.'

Mr. Stanley and Mr. Bonny know better than
this. When Major Barttelot gave Bonny instructions in April they were alone, except for the return
of Mr. Troup, very ill, to camp). Mr. Jameson was
over 500 miles away, at Kasongo, pursuing Tippu-
Tib for the carriers; and Mr. Ward was 1,300 miles
away, at St. Paul de Loanda, with a cablegram
home. The instructions of April referred only to
April, and were entirely cancelled by subsequent
instructions. Mr. Stanley suppresses all these facts.
He knows that Major Barttelot and Mr. Jameson
loved one another as seldom men do, and had that
implicit trust and confidence in each other, as the
result of the long companionship of two honourable
natures. They stood two friends, true as steel; and
now Mr. Stanley—to his shame be it spoken!—tries
to make the public believe that Major Barttelot had
passed over his officers to place Mr. Bonny, a non-
commissioned officer, in command—had treated his
well-loved friend and most trusted officer, Mr. Jameson, with cruel indifference, and reduced him in
order to elevate Mr. Bonny to the command! What
a palpable absurdity! They should go further, and
say Major Barttelot procured his own death to
place Mr. Bonny in command. It is most harrow-
ing to write of these things. Surely, in attempting
to prove too much against the poor officers of the
rear column the good advice is disregarded:

' Heat not a furnace for your foe so hot
That it do singe yourself.'

But yet more.   Mr. Jameson, after Barttelot's
death, having offered Tippu-Tib £10,000 out of his
own pocket, and failed to secure his services, dies at
Bangala.   Mr. Stanley and Bonny receive a letter
from Mr. Jameson, dated August 12, relating what
he has done and proposes doing.   Mr. Stanley
writes :

' Mr. Jameson's letter from Stanley Falls arrived,
dated August 12.   Though the letter stated he pur-
posed to descend to Bangala, the messenger reported
that he was likely to proceed to Banana Point ; but
whether Banana Point or Bangala mattered very
little.   When he descended from Stanley Falls
he deliberately severed himself from the Expedition.'

' It is only with anger,' says an able article in
Blackwood's Magazine, ' that one reads the glaringly
unjust reference to him ' (Mr. Jameson) ; ' with the
faithful man's letter in his hand, showing how eagerly
he was exerting himself to repair the disaster . . .
Mr. Stanley accuses Jameson of deliberately severing
himself from the Expedition.'

Not only so, but a letter was sent to Mr. Jameson
to tell him that he had deserted the Expedition, and
upbraiding him.   Then Mr. Stanley demanded from
Bonny the papers belonging to Mr. Jameson (Mr.
Bonny told me this).   Mr. Bonny refused to give
them.   Mr. Stanley ordered them to be given, and
they were handed to him, sealed up.   (Mr. Bonny
had been requested by Mr. Jameson, in case of anything happening to him, to take them home to his
wife.)   Mr. Stanley broke the seals, read the private
diary and papers, kept them till his return to England, when he left them at a bank at Cairo, and it
was only after several communications and a lawyer's
letter that Mrs. Jameson got them.

I have noted these facts here instead of in their order of date, as I wish to close the book with the account of Major Barttelot's death. These painful incidents need no comment ; they show extraordinary malignity and ingratitude.

CHAPTER XVI.

LAST DAYS.—'FAITHFUL UNTO DEATH.'

JUNE 24—JULY 5, 1888. END OF DIARY.

March to the Falls Station—Ill and Footsore—Interview with Tippu-Tib—Last Letters to his Father and Major Sclater—A Comparison of the Losses of the Advance and Rear Columns—An Examination of Events—Major Barttelot's Last March—Banalya, July 17—Mr. Bonny and Major Barttelot fired at in their House — July 18 — July 19 — Major Barttelot is shot by the Manyuema Sanga—Letter from Mr. Jameson to Sir Walter Barttelot—Mr. Jameson's Sorrow—His Death.

To continue the diary :

'*June* 24.—Wet morning early. I fell in all the men ; one man absent—he has probably deserted. At 8 a.m. I started with twenty-one people, and camped at 4 in the afternoon. There were tracks all along our road, as of four or five men, and a small foot-mark. Fine day.

'*Monday, June* 25.—We started at 6.30 a.m., camped in Wobai Village at 4 p.m., and there one of my men, Trokodero, caught the boy Sudi, with my revolver, etc. He said he was with the other deserters. but that they had left him as he slept. I don't think this is true, otherwise they would have taken the revolver also. I did not punish him, as it was partly my fault that he ran away, and the boy is not a bad one. Fine day.

' *Tuesday, June* 26.—Heavy rain till 8 a.m. We left camp at 9.30 a.m., and got to Sala Sala's at noon. Last night I had sent on my three Soudanese to search the village ; I had made offers to the interpreter Bartholomew. On arrival, the Soudanese could give me no news. Sala was away, but returned late last night. He was astounded at my return, but professed all ignorance, which I told him was planned. He asked me why I was going to Tippu-Tib, but received no definite answer. He gave me guides to send my messenger and letter to Jameson. In the letter I told Jameson to go and aid Bonny, and in conjunction with Muni Somai to form a camp at *Nurenia, Abdulla's place, and await me there.

' *Wednesday, June* 27.—I left Sala's at 7 a.m., got to Yambuya at noon, and camped at 4.30 p.m. In passing through Suedi's village I found Bonny's ass, and brought him to Yambuya. On leaving Yambuya, in Salem Mohammed's old camp, I found one of the Zanzibaris and others. These were the sick we had left in Tippu-Tib's charge.

' *Thursday, June* 28.—Left at 7 a.m.. arrived at

* Another name for Banalya.

Yaraweko at noon, Yarilua at 4.30 p.m. ; a heavy rain came on just as we got in. I put up in the old ant-house. I passed five dead men on the road, two of whom were soldiers—Abdulla Hamdeh, and Sergeant Murad Ali. I was suffering from sickness and a bad foot. This day last year Stanley left Yambuya, and still no news.

'*Friday*, *June* 29.—I suffered all night, and my foot was very bad. I started at 5.30 a.m., and got to Yangambi at 4.30 p.m., dog-tired, footsore, and weak. All along the road single and small parties of Zanzibaris were found, who had been handed over sick to Tippu-Tib. They were without food or water. My carriers had gone on, so I could give them nothing. They amounted to ten, also one dead. Light rain in the afternoon.

'*Saturday*, *June* 30, *to July* 1.—Left Yangambi at 7 a.m. by canoe ; Yarageli, Nasiboo's place, at 1 p.m. ; he gave me and my men food. We reached Yarukombé at 7 p.m., had dinner, got into the canoe at 9 p.m., reached Lower Yatakusé at 2 a.m., and Upper Yatakusé at 6 a.m. I started at 9 a.m., reached the Falls 2.30 p.m., and was put up by the Belgian officers, M. Bodsan, Baert, and Henk. Tippu was surprised, but gave me what I wanted, though Salem Mohammed begged him not to. Fine day.

'*July* 3.—Singatini. I had a big palaver with Tippu ; all my men arrived. One of the sick Zanzibaris begged to come with me, so he has.

' *Wednesday, July* 4.— Singatini. I was shown a letter of false testimony against Jameson which Assad Farran had written to the State, in spite of his agreement with me. I wrote to Jameson's brother, and went to see Nassir Masudi ; he fed me. Tippu was obliging. A fine day.

' *Thursday, July* 5.—I wrote to M., father, Harry, and Mackinnon.'

Here the diary ceases.

Copy of the last Letter of Major Barttelot to Sir W. Barttelot, Bart.

'Singatini,
'*July* 5, 1888.

' My dearest old Father,

' I have had to come back here on business, and am glad to say have settled it satisfactorily, and shall depart to-morrow for up country. Our march altogether up to the present has not been a success, but I think now I have so arranged matters that I shall have no more stoppage. I did 300 miles in eight days coming here, and shall hope to do the same going back. Can get no news of Stanley. Am sorry to hear of the death of the Emperor of Germany. I hope I may miss nothing.

' I hope you are all well ; there is not much news with us.

' Give my love to all, and believe me,

' Ever your very affectionate son,

' Edmund M. Barttelot.

COPY OF LETTER TO MAJOR H. C. SCLATER, R.A.

'Singatini,
'*July* 6, 1888.

'MY DEAR HARRY,

'I am back again. Our Zanzibaris are deserting us at all turns; twenty-two gone in four marches, and many more intending to desert. I have deprived them of their arms, and left them camped in the bush, surrounded by natives, so that they dare not run away.

'Jameson and Bonny, when Muni Somai can give them an escort, will take them on to Nurenia, Abdulla Korona's camp; camp there and await me.

'I marched eight days here, doing thirty miles per diem, tackled Tippu, and got him to give me what I wanted, though Salem Mohammed begged him not to.

'I am very well and fit; we all are. We shall have a lot of trouble with that caravan, I am sure.

'The interpreter, Assad Farran, whom I sent home, has been making the best of his time traducing all of us, and spreading the most abominable stories about us. He has written an official letter to the State about Jameson, and Troup, who was on board the *Stanley* with him, never attempted to stop it.

'Should you see anything particularly abusive against Jameson or me in the *Bosphore*, or other papers, find out the source, and should it be Assad

Farran, go to the Consul-General and demand redress for us.

'I hope you and E. are well.

'Ever your affectionate friend,

'EDMUND M. BARTTELOT.'

NOTE.—Mr. Troup was so ill when on board that he could know nothing of what Assad Farran might do or say. Assad Farran, when he came home, denied the truth of the statements he is said to have made.

As Mr. Stanley draws attention to the terrible losses of the rear column, the following figures, taken from his own book and brought together for verification, are interesting. There is nothing like the truth properly told.

TERRIBLE MORTALITY.

A Comparison of the Losses of the Advance Column, under Mr. Stanley, and of the Rear Column, under Major Barttelot.—Terrible Mortality of the Advance Column.

ADVANCE COLUMN.

On February 14 Mr. Stanley calculates his force :

Present at Fort Bodo	184
,, ,, Ipoto.	11
,, ,, Ugarrowwa's . . .	56
Total	251
Deduct 26 who have died at Ugarrowwa's	26
Actual total . .	225

Mr. Stanley left Yambuya in June, 1887, with a force of 389 picked men. On February 14, 1888, he has 225. He has lost 164 by death and desertion.

On February 3, 228 present at Yambuya.

Total force of the rear column left by Mr. Stanley, 271. On February 3, 1888, there are present 228—a loss of 43 only.

The advance column had suffered terrible mortality, and had lost nearly four times as many men as the rear column, although the sick, diseased, and worst characters were mostly left behind. Even after another six months of most bitter anxiety and privation, when Mr. Bonny, on August 17, hands in his official report to Mr. Stanley, after the death of Major Barttelot, the rear column has only lost 139 men—which compares favourably with the 164 lost by Mr. Stanley up to February.

On Mr. Stanley's journey again back, from Banalya to Fort Bodo, which took from August 31, 1888, to December 20, he lost another 106 lives (p. 105, vol. ii., 'Darkest Africa').

When Mr. Stanley, on April 10, 1889, marched from Kavalli's on the Albert Nyanza on his start for the journey to the coast, the total number of men he has left of the Expedition has dwindled to 230 all told, all that were left of 680, being a total loss of 450. Lost with Barttelot, 139; lost with Stanley, 311.

Major Barttelot now leaves the Falls Station, and

makes his last march through the forest, arriving on July 17 at Banalya, called by the Arabs Unaria, where Abdulla Korona has his camp. This is the same Arab chief Abdulla who visited the camp at Yambuya on August 18, 1887—eleven months ago —and was the first to commence that crafty system of espionage, cajolery and deceit (telling the officers that Tippu's men had come part of the way, but had turned back), which having failed, was shortly to culminate in the murder of the courageous man who had defied their intrigues so long.

If Major Barttelot had not been assassinated, and the rear column had struggled on another thirty days, he would have handed over the column to Mr. Stanley at the very place, Mugwye's, where he was instructed (in the letter Mr. Stanley sent him, and which he never received) to halt and await Mr. Stanley, Mugwye's being only some ninety miles beyond Banalya. Mr. Stanley arrived there August 10, though in the letter referred to he said he would be there the end of May. (Where the rear column is concerned, Mr. Stanley forgets that he is a man of punctual performance of promise.)

If Major Barttelot had met Mr. Stanley, he would have demanded explanations from him of his treatment of the rear column, in leaving them without carriers or proper food in the hands of the Arabs, and in a place of such supreme danger for fourteen months; why he broke his promise, and why he never communicated with them—and his reply being unsatisfactory, Major Barttelot's report to the authorities at home would have damaged Mr. Stanley's reputation exceedingly. But the hand of the poor Manyuema slave was to smooth away these difficulties from Mr. Stanley's path—in Tippu-Tib's furthest station the crime was to be committed—under the eyes of Abdulla, who so long had faithfully kept watch for his master.

The Falls Station was only six days distant from Banalya by an Arab track, and communication was easy for messengers from many points on the Aruwimi, along Mr. Stanley's path.

These tracks are troublesome and tedious for a large caravan to pass along in single file, but for one or two alone they offer no insuperable difficulties. Major Barttelot used often to walk twenty-five miles a day.

Ugarrowwa and Tippu-Tib communicated with ease. On August 17, Mr. Stanley communicated with Tippu-Tib, and sixteen days later, September 2, Salem Mohammed of Yambuya, nephew of Tippu-Tib, came with Ugarrowwa to see Mr. Stanley. We must remember that Mr. Stanley and the King of the Belgians had made Tippu-Tib Governor of the Falls Station, and that great territory on the Congo above, over which Tippu-Tib ruled, and over which he now, in virtue of this contract with the King of the Belgians, practised all the horrors of slavery, under the sanction of the Belgian flag. That he had broken his contract, and raided the

whole district between Singatini and the Aruwimi—
all *south* of the Falls—is not to be noticed ; that the
Belgian officers invited him to raid the Ubangi River
is only natural ; and slavery and its attendant horrors
had certainly increased a thousand-fold around
Yambuya, south of the Falls and up to the Ubangi,
since Mr. Stanley had taken Tippu-Tib there. So
active has trade become on the Upper Congo, that
at the close of 1889 nearly fifty tons of ivory were
sold in the Antwerp market from the territory of
King Leopold.

Mr. Stanley says (p. 230, vol. i., ' Darkest Africa ') :
' Every pound-weight has cost the life of a man,
woman, or child ; for every two tusks a whole village
has been destroyed.' The Arabs hunt the natives to
obtain slaves and ivory. Anti-slavery meetings have
been numerous, and those who placed this slave-
trader in power at the Falls Station have been
present. No blame is bad enough for the poor
officers of Mr. Stanley's rear column, who are made
the scapegoats, as their lives were the sacrifice to
his actions.

True, Tippu-Tib is to be tried for breach of contract in not supplying the carriers, and the sum of
£10,000 in damages is demanded from him ; but that
is an easy arrangement for both parties—a very convenient manner of slipping away from justice. Tippu-
Tib will gladly arrange that ; the ruler of Central
Africa, with full powers to make enormous wealth out
of the teeming population of his great territory, will

laugh at such a flea-bite.   Southwards, from near to
the watershed of the Zambesi, to the Ubangi on the
north ; from Lake Tanganyika on the east, towards
Bangala on the west, stretch the dominions of this
enemy of the human race.   What understandings
and sympathies exist between Mr. Stanley and this
man we do not know ; all we are told is that Mr.
Stanley placed him there, that he is destroying
human life from day to day in his terrible greed of
gain, and that he ordered the life of Major Barttelot
to be taken.   Mr. Stanley, of course, defends his
friend, and denies that he had any hand in the
matter : he has to do that in self-defence.   Perhaps
one of the worst features in this strange case is the
way in which, after travelling amicably with Tippu-
Tib all the way from Zanzibar, and telling his officers
that he trusted Tippu-Tib as any white man,
Mr. Stanley completely changes his front at
Yambuya, and tells Major Barttelot he would not
trust him at all.   On June 23, at the same date, he
writes to Mackinnon that Tippu-Tib will prove
worthy of trust, and make the ' very best Governor '
possible.   ' The consequences of their own actions
men sometimes call fate,' and that fate Mr. Stanley
is not going to attribute to the action of Tippu-
Tib, for by so doing he would condemn himself. If Tippu-Tib connived at Major Barttelot's
murder, it was Mr. Stanley who left Major Barttelot
at Yambuya without sufficient food or carriers—it
was Mr. Stanley who placed Tippu-Tib at the Falls

Station, knowing the camp at Yambuya to be at his mercy.

The writer of an able article in *Blackwood's Magazine* for August, 1890, referring to the defence of Tippu-Tib by his friend Mr. Stanley, says : 'He is probably the only man in Europe or Africa who thinks so (that Tippu-Tib was not guilty of the death of Major Barttelot). The advance column passed on from Yambuya, leaving Major Barttelot to follow, at what time the sable Governor of the Falls should supply him with the 600 carriers promised. Then followed those months of insolent and "systematic delay," the high-handed seizure of as much gunpowder as possible, and the sending of the gallant officer into the desert, accompanied by miscreants instructed to shoot him . . . We now know . . . that the Major's assassination was not a thing of sudden passion, but a regular "plant"—the woman annoying and disobeying him, the murderer not in the open, but watching from a loophole in a hut.'

' What hast thou done ? the voice of thy brother's blood crieth unto Me from the ground.'

It now only remains to give a short account of Major Barttelot's death, and close this sad narrative of the last days of his young life.

I gather the following from Mr. Bonny's official report, from the conversations I had with him, and from a letter he wrote to my father, after Mr. Stanley had arrived at Banalya, dated August. He had previously sent a short announcement to my father, which it appears was lost. Major Barttelot arrived at Banalya on July 17, Mr. Bonny having got there only two days before him, and having had great trouble with the men on the march. According to Mr. Jameson's log, he also had had much trouble. On the night of July 9 the Manyuema fired shots close to his tent ; Mr. Jameson jumped out of bed, got his rifle, and said he would shoot the next man who fired close to his tent.

When Major Barttelot saw Bonny, he told him that he had seen Tippu-Tib, who had given him power of life and death over the 430 Manyuema. He had also got an order from Tippu-Tib for Abdulla Korona, the chief, to provide them with bananas, plantains, etc., also for 60 more men, to replace the Zanzibaris, who were continually deserting.

Abdulla said he could give none of these things. Soon after this the Manyuema, to annoy them, began firing off their guns, and Muni Somai refused to stop them. Major Barttelot and Mr. Bonny, while sitting later on in the back of Mr. Bonny's house, were startled by a shot, which passed over their heads and lodged in the roof. Major Barttelot caught the man and punished him severely.

July 18.—Major Barttelot continued to press Abdulla for the carriers, apparently without success. About 10 p.m. drums were heard and singing, and Barttelot sent his boy to stop it. The noise ceased.

July 19.—Early this morning a Manyuema woman commenced beating a drum and singing. Major Barttelot sent his boy, Sudi, to stop this ; loud and angry voices were heard, followed by two shots. The Major then ordered some Soudanese to find the men who were firing, and at the same time he got up from bed and took his revolvers from the case. He said, ' I will shoot the first man I catch firing.' He went out, revolver in hand, to where the Soudanese were. They told him they could not find the men who were firing. The Major then pushed aside some Manyuema, and passed through them towards the woman who was beating the drum and singing, and ordered her to desist. Just then a shot was fired through a loophole in a house opposite by Sanga, the husband of the woman. The shot passed through Major Barttelot's body below the heart, and lodged in a post supporting the veranda, under which he fell. Mr. Bonny went and, with one Somali and one Soudanese, found the body, and carried it to the house. There were about 1,000 people in the camp, nearly all cannibals. The wild scene that followed must have been fearful to witness. Mr. Bonny sent a message to Mr. Jameson and to Tippu-Tib and Mr. Baert at the Falls Station. Mr. Bonny then, having restored a certain amount of order and recovered some of the loads that had been stolen in the stampede, proceeded to bury Major Barttelot's body, after sewing it up in a blanket. ' I dug a grave just within the forest,

placing leaves at the bottom of the grave, and
covered the body with the same. I then read the
Church Service from our Prayer-book over the
body.'

COPY OF A LETTER FROM J. S. JAMESON, ESQ., TO
SIR WALTER BARTTELOT, BART.

' TO COLONEL SIR WALTER B. BARTTELOT, BART., C.B., M.P.

'Stanley Falls,
'*August* 3, 1888.

· SIR,

'It is with extreme regret that I have to
announce to you the untimely death of your son,
Major E. M. Barttelot, which took place at Unaria
early on the morning of July 19, he being shot by
one of the Manyuema in charge of some of the men
supplied to the Expedition by Tippu-Tib. I myself
was not present when this happened, but gathered
the following particulars from Mr. Bonny, the only
other officer of the Expedition who was there, and
who has also forwarded to you an intimation of the
occurrence. It appears that just at daybreak, on
the morning of the 19th ult., some of the Manyuema
camped in the village close to Major Barttelot's
house (he having arrived at Unaria from Stanley
Falls on the evening of the 17th) began to beat
their drums and sing, which is their constant practice.
Major Barttelot had been annoyed by the same noise
early the night before, between 9 and 10 o'clock,
and had sent his boy to them, upon which the music

ceased. He sent his boy again in the morning, when loud murmurs were heard, and two guns were fired off in the air. He then jumped out of bed, taking his revolver in his pocket, and went out of the house. Immediately afterwards a shot was fired, and shouts were heard that he was killed. A fearful scene of panic followed. Mr. Bonny went out, and could not find a Zanzibari; called for Muni Somai (the head Arab in charge of Tippu-Tib's men), but he did not appear; ordered the Soudanese soldiers to follow him, but they stood to arms, refusing to follow. Then he went towards the spot where the shot had been fired, Chana, a Somali, and Omana, a Soudanese officer, following him, and went on until he came to the body of Major Barttelot, which was lying face upwards, with one hand under the body, holding his revolver, which had not been discharged. He must have been shot quite dead on the spot, as not a muscle of his face had moved. At the time this occurred I was three days' march from Unaria, bringing up a lot of loads in the rear. On the 21st inst. I received a note from Mr. Bonny, stating the fact of your son's death, and that the head-man and all the Manyuema had run away. I left the loads to follow me in charge of a Soudanese escort, and marched through to Unaria in one day, where I found all quiet. Mr. Bonny could not possibly have taken any active measures against the Manyuema, as the Zanzibaris, if given their guns, would only have deserted with them; and there were not twenty

23

Soudanese left to fight with, there being over 400 Manyuema, so that any act of reprisal on his part at the time, or on my part after I arrived, would have been fatal to the whole Expedition.

'Mr. Bonny had already offered a reward for the arrest of the murderer; and on my arrival I succeeded in getting the head-men to come into the village and speak with me, when they informed me that Sanga, the man who had caused your son to be shot, had gone to Stanley Falls.

'I left Unaria on the 25th, and reached this place at daybreak August 2. I at once saw Tippu-Tib, and told him I had come to demand justice on the man Sanga and to ask his aid, so that the Expedition might proceed with as little delay as possible. He told me he had Sanga here in chains, and would deliver him over to me for justice. I told him that the new Belgian President having arrived the day before, and the act being committed in their territory, I should communicate the facts to him at once. I got a canoe, and crossed over to the Belgian station. The President told me he would hold a council with Tippu-Tib, call out a file of men, and have the man shot. This happened yesterday, and there has not been time yet to carry it into effect. The steamer with this letter leaves to-morrow morning at daybreak, so that I cannot write you fuller particulars, but will do so before leaving Stanley Falls; and I give you my word of honour that I will see justice done to the man, even if I have to shoot him myself. Your son was one of the closest friends I ever had. He was disliked by the Arabs, because he was far too open and honest himself to stand their mean, roundabout ways of doing things, and showed it to them.

'Should any reports derogatory to your son's character when in command at Yambuya ever occur, please call upon me to answer them, should (D.V.) I ever return to England. The chief source of these reports, I am afraid, will be Assad Farran, the dismissed Soudanese interpreter, who has already begun to spread the foulest reports about me; but, thank God, I am alive to answer them, and hope to be alive if it is ever necessary to do so for your son. I am sending home by this steamer, through the agency of the Dutch House at Banana, one of your son's boxes, containing all his effects which Mr. Bonny and myself considered it necessary to send, and of which I enclose an inventory, as well as a list of his other effects and their disposal.

'Please accept my most sincere expression of regret and sorrow for the untimely death of your son, and I will always be willing to answer anything you may wish, should I return to England.

'I have the honour to be, sir,

'Your obedient servant,

'JAMES S. JAMESON.

'P.S.—Major Barttelot also had a large waterproof bag containing bedding, clothes, etc., and letters for Mr. Stanley and the officers with the advance force ; but this was lost on the march from Stanley Falls to Unaria, the carrier rushing away with it.* I have done my best to recover this bag, but without success. I enclose a letter written to you by your son which had not left on my arrival here, and have forwarded other letters to their addresses. I also enclose a letter from the Horse Guards, and contract with Mr. Stanley. All papers relating to the Expedition business I have kept.'

List of Things sent Home in Iron Box.

1 piece of Kasongo cloth.

1 Afghan praying-mat.

1 case handkerchiefs.

5 pairs socks.

1 writing case containing all private letters, etc.

1 housewife.

1 private diary.

1 Bible.

1 case hair-brushes.

1 silver tankard.

1 telescope.

1 silver chain and money box attached containing 1 sovereign.

1 small box of silver links.

2 silver compasses.

1 silver aneroid.

---

* Mr. Bonny told me he recovered this bag, and handed it over to Mr. Stanley.

1 silver card-case.

1 gold chain with seal and keys attached.

2 pocket-knives.

1 pincushion with 1 pearl, 1 coral, 1 platinum
    pin in it.

1 pair scissors, 1 pair compasses.

1 button-hook, 1 silver match-box, 1 ink-bottle.

Sanga was duly tried and shot.

Mr. Jameson then tried to induce Tippu to help
the Expedition.

To Bonny he writes August 12, 1888 : 'My
hopes have been raised to the highest pitch, and
then thrown to the ground the next moment.   When
Tippu-Tib said he would go for £20,000, I told him
I did not think the Committee would give it, but if
he would give me certain guarantees, I would pay
half the sum myself as a subscription to the Expedition.   But after what he had said, no one would
take him.'

Mr. Jameson went, therefore, down the Congo
by canoe to meet Ward at Bangala, and to hear
if there were any orders or news from the Committee.
On the journey, it is said, he got a fever, and
arrived at Bangala only to die, August 17, 1888.*

That same day Mr. Stanley arrived at Banalya.
Thus the deaths of these two dear friends were not

---

* It is a very remarkable circumstance that Mr. Jameson kept
his diary written up to the day of his death ; there is actually an
entry in the diary on the 17th, and no mention of severe illness.

far divided—Edmund M. Barttelot on July 19, and James S. Jameson on August 17, 1888. And truly this friendship is the only music—sad, indeed, but sweet—that accompanies in any way the telling of the story of Mr. Stanley's rear column. We may say in the words of David's beautiful lament :

'They were lovely and pleasant in their lives, and in their death they were not divided.'

EXTRACT FROM MR. J. S. JAMESON'S DIARY, BY KIND PERMISSION.

'*Saturday, July* 21, 1888.—Poor Major Barttelot was shot dead by one of the Manyuema early on the morning of the 19th inst. Such is the news I have received from Bonny to-day. It was a case of deliberate murder, as far as I can judge from the scant knowledge his messengers have of any details. Bonny's note is shorter than a telegram ought to have been, merely stating the fact that he was shot, and that all the Manyuema, Muni Somai, and Abdulla Korona have left ; also that he has written to Tippu-Tib. As far as I can learn from the messengers, early on the morning of the 19th, before daylight, some of the Manyuema were making a great noise beating on their drums. Major Barttelot sent his boy Sudi to tell them to be quiet, as he could not sleep. They still kept on beating their drums, and fired a couple of shots. He then went down to stop this himself, and all the men know is that he was shot stone dead, through the heart, the bullet passing out and grazing another man's face. It is a fearfully sad piece of news for me, for ever since we were left together at Yambuya Camp, more than a year ago, there has been the closest friendship between us, never so much as a single quarrel. In all difficulties we went to one another for advice, and many a happy picture did we draw of times at home together after all this unlucky Expedition was over. He was a straightforward, honest English gentleman—his only fault was that he was a little too quick-tempered. He loved plain straightforward dealing far too much to get on well with the Arabs. He hated their crafty, roundabout way of doing everything, and showed it to them, and of course was disliked in turn. He was far too good a man to lose his life in a miserable way like this, and God knows what I shall do without him.'

'They say the tongues of dying men
Enforce attention, like deep harmony ;
Where words are scarce they are seldom spent in vain ;
Or they breathe truth that breathe their words in pain.
He that no more must say is listened more
Than they whom youth and ease have taught to glose :
More are men's ends marked than their lives before ;
The setting sun and music at the close,
As the last taste of sweets, is sweetest last ;
Writ in remembrance, more than things long past.'

NOTE.

On the opposite page is a copy of the brass tablet erected in Stopham Church to the memory of Major Barttelot by his brother officers of the Royal Fusiliers.

In addition to this a brass tablet has also been placed to his memory by his companions of the Emin Relief Expedition in Stopham Church. A tablet has also been erected in the Memorial Chapel, Sandhurst, and a stained glass window has been placed in the parish church, Storrington, by his associates when reading at the Rev. G. Faithfull's for the army.

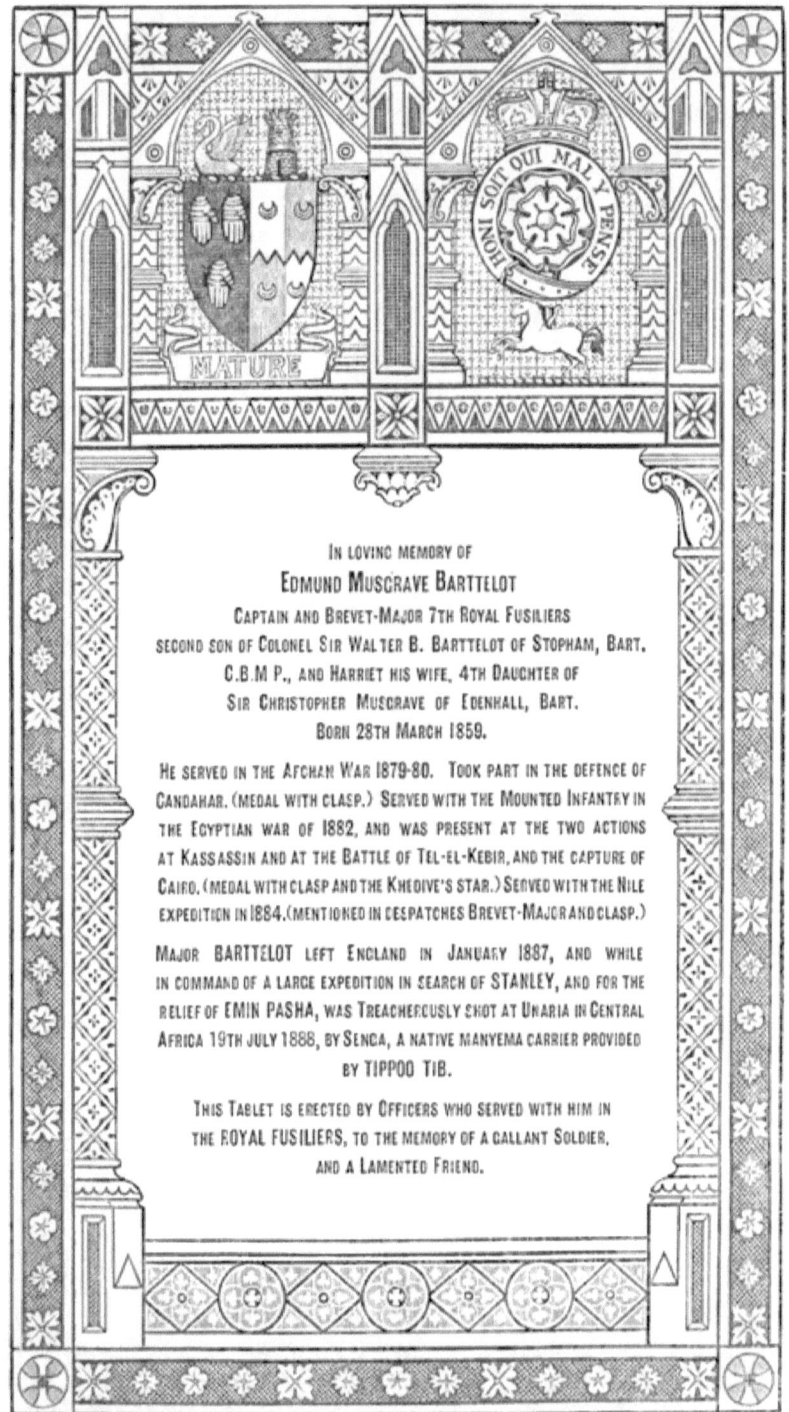

IN LOVING MEMORY OF
EDMUND MUSGRAVE BARTTELOT
CAPTAIN AND BREVET-MAJOR 7TH ROYAL FUSILIERS
SECOND SON OF COLONEL SIR WALTER B. BARTTELOT OF STOPHAM, BART,
C.B. M P., AND HARRIET HIS WIFE, 4TH DAUGHTER OF
SIR CHRISTOPHER MUSGRAVE OF EDENHALL, BART.
BORN 28TH MARCH 1859.

HE SERVED IN THE AFGHAN WAR 1879-80. TOOK PART IN THE DEFENCE OF
CANDAHAR. (MEDAL WITH CLASP.) SERVED WITH THE MOUNTED INFANTRY IN
THE EGYPTIAN WAR OF 1882, AND WAS PRESENT AT THE TWO ACTIONS
AT KASSASSIN AND AT THE BATTLE OF TEL-EL-KEBIR, AND THE CAPTURE OF
CAIRO. (MEDAL WITH CLASP AND THE KHEDIVE'S STAR.) SERVED WITH THE NILE
EXPEDITION IN 1884. (MENTIONED IN DESPATCHES BREVET-MAJOR AND CLASP.)

MAJOR BARTTELOT LEFT ENGLAND IN JANUARY 1887, AND WHILE
IN COMMAND OF A LARGE EXPEDITION IN SEARCH OF STANLEY, AND FOR THE
RELIEF OF EMIN PASHA, WAS TREACHEROUSLY SHOT AT UNARIA IN CENTRAL
AFRICA 19TH JULY 1888, BY SENGA, A NATIVE MANYEMA CARRIER PROVIDED
BY TIPPOO TIB.

THIS TABLET IS ERECTED BY OFFICERS WHO SERVED WITH HIM IN
THE ROYAL FUSILIERS, TO THE MEMORY OF A GALLANT SOLDIER,
AND A LAMENTED FRIEND.

TABLET ERECTED IN STOPHAM CHURCH.

APPENDIX I.

LETTER FROM MR. STANLEY TO SIR WALTER BARTTELOT, BART.

'Villa Victoria, Cairo,
'*April*, 1890.

'DEAR SIR,

'It is impossible for me ever to think of the fatal event at Banalya without becoming filled with sympathy for you. I think my almost earliest thought after recovering from the shock of the news, was how terrible were the tidings that awaited you in the letter which I was told Mr. Bonny had written. But when I heard how things—petty incidents and events—had preceded the catastrophe, converging towards and finally grouped round that one supreme event, and not one of the five officers of the rear column at all aware that any, or all, boded anything dreadful, my amazement was as great as my grief, and I certainly would have wished that you could have dispensed with hearing from me a word about it. I was warned over and over again by presenti-

Major Barttelot was murdered August 17, 1888. *Mr. Stanley does not write this letter till April,* 1890.

Mr. Stanley's information on this matter appears quite at fault. See Major Barttelot's diary, June, 1887, *to June,* 1888.

ments, and by an increasing
anxiety that would not be satisfied by anything any of my companions said, that something was
brooding of a fateful character
with the rear column ; and every
member of the Expedition, black
and white, will remember the day
when I called everyone to muster
and confessed to them that I was
more uneasy about Major Barttelot
than about Emin Pasha. Finding
that every officer was dead against
returning, I shunned doing what
I would have done had I not
been so influenced. We turned
our faces to seek Emin Pasha the
second time, instead of going to
search for the Major. But I
was comforted when the couriers
volunteered to do what was denied to me. You know, perhaps,
what a series of misfortunes met
them on the way ; how one thing
followed another to depress them,
worry them, and finally to cause
them to return, of somewhat the
same character to what was trans-
piring with the rear column to prevent anyone from being alarmed
at the inevitable to which every
act was tending. We all get to
be fatalists as we get older.
What is to be, will be. "*Mambu
Kwa Mumgu.*" The trouble is
with God. His companion officers
were to remain sullen, angered,
or too blind to perceive whither
they were all drifting, and from

*Mr. Stanley here tries to
place the blame attaching to
himself, for not returning to
his rear column, on his officers
of the advance force.*

*The Christian reader will
hardly agree with this.*

the eastward no message of comfort or good cheer could reach him. Ugarrowwa's forty scouts failed ; my twenty couriers nobly tried to reach him, and failed also ; consequently the event was to happen, and did happen, and it strikes me as a curious fact in psychology, that every one of your son's companions is as blind to-day as then. The Major was no more to blame than any of the others. If the Major is culpable in any one act, they are equally so ; and say what I may, I can only trace a disposition to shield themselves from blame for error of judgment under the plea that the Major was chief. The Major certainly was in command, but as the executive officer of the council of four—Barttelot, Jameson, Troup and Ward. Every vital step was to be discussed, and no step was to be taken without the voice of the majority deciding that it was best, and then Major Barttelot was to see that it was carried out. But I find that at an early period the Major assumed all authority, and they all seem to have submitted without a word, though evidently they seek to find comfort in their diaries and journals ; and whatever misgivings they may have had, they seem to have taken particular care that to the one who ought to have heard them they

The arguments here are very curious, confused, and contradictory.

Major Barttelot carried out Mr. Stanley's letter of instructions (which placed him in command) literally and absolutely, and accepted the responsibility.

If Major Barttelot had lived to meet Mr. Stanley, it would have been Major Barttelot alone who would have been held responsible.

are dumb. Consequently the Major, who is the youngest but one of the party, is permitted to follow his own bent ; there is none generous or magnanimous enough to pass over any little resentment, and plead and show to him kindly and respectfully what they believe is wise or unwise, right or wrong. Among themselves there are meetings, and various opinions and ominous shakings of the head, when a little firmness and a little frankness would have cleared every little misunderstanding, and united them all for the common good. It was not to be expected that five human beings, daily suffering tortures, could pass months together without some little unpleasantness marring the harmony of life. For all the surroundings were of such a nature as to produce friction—the hot climate, the damp atmosphere, the pinching, meagre diet, the indolence and rancorous carelessness of the blacks ; the strange proceedings of the Arabs, their veiled threats and cruel indifference to their needs, and the altogether dark prospect around them. I do not wonder that the Major got more and more vexed, and became more and more harassed. According to his light he could rightly plead that he was doing what he thought right. Jameson evidently sympathizes with him in

Previously Mr. Stanley states : ' Not one of the five officers at all aware that any, or all, boded anything dreadful ;' and later in this letter he states : ' But I have not heard that anyone suggested to him that they (the Arabs) were a source of danger and trouble.'

his distressful moods, and ex-
hibits an unvarying cheerfulness
of temper. But for the others,
who seem to think that the Major
was doing wrong, the cure seems
to be absolute silence. Probably
what I write may not be very
clear to you, unaware of the vin-
dictiveness manifested, not by
overt acts, but by a scornful, or
shall I say unkind, silence to the
Major; but really to me there is
nothing more pathetic than that
a little resentment, originally,
should ferment in the minds of
that very small community of
white men, until they became
totally estranged to one another.
One little frank word, and the
matter would have been buried.

'It is not likely that you will
forget what your son's nature was,
any more than we will the impression he made upon us.
Ardent, impetuous, outspoken,
prompt as tinder to utter the
thoughtless word, but generous,
zealous, brave, and the beau idéal
of a jockey of Mars—fit to have
ridden that fatal race into the
flames of Muscovy's cannon, side
by side with the boldest of the
Light Brigade, or to lead a forlorn
hope to bid men "stand" when
all would fly — Major Barttelot
will ever be remembered by us.
Such an one, left to himself, if
irritated and goaded by petty
miseries, would naturally and off-

*Mr. Stanley here tries to
throw blame on Major Barttelot's companions, for their conduct to Major Barttelot—for
what purpose ?*

*It seems curious, if this is Mr.
Stanley's estimate of Barttelot's
character, that he should be the
one selected to deal with the
Arabs and Tippu-Tib, and to
be left behind in command of a
camp so dangerously situated as
Yambuya.*

hand utter some words that had better be left unspoken, and probably wound susceptibilities of others; but the pity of it is that such words and acts were too much remembered.

'After promising us in the advance that he would not stay a day at Yambuya after the arrival of Troup and others from Bolobo, he was wrong to break his word; but I think all of his companions were of one mind.

'After seeing that Tippu-Tib broke one promise, the Major was wrong to trust him again; but I do not learn that any dissuaded him from staying and trying him again.

'The Major ought not to have listened to the stories of deserters who appeared before him with silver watches and Arab cloaks; but I cannot find that others older and more experienced in African craft were any wiser.

'The Major ought never to have permitted the Arabs to have invested him at Yambuya; but I have not heard that anyone suggested to him that they were a source of danger and trouble. The Major ought never to have broken open my luggage publicly, and deported it down stream; but the act never struck any of his companions as unkind to the chief whom they professed to believe was alive.

Mr. Stanley forgets that 600 carriers were to arrive, as well as the Bolobo contingent; and he omits to mention his last words to Major Barttelot, that he would return to Yambuya himself in November.

Mr. Stanley omits to state that Major Barttelot could not move without carriers, and that Major Barttelot was placed in Tippu-Tib's hands by himself (Stanley).

As Mr. Stanley failed to keep his promise to return in November, and did not communicate with his rear column, it was Major Barttelot's duty to get information where he could.

Mr. Stanley does not point out how Major Barttelot could have avoided the Arabs. If Mr. Stanley did not know they were a danger and trouble he must have been badly informed of Major Barttelot's opinions.

Mr. Stanley omits to state that all the loads at Yambuya had to be reduced in weight, and that to carry the ammunition and gunpowder it was compulsory to leave many things.

'The Major ought never to have sent European provisions and old madeira wine down river while in the act of abandoning thirty-three men, so wretched and feeble as to be unable to move ; but his companions looked on approving.

Major Barttelot provided for the men he left behind him with Tippu-Tib ; he deserted no one.

'The Major ought never to have travelled backwards and forwards between Yambuya and Stanley Falls — 800 miles of aggregate journeys ; but it does not seem to have impressed any of his companions that he and they were only "marking time." The acts were but the relative consequences of that resolution which was taken, to set aside the promise we received from the Major and Mr. Jameson on parting from them, that they would not rest "a day after the Bolobo contingent had arrived." One wrong step led to another. The work was gigantic to which they were committed ; but if death and failure is to be the result of loyal work, who cares ? A soldier does not shrink the deadly task because he believes it will be the death of him.

If Major Barttelot had made no attempts to obtain the carriers, what would Mr. Stanley have said ?

These accusations of Mr. Stanley's, written to Sir Walter Barttelot after his son's murder, are contemptible, and are evidently only made to draw away attention from other serious matters.

This amounts to accusing Major Barttelot of cowardice to his father.

'The Major, seeing the awful pile of goods to be carried by repeated stages along our track, prefers to try Tippu-Tib once more, after he has clear proof that he did not wish to fulfil his contract. When, after repeated breaches of promises, he still pins his faith to Tippu Tib, it becomes incomprehensible; and yet, alas! what could he do? His own men have in the meantime died, and he is quite stranded, unless he perseveres in the attempt to persuade the prevaricating Arab to assist him, which he does, and then comes the catastrophe. I do not think that the annals of African travel present anything so lamentable as the story of the rear column; and the most remarkable feature of it all is the indisputable loyalty by which every person in it is animated, and the perverse issues of every effort, as though there was some uncanny influence thwarting every noble aim.

Mr. Stanley here replies to his own arguments.

Mr. Stanley describes the result of his own arrangements.

'I greatly regret that I can do no more than assert my perfect belief that every thought that animated your son was for the well-being and success of the enterprise for which he had volunteered; and I do not think there is one man out of ten thousand living, who, after resolving to discover what persuasion could effect with Tippu-Tib, would have done otherwise than persevere in the attempt; and none possessing the zeal and ardour and passion for work which distinguished your son could possibly have evaded the fate which overtook him. However erring the conception of his duty, his com-

This, after the accusations before, is mere farrago.

Mr. Stanley omits to state that Major Barttelot only

panions concurred in it, and he, being the responsible chief, suffered while performing what he and they considered to be his duty. I have the satisfaction of remembering that, during our acquaintance, and when we parted at Yambuya, we lived as friends, and separated as such ; and I only regret that I could not have been twenty-eight days earlier, to have rescued a young fellow whose heart, I shall always believe, was in the right place.

carried out the letter of instructions given by himself.

Mr. Stanley had promised to return to them some 270 days earlier.

'If anything in the above lines jars on your parental feelings, I pray you attribute it to the facts. I would wish they were otherwise, but whatever they may be, as I loved your son, and admired him for many excellent qualities befitting a brave and noble soldier, I hope you will accept the sincere expression of sympathy for his untimely loss, of

'Yours most faithfully,
'(*Signed*) HENRY M. STANLEY.

'TO SIR WALTER BARTTELOT, BART.'

APPENDIX II.

'Brookdean, Pulborough,
'*May* 2, 1890.

'Sir,

'At the request of my father, I reply to your letter to him dated April, 1890, concerning the death of Major Barttelot, which took place in July, 1888. By your omission of several important facts, that undoubtedly influenced and decided Major Barttelot and his companions in their conduct at Yambuya, you do him and them a cruel injustice : you cast blame on their memory and sully good reputations. True, in this letter you write many kind things of my brother, but the essence of it lies in the formulated array of eight specific charges against him, some of which you have before published to the world, without the sympathy you now express to Major Barttelot's father for the first time since the event occurred—one year and nine months ago.

'Your actual feeling at the time of your arrival at Banalya, on meeting the rear column under Mr. Bonny, was plainly expressed in letters you wrote home at the time. When you gave your first account of Major Barttelot's death, you wrote as follows to Sir W. Mackinnon, August 28, 1888: "Well, my dear Bonny, where is the Major?" "He is dead, sir ; shot by the Manyuema about a month ago." "Good God !" is all your comment ; but to the subject of your personal inconvenience in the loss of your clothes you devote some twenty-five lines of the same letter. Again, on August 5, 1889, a year later, you wrote to Sir W. Mackinnon : "If you will bear in mind that on August 17, 1888, after a march of 600 miles to hunt up the rear column, I met only a miserable remnant of it, wrecked by the irresolution of its officers, neglect of their promises and indifference to their written orders." To this is added no word to qualify in any way the blame you unsparingly cast on those who were dead and could not reply. I refer you to the above letters because they do not tally with the tone of the letter to my father now under consideration, and which I will proceed to examine in detail.

'You write: "But when I heard how things, petty incidents, and events which preceded the catastrophe, converging towards and finally grouped round that one supreme event, and *not one of the five officers* of the rear column at all aware that any or all boded anything dreadful, my amazement was as great as my grief." On the contrary, Major Barttelot knew very well that his life was threatened, that he might be assassinated at any moment, that the camp was in great danger from the Arabs, and that never was any body of men left in a more deplorable position. Pinched with hunger, emaciated with fever, in perpetual fear of an attack by the Arabs, threatened and insulted by the Arab chiefs, the anguish of Major Barttelot was rendered more bitter by the necessary severity of the daily camp life. Upon him as chief fell the hatred and the blame for all the miseries the poor fellows had to endure. Major Barttelot, I can assure you, knew his position very well, and that such terrible knowledge was his to endure adds a hundredfold to the grief of his relations and friends. You write: " I was warned over and over again by presentiments, and by an increasing anxiety that would not be satisfied by anything any of my companions said, that something was brooding of a fateful character with the rear column." Sir, your presentiments and your anxiety were, as a matter of fact, actual knowledge that the rear column, whether it remained at Yambuya or moved on, was in a position of great danger owing to the Arabs. If you found the forest journey so difficult and so deadly with your 384 picked men and few loads, you must have known of the greater difficulties awaiting Major Barttelot with his enormous quantity of stores, whether with the terrible Manyuema carriers, or only with the wretched lot of Zanzibaris that you left behind at Yambuya. You, of course, are aware that the position of the camp at Yambuya was on the very site where some months before a number of Arabs

374 LIFE OF EDMUND MUSGRAVE BARTTELOT.

were destroyed by the natives, and that Stanley Falls Station was taken by the Arabs, under a relation of Tippu-Tib's, by force, and Mr. Dean, an Englishman, driven into the bush only a year before, viz., in 1886.

'You are apparently aware of Tippu-Tib's treacherous character. In a letter written to Major Barttelot, dated February 14, 1888, you write: "We first met the Manyuema on the last day of August, and parted from them in January. In this interval we lost 118 through death and starvation. In their camps it was as bad as in the wilderness, for they ground us down by extortion so extreme that we were naked in a short time. They tempted the Zanzibaris to sell their rifles and ammunition, ramrods, officers' blankets, etc., and then gave food so sparingly that these crimes were of no avail. Finally, besides starving them and tempting them to ruin the Expedition, they speared them, scourged them and tied them up." This was your experience of the Manyuema, yet on them you left the rear column dependent for carriers, if Tippu-Tib fulfilled his contract; for they do all the Arab work in that region. You also knew the custom of the Arabs to at once follow up the track of any expedition, and could not but be aware that the vast quantity of stores at Yambuya would attract the greedy eyes of all the neighbourhood—Arabs, Manyuema and natives. No wonder such knowledge as this warned you "that something was brooding of a fateful character with the rear column." You go on to say, "Finding that every officer was dead against returning, I shunned doing what I should have done had I not been so influenced. We turned our faces to seek Emin Pasha the second time, instead of going to search for the Major." Sir, you alone had the knowledge of the actual position of the rear column, and with you alone rested the responsibility of the arrangements you had made—arrangements in which your companions had no voice at all. You alone are responsible for not communicating with your rear column. As to your remarks upon the equal responsibility of Major Barttelot's companions with himself, I will only say that in no report of Major Barttelot does he attempt to cast any blame on others. He took, on the contrary, the full responsibility of his actions. You write: "There is nothing more pathetic than that a little resentment originally, should ferment in the minds of that very small community of white men, until they became totally estranged to one another." In reply to this, I would say that the one bright feature in the camp-life at Yambuya was the close, intimate friendship which sprang up between Mr. Jameson and Major Barttelot, whose letters are full of the consolation and support he derived from it. You cannot call this total estrangement.

'I now come to the specific charges you bring against Major Barttelot.

'1. "After promising us in the advance that he would not stay a day at Yambuya after the arrival of Troup and others from Bolobo, he was wrong to break his word; but I think all of his companions were of one mind."

'In a letter you wrote Sir Francis de Winton, finished at Yambuya Camp, dated June 19, 1887, you say : "We release our captives at once with small gifts and good words, seedlings, I hope, of a future amicable intercourse. If Barttelot will exercise patience with them, *long before we return* they will be a prosperous community, and friendship will be firmly established." On June 19, therefore, you expected to return to Yambuya after reaching Emin Pasha. In an earlier portion of the same letter, dated May 31, 1887, you write: "In my letter from Cairo I estimated that the journey to Wadelai could be performed, *viâ* the Congo, in 157 days from Zanzibar : 100 days have already passed. If we meet with no accidents, we may safely reach the rapids sixteen days hence. We shall then be 360 geographical miles from the Albert . . . . say that we have but thirty days left of the estimated time when we attempt the first march, we shall have a task of twelve geographical miles to each day . . . . nevertheless, though it is scarcely possible to march twelve geographical miles a day steadily through an utterly unknown country, without guides or interpreters, we shall do our very best." I gather from this letter that you expected to reach Wadelai in about five or six weeks after leaving Yambuya Camp, and that then you would return and would be back, allowing another five or six weeks, about November.

'Major Barttelot understood from you that you would be at the camp the end of October or November. He also was anxious to be allowed to follow you and the advance party as soon as possible. In a letter to a friend Major Barttelot writes : "June 23, Camp, Aruwimi Falls.—We arrived here last night ; the others had

been here six days ; there is nothing to eat but manioc. Stanley
intends to leave Jameson and me here ; we are to await his
return, which will be about five months ; but I am going to try
and persuade him otherwise." That same day, June 23, Major
Barttelot had a talk with you, and obtained your permission to
follow you and move eastward directly Ward and Troup came up.
The next day, June 24, you write your instructions to Major
Barttelot, in which you say : "If you still cannot march, then it
would be better to make marches of six miles twice over, if you
prefer marching *to staying for our arrival*, than throw too many
things away." The desire of Major Barttelot, therefore, was to
advance ; he had asked your permission to do so, and by your
instructions you permitted him, if he felt himself "*competent*," and
he "*preferred*" to do so ; but you had yourself originally intended
him to remain at Yambuya, and you apparently, from *the written
instructions* you gave, very much doubted whether Tippu would
give the men, or whether the rear column could advance. On
leaving the camp, you gave Major Barttelot and Mr. Jameson
to understand you would be back in October or November. You
said, " Good-bye, Major ; shall find you here in October, when I
return." That does not look like expecting them to move. Then
you started. You know the wretched lot of men you left at
Yambuya ; out of seventy-five Zanzibaris, thirty-nine sick and fit
for nothing ; these were the porters, for the Soudanese were not
used for carrying. Life in this wretched camp, without proper
food, did not increase their vitality, but killed them off. When
Ward, Troup and Bonny arrived with the 500 loads and 125 men
at Yambuya, there were not more than 160 men fit to carry altogether, besides the Soudanese.

'What was the position of affairs ? Some 600 loads to carry,
160 people to carry them ; a camp to be guarded (if they advanced)
at either end of the six-mile march, the sick to be carried as well.
The Arabs were commencing to occupy the villages on your track,
and it was very difficult to obtain food. The Zanzibaris could not
be trusted, but would desert to the Arabs if they could.

'The officers of the rear column at once recognised the foolhardiness of the march without carriers, and knew that at all
events they could maintain intact the camp and the goods, upon
which you set so much store (as shown in your letter of instruc-

tions, in which you say, "The loss of these goods and the men would be certain ruin to us "), until your return in November. I believe they could not have done otherwise, however much they may have desired to move, or even if they did promise to move, for which there is no authority but your own word, the two men, Barttelot and Jameson, both being dead. If you consider that Major Barttelot, under these circumstances, foolishly and wilfully, without justification, broke his promise, because being unable (owing to the arrangements you had made) to advance he did not advance, in what light is your promise to Major Barttelot and Mr. Jameson to be regarded, viz., that you would be back before November?

'It was possible for you to send back a white officer with an escort, or to come back yourself when you found, after five weeks' march, that you were only a few miles on your way in a wilderness of forest instead of being at Wadelai, as you hoped, and to have given the rear column definite instructions under circumstances which differed so widely from all your calculations; and it seems to me that as the rear column had the stores which were supposed to be for the use of Emin Pasha, and you knew the officers would be expecting you about November, it was culpable, considering the danger of their position, not to communicate with them before you advanced further, and so fulfil your promise.

'2. Your second charge is : "After seeing that Tippu-Tib broke one promise, the Major was wrong to trust him again."

'The Major never trusted him ; in fact, he told you at Yambuya in June that Tippu-Tib considered you had broken faith with him, and that, as you had not given him the powder promised, he would not give you the men ; but afterwards he relented, and said he would. You told Major Barttelot that it did not matter if Tippu did not send the men, as you could do very well without them. But the rear column could not advance without them, and so they tried all they could to get them, and as time went on, and their position became more and more desperate, no news of you or from you, and their force reduced by sickness and death, it became a question of life and death to obtain the carriers. They would try to get the carriers, and if they could not, then they would have to sit still and await events.

'3. "The Major ought not to have listened to the stories of

deserters who appeared before him with silver watches and Arab cloaks."

' I do not know to what men you refer; nor can I find any mention of deserters appearing with silver watches before my brother; nor do I understand where you gained information of such a frivolous character, or from whom. My brother questioned all deserters, sifted their stories, and found them unreliable.

' 4. "The Major ought never to have permitted the Arabs to have invested him at Yambuya; but I have not heard that anyone suggested that they were a source of danger and trouble."

' Major Barttelot certainly would have prevented the Arabs forming a camp close to him and cutting off his food supplies if he could have done so. Two methods were open to him: one to fight, which you will recognise as ridiculous, as the Arabs and Manyuemas could have overwhelmed them in the forest, and Tippu's aid would have been altogether lost: the other method was to try to induce the chiefs to move the camp, and to forbid their men interfering. Major Barttelot and his companions were constantly trying, by every means in their power, to work amicably with the Arabs, whose design he feared was to try and rush the camp. I have pages before me of letters, and diary full of the Arab doings, and Major Barttelot's great and growing anxiety for the camp on their account, in his own writing. For instance, take this entry: " While I was at the Falls there was a woman palaver here at Yambuya. The Manyuema complained of our men; a trap was set for a man of mine—Munichandi—and they took all his clothes from him. The affair was settled, but Salem Mohammed (the Arab chief) was heard to say, 'This will be a second Stanley Falls palaver.' Subsequently our men chaffed the Manyuema because they found them eating human flesh; this embittered the already bad feeling between them."

' Major Barttelot could no more prevent the doings of the Arabs than you could prevent your Zanzibaris being tempted to " sell their rifles and ammunition, ramrods, etc," to the Manyuema, with a view to ruin your Expedition. I do not think that you can be well informed if you are not aware of what Major Barttelot suffered from his knowledge and fear of danger to the camp from the Arabs and Manyuema, and of his strenuous and successful efforts to keep the Arabs out of the camp.

' 5. "The Major ought never to have broken open my baggage publicly, and deported it down stream ; but the act never struck any of his companions as unkind to the chief whom they professed to believe was alive."

' This is a matter of personal inconvenience to yourself which my brother would much regret ; but you do not appear to take into consideration the pressure under which he effected his departure from Yambuya. Bonny and Troup both ill at the time ; every load in the camp had to be reduced from 60 lb. to 40 lb., as the Manyuema would carry nothing heavier ; and only Barttelot and Jameson, with such help as they could get from Mr. Werner and his people on the steamer, to alter all the loads, write their letters home, and arrange the details of the start. They took such things only as they deemed you would think necessary ; the rest were sent with the other goods to Bangala for safety. Major Barttelot, in his letter to Sir W. Mackinnon, dated June 4, 1888, writes : " I have been obliged to open Mr. Stanley's boxes, as I cannot carry all his stuff, and I had no other means of ascertaining what was in them. Two cases of madeira were also sent him. One case I am sending back ; the other has been half given to Mr. Troup, the other half we take as medical comforts."

' 6. "The Major ought never to have sent European provisions and old madeira wine down river while in the act of abandoning thirty-three men, so wretched and feeble as hardly to be able to move ; but his companions calmly looked on approving."

' Major Barttelot never abandoned thirty-three men ; on the contrary, he made a pecuniary arrangement with Tippu-Tib to take charge of the sick men, and handed them over to him when he left Yambuya. He never abandoned men as Captain Nelson and the fifty-two Zanzibaris who could not march were abandoned by you at Nelson's "starvation camp," without food for twenty-three days, and of whom you lost forty-seven.

' 7. "The Major ought never to have sent the officers' rations to the Belgians of Bangala ; but Troup and Bonny appear to see no harm done."*

' I think, if you care to remember, you will call to mind that

* I find Major Barttelot did not give any rations to the Belgians at Bangala, except one box of pressed meat and some private stores of his own. See Major Barttelot's instructions to Mr. Ward, dated June 4, 1888.

when coming up the Congo you made accusations that the officers had been tampering with the food provisions, which accusations were not justified. Major Barttelot, I gather, determined to have nothing more to do with your provisions than he could help after your peculiar treatment of the officers of the Expedition. He wrote as follows : " I am sending a terrible lot of stores to Bangala which I cannot carry—amongst other stuff, a lot of food like jam, and herrings. I could eat them here, of course, but knowing Stanley as I do, I prefer to be quit of them ; and jam, candles, herrings, and soap ain't going to keep us alive. They weigh a lot, and are bulky, and for light there is always palm-oil, and for soap native soap."

'8. "The Major ought never to have travelled backwards and forwards between Yambuya and Stanley Falls—800 miles of aggregate journeys ; but it does not seem to have impressed any of his companions that they were only 'marking time.'"

' Major Barttelot's journeys to the Falls Station were partly to obtain carriers, partly to get aid to frustrate the designs of Salem Mohammed and his Arabs on the camp at Yambuya. It was a very particular object with Major Barttelot to keep his communications open with Stanley Falls Station, the nearest Belgian station ; and it was the knowledge of that communication which kept Salem Mohammed in check, and which enabled Major Barttelot to hold the camp. These journeys appear to me more reasonable than the inexplicable arrangement by which you made so many double journeys yourself—notably, the double journey between the Albert Nyanza Lake and the rear column, which you had planned from the first, as shown by your letters, and which would altogether have been avoided by a proper provision of carriers, with proper communication between your front and rear columns, and have saved a multitude from death and misery unspeakable.

' You reached the Albert Nyanza in December, but it is not till the following June, after six months' "marking time," that you think of returning to the rear column, although in the letter addressed to Major Barttelot you recognised the fact that if Tippu did not provide carriers the rear column could not have advanced very far. You write, February 14, 1888, to Major Barttelot : "If alone, we understand that you are very far from us." And again

you write : " If (as it might chance for all we know to the contrary) you have not started "—an observation which shows that
you quite thought it possible they might not have started. As to
"marking time," poor fellows ! the rear column knew it only too
well. Major Barttelot writes, June 1, 1888 : "What a fiasco it
has all been, and what a waste of time for me ! Stanley should
never have gone till Tippu's men had been forthcoming." You
took a fatal step in impatiently hurrying on from Yambuya without
providing the carriers required to carry the vast stores which you
left in charge of five officers with a worthless lot of Zanzibaris, the
residue of the Expedition, you having picked the men over twice
for the advance party—first at Bolobo, and again at Yambuya—
unless, as you said to Major Barttelot, you " did not want Tippu's
aid," in which case you could not have wanted the rear column to
move. Then why did you not say so, and give explicit instructions ?

'You leave the whole responsibility of moving or not moving
with Major Barttelot, *vide* your written instructions ; you leave the
camp with a full knowledge of its extreme danger, both from Arabs
and natives, and with miserable supplies of food, in the power of
Tippu-Tib (whom you regard apparently as faithful or faithless, as
suits your pen), and without carriers ; you leave him and his companions helpless to move unless Tippu gives the men, and now
turn round on Major Barttelot and say that he promised to advance,
and ought to have done so. But I find no mention of this
promise anywhere other than your own unsupported statement,
not made till after his death. You then aggravated the position
by neglecting to secure communication with the rear column, even
if you could not fulfil your promise to return yourself in November;
and from this act of desertion arose the great misery of the officers
of the rear column, who, committed as they were to a work you
call "gigantic," but which in the circumstances you had created
for them was impossible, nevertheless displayed a dauntless
energy in maintaining their camp and stores intact, and in securing
at length the carriers you neglected to obtain for them.

'Brave, true and loyal, carrying out their instructions in face
of overwhelming odds, deserted and alone, the three officers,
Barttelot, Jameson and Bonny, started on the march from Yambuya only to be betrayed, and in death to be covered with blame

by yourself, sir, their chief, for whom they had toiled and suffered so much, and in whose service two of them died. The true history of your Expedition is a very sad one, and not the least regrettable fact is that where arrangements made by yourself are not successful, the unfortunate result is always attributed by you to the fault of your officers.

'It was always a grief to my brother that during the journey up the Congo, and at Yambuya, no matter how hard he worked, or how much he tried to please you, he got no word of thanks or appreciation, but plenty of blame and threats.

'In pointing out to you that you broke your promise and deserted your rear column for fourteen months, I do not forget that you say you sent messengers back to them twice with letters, and that these letters were handed to you on your way back to the rear column. But it was scarcely probable that these couriers would get through, even if they tried, when you yourself have related in these very letters the utter demoralization that ensues to the Zanzibaris who pass through a Manyuema camp. No doubt in playing off Tippu-Tib against Major Barttelot you hoped that all eyes would be turned on the camp, rich in stores, at Yambuya, while you secured to yourself an easy passage to the Lakes, where a large caravan of goods awaited you, of which Major Barttelot was not aware, unmolested by the Arabs. Unfortunately, however, they were before you in the forest. On August 31, 1888, you write: "We met for the first time a party of Manyuema; our misfortunes began from this date, for I had taken the Congo route to avoid the Arabs, that they might not tamper with my men and tempt them to desert." Yet you left Major Barttelot unable to move, without carriers, and dependent on Arabs and Manyuema for carriers. You now blame Major Barttelot for trying to get the carriers from Tippu, and yet he was the man you had carried round half a continent and conveyed thousands of miles in order to make him Governor over vast regions, and to place in his hands the supreme power under Belgium in Central Africa, and to provide carriers, of whom you write, June 23, 1887, "That he will restrain his own people is of course certain, and with a small force of soldiers, such as he asks for, and with Europeans to supervise, advise and encourage him, Tippu-Tib will make the very best Governor that could be found for that distant station." But on

August 31, 1889, you write : "*In re* Major Barttelot and Tippu-Tib, I have seen more nonsense on this subject than on any other, etc. . . . Thank God I have long left that immature age when one becomes a victim to every crafty rogue he meets. I am not a gushing youth, and we may assume Tippu-Tib's prime age was far from dotage. We both did as much as was possible to gain the advantage. I was satisfied with what I obtained, and Tippu-Tib obtained what money he wanted . . . Tippu-Tib, the pirate, the freebooter, buccaneer and famous raider." Sir, it is curious and incredible that you should say you were satisfied with what you obtained. As far as the Belgian Free State is concerned, you did them, I suppose you and they consider, a great service in giving them this fine slave-trading Governor at Stanley Falls at the sacrifice of your rear column, who were perpetually and always being harassed by these Arabs; and Tippu* finally gave the word to the Manyuema that if the Major did not treat them well, or did what they did not like, they were to shoot him ; the Belgian officers, who knew this and were on the spot, taking no steps in the matter. Of this you take no notice—a common African experience, perhaps, for I know of similar threats being used towards English officers by yourself on your journey up the Congo, when you told the Zanzibaris one day that if two particular officers did what annoyed them, the Zanzibaris should take them and tie them to trees ; and, turning to the two officers, to whom you used much abusive and insulting language, you informed them, "One word from me, and the Zanzibaris shall drive you into the river," or words to that effect.

'I would point out to you that such language and behaviour towards your officers in the presence of the men tended greatly to weaken the authority of the officers, and to create mutiny and insubordination among the Zanzibaris, and endangered the safety of the Expedition. This is not a solitary instance of such treatment.

'To conclude, not content with taking credit to yourself for all that you have done, and receiving glory and honour such as is seldom given to the leader of the most successful enterprise, you have sought to enhance your own merits, and to cover your mistakes by the ignoble act of depreciating others and flinging about

* According to the statement of Mr. Werner and Mr. Troup.

accusations against those who served you devotedly, and who are no longer here to defend themselves.

'It is this attitude on your part which forces me to recall to your mind some truths concerning the manner you dealt with your rear column, as shown by the private letters and papers of my brother, by Mr. Werner's book, by the statements of surviving officers of the Expedition, and by your own published letters.

'We anxiously await your reply, and reserve to ourselves the right to publish this correspondence should we deem it necessary.

'I am, Sir,

'Your obedient servant,

'WALTER G. BARTTELOT.

'To H. M. STANLEY, Esq.'

APPENDIX III.

Copy of a Letter from Mr. Jameson to Major Barttelot.

'Kibonge, *March* 26, 1888.

' Dear Major Barttelot,

'I arrived here, after an eventful journey, yesterday evening. The chief of this place, an Arab called Kibonge, is away; but Tippu-Tib's representative here, a man called Saleh bin Ali, looked after me. On the fourth day after leaving the Falls, early in the morning, I passed ten canoes from Kasongo in charge of an Arab called Raschid bin Serur. I stopped his canoe, and he came into ours. In answer to my questions, he said that he could not say if any of the other men were for us, but that five canoes were for Nzigé, the rest belonging to other Arabs. He did not know how many men were in the five canoes. I could not count them, for they were all

mixed up with women and boys. He told me that
Tippu-Tib had sent an Arab to Ugigi for men, and
that he did not think Tippu-Tib would leave Kasongo
until Ramadan, which is in May; but his head Arab
here tells me he has had letters which say that he
will leave next month. This Arab had no other
news. We have three times met with bad rapids, in
each case having to carry everything overland. I
have done everything I can to find out any men
of Mr. Stanley's here; but the chief and everyone
assure me that there are none here, and never have
been. What gave rise to the report is that men from
this place met Mr. Stanley very far upon his road to
the Lake, at a place called Eturi, where the Kibonge
men had made a camp. Mr. Stanley there left forty
sick men in their charge, leaving their guns not with
the forty men themselves, but under charge of the
Arabs, with orders not to give them to the men
until his return on that road. It had taken the men
from this town seven months to reach the place
where they met Mr. Stanley; but they have been
going very slowly, fighting natives and capturing
women and ivory. Their meeting occurred at least
six months ago. He then informed me that some of
their men were leaving this town very soon for the
same place, taking up guns and powder, and that
they would take any message for me to Mr. Stanley
in case they met him. I therefore wrote the enclosed
letter, in doing which I trust you do not think I have
exceeded my duty. Please keep the copy, as I have
not had time to make another. I have been very
seedy, having had a very narrow squeak of dysentery,
but hope I have escaped it. I have had to sleep
several nights in the canoe, in order to make an
early start in the morning. This is a very big place,
three or four times the size of Singatini, and full of
Arabs from every part—Madagascar, Bagamoyo,
Muscat, and Zanzibar. I will have to sit up to-night

and put Stanley's letter and this one into ink, as I
have been badgered out of my life by every Arab in
the place all day, so I have not time for more ; but
I am sure I have told you everything of interest
since I left.

' Trusting this will find you all right again and fit
and well, and with kind remembrances to all other
officers at Yambuya,

'I remain, sincerely yours,

'JAMES S. JAMESON.

' P.S.—I would not have written the enclosed
letter to Mr. Stanley had I not thought that it would
have been your wish that I should take this opportunity of doing so. It is the opinion of all the head-
men here that Mr. Stanley is not in a difficulty, and
they fully expect him to return. They tell me I
ought to reach Kasongo in seventeen days from
here.

' *Tuesday, April* 3.

' Reached Riba Riba yesterday. Have just met
two canoes for Singatini, the first since leaving
Kibonge. Am well, and (D.V.) will reach Kasongo
in eight days, counting this one. No news of any
kind.'

COPY OF A LETTER TO MR. STANLEY FROM MR.
JAMESON, FOUND IN MAJOR BARTTELOT'S WRITING-
CASE.

' Kibonge, — days above Stanley Falls,
' *March* 26, 1888.

'SIR,

'I arrived here yesterday, on my way from
Stanley Falls to Kasongo, and the chief Arab here
(in the absence of Kibonge himself), Saleh bin Ali,
told me that some of the men from this town had
met you at a place called Eturi, a long way on your

road to the Lake, about six months ago, and that
there you had left forty sick men, and given their
rifles into the charge of the Kibonge men until your
return on that road. They also told me that some
men were leaving this town very soon for Eturi, and
therefore I take this opportunity of sending you a
brief outline of what has taken place at Yambuya
Camp since your departure, and the causes which
led to my mission to Tippu-Tib at Kasongo, trusting that it may meet you at Eturi on your return
journey, or before we meet you. The steamer
Stanley arrived at Yambuya Camp on August 14,
with the loads from Stanley Pool in charge of Mr.
Troup, and the men from Bolobo in charge of
Messrs. Ward and Bonny, in perfect safety. They
brought the news that the steamer *Henry Reid* had
been seized by Mr. Van Gèle at Bangala, he having
come there from Equator Station before the steamer's
arrival. Up to the arrival of the *Stanley* we had
seen or heard nothing of the men promised by
Tippu-Tib; but a few days before this the natives
had told us of some Arabs who were encamped
some distance up on the opposite side of the river.
On the day of the *Stanley's* departure, or on that
following, the village opposite the camp was attacked
by Arabs, and although Major Barttelot sent across
as soon as possible, the Arabs could not be found.
He then sent some men up with the natives in a
canoe to the Arab camp, to find out who they were.
These men returned with the head Arab, Abdulla
Korona, and some of his men. They told us that
they were encamped on the opposite side of the
river getting ivory, and that they were quite willing
to conduct any of the officers to Stanley Falls in
order to see Tippu-Tib. Abdulla told us that a
long time before Tippu-Tib had sent a large number
of men to us, but after some fighting on the Aruwimi
River they had never reached our camp, and had

eventually dispersed, most of them being on the
. . . . River.

'Major Barttelot, after consulting the other
officers, then decided to send Mr. Ward and myself
to Stanley Falls to see Tippu-Tib, with orders to
try and obtain the men promised by him as soon
as possible. We accordingly left Yambuya Camp
on August 23, reaching Stanley Falls on Sunday,
the 28th inst. The same evening I presented
Tippu-Tib with a letter from Major Barttelot.
After reading it, he proceeded to explain to me the
reason of his men not having reached Yambuya
Camp. He said that 500 men, he himself being
with them, left Stanley Falls in canoes for Yambuya
very soon after the departure of the *Henry Reid*
from that place. On arriving at the Aruwimi River
they had a fight, and lost one man at the first
village, and one man at the next, and so on, until
arriving at a big village (as far as one can make
out) within half a day by steamer of our camp.
Here Tippu-Tib was encamped at a small village
on the opposite bank, and sent some men over to
the large one for food. The natives all ran away
at their approach; but they had no sooner taken
some fowls and plantains, and were returning to
their canoes, than the natives rushed over and killed
four of them, cutting them up and dividing the
meat at once. Tippu-Tib then attacked the village
that evening, and burned it next morning. He
then found that all the Stanley Falls natives who
were paddling the canoes refused to go any further,
stating that they either had fever, or that their
bowels were in such a state that they could go no
further up-stream, and so he was forced to return.
He here stated that he had understood from you
that the camp was very much lower down the
Aruwimi River. He then sent 200 men, going
overland, to find out the camp, but they returned

saying they had failed to find it. He next sent Abdulla, a man who conducted us to Stanley Falls, with 200 men, ordering him not to return until he had found either the camp or your road. Tippu-Tib then told me that morning he would send out his head-men to collect as many men as possible at once, and after three days' time, when it was their Christmas, he would start himself for our camp with all the men then collected, and that his brother Nzigé would send on the rest after they were collected.

'I could get no definite answer from him as to the number of men we might expect; so next morning I urged upon him the necessity of our knowing how many men he could give us, and at what date, and that I thought if he were willing to remain a few days longer than the three before starting, so as to have more men, and to know definitely how many he could let us have, it would be better. He then told me his reason for starting in three days. He said that the majority of the men are in villages below the Falls, and that if he goes down with as many men as he will then have to our camp, he will have far less difficulty in collecting them, as they will all have orders to come on straight to him there, without the delay of collecting in one place first. Tippu-Tib finally had canoes ready for us to start on September 2, a day later than he at first stated, and told us that he was sorry he could not come with us that day, but would send Salem Mohammed with us, and follow the next day.

'We accordingly started, and I eventually reached Yambuya Camp on Monday, September 12, having sent Mr. Ward on ahead with the news to Major Barttelot. We waited in vain for the arrival of either Tippu-Tib or the men, being always assured that they were coming, until at last the truth came out that Tippu-Tib was very much ashamed that he

could not get us the men, but would have to go to
Kasongo for them, only 64 men having arrived in
the meantime at our camp. Major Barttelot then
left for the Falls with Mr. Troup at the end of the
first week in October, and returned on the 31st of
that month, having obtained a promise from Tippu-
Tib that he would send the men from Kasongo as
soon as possible. He, leaving for Kasongo at the
end of the first week in November, would reach
Kasongo in the first week in December, and the
men ought to be with us in January.

'Your non-arrival in November, December,
January, and the beginning of February made us
more anxious ; but it was impossible to make a move
of any kind, for already over 50 of the men had
died, and there were many more sick, and no help
was forthcoming from Tippu-Tib ; so on February 14
Major Barttelot, after consulting the other officers,
decided to take me with him to Stanley Falls, and
find out what Tippu-Tib was really doing, and place
new proposals before him, which had become necessary, owing to your prolonged absence and no communication with us. On our way to Stanley Falls
we passed a number of men from Kasongo going
to our camp, 150 in all, with orders to await
Tippu-Tib's return, under the command of Salem
Mohammed ; 50 more we found had arrived before
this lot, but were stationed elsewhere ; 52 more men
arrived during our stay at the Falls, making 252
in all.

'At the Falls we could learn nothing definite
about Tippu-Tib's return from Kasongo, or about
the number of men he was sending ; nor could we
obtain the slightest information about your movements, except that you had been met by men from
Kibonge, which news was brought by an Arab
called Moro ben Reg, who had seen two deserters
from your force at a place called Unaria, where

Abdulla Korona has formed a camp. These two men had escaped with five others from this place, which took you five months to reach from our camp, and it had taken them a month in a canoe to reach Abdulla's camp, the canoe being upset, and five of them lost.

'This lack of all news, either about you and your force or about Tippu-Tib's movements, made Major Barttelot decide, after talking the matter over with me, to send me to Kasongo at once to place fresh proposals before Tippu-Tib, and to send Mr. Ward down the Congo in order to telegraph our situation to the Committee, and let them know what we are doing. No steamer has arrived at Stanley Falls during the whole of our stay at Yambuya Camp. The great reason always given to us for the non-ability of Tippu-Tib to get carriers for us is the size of the loads, or, rather, I should say, their weight, so Major Barttelot has decided that he will allow Tippu-Tib's men to carry half-loads, as we cannot help thinking that you are in a difficulty, and we must reach you as soon as possible. I am also to obtain from him as many fighting men as possible up to 400, to get him to sign an agreement as to date of delivery of these men, and as to amount of money required, whether a lump sum, or whether so much per month per head, paying the carriers less than the original amount, as they only carry half-loads; and the same will apply to the fighting men, who will carry no loads at all. Major Barttelot and myself will sign our names as security for the money, he having telegraphed to the Committee to this effect. I am also to urge upon Tippu-Tib the great necessity of haste. We are entirely dependent upon him, as from the number of deaths and the amount of sick men in our camp we could not muster more than eighty carriers; and when you, with the force you took with you, have presumably met with some serious opposition preventing you either returning or communicating with our camp, it would be useless for us to start without such a force as to be of efficient aid to you.

'In the agreement with Tippu-Tib a clause will be inserted stating that the moment we meet with you the command, of course, will be handed over to you, and in case you do not require his men they will be dismissed, being paid up to date.

'In consequence of my very short stay here, I cannot enter into further details in this letter, but I trust it will give you a clear view of the whole situation since your departure from Yambuya Camp. All the officers at Yambuya Camp were well when I left Stanley Falls, and I am happy to say that Major Barttelot and I are also in good health. He was to return to Yambuya Camp two days after my departure with the last arrival of fifty-two men from Kasongo. Trusting that this letter will find you and your officers in equally good health, and that we may soon meet,

   'I remain, sir,
    'Your obedient servant,
     'JAMES S. JAMESON.

'H. M. STANLEY, Esq.,
 'Com. Emin Pasha Relief Expedition.

'Before closing this I must add that we have lived in perfect peace with all the natives during the whole of our stay at Yambuya Camp.'

COPY OF LETTER FOUND IN MAJOR BARTTELOT'S WRITING-CASE, MUCH TORN, AND IN SOME PLACES ILLEGIBLE, FROM MR. JAMESON TO MR. MACKINNON.

'SIR,   'Kasongo, *April* 15, 1888.

'I arrived here on April 11, in pursuance of orders received from Major Barttelot at Stanley

Falls, to proceed to this place with all possible speed
and obtain an interview with Tippu-Tib, in order
that I might impress upon him the great necessity
of hastening the despatch of his men to us, and try to
obtain from him a further supply of 400 fighting men,
not to carry loads, besides the 600 carriers already
promised.   I was also to ask him to name a definite
date upon which the delivery of all the men will
have (been) completed ; for (what sum of ?) . . . .
. . . .
fighting men none, a (less ?) sum than that originally
agreed upon, namely, five dollars per month per
head, ought to be accepted by him.   Another
subject of inquiry was, as to whether the Arab
chief over Tippu's men, Major Barttelot being in
supreme command, would receive all orders as
regards marching and fighting from him.   Also to
obtain from Tippu-Tib his promise to aid us as
regards purchasing supplies, hiring of guides
(canoes ?), etc., in his territory, and where he has
garrisons, and escort and guide to coast in case
of our return by this route ; also as to what sum
he would agree to being struck off in the case of
deserters, so much to be deducted if deserting without loads, and if with loads, the value of the loads
to be added to this amount—in case of sickness
or death the men being paid up to the date of their
being rendered incapable or death. A form of agreement was then to be drawn out embodying all the
above matter between Tippu-Tib on the one hand
and Major Barttelot on the other, to which I was
to obtain Tippu's signature, Major B. and I both
signing the guarantee as regards the payment of
the money for carriers, etc.   A clause was to be
inserted in this agreement which stated that, in case
of our having definite news of Mr. Stanley's return
before we left Yambuya Camp, the agreement would
become void, and in case of our meeting with him

he would at once assume supreme command, in
which case . . . . . . with him to say . . . . .
. . . .
him the proposal mentioned in the forepart of this
letter.   On our arrival there we could obtain no
definite news as to the date of his return, nor as
to the number of men he was sending, he having
then only sent 200 men.   Nor could we obtain any
news of Mr. Stanley except that brought to us by
an Arab, who had been a long way up the Aruwimi
in search of ivory, who told us that at an Arab camp
six days' journey above Yambuya Camp he had met
two deserters from Mr. Stanley's force.   They had
been there for over five months, and said that Mr.
Stanley had taken five months to reach the point at
which they left him.   Seven of them had deserted,
and it had taken them a month in a canoe going
down stream to reach Unaria, the name of the Arab
camp.   The canoe had been upset and five of them
lost.   They told him that before leaving Mr. Stanley
he had been met by a party of Arabs from Kibonge,
a village belonging to Said bin Abede, about seven
days' journey above Stanley Falls on the Congo.
Mr. Stanley had left forty sick men with these
Arabs.   Our not being able to obtain any news of
Mr. Stanley or of the movements of Tippu-Tib
made Major Barttelot decide on sending me to
Kasongo in order to have a personal interview
with Tippu-Tib ; Major Barttelot himself being
unable to proceed there, as he could not leave his
post in command of Yambuya Camp for so long a
period.

'During our stay at Stanley Falls the camp was
left in charge of Mr. Troup, he having under him
Messrs. Ward and Bonny.   Major Barttelot, when
I left him at Stanley Falls, on March 18, intended
sending an officer down the Congo to forward a
letter and telegram to you from Banana Point.   In

this letter I believe the whole of the above was mentioned; but I have repeated it, as there may have been some miscarriage of that letter.

'I left Stanley Falls on March 18, arriving here at mid-day on April 11, having taken twenty-five days to complete the journey, the usual time taken to do it being thirty days.* I could not travel faster, as I had to accompany several carriers conveying . . . . but through . . . . . . wishes a

[*Three or four lines illegible.*]

. . . eats . . . . wing their guns into the . . . . until on that road. This is the same news as that brought to us by the Arab at Stanley Falls, and obtained from the deserters at Unaria. He also told me that in a very short time there were men from Kibonge going up to Eturi, the name of the place where Mr. Stanley was last seen; and any message or letter I had to send would be sent with them on the chance that it might reach Mr. Stanley either on his return on that road or before we met him. I therefore wrote as long a letter as my short stay there permitted, clearly placing before Mr. Stanley everything that had taken place at Yambuya Camp since his departure from there, and the causes of my present mission, sending a copy of the same to Major Barttelot at Yambuya Camp.

'I cannot give you a clearer idea of what took place at my interviews with Tippu-Tib than by quoting from my diary, which was written immediately after those interviews took place:

'On April 11, the day of my arrival, I went straight to Tippu-Tib's house, and, after greeting him, told him I had been sent here by Major Barttelot to place certain proposals before him; and

---

* It is about 360 miles from the Falls Station to Kasongo, which is on the Congo, and the journey is made by canoe; the distance from Yambuya to Kasongo would be about 500 miles.

that, as soon as I had changed my wet clothes, the time being suitable to him, I would see him. He told me that there was a house ready for me, and that he would come up there to speak with me. Major Barttelot had given me definite orders on no account to use any other interpreter than Assad Farran, the interpreter accompanying the Soudanese on this Expedition, who speaks Arabic fluently; especially not to make use of Salem Masudi, Tippu-Tib's interpreter, as he could not trust him. Salem Masudi called on me that afternoon; and I told him, in the presence of Assad Farran, who had then just arrived, taking longer on the road than I did, that it was Major Barttelot's wish that I should use Assad Farran as interpreter, and that he might ask Tippu-Tib to bring someone with him who spoke Arabic fluently. I waited in all that afternoon, but Tippu-Tib did not pay me his promised visit.

'*April* 12.—I went down and paid my respects to Tippu-Tib early in the morning, but he was very busy writing letters, so I did not wait long. After returning to my house, Salem Masudi came in, and I asked him if Tippu-Tib was coming to see me, and he said "Yes." After a short time he said: "There is no one here now; it will be a good time for Tippu-Tib to come," and went out. He soon returned, and told me that Tippu-Tib said that he knew, from a letter received from . . . . brother at Stanley Falls all I had come about; there was no special (hurry?) for . . . . interview, and that he (would give?) all the men we (required?) and be ready to start on . . . . . . which is the (20th?) of this . . . . . . a brother . . . . . . from . . . . ge did . . . . . . to ask him . . . .
[*Several lines totally gone.*]
. . . of men, especially the 400 . . . .

for them.   He then said . . . . undoubtedly give
us the m . . . . 400, then 300, that as
(regards ?) the money for the 600 he . . . . . that
with Mr. Stanley and . . . the 400 with us when
we ret . . . . . . him, that as the men had been so
long in being sent Mr. Stanley . . . refuse to pay
the money, and that an agreement with Major
(Barttelot ?) was really a safeguard for himself,
Major Barttelot and I (guaranteeing ?) the money.
He then said he would settle everything with Mr.
(Stanley ?), and would evidently have nothing to do
about an agreement with Major Barttelot.   He kept
assuring me three or four times that I need not be
anxious, and he promised me to leave here on the
10th of next moon ; that I was to wait quietly here
until then and go with him ; that all the men we
wanted, if not 400, then 300 extra, would be forthcoming ; and that he had received letters from
Zanzibar, where it was reported Mr. Stanley was
dead, asking him why there was no news of him,
and what he (Tippu-Tib) was doing.   He had
replied, saying Mr. Stanley was not dead, and,
" Inshallah," he would get news of him.   Two or
three times I tried to impress upon him the necessity of speed, and of an agreement which was for
his good ; but he simply answered as before, and
seemed rather annoyed.   He once or twice tried to
use other interpreters who spoke a little English,
evidently put out because he did not use his own ;
but I told him that I did not understand them, so
he used Assad Farran.   The reason of a second
interpreter being necessary is that Tippu-Tib has
always been supposed not to speak much Arabic,
and Assad Farran does not speak Swahili, so that a
man who spoke both was necessary.   Tippu-Tib
had an Arab present for this purpose.   (Assad
Farran tells me to-day that Tippu-Tib has been
speaking to him in the most perfect Arabic.)   I

decided to accept his promise and leave, as he was evidently just as anxious as we are to see us start with all the men, the letters from Zanzibar having blamed him for delay.

'Before I left he told me that he had received news, but did not know if it was true, that the King of Unyoro had been collecting men for the carriage of Emin Pasha's ivory to the coast, and to escort him there. He said that most probably, if this news was true, Mr. Stanley had gone down the other road by Unyoro and Uganda either with Emin Bey or behind him. I told him that had Mr. Stanley done so he would certainly have sent messengers back to us, and it was the want of this news which made us so anxious. He finally said again, " Do not be anxious ; wait quietly here until the 10th of next moon, when I will truly start, and come with me. You will have all the men. I won't wait for . . . . . brother . . . id we will get news of (Stanley ?) . . . . . I . . . (did ?) him . . . .
[*Several lines totally gone.*]
leave Yambuya Camp . . . told me the . . . of June (would ?) be the very latest, and he (thought ?) certainly before that (date ?), as he would only wait at Stanley Falls one day, and go straight on to Yambuya Camp. I found out that some men were leaving at once for Stanley Falls, so I went home and wrote to Major Barttelot, telling him the result of my interviews with Tippu-Tib, and of my decision to stay here and go back with him, as I can be of little use at the camp at present, and my presence here, in case of any delay, may be useful, and any news of Mr. Stanley I believe will be first known here ; but a number of them had run away, a good many men being recaptured. He has made no excuses to me for the delay in the delivery of the men, but it appears he has been greatly hampered in his movements by a dispute with another Arab

chief, called Said bin Abede. Our movements
until a start is made from Yambuya Camp ought
to be as nearly as possible the following :

'I will leave here with Tippu-Tib and as many
more men as are going to be sent from here (I
believe his brother . . . . is bringing some) on
April 24, arriving at Stanley Falls on May 10, wait
there one day, then start for Yambuya Camp. It
will take us two days in canoes to reach (Yallasula ?)
—the point where we leave the canoes and go overland—then three days to Yambuya Camp; therefore I may. say that, if we travel as quickly as
possible, with no delays, we will reach Yambuya
Camp on May 16. During this period I believe
Major Barttelot will have removed all the loads,
which are being left behind at Stanley Falls under
the charge of a European officer, to Yallasula, ready
for conveyance to the Falls in canoes. It will take
Tippu-Tib . . . . to collect and put in order the
300 or 400 fighting men he is going to give us,
so that we may calculate upon finally leaving Yambuya Camp about May 23. I assure you that Major
Barttelot has made every effort, and used every means
at his command to make a start after Mr. Stanley,
ever since the arrival of the ss. *Stanley* at Yambuya
Camp in August with the men from Bolobo and the
loads from Stanley Pool. When I left Stanley Falls
between fifty and sixty men out of our small force at
Yambuya Camp had died, and there were over thirty
sick. We could not muster more than (eighty ?)
. . . altogether . . . ing . . . handful of . . . . .
[*Several lines totally gone.*]
. . . til our lef . . re has . . . .
. . . from . . . .
. . . was . . . .
. . . . able . . . .
. . . from Stanley Falls . . . . . . rttelot . . . .
in Yambuya Camp w . . . . . good health, and that

we lived in perfect peace with all the natives during the whole of our stay there.

'Trusting that the next news you will receive will be of our return from a successful journey to the Lake,

'I have the honour to be, sir,
'Your most obedient servant,
'JAMES S. JAMESON,
'Officer of the Emin Pasha Relief Expedition.

'WILLIAM MACKINNON, Esq.,
'President of Committee
of Emin Pasha Relief Expedition.'

APPENDIX IV.

AGREEMENT BETWEEN MR. STANLEY AND TIPPU-TIB.

No. 39.—Agreement.

'Mr. Henry Morton Stanley, on behalf of his Majesty the King of the Belgians, and Sovereign of the Congo State, appoints Hamed-bin-Mohammed Al Marjebi, Tippu-Tib, to be Wali of the independent State of the Congo at Stanley Falls district at a salary of £30 per month, payable to his agent at Zanzibar, on the following conditions :

'1. Tippu-Tib is to hoist the flag of the Congo State at its station near Stanley Falls, and to maintain the authority of the State on the Congo, and all its affluents at the said station downwards to the Bujine or Aruwimi River, and to prevent the tribes thereon, as well as the Arabs and others, from engaging in the slave-trade.

'2. Tippu-Tib is to receive a resident officer of the Congo State, who will act as his secretary in all his communications with the Administrator-General.

'3. Tippu-Tib is to be at full liberty to carry on his legitimate private trade in any direction, and to send his caravans to and from any places he may desire.

'4. Tippu-Tib shall nominate a *locum tenens*, to whom in case of his temporary absence his powers shall be delegated, and who in the event of his death shall become his successor in the Wali-ship ; but his Majesty the King of the Belgians shall have the power of veto should there be any serious objection to Tippu-Tib's nominee.

'5. This arrangement shall only be binding so long as Tippu Tib or his representative fulfils the conditions embodied in this agreement.

(*Signed*) 'HENRY M. STANLEY.

(*Signed*)   'TIPPU-TIB (in Arabic).

'FREDC. HOLMWOOD,

'KÀNJI RAJPAR (in Hindi).

'Zanzibar,

'*February* 24, 1887.'

APPENDIX V.

EXTRACTS FROM CORRESPONDENCE RESPECTING THE EXPEDITION FOR THE RELIEF OF EMIN PASHA, 1886, 1887.

PRESENTED TO BOTH HOUSES OF PARLIAMENT, BY COMMAND OF HER MAJESTY, DECEMBER, 1888, IN A PAPER, 'AFRICA,' NO. 8 (1888).

INCLOSURE IN NO. 11.—MEMORANDUM ON THE SUBJECT OF THE RELIEF OF EMIN BEY.

'It is suggested, for the consideration of her Majesty's Government, by Mr. W. Mackinnon, acting for himself and others, that a small Committee be formed to organize and send out a private Expedition to open communications with, and carry relief to, Emin Bey.

'It has been estimated by the most competent authorities that for this purpose a sum of £20,000 will be needed, and it is proposed that, the sum being provided, the Committee should entrust the leadership and sole conduct of the Expedition to Mr. H. M. Stanley, who offers his services gratuitously, and proposes to engage only Zanzibaris and other East Africans. He is ready to accept all the personal risks involved, and to relieve everyone else of responsibility.

'It would be necessary, in order to carry out this proposal, that Government should assist the Expedition by instructing its agents and naval officers to render every assistance and exert themselves in its favour, and that Government should facilitate the supply of the arms and ammunition necessary to Mr. Stanley's native escort.

'Mr. Mackinnon and friends will endeavour to provide £10,000 towards the expenses of the Expedition, on condition that a similar amount be placed at the disposal of the Committee through her Majesty's Government.

'Mr. Stanley would be left to decide what would be the best and quickest mode of reaching Emin Bey. He would, in consideration of the Government grant, be instructed to convey any communications with which he might be entrusted by her Majesty's Government or by the Egyptian Government, and to assist the withdrawal to the coast of the Egyptian garrison.

(Signed)   'W. MACKINNON.'

No. 12.—The Earl of Iddesleigh to Sir E. Baring.

'Foreign Office,
'December 3, 1886.

'SIR,

'I have informed you to-day, by telegraph, that some private persons personally interested in Emin Bey are organizing a small Committee with the view of setting on foot an expedition for his relief of a purely pacific character. The sum of £10,000 will be raised by them for the purpose, and they will take on themselves all responsibility, provided that a similar sum is given by the Egyptian Government.

'The Expedition will be under the direction of Mr. H. M. Stanley.

'Her Majesty's Government approve the proposal, and the persons by whom the offer is made have been informed that it is understood by us that the agreement of the Egyptian Government is assured.

'I am, etc.,
(Signed)   'IDDESLEIGH.'

No. 13.—Sir E. Baring to the Earl of Iddesleigh.— (Received December 4, 10.30 a.m.).

'Cairo,
'December 4, 1886.

'(Telegraphic.)

'Egyptian Government fully concur in the arrangement, and agree to contribute £10,000 towards the expenses of the Expedition.'

No. 18.—Sir F. de Winton to Foreign Office.—(Received January 3, 1887.)

'160, New Bond Street,
'*December* 30, 1886.

'Sir,

'I have the honour to inform you, for the information of the Right Honourable the Secretary of State for Foreign Affairs, that a Committee has been formed of the following gentlemen, to conduct the affairs of the Emin Bey Relief Expedition :

'Mr. W. Mackinnon, Chairman ; Honourable G. Dawnay ; Mr. H. M. Stanley ; Sir L. Pelly ; Mr. A. F. Kinnaird ; Colonel Grant ; Reverend H. Waller ; Colonel Sir F. de Winton, Acting Secretary.

'A meeting of this Committee was held on the 29th instant, when the action of Mr. Mackinnon, and the appointment of Mr. Stanley to command the Expedition, were confirmed.

'I have, etc.,

(*Signed*)   'F. de Winton.'

No. 19.—Emin Relief Committee to the Marquis of Salisbury.—(Received January 13.)

'160, New Bond Street, London,
'*January* 12, 1887.

'My Lord,

'I have been instructed by the Committee of the Emin Pasha Relief Expedition to request the favourable consideration of her Majesty's Government to the question of transport of the Expedition from Zanzibar to Banana, the mouth of the Congo, for the following reasons :

'That his Majesty the Sovereign of the New Congo Free State has placed a sufficiency of transport on the waters of the Haut Congo, at the disposal of Mr. Stanley, for the use of the Expedition, gratuitously.

'That the adoption of the Congo route would prevent any misfortune happening to the missionaries, French and English, now in the power of Mwanga, the King of Uganda.

'That the funds of the Committee are not sufficient to enable them to carry out the whole object of the Expedition, *via* the Congo route, in consequence of the cost of transport from Zanzibar to Banana Point.

' The Congo route has the further advantages, that it offers far greater facilities for the withdrawal of the women and children at present with Emin Bey.   It would also open up a sure and certain route for any further relief to Emin Pasha, and for his own ultimate retreat.

' The Committee have therefore to request, as the Congo route is for so many reasons the more suitable, that her Majesty's Government may see fit to place a steam-vessel at the disposition of the Expedition, to carry out the service of transport of 500 Zanzibaris and the material belonging to the Expedition, from Zanzibar to Banana ; and, if the request be granted, that the steamer may be at Zanzibar not later than February 21, to await Mr. Stanley's orders.

' I have, etc.,
(*Signed*)   ' F. DE WINTON, Colonel,
' Acting Secretary, Emin Pasha Relief Expedition.'

'(TRANSLATION.)

' Cairo,
' *February* 2, 1887.

' MY DEAR EMIN PASHA,

' I had sent you, by the kind favour of her Britannic Majesty's Consulate at Zanzibar, a letter addressed to you by his Highness complimenting you on your conduct, and congratulating you, your officers, and your soldiers on having overcome the difficulties with which you had to cope.

' His Excellency made you aware in that letter that he had promoted you to the rank of General, and would confirm all promotions and rewards given by you to your officers and others.   I informed you myself of the preparation of an Expedition for your relief.   The Expedition is now formed ; it is commanded by Mr. Stanley, who will himself hand you my letter, with that which his Highness is writing to you, and another which I am writing to you in Arabic.

' The Expedition commanded by Mr. Stanley has been formed and organized in order to go to you with the provisions and stores, of which you must certainly be in want. Its object is to bring you, your officers and soldiers, back to Egypt by the way which Mr. Stanley shall think most suitable. I have nothing to add to what I have just said of the objects of the Expedition. Only, his Highness leaves you, your officers, your soldiers and others, entirely free to stay where you are, or to make use of the help he sends for your return.

' But, of course—and this must be made clear to your officers, soldiers, or others—if some do not wish to return they are free to remain, but at their own risk, and by their own desire, and that they cannot expect any other help from the Government. That is what I wish you to make clear to those who may wish to remain.

' I have only to add that you, your officers, your soldiers and other officials will have your accounts settled, and be paid on your arrival in Egypt what is due to you on account of salaries and other allowances, as all your promotions have been already confirmed by his Highness.

' I hope, my dear Pasha, that Mr. Stanley will find you all safe and sound, and enjoying good health. That is what we all wish with all our hearts, and it is with these wishes, etc.,

(Signed) ' N. NUBAR.'

' No. 25.—EMIN RELIEF COMMITTEE TO FOREIGN OFFICE.— (RECEIVED FEBRUARY 11).

' 30, Old Burlington Street, W.,
' February 10, 1887.

' SIR,

' I have the honour to report, for the information of the Marquis of Salisbury, that the Emin Relief Expedition has departed, that it will reach Zanzibar on or about February 21, and unless Mr. H. M. Stanley, on his arrival there, receives intelligence from the interior necessitating an advance from the East Coast, he will proceed with his Expedition from Zanzibar in the British India Steam Company's steamship *Madura*, 2,000 tons, to Banana, off the mouth of the Congo, where he expects to arrive about March 23. The Expedition will then push as rapidly as is possible up the Congo to a point about 23° east longitude ; from this point it will take about thirty-five days to march to the Lake Albert Nyanza, when the object of the Expedition will have been accomplished.

'The earliest date at which Mr. Stanley can arrive at Wadelai is about the middle or end of July.

'With reference to this Congo route, it is very probable, after Mr. Stanley has opened up a road from the Congo to Wadelai, that Emin Pasha will send the women and children, and other Egyptians who may be desirous of returning to their country, by this route, which will have a land journey of about 600 miles, as against 1,200 miles by the route to the East Coast.

'The Committee are therefore desirous that such a possibility may be brought to the notice of the Egyptian Government, in order that the co-operation of the authorities of the Congo Free State may be invited to assist these people down the Congo, and also that suitable stores of food may be established at certain parts of the route where drought extending for a period of three years has caused a scarcity of provisions.

'They have deemed it their duty to bring the fact to the notice of her Majesty's Government, for although Mr. H. M. Stanley will afford Emin Pasha all the assistance in his power, arrangements for transport and food for refugees, whether men or helpless women and children, must be made by the Egyptian Government, the Committee undertaking only the expense of the Expedition, and they have made no provision for the passages down the Congo and back to Egypt of any refugees. Neither would it be, in Mr. Stanley's opinion, advisable to convey such by the land route to the East Coast, on account of the length of the land journey, as the women and children would have to be carried all the way, with the probability of meeting fierce and hostile tribes between Wadelai and Karagwe.

'Should it be deemed desirable, the Committee will be happy to submit a short memorandum showing the probable requirements of such a service as they have indicated.

'I have, etc.,

(*Signed*)　　　'W. MACKINNON,

'Chairman of Committee.'

'No. 28.—The Marquis of Salisbury to Sir E. Baring.

'Foreign Office,
'*February* 17, 1887.

'Sir,

'I enclose herewith copy of a letter which has been received from the Chairman of the Emin Bey Relief Committee with reference to the withdrawal of Emin's party through the Congo territory ; and I have to request you to ascertain whether the Egyptian Government would wish the Committee to be asked to supply any further information. You will see that the Committee is prepared to furnish a memorandum if required.

'I am, etc.,
(*Signed*) 'Salisbury.'

Emin Relief Committee to Foreign Office.—(Received March 26.)

'28, Wynnstay Gardens, Kensington,
'*March* 25, 1887.

'Sir,

'In the concluding part of your letter of the 16th instant allusion is made to the question of ivory, and the hope expressed by Nubar Pasha that the expenses incurred by the Egyptian Government would be covered by the sale of the ivory they possess at Wadelai.

'Referring to a letter from Mr. W. Mackinnon to the late Lord Iddesleigh, dated November 27, 1886, the following paragraph occurs :

'"It appears from information in the newspapers that Emin Bey is believed to have considerable quantities of ivory which might be utilized for repayment of outlays connected with any scheme of relief. The Committee would naturally expect that, if this anticipation be realized, a just proportion should be made over to them."

'I have now the honour to request that her Majesty's Secretary of State for Foreign Affairs may see fit to have the just claims of the Committee for their proportion of their ivory at Wadelai acknowledged by the Egyptian Government, in order that no misunderstanding may arise in the future, and that the utmost harmony of purpose may exist between the objects of the Committee and that of the Egyptian Government.

> ' I have, etc.,
>
> (*Signed*) ' F. DE WINTON, Hon. Secretary,
>
> ' Emin Relief Committee.'

No. 34.—EMIN RELIEF COMMITTEE TO FOREIGN OFFICE.— (RECEIVED MARCH 27.)

> ' 28, Wynnstay Gardens, Kensington,
>
> ' *March* 25, 1887.

' SIR,

'In further reply to your letter of March 16, relative to the withdrawal of Emin's party through the territory of the Congo Free State, I have the honour to transmit a memorandum, adopted by the Committee, to which is appended an estimate showing probable expense for 100 persons, for the information of the Egyptian Government.

' In framing this estimate, it is presumed that a sufficient escort will be provided by Emin Pasha to transport all the loads required by the party, as well as to carry the women and children.

' The estimates are based upon the prices paid by the Congo Free State to feed their employés.

' With reference to the assistance of the Congo Free State, the Committee, as they have no official position, would suggest, if the Egyptian Government approve of this route, that her Majesty's Government communicate with the Sovereign of the Congo Free State, in order to obtain the necessary authority for the carrying out of the following services :

' 1. The engagement of the steamer *Stanley*, to proceed to Stanley Falls about the last week in September.

' 2. To send to the Congo in June, or to arrange with the authorities of the Congo Free State to have in their stores, six tons of rice, to be distributed as follows :

> ' Two tons at Stanley Pool.
>
> ' Two tons at Lukungu.
>
> ' Two tons at Matadi.

' 3. To obtain authority for the purchase from the stores of the

Congo Free State of such cloth and goods as the Emin party may reasonably require.

'It is probable that about next June or July the Committee will be in possession of further intelligence from Mr. Stanley, which might modify these arrangements as regards time ; but they earnestly advise that the general scheme they have suggested be carried out.

'In conclusion, the Committee append a comparative table of the distances of the different routes from Wadelai to the East Coast, and to the West Coast *via* the Congo. These distances only refer to the land portion of the different roads, and are given according to the number of days each would take.

'I have, etc.,

(Signed)   'F. DE WINTON, Hon. Secretary,

'Emin Relief Committee.'

'NO. 41.—EMIN RELIEF COMMITTEE TO FOREIGN OFFICE.—
(RECEIVED APRIL 26).

'28, Wynnstay Gardens, Kensington,
'April 25, 1887.

'SIR,

'I have the honour to acknowledge the receipt of your letter of April 1, having reference to the subjects contained in my three letters of the 25th ultimo, and I am requested by the Emin Relief Committee to convey their grateful acknowledgments to the Right Honourable the Secretary of State for Foreign Affairs for the reference he has caused to be made to the Egyptian Government concerning the ivory stated to be in the possession of Emin Pasha.

'With regard to the repatriation of the Egyptian troops, and their women and children, *via* the Congo route, the Committee beg to refer you to the letter of Mr. W. Mackinnon, dated February 10, 1887. In this letter the position of, and the duties undertaken by, the Emin Relief Expedition are clearly defined.

'The Egyptian Government, as we are informed by Sir John . Kirk, have already made arrangements, through her Majesty's Consul-General at Zanzibar, for the payment of all expenses incurred by Emin Pasha's forces should they return *viâ* the East Coast.

'It would therefore appear proper they should make arrangements such as are suggested by the Committee, and forwarded, under cover, in my letter of the 26th ultimo, for the West Coast, so as to ensure the return of the refugees without fear of possible disasters which might arise from want of proper arrangements for their transport from the Congo to Egypt, and of a proper food supply. As regards the transport on the Haut Congo of the relieving force by the boats of the Congo Free State, this service was offered to the Expedition by his Majesty the King of the Belgians, and was the chief inducement to adopting that route; but for the transport down the Congo required by the Egyptian Government for refugees, the Committee suggest that the Government of his Highness the Khedive should apply for such service direct to the Sovereign of the Congo Free State, which is under no engagement to the Committee to provide any transport downwards.

'In conclusion, the Committee desire to repeat that the only duty they have undertaken is that of attempting to relieve Emin Pasha, and to open up communications with him, as will be seen by the enclosed copies of a letter written to the late Lord Iddesleigh, and the memorandum which accompanied it.

'Mr. H. M. Stanley will, of course, co-operate with Emin Pasha, and help him to the utmost of his ability; but the Committee are unable to undertake the repatriation of any refugees, or to provide for the expenses of the journey either by East or West Coast, though they are desirous to give every information and afford every assistance that may lie in their power.

'I have, etc.,

(*Signed*) 'F. DE WINTON, Hon. Secretary,

'Emin Relief Expedition.'

THE END.

BILLING AND SONS, PRINTERS, GUILDFORD.

G. C. & Co.

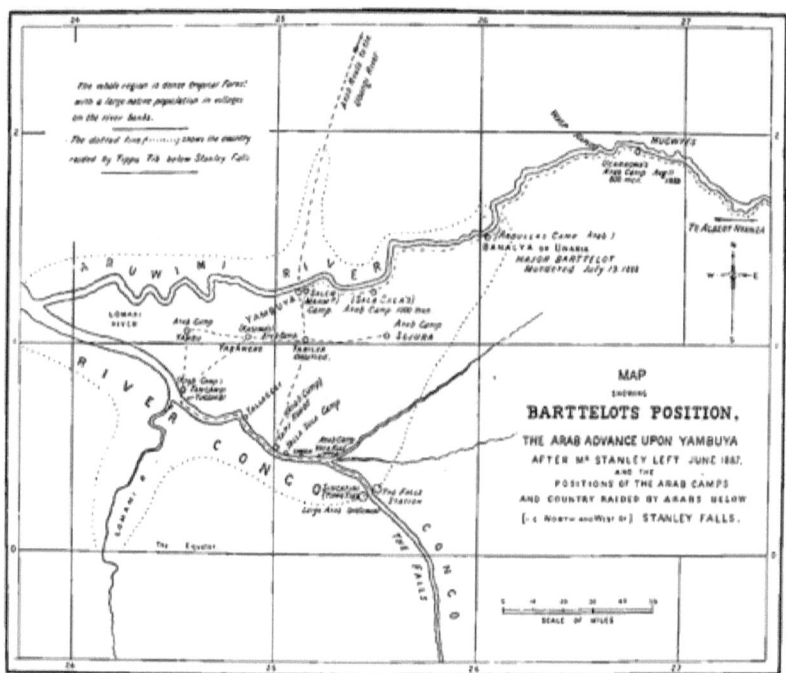

The whole region is dense tropical Forest
with a large native population in villages
on the river banks.

The dotted line .... shows the country
raided by Tippu-Tib below Stanley Falls

MAP
SHOWING
BARTTELOTS POSITION,
THE ARAB ADVANCE UPON YAMBUYA
AFTER Mr STANLEY LEFT JUNE 1887,
AND THE
POSITIONS OF THE ARAB CAMPS
AND COUNTRY RAIDED BY ARABS BELOW
(i.e. NORTH AND WEST OF) STANLEY FALLS.

SCALE OF MILES